GRAIL KNIGHT

GRAIL KNIGHT

ANGUS DONALD

sphere

SPHERE

First published in Great Britain in 2013 by Sphere

A CIP catalogue record for this book
is available from the British Library.

ISBN 978-1-84744-508-7

Typeset in Goudy by Palimpsest Book Production Limited,
Falkirk, Stirlingshire
Printed and bound in Great Britain by
Clays Ltd, St Ives plc

Papers used by Sphere are from well-managed forests
and other responsible sources.

MIX
Paper from
responsible sources
FSC
www.fsc.org   FSC® C104740

Sphere
An imprint of
Little, Brown Book Group
100 Victoria Embankment
London EC4Y 0DY

An Hachette UK Company
www.hachette.co.uk

www.littlebrown.co.uk

For Mary, Emma and Robin,
with all my love

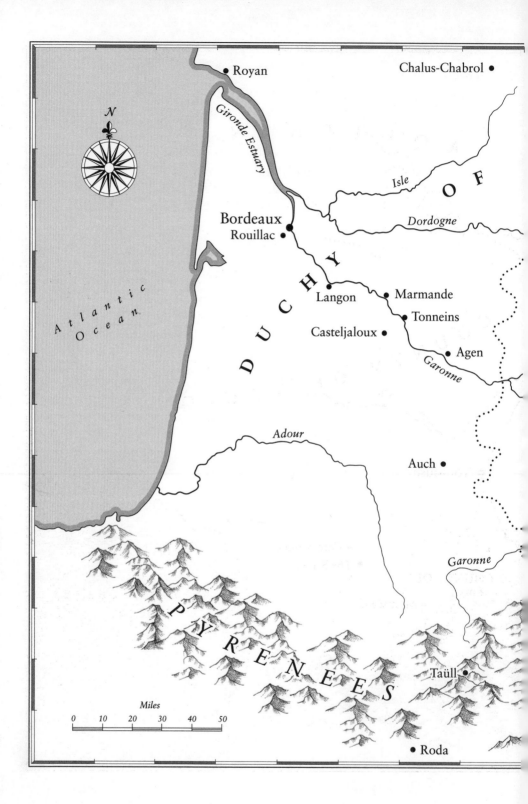

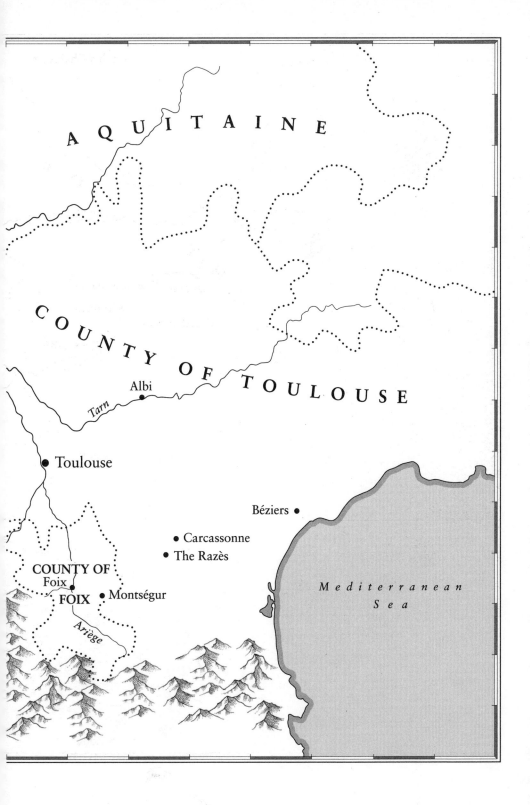

Part One

Chapter One

My immortal soul is in grave peril, I have been informed, for the sin of blasphemy. And, as I am now in my seventh decade, a weary old man approaching my end, I suppose I must try to treat this sort of thing with a degree of seriousness – even if this extraordinary knowledge was imparted to me by a bouncy stripling barely out of childhood with a wispy upper lip and a brutally fresh tonsure . . . But I must strive to be fair in these writings; I must not indulge my envy of his youth: Father Anselm, our village priest, is no callow stripling, he is fully twenty-three years of age. It is only that he looks to me like an untried lad of twelve summers. Perhaps, when the ripe pimples that stud his small, eager face have cleared up, I will be able to show him the proper respect due a man of God.

But somehow I doubt it.

How did I blaspheme? I laughed in church today during Mass, long and very loud, joyously and uncontrollably; indeed, such was my mirth that I was forced to excuse myself and leave in the midst of the lesson. I was reproved for my levity afterwards, and I may, Father Anselm warned me, even be guilty of blasphemy as well – a mortal sin. I showed a gross lack of reverence for a holy object and I must do a penance.

3

When he told me this after the service this morning, it was only with a deal of difficulty that I did not begin to roar like a donkey once again.

It happened like this: Father Anselm was delivering his usual Sunday homily to the villagers and using the Flask of St Luke the Evangelist, as it is known, our village's only relic, as the basis for his theme, and the words from the Gospel of Matthew about the power of Faith as his text. I'm sure you will know it. Our Lord Jesus Christ said, 'If ye have faith as a grain of mustard seed, ye shall say unto this mountain: "Remove hence to yonder place", and it shall remove; and nothing shall be impossible unto you.'

Father Anselm claims that he had a vision in which St Luke himself came to his bedside and gave him the flask – which is an ancient leather bottle, sealed on the inside with pitch and at the neck with a wooden stopper. It has a rather indistinct image stamped into the leather of a prone man and a bovine animal of some kind. Father Anselm claims that it is an image of St Luke himself and his symbol of an ox, and that the saint told him to use it for God's work in the manor of Westbury in the county of Nottinghamshire. My manor, where I am lord over all, except perhaps over my sharp-tongued daughter-in-law Marie, mother of my grandson and namesake Alan. It is my church, in fact, that Father Anselm preaches in. It stands on my land, the living is within my gift, and it was my silver, not five years ago, that paid for the new roof. If I choose to laugh there about his ridiculous stories of visions and holy flasks, surely that is my right.

I know that Father Anselm is lying about the vision; that water flask used to belong to me, and I gave it to the old village priest of Westbury – not Anselm's predecessor Father Gilbert, but the incumbent even before him, a little owlish man named Father Arnold – long ago when I had returned from my travels in the south. Nobody but me remembers him now – they are all in their graves. I do not know exactly where Arnold hid the bottle away in his little cott behind the church but, evidently, Father Anselm has newly discovered it and he is now

4

pretending that because, like me, it is very old, it must be a sacred relic. It is not – the ox is, in fact, a bull and the man depicted on the leather is St Sernin, a holy man who lived and died in the far south, and whose image can be found, I would imagine, on hundreds or even thousands of similar water bottles that are sold to pilgrims in the beautiful, rose-coloured city of Toulouse. I know because that is where I bought this particular bottle, merely as a container for refreshment during my journeying, when I was in that city some forty years ago.

I will refrain from exposing the priest as a liar, although I would enjoy that a good deal. That would no doubt also gravely imperil my soul, I suspect, but I choose not to expose him for another, better reason. Father Anselm is a distant kinsman of the Earl of Locksley, a landowner in the counties of Yorkshire and Nottinghamshire, and I have given the priest the living here at Westbury as a boon to the Earl. This magnate is not my old friend Robert Odo, the hero of all those lively ale-house rhymes, and the man who was my liege lord and companion on many a bloody adventure – no, alas, my old friend Robin has long been in his grave – this is his son, a bird of a very different feather. Yet I would not wish to offend him by embarrassing his priestly kinsman. So I will remain silent about the true provenance of the Flask of St Luke, and I will try to control my mirth when he prates about the power of faith to move mountains and how the flask will perform miracles if only the villagers will believe in it. I am too old to make fresh enemies, and fight yet more futile battles over something as slight as a boy priest's foolish lies.

I have seen enough of battle in my long life. Quite enough.

I must husband my strength, too. I do not know how long I have left in this sinful world – it cannot be long – and before I depart I have a tale to set down upon this parchment by my own blotched and shaking hand. By strange coincidence, it too is a tale of faith, and of a mountain. A tale of that journey to the rosy city of Toulouse when I was not much older than Father Anselm – a young knight of five and twenty years. It is a tale of that old leather flask, and a tale about my

5

friend, the thief, the warrior, the cruel and generous lord – the current Earl of Locksley's father, whom all the people knew then as the outlaw Robin Hood . . .

The sound of a screaming horse ripped through the warm, dusty summer air in the hall at Westbury: a raw blast of scalding pain and rage, barely recognizable as coming from a living thing and not some monstrous creature from a sweat-drenched nightmare. I was leaning over the long table at the north end of the hall, with my steward Baldwin, and Father Arnold, the old village priest, frowning over a scatter of parchments and rolls at the tally of rents and dues from the previous year, and building myself a mild headache after several hours of close study.

At the first equine squeal, I jerked upright, turned from the table and sprinted towards the door of the hall, vaulting the central hearth that lay directly in my path and bursting out through the portal into the bright July light of the courtyard. I knew the animal that was making that terrible sound: a gigantic, noble beast, dark as sin, strong as a mountain and worth two years' revenues from Westbury. It was my destrier, my trusted friend and mount in many a desperate mêlée: it was Shaitan. And when Shaitan was angry, hurt or frightened, he was as lethal as a maddened bull – just as powerful and twice as vicious. As I burst out of the hall doorway, I saw that my warhorse, saddled, bridled and accoutred for a morning gallop, had already taken a toll on the human population of Westbury. A young groom called Matthew lay on the dried mud of the courtyard, whey-faced and clutching an obviously broken arm, his eyes wide with agony. Shaitan was pawing the ground, skittering, capering and snapping his teeth at the centre of a loose ring of my people, men-at-arms, grooms, farm servants and maids. The Westbury folk, all of whom seemed to be shouting advice over each other, were wisely keeping their distance from the vast prancing, kicking, bucking bulk of the horse. All except one: my squire Thomas, a young man of seventeen or so summers, with peat-brown hair and dark Welsh eyes, and an air of oak-hard sturdiness, who had followed me to the wars in France. Thomas had the horse's leather reins wrapped around both of his fists, pulled taut, his weight leaning back in an attempt to keep the animal at least partly anchored. Shaitan suddenly stopped his weird capering and raised his massive head in one quick jerk, hauling Thomas forward willy-nilly; the horse then let out a massive squeal of displeasure and shook his heavy head, causing Thomas to scuttle to one side, then the other. The animal's wide shoulders bunched, the head dipped and, like twin black battering rams, his hind legs pounded out, iron-shod hooves slicing the air inches from the face of an incautiously close man-at-arms behind him. It was a manoeuvre that Shaitan had been patiently taught, long before I had owned him – and his ability to do this was part of his enormous value: the backwards double-kick was a deadly strike in the fierce press of battle that could crush an enemy's skull or stave in his chest, and it was only by the grace of God that no one had been killed so far on this day. Thomas had been dragged to his knees in the courtyard dust by then, and had lost one of the reins. He grimly held the other in both hands; but Shaitan, his chestnut eyes rolling in fury, grunting neighs exploding from his nostrils, clearly resented this slight check on his liberty; the huge black head swooped down, lips peeled back to expose pink gums and big, square yellow teeth, and, fast as a pouncing cat, my warhorse lunged forward and bit down hard on Thomas's shoulder, eliciting a scream from the young man and a satisfied snort from the beast.

Into this maelstrom of angry horse and anguished squire, shouting folk and weeping, terrified servants, stepped my beloved, my utterly beautiful wife Godifa. She came out of the dairy, a white apron tied around her slim middle, the sleeves of her gown rolled up beyond her elbows, hands slightly reddened with hard work: blonde hair tucked under a neat white cap, pale cream face, sparkling violet-blue eyes – and an air of calm, quiet womanly authority, more remarkable for the fact that she had only recently passed her twentieth birthday. She seemed to glide smoothly towards Shaitan like a swan, her feet invisible beneath the hem of her long blue gown, her arms were held wide, outstretched to make the shape of the cross, and I saw then that she had a short cheese knife in her right hand. She was making a low meaningless noise in her throat as she advanced relentlessly on the destrier, who was now scuttling and prancing crabwise, shaking his back and hindquarters as if trying to wriggle his huge barrel of a body out of his tight riding saddle.

Stepping forward myself, I shouted, 'Goody, get back. For God's sake, keep away from him!' But my determined wife appeared not to hear me; she continued her calm, graceful walk towards Shaitan, crooning soft nonsensical phrases, arms out; and the crowd split before her, the folk moving aside to clear her passage like a swept-back pair of bed curtains. Shaitan saw my lady coming; he twisted his head and fixed her with his dark, malevolent eye. Then he nodded once, as if making his mind up about something, brayed deafeningly with furious outrage, and reared high on his hind legs, his broad forefeet wind-milling above Goody's head; heavy, iron-rimmed hooves the size of roof shingles pawing the air above her fragile skull.

My heart stopped. The moment was frozen: the massive, furious, tar-black animal rearing up high against a pale sky, and before it, the slender figure of Goody, arms spread abroad like Our Saviour in his Passion on the Cross.

I screamed, 'No, no!' And took a fast step closer, reaching out blindly for a trailing rein. And then Shaitan came down. He laid his hooves down softly, one after the other, with a delicate precision, on the ground in front of Goody, scarcely creating a puff of dust. His long dark head bowed before my wife, nostrils warmly puffing, forehead knocking playfully against her breasts and belly;

8

and Goody stroked his muzzle and satin neck with her left hand, still crooning, and her right arm moved smoothly along his flank. The cheese knife slipped between his belly and the twin girths holding the saddle in place, slicing through the tough binding leather in a couple of jerky thrusts. It was only then that I noticed the blood, dark fluid on his dark hide, seeping down Shaitan's flank from beneath the high saddle, showing up scarlet on Goody's white hand.

'Help me, Thomas, quickly now,' said Goody to my squire, who had got to his feet and was brushing the dust of the courtyard from his hose. And between them they carefully lifted the heavy wood-framed saddle from Shaitan's back, and the blood-and-sweat-stained blanket beneath it, and Thomas bore them away and into the gloom of the stable.

I found myself at Shaitan's head, his bridle in my shaking hand and I stroked his broad nose, and silky-hard jaw bones for a hundred heartbeats, blowing softly into his nostrils and murmuring apologies to him. I looked between his ears over the muscular arch of his neck and down into the broad hollow of his back, and I could see the wound clearly, a gash a couple of inches long running laterally to the left of his spine, just above the glossy black bulge of his haunch.

'This is the culprit, sir,' said Thomas returning from the stable with a small grey-brown object in his right hand. It was a bent three-inch nail, a little rusty and oddly small in his strong brown hand but still sharp, and now smirched with horse blood and hair. 'This must have become wedged under the saddle somehow, then worked its way through the blanket when Matthew rode him across the courtyard.'

'How is Matthew?' Goody's voice broke in.

'He'll live, my lady,' Thomas replied, his natural grave cheerfulness already reasserting itself. He smiled in admiration at Goody. 'That arm is certainly broken – but it will be a good lesson for him. It will teach him that grooms should always check their gear carefully before saddling expensive destriers – and that they should not try to ride their master's mounts without permission!'

I put my arms around Goody then, and crushed her to me, that awful moment – when Shaitan had towered above her like a solid black mountain, ready to fall on her head – still echoing shrilly in my soul. 'Promise me, promise me, my love, that you will never do something as foolish as that again,' I said, my words muffled by the white linen cap atop her head. I could smell the scent of her hair through it; and a perfume made of crushed summer roses that she sometimes wore. 'You must be careful, my darling; I do not think I could bear it if . . .'

Goody broke our embrace. She pushed back her body in the loose circle of my arms and smiled up at me. 'Oh do shut up, you silly man,' said my beloved, her violet-blue eyes glinting. 'I knew Shaitan would never really hurt me. What a fuss you do make!'

I had planned, with Thomas as an escort, to take Shaitan out for a good long gallop that morning – nowhere wild and dangerous, he was too valuable a beast to risk a carelessly broken leg by some mishap over rough ground – but the destrier was badly in need of some exercise. And while I did not fear that his wound was serious – it was a deep cut, no more nor less, and the head groom had already doctored it with a poultice of old bread and goose fat – I could certainly not ride him for some weeks. I was, however, reluctant to relinquish my own urge for fresh air – I had not left the compound of Westbury for some days, and I itched for the sensation of speed and freedom. I was more than ready that day to leave the mysteries of tallying the manor's revenues to Baldwin and Father Arnold, and enjoy some sunshine on my face and feel the wind in my hair. So I ordered a feisty bay mare from the stables to be saddled instead, strapped on my sword and found an old riding cloak. While I was waiting for my mount, I took a look at Thomas's shoulder.

My squire told me it was nothing but I made him strip off his chemise and inspected the two matching bright-red curves of swelling flesh on his chest and back that were the result of Shaitan's savage bite. He was right: no bone was damaged, the skin was barely broken, but I knew that the bruising would be spectacular and so, while my squire bore his wound stoically, I left Goody to apply a herb-laced salve of her own devising and cantered out of the main gate, leaving all my cares behind me.

And so it was that I found myself alone, on a fresh horse, riding out into the Nottinghamshire countryside that fine July morning. The fright that I had taken over Goody and Shaitan had made me a little reckless, and I put my spurs to the bay's sides and we galloped for a mile or so, taking the road towards Nottingham and heading due south. The sun was warm on my face, the horse moved smoothly under me and we ate up the ground together. On a whim, I took a path off the main road down a long tunnel of trees and, pounding along at a canter, my breath coming easily, I felt my anxiety over Goody recede. I was conscious of a deep sense of well-being: I was healthy and strong, not yet twenty-five years old; married to a wonderful woman and lord of a small but bountiful manor. On that morning, it seemed, all was well. I had proved myself as a man in war, many times, but I had no urge to seek out battle again. I had silver in my coffers and strength in my limbs. I was content to husband my lands and raise fine sons and daughters with Goody for the rest of my days.

As I cantered along the tunnel between the trees, I reflected that in the full robes of midsummer, Sherwood was as fair as a maiden on her wedding morning: the oak and elm and ash each cloaked in glowing green hues; each trunk plump with sap and bursting with life; each sun-blessed clearing fecund with bright wild flowers. The forest floor was alive with the scuttle of rabbits, the boughs rattled with the chasings of squirrels, the calling and clatter of pigeons through branches and the quick-moving shadows

11

of large game, red deer and the very occasional glimpse of wild boar.

I surged along that narrow track, urging the bay ever onward, out of sheer exuberance. The quickening forest life all around, the rhythm of my breathing, the cleansing feeling of swift forward motion, all added to my bubble of well-being. A hart bounded out in front of my horse's nose, surprising both me and my mount and I tugged the reins to check my pace, clamped my knees to keep my seat and hauled the bay to a halt. I found then I was laughing in the saddle after that slight shock, laughing for no reason but from a profound lightness of heart; a beneficent balance of the humours I had not felt in many months.

The mare was tiring, pecking against the reins and the sun was now soaring above me, not far off noon, so I turned my mount back towards the main road, and was content to walk her sedately along the leaf-padded track through the trees. I was thinking then about dinner at Westbury, and how pleasant it would be to sit at the table with Goody and share a dish or two of meat with her and a flagon of good wine; and after dinner, perhaps, we would retire to our chamber together during the long, hot afternoon, and close the wooden door on the world. Perhaps this afternoon we might between us make our first strong son . . .

I heard a rustling in the wall of leaves to my right, the sound of a large animal moving through the undergrowth with little attempt at stealth. And ahead of me to my left I heard the crack of a breaking stick. In my joy-fuddled state, I merely frowned, puzzled as to what could be making these unusual noises – a clumsy deer, a sick boar? And then, simultaneously, four men stepped out of the greenwood and stood in the track to bar my path ahead. They were very dirty, ill-clad peasant folk in greeny-brown rags, three of them favouring dark hoods, and armed with a motley collection of weapons: cudgels, quarterstaves, an axe; two held rusty swords, one a spear. I had my hand on my own sword hilt by then, and whipped my head around when I heard a noise behind me. Three men of similar ilk stood on the path behind my horse.

Seven desperate men were now ranged against me; wild men of the woods, no doubt; thieves and killers . . . well, I had fought and won against longer odds – I was well schooled in war, well armed, well mounted, young and dauntless. I took a deep breath, my stomach muscles tightened and . . .

'Look up there, Sir Alan, if you please,' said the foremost man, a slim, almost girlishly good-looking rogue, with dark curly hair on his bare head and a vicious-looking woodsman's axe resting on his shoulder. His right arm was pointing upwards, ahead of the mare's nose and to my left. My eye followed his pointing finger and my heart sank. Standing on a stout branch of a tree, twelve foot above the forest floor, was an archer: a long yew bow was in his powerful hands, an arrow nocked and aimed at my heart, the trembling hemp string in his fingers pulled back all the way to the man's grubby right ear.

'Take your hand off your sword hilt, Sir Alan – and sit very, very still if you wish to live,' said Curly-hair.

I did as I was ordered. The men swarmed around the bay, two of them taking a firm hold on either side of the bridle, and Curly-hair pulled my long sword from its scabbard and held it up in the air with a whistle of admiration, as well he might. It was a beautiful object: a long slim blade of Spanish steel, sharp as a barber's razor and engraved in tiny gold letters along the fuller with the word 'Fidelity'. Above the wide steel crosspiece, a long leather-wrapped wood-and-iron hilt balanced the unusual length of the blade and the pommel was made of a thick, heavy ring of silver encasing a magnificent jewel, a sapphire of palest blue. It was a costly sword, worth almost as much as Shaitan, and a blade that I had won in single combat to the death with its previous owner: it soured my belly like a draught of bad wine to see it in another man's hands.

13

Curly-hair's greed for that blade was plain to see. 'I shall safeguard this for you, Sir Alan,' he said, in a voice thickened with a kind of lustful envy.

Surrounded by these men, I was led, still a-horse, off the main tunnel-like track and into deep forest. For several miles, indeed for more than an hour, we plodded along pathways that were often no more than deer tracks a few inches wide. The men were silent, watching me closely from under their hoods, with Curly-hair leading the way, my sword Fidelity on one shoulder and his axe on the other. They offered me no harm as we travelled along, and when I asked them where they were taking me, their only response was to mutter that I had been invited to dinner. And I began to relax, for I knew who it was that had ordered these men, these desperate outlaws, to fetch me. It could only be one man; and, as far as I knew, he did not wish me any harm.

At last we came upon a wide clearing in the forest, an encamp-ment of some permanence. A few crude shelters had been constructed at the edge of the space from cut wood and branches. A deer carcass turned on a spit over a fire in the centre, and two dozen or so men, women and children busied themselves; the men sitting in groups and drinking from a barrel of ale, or playing at dice or cleaning their weapons; the women sewing furs, mending their rags, moving about with bundles of firewood or bawling lovingly after scampering children. Two tall figures stood on the far side of the open space: one, a giant nearly seven foot tall, with shaggy blond hair that fell below his shoulders, was leaning on a vast double-headed axe. He was in earnest conversation with his companion. This fellow, though a little shorter, was still a well set-up, handsome man of about thirty-five years old, unshaven, dressed in a scuffed leather jerkin and black hose, a long sword at his waist. He watched me advance across the clearing and dismount before him, a smile on his lean, stubbled face, his lively grey, almost silver eyes sparkling with mischievous joy.

'Ah, there you are at last, Alan,' said Robin. For before me stood Robin Hood, Earl of Locksley, my friend, mentor and liege lord. 'Don't you ever leave the comfort of your hall for a healthy breath of fresh air these days? I've had men all over Sherwood waiting to waylay you for some days.'

I turned to my curly-haired captor, who was now standing beside the blond giant, and held out my right hand. 'I'll take my sword now, if you please.' The young man glanced quickly across at Robin and with a deep sigh of regret he flipped the blade off his shoulder and put the leather hilt of Fidelity into my hand.

'God's bulging ball-sack, I'm surprised to see you out and about, young Alan! I imagine you've barely left your bed, these past few weeks,' said the huge man, chuckling lewdly. He turned to Robin and said, 'You know what these lusty newly-weds are like: rut, rut, rut, all day, all night . . . I'll wager Alan and Goody have been banging away five times a day like a pair of love-drunk rabbits.' He affected a hideous, false woman's voice. 'Ooh, Alan, do come back to bed and bring your big sword with you . . .'

I paused in the act of sliding Fidelity back into its scabbard and glared at the giant. 'I give you fair warning, John Nailor: if you ever speak about my wife in that disrespectful way again, I will shove this blade so far up your fat arse that you'll be using the point as a tooth-pick.' I looked hard at the big man, holding his eye, then slammed the sword home into its sheath.

Little John's mouth opened but he said nothing for a couple of heartbeats; out of shock, I am quite certain, rather than fear. But I do not believe he had been seriously threatened for many a year. Young Curly-hair took a step forward, but John put a massive hand on his chest that stopped his advance and said, 'Hold up, Gavin.'

There was a long, awkward silence, during which John and I stared at each other. It was finally broken by Robin. 'He's right, John. That was most discourteous of you. I think you should make an apology to Alan for speaking ill of his lady.'

15

Little John looked over at Robin in disbelief. 'Apologize? You want me to say I'm sorry?'

'I accept your apology, John,' I said, grinning at him. 'And I particularly appreciate the handsome way in which the apology was made. Now, this fellow here made a mention of dinner. Was that merely a ruse to bring me here without a fight?'

That golden July afternoon, at a long trestle table of greenwood planks set up in the centre of the clearing, we ate roasted venison, pigeon pie and barley bread and a simple sallet of wild leaves and herbs, washed down with a goodly quantity of freshly brewed ale. As we ate, I studied my lord, the notorious Earl of Locksley, and I was struck by his simple, radiating happiness; his deep, uncomplicated enjoyment of life. Here was a man entering the middle years, although still as slim and fit as a twenty-year-old, who had been one of the greatest nobles at the court of King Richard, and one of his greatest warriors – and he was living like an animal in the wilderness of Sherwood, surrounded by a score of cut-throats, with a price on his head. Yet, while I'd known Robin for ten years or more, and knew him as well as any man, I'd never seen my lord more contented.

He had been recently outlawed, of course, and not for the first time. As a youngster he had been declared beyond the law – after he had killed a bullying, abusive priest – and Robin had taken to the predatory life of a thief in the woods like a pike to a fishpond. He had robbed from the rich who were foolish enough to travel through his part of Sherwood, and taken their silver by the sackload, and he had given protection to the poor from other bandits and evil men, and even from the law – for a price. Robin was known then across the land for his ruthlessness to his enemies and for his reckless generosity to his friends – to cross him meant death or mutilation, but if you were inside his circle, quite simply, he would die for you. At the height of his fame, he was one of the most powerful men in the country, able to purchase a full pardon from King Richard with barrels of stolen silver, and be granted the fair hand and fair estates of the Countess of Locksley, his sweetheart Marie-Anne.

After his pardon, Robin had served Richard well: in the Holy Land fighting the Saracens, in England during the rebellion, and in the long bloody wars in Normandy against Philip of France. But our hero-king Richard was dead, killed by a crossbow bolt outside an insignificant fortress in Aquitaine. And the new King, Richard's weak, vengeful and duplicitous brother John, had no love for Robin and had repaid my lord's loyalty to his older sibling by declaring the Earl of Locksley an outlaw, whose head was worth a small hill of silver to any man bold enough to try to take it.

There had been no trial, no assembly of the barons to weigh the merits of the case: a proclamation had been issued by the new Sheriff of Nottinghamshire – a greedy, short-legged crony of King John's named Sir William Brewer – and a strong force of knights and men-at-arms had galloped north to occupy Kirkton, Robin's castle in South Yorkshire that overlooked the Locksley Valley. They had found the place deserted; an echoing shell without a soul in residence, without beasts, fowls or a roaming stray dog. Even the fishpond had been emptied, every pot and pan packed up; every bale of hay and peck of corn long gone. Robin had given his goods and chattels to his friends, sent his horses, trained men and armour to his elder brother William, a petty baron who held the honour of Edwinstowe, and sent his wife and two boys across the sea to live under the protection of the Queen Mother, the venerable Eleanor of Aquitaine, where they would be safe from John's vengeance. Robin himself had slipped away into the vast, tangled depths of Sherwood, the haunt of wild men cast out by decent society, my lord's old playground – and his true home.

I had served King Richard too. He and I had even made music together, as we were both *trouvères* – poets who 'found' or composed songs during our leisure hours. And I mourned the loss of the

Lionheart deeply, I had liked and admired him as a man and a fellow warrior, and he had been most generous and kind to me – knighting me personally, despite my lowly origins, and granting me lands and a place among his trusted companions. But I mourned him too because I hated his brother John perhaps even more than Robin did. I had served John once, reluctantly, and had vowed that I would never do so again. Indeed, I had no obligation to do so: one of John's first acts as King was to appropriate the lands that Richard had granted me: the rich manors of Burford, Stroud and Edington in England, and the war-ravaged manor of Clermont-sur-Andelle in Normandy. But I considered myself lucky – I had not been outlawed like Robin and, had I still had possession of these lands, I would also have owed John my service as a fighting knight. However, on that gorgeous summer afternoon, as I feasted with Robin and Little John, and jested and swapped stories, all that I had to uphold the dignity of my rank was the small manor of Westbury, which I held of the man sitting across the table from me, the outlawed Earl of Locksley.

While we ate, we passed the time in idle conversation: how was Marie-Anne, and her two boys? All well, Robin assured me, the boys growing up fast in Queen Eleanor's travelling court. And was Goody pregnant yet? Robin knew that a son to follow in my foot-steps was my heart's desire. No, not yet, but it was still early in the day. I looked at John sternly, half-expecting him to utter some crude comment about our attempts to make a baby – I had meant what I said about fighting him if he showed the least disrespect to Goody – but he seemed to have taken my threat to heart, and the big man merely grinned at me, winked cheekily and busied himself stripping the flesh from a whole haunch of roasted venison with his teeth.

'So you've had men looking for me about Nottinghamshire,' I said, when I had finally eaten my fill and I was sitting back, picking my teeth with a splinter from the table. 'Why did you not just send a messenger to Westbury? Or come and see me yourself. Goody would have been delighted to receive a visit from you.'

'I'm a wanted man, Alan,' said Robin with a happy grin, 'I can't go wandering about the countryside paying calls on the gentry whenever I feel like it. The Sheriff of Nottinghamshire is after my blood and I tremble at the thought of his terrible wrath.'

'Could it be, just perhaps, that the Sheriff is wrathful because a party of his tax gatherers was ambushed last week and robbed of nigh on ten pounds in silver up by Southwell?' I asked.

'Could be, could well be.' Robin's grin had become dangerously close to a smirk. 'Who knows what makes that funny little mountebank angry? Silly man. He stamps around Nottingham Castle, ranting and raving, pulling his own hair out – his *own* hair, mark you – and issuing dire threats that he cannot possibly fulfil – no sense of moderation, no sense of dignity and no manners either. I sent him a pair of venison the other day, two fine plump hinds. A noble gift, you might well think. But did he have the courtesy to thank me? No. My people in the castle tell me that he harangued his men-at-arms for an hour, then raised the price on my head to fifty pounds! Fool.'

I laughed. 'Are you deliberately trying to goad him?' I asked. 'Sending him a brace of the King's deer, poached from under his nose? What did you expect – a big wet kiss and an invitation to keep Christmas with his wife and family this year?'

'I have no desire at all for his company, still less that of his appalling wife and her snotty brats – a simple thank-you would have sufficed. People are so ungrateful these days. But that brings me rather neatly to the reason why I wanted to see you.'

'No,' I said quickly. 'The answer is no.'

Robin looked hurt. 'I haven't even asked you the question.' He looked over at Little John. 'You see what I mean – there is no gratitude in the world. None at all.' Then to me: 'Come now, Alan, don't you even want to hear my proposal?'

19

'You want me to help you do something bad, I feel it in my bones, something far beyond the law and very likely immoral too – you want me to murder or kidnap someone; or, most probably, to help you steal something valuable that you have set your heart on. And that will put me afoul of the Sheriff, and have him coming after *my* blood. The answer is, no, thank you, Robin. I just want to stay quietly at home at Westbury, write a few half-decent *chansons*, tend to my lands and put a baby in my wife's womb. That's all I want. I don't want to go on a wild escapade with you; I don't want to hurt anybody. I'm sorry, Robin, but whatever your proposal is, the answer must be no.'

'I want you to help me right a great wrong,' said Robin, looking absurdly pious. 'I want you to help me help a poor man, a friend of a friend of ours, who has been cruelly ill-used by a powerful lord. I have always thought of you as a decent man, Alan, a man on the side of all that is good and right. And now you have the chance to do something fine in this ugly world.' Robin fixed me with his odd silver eyes. 'Surely, as a good Christian, you want to make the world a better place, to help the poor and weak. Will you do that, for me, Alan? Help me to help someone. For the sake of all that we have done together, for our friendship?'

I said nothing, but I felt my heart beginning to sink.

'Allow me to tell you a little story,' said Robin, smiling like a fox outside a chicken run. 'Then you can give me your answer.'

Chapter Two

'Malloch Baruch is not a rich man,' Robin began, 'although to make his livelihood he deals with expensive materials, and must keep a goodly store of them. He is a goldsmith by trade, a Jew, of course, and he and his family lived in York – until ten years ago.'

My lord paused and looked at me, to see if I was attending closely to his words. I nodded, and swallowed thickly, as the memories came flooding back. A couple of years after I had joined Robin's men, he and I had been caught up in a bloody, Devil-inspired frenzy in York, during which almost the entire Jewish population of that city had been hounded to death by crowds of Christians fired by religious zeal. The Jews had been assaulted and robbed and forced to take refuge in the King's Tower at York Castle – and there, for several days of brutal siege, they were surrounded by a boiling sea of Christian citizenry crazed with hatred for the unbelievers. Until the entire surviving community of York Jews – about a hundred and fifty men, women and children – decided to take drastic action. On the ground floor of the tower, trapped and desperate, the men of each family cut the throats of their wives and children, and then took turns to end each other's lives. For a moment, I recalled the lake of gore and its meaty stench, and the pathetic curled bodies carpeting the slick floor, their white throats sliced open by loving familiar hands. Robin and I, and our Jewish friend Reuben, had escaped only by the skin of our teeth, and Reuben's only daughter Ruth was killed in the mêlée while we were cutting our way free.

It was not a memory I relished.

Robin could see that he had my full attention. 'By luck, or the Hand of God, if you prefer, Malloch Baruch happened to be away from York on an errand in Lincoln during that time of madness,' he said, 'although his wife and young children perished in the King's Tower with all the rest of them.'

Robin paused again and scratched his growing beard. He had stopped smiling by now. 'So Malloch lost everything: his family were dead, his precious metals stolen from his workshop, his house burned to the ground. But he did not give in to despair, as might many a man. After he had buried his wife and children in York, and said the traditional words of mourning over them, he returned to Lincoln and began again. Reuben helped him in those early days: he arranged for Malloch to borrow money to buy gold to work with; he found him a new workshop and generous clients in and around Lincoln. Malloch worked hard, long days and nights hunched over his workbench patiently fashioning gold and silver trinkets for his clients, and with the passing of time his spirit revived. He married again, his new wife bore him a son, and then a daughter, and his fame as a goldsmith grew with his new family. Ten years on, and his reputation as a goldsmith is as one of the finest craftsmen in England. But, in spite of this, his living is still precarious; he took on heavy debts to rebuild his life, and he has not yet redeemed them. You must remember that he lost half a lifetime of savings in the disaster at York and that scale of loss is not recovered by a few years of hard labour. Then, two years ago, Malloch had a stroke of fortune – or so he believed.'

The shadows were lengthening in the clearing and the men and women of Robin's band were making their preparations for nightfall: wide deer skins were being laid out on the grass for the family groups over by the tree line, while the single men and women laid their blankets and furs by the fire. Cut branches were being stacked in high tottering piles by the stone-lined hearth to fuel a damped blaze during the night. In the rough wooden shelters, mothers washed their children's grubby faces, men took a last tankard of ale or scrubbed their teeth with salt and well-chewed willow twigs.

'Gavin,' called Robin to the ruffian who had brought me here, as he passed by the long table with an armful of firewood, 'fetch us some of that cheese, would you, and some more ale.' He turned to me: 'You'll stop with us tonight, Alan?'

I muttered something to the effect of Goody worrying about me, but Robin waved that idea away. 'I sent word that you were with me,' he said. 'She's a sensible lass who won't be overly concerned if you don't come home till the morrow.'

I privately noted that Robin had messengers at his beck and call who *could* visit Westbury any time they pleased. And realized that the only reason I had been waylaid in that alarming manner earlier was because Robin wished it so. He could easily have summoned me in many other ways. I wondered why he had chosen that dramatic method, and knew then that the answer lay within the question: Robin often loved to pose and strut and perform like an actor in an Easter mystery play – it was in his very bones. He loved the idea that he was the hero of his own *chanson* or epic poem, and he was prepared to go a good deal out of his way to make his actions seem larger than life. But Robin had picked up the threads of his speech, and I was caught up once again in the tale of the unfortunate Jewish goldsmith.

'So Malloch had a stroke of good fortune: he was visited at his workshop by a Sacrist, a canon of Welbeck Abbey. You know the place, of course?'

23

I did. It was a remote house of Premonstratensians in the depths of Sherwood, not far from Worksop. The canons were reputed to be zealous and extremely wealthy. I nodded warily. Robin's relationship with wealthy Houses of God might be likened to the relationship between a hungry wolf and a newborn lamb.

'Abbot Richard, it seemed, had a desire for a set of golden altar paraphernalia, liturgical vessels and the like, for his Church of St James the Great, and he had heard of the growing fame of Malloch the goldsmith of Lincoln. The Sacrist had a marvellous commission to dangle in front of the craftsman: a full set of altar ornaments – chalice and ciborium, monstrance, holy water vat, wine jug, paten and pyx, a pair of candelabra – and a magnificent crucifix as the centrepiece – all in solid gold, carved and inscribed and decorated with rubies, enamels and pearls and other precious items. "Spare no expense," the Sacrist said to our friend. "Count not the cost, my good man: magnificence is required!" It was to be Malloch's masterpiece, a work that would be the wonder of Christendom.'

I murmured in appreciation: in my mind's eye I could see the altar spread with these precious items, the sacred heart of the Abbey church glowing warmly with yellow candlelight reflected from these golden ornaments. It would indeed create a wondrous sight for worshippers – and ensure that Welbeck Abbey received a stream of pilgrims wishing to view such a splendid display. The Abbey would become justly famous; the Abbot's influence and power would grow.

'Malloch asked for a small deposit in silver to pay for his materials; he showed his sketches to the Abbot himself and they were approved – even highly praised. And then he began to work. For six long months he toiled on the Welbeck pieces, eschewing all other employment, putting his heart and soul into creating the most wonderful objects the world had yet seen. He constantly improved his designs, making them ever more costly, ever more fabulous, and borrowing money from his fellow Jews to pay for the finest jewels, for the extra gold and silver required. Then, at Easter last year, he presented his work to the Abbey.

'Abbot Richard and all the canons were duly struck dumb with wonder at the artistry of his finished objects, and they were received with much rejoicing. Then Malloch presented his bill of accounts, detailing the monies he had outlaid on metals and jewels, the wages he had paid his apprentices and journeymen, and asking most humbly if he might be recompensed at the Abbot's earliest convenience.

'At first the Abbot was all kindness and reassurances; the money would certainly be forthcoming once the Welbeck estate wool revenues had come in at Michaelmas. But, as the months passed, the Abbot's tone changed. He spoke of the deposit in silver as if that sum were a full and final settlement; then he spoke of Malloch's duty to God, of the historical crimes of the Jews, and suggested that the "gift" of the golden altar ornaments might be seen as an act of atonement. Malloch's increasingly vociferous pleas for payment – for at least a part of the huge sums he had outlaid – were ignored. A year passed and his fellow Jews began to demand that he make good his loans to them, but the goldsmith was unable to honour his debts. Malloch was staring ruin in the face; he went to Welbeck earlier this summer and begged for even a part of the money to meet his bills: he went down on his knees in front of the Abbot. But the Abbot's men-at-arms dragged him away, and beat him and ejected him from the Abbey. Finally, in despair, and not knowing where else to turn, he came to me.'

My heart had been touched by the story of the Jew but this was not an unusual tale. The Jews were despised by many for their rejection of Our Saviour and for their usurious activities; while many a nobleman or bishop was happy to borrow from them, even agreeing to very high annual repayments, it was not uncommon for the same lord to refuse to repay the sum when it was called in. Indeed, some people whispered that the persecution of the Jews

25

in York ten years ago had been at least partly fired by landowners who wanted to see those they owed money to destroyed and their mortgages consumed in the flames of the riot.

Robin had been watching me as I thought. Indeed, he seemed to have been reading my mind: 'Do you remember that fellow, Brother Ademar, from the siege of the King's Tower?'

I shook my head.

'He was a monk dressed all in white, something of a skilled orator, who used his talent to exhort the crowds to kill the Jews.'

I remembered him then; and I remembered Robin hurling a great stone down on him from the battlements of the tower, which smashed his skull like an egg.

'Brother Ademar came from Welbeck – he was an official of the Abbey, the cellarer, I believe, for many years,' said Robin. 'Indeed, he was Abbot Richard's younger brother. That is a family that clearly has little love for the Jews of England.'

I sighed, beaten. 'What does Malloch want us to do?'

Robin smiled at me, his bright eyes reflecting the last gleams of sunlight. 'I knew I could count on you, Alan,' he said, and he reached forward across the table and gripped my forearm for a moment. 'I have promised Malloch that I will go to Welbeck, take the golden pieces from the altar and return them to him.'

'And we do this for a fat fee – for a suitable recompense, I mean,' I said, with a smile to take the sting from my words.

'For a suitable recompense, yes,' said Robin gravely. 'Should I put my life at risk, endanger the lives of my men, for nothing?'

I rode back to Westbury the next morning with my heart in turmoil. I had, of course, agreed to go with Robin to Welbeck in three days' time to steal back the golden altar items for poor Malloch – how could I refuse, after that doleful story? And the goldsmith was a friend of Reuben's, which meant that Robin wanted to help him, and I did too – I owed Reuben my life several times over. So despite what I had promised myself, I was about to embark on a wild, unlawful escapade – and I wasn't sure how I felt about it. What I had said to Robin was quite true: I did want to live the quiet life with Goody, tend my lands, husband my crops and raise strong sons; but a part of me was vibrating like a vielle string at the thought of action. I had been a thief before I was a warrior, and long before I was a lord of lands, and I had never forgotten the thrill of larceny that I'd loved as a snot-nosed cut-purse in the crowded streets of Nottingham.

But I did not think it would be an easy task – we had to enter an abbey filled with dozens of vigorous young canons and muscular lay workers, plus a dozen of the Abbot's personal men-at-arms, break into their church, purloin their most holy, treasured possession and escape – all without being recognized. On top of that, I had made Robin swear that we would not kill or hurt any of the Abbey folk – they were not enemy soldiers to be slaughtered; most of them were doubtless good, decent Englishmen trying to live a quiet life of religious devotion – and, with a fine show of reluctance, my lord of Locksley had agreed to my conditions.

Finally, there was Goody. What would she say when I told her I was riding off on a madcap adventure with Robin that could easily end in death, disaster or outlawry? Robin had made the obvious suggestion that I should not tell her where I was going or what I was planning to do, but I had rejected that. I did not wish there to be any falsehoods between myself and my beloved.

In the event, when I told Goody about Malloch and his golden ornaments her response surprised me. 'Of course, you must do it,' she said. 'God made you a knight for a purpose and, as a knight, it is your Christian duty to protect the weak – even a Jew – and see justice done. A poor man has been cheated by a rich and powerful one: you must set things right, if it is in your hands to do so.'

I should not have been surprised. Goody had taken to reading romances recently and had developed a conception of knightly conduct that was very far from the brutal, gore-sodden reality. Her friend, Robin's wife Marie-Anne, Countess of Locksley, had sent her a copy of a poem by Christian of Troyes called 'Lancelot, the Knight of the Cart', and she had read it all the way through at least three times to my knowledge. It tells a tale of the noble knight Lancelot and his adulterous relationship with Guinevere, the wife of King Arthur. This has long proved a popular theme with the ladies – as a *trouvère*, I had even composed a few *cansos* on the subject myself. I had found, though, that my attitude had changed somewhat since I had become a married man, and lord of a moderate estate. And while I did not suspect my lovely Goody of a liaison with a younger man – I found her enthusiasm for these fanciful tales disconcerting.

With Goody's blessing, then, I set about preparing myself for my mission of justice with Robin. My primary concern was that I should not be recognized as Sir Alan Dale, lord of the manor of Westbury, by the canons of Welbeck – the Abbey was, after all, only a day's ride from Westbury, and though the canons kept to themselves, for the most part, and resided in a very remote part of Sherwood, they could conceivably be considered my neighbours. I did not care to run into the Abbot at, say, Nottingham Castle in the years to come and have to explain why I had robbed him and his brothers of their golden hoard – I cared even less for the idea that they might complain to King John and petition to have me brought before his courts. I could expect little justice, and even less mercy, if I found myself there. So I cut myself a broad strip of soft cowhide and tied it diagonally around my head in the manner of someone who has lost an eye. And I began to experiment with a weak glue of boiled beef tendons, a few drops of blood squeezed from a pin-prick in my finger and a bowl of milled oats. The day before I was due to depart with Robin, I had completed my disguise and I was admiring myself at the far end of the hall in a large polished-silver mirror that belonged to Goody.

28

My own mother – God rest her soul – would not have owned me. A desperate villain looked out at me from Goody's fine mirror: I was dressed in rags; my blond hair was hidden by a tightly fitting woollen workman's cap; half my face was covered by the broad leather eye-patch and the rest of my face and my hands were covered with a disgusting-looking skin complaint, created by sticking individual oats to my skin in little clumps and colouring them with drops of dried blood. I looked rather like one of the misbegotten lepers I had seen in the Holy Land during the Great Pilgrimage – indeed, for a moment, I was concerned that the canons would not allow me entrance to Welbeck, fearing that I would spread some awful contagion. But I was satisfied that no one would recognize the handsome young knight, Sir Alan of Westbury, in the foul-looking vagabond who stared out at me from the silver. As a final touch, I wadded a piece of clean linen and pushed it inside my left cheek, and that gave the effect of distorting the line of my jaw and cheekbone on that side. It made my speech seem muffled and odd – which pleased me, for I did not want my voice to be recognized either – but I did not expect to be doing much talking at Welbeck. I was just admiring my villainous reflection, grinning in satisfaction, when I heard a polite cough behind me, and whirled around. It was Baldwin, my usually very competent steward, looking a little shame-faced.

He was not alone.

'Excuse me, Sir Alan, but we have a visitor: Sir Nicholas de Scras has just arrived and he insists on paying his respects to you. I've arranged for his horse to be stabled and his belongings to be taken to the guest hall; I hope that is all satisfactory.'

And I looked beyond my retainer at the sturdy familiar figure of the knight. Sir Nicholas was still the same slim, fit-looking man I had known in the Holy Land; his iron-grey hair had perhaps a few more flecks of silver in it; but his browny-green eyes were still sharp. He looked utterly appalled.

'By the Cross, Alan – is that really you?' said my old friend.

I could feel myself blushing as I hastily pulled the cap and eye-patch off my head, and scrubbed at the dried oats with my cuff in an effort to dislodge them.

'Why in the name of all that is holy are you got up like a thrice-poxed beggarman?'

'It is for an entertainment,' I mumbled through my sodden cheek cloth. 'A bit of mummery for the village, er, for the Church, to celebrate the Assumption of the Blessed Virgin in a fortnight.'

'Is that really suitable attire for a church? Under the eyes of Almighty God? Well, my friend, it is your business, of course, but . . .' Then Sir Nicholas stopped, his face seemed to be contorting, bulging and writhing, his skin above the neck was turning the colour of a peeled beetroot. I realized then, with a dismal sinking of the heart, that he was trying not to laugh.

'To be honest, Sir Alan,' wheezed this pious knight, gasping, and causing his muddy eyes to protrude in a quite unnerving manner, 'You look rather . . . absurd . . . forgive me . . . like a pantaloon . . . ha-ha . . . like a seller of quack remedies at a fair . . . ha-ha . . . who has cut himself shaving and then fallen face-first into a bowl of porridge. Oh. Ha-ha-ha-ha-ha!'

Then Sir Nicholas, former Knight Hospitaller, warrior of Christ and pitiless scourge of the Saracen hordes, surrendered at last to his mirth. He threw back his head and brayed like a drunken donkey at his own enormous wit.

I straightened my back. 'Welcome to my hall, Sir Nicholas,' I said coldly. 'What a wonderful surprise. Baldwin, stir yourself and bring us wine, will you? And hot water and a towel.'

Sir Nicholas de Scras poured the wine while I scrubbed the dried oats from my face; and in a little while I recovered my usual good humour and began to enjoy the company of my old friend.

'What brings you here, Nicholas?' I asked. 'I had thought you would have your hands full in serving William Marshal, the newly

30

made Earl of Pembroke. Does he no longer require your skill at arms?'

'Hmm. Yes. Well, in truth, I have left the Earl's service. I'm an idle fellow these days, Alan, a gentleman of leisure,' said Sir Nicholas with a tight smile. 'Plenty of time on my hands. My nephews are away training to be knights in Kent. Our lands at Horsham are run by the steward. There's not much for me to do.'

'The King would surely welcome a knight of your experience,' I said, somewhat unkindly, for he had once been John's man and had tried to persuade me to join that household. Sir Nicholas looked at me hard over the rim of his cup.

'The Earl of Pembroke now serves King John. But I will not. That is why I left his service. I will not serve that impious, royal, red-haired little shit-weasel again,' he said flatly. 'He humiliated me after we surrendered Nottingham to Richard – called me a coward to my face, would you believe it?' Nicholas laughed grimly. 'I'll roast in Hell before I will wield my sword for that croaking, God-mocking popinjay.

'Do you know that he once asked me if I truly believed that the Devil existed? And then he mocked my answer. No, Alan, I will not serve John or his man the Earl of Pembroke; and so I think my fighting days must be behind me. In a year or two, when my nephew William is old enough to shoulder his responsibilities for my brother's lands at Horsham, I will leave this world behind and offer myself as a novice at Lewes Priory, our family has long had connections there. I plan to spend the rest of my days praying for my family and the forgiveness of my sins.'

He did not seem old enough yet to retire from the world and take the black habit of a Cluniac monk. However, I could feel a deep sadness in him; I believed that he had always regretted his decision to leave the Order of the Knights Hospitaller, and I sensed that he felt that by joining another religious institution – even as a novice – he hoped to regain some of the comradeship that he'd enjoyed among the Hospitallers.

'I'd better give you a decent dinner before you take your vows, then,' I said with a smile. 'You'll be on stale bread and cold cabbage broth, with the brothers at Lewes, and nothing to drink but water.'

'Well, I won't say no to a decent meal,' Sir Nicholas replied, smiling, 'but I'm not hanging up my spurs just yet. I plan to travel a little, see some old friends, make a small pilgrimage or two.'

Over dinner, the best that the servants could prepare at such short notice, I tried to raise Sir Nicholas's spirits, and we spoke of battles won and lost, or brave men we had known – many of whom were now dead. Goody left us to our manly talk, and in the dusk of twilight, we pulled up stools beside the hearth at the centre of the hall and finished our wine as we toasted our boot soles.

'There is another reason why I have come to see you, Alan,' said Sir Nicholas, at last. 'I apologize for springing myself on you without a word of warning: but what I have to say is important, and I wanted to tell you as soon as possible.'

I had been half-expecting something of this kind. Nicholas de Scras was not an aimless man and I suspected that there was some deeper reason for his sudden arrival, deeper anyway than the urge to see an old comrade. I refilled his wine cup and kept silent.

'I still have friends in the Hospitallers,' Sir Nicholas said. 'A few who understand why I felt it was my duty to leave the Order. And I write to them, and meet up with them from time to time.' He took a sip of his wine; he seemed almost a little embarrassed. I sat back on my stool and waited for him to come to the point.

'As you know, there has always been a great rivalry between the Templars and the Hospitallers – we should be as brothers, I know, united in our love of Christ and serving God shoulder to shoulder with humble hearts; but the truth is that the Templars are an arrogant, headstrong lot, obsessed with money and power, for the most part, and we often see each other as our opponents, to be overcome, outdone; that is to say . . . there have been times when we have, God forgive us, rejoiced at the Templars' misfortune.'

He took a sip of wine and continued. 'I heard a rumour of such a misfortune when I was visiting a Brother Hospitaller in Leicestershire – how we chuckled about it together. The misfortune happened to the Templars of France, of the Paris Temple, to be precise – and I'm sorry to say that this rumour concerns you.'

I noticed that he used the words 'us' and 'we' to describe the Hospitallers, although he had left his Order nearly ten years ago; also, I had a fairly good idea what he was referring to by this 'misfortune', but I held my tongue. I wanted to hear what the Knight Templars were saying about me and my dealings in Paris.

'My Hospitaller friend told me that the Templars had been deprived of a significant sum in silver last year by a clever forgery. Apparently, the thief had got hold of one of the Templars' promissory notes, the parchment letters that, on production, allow the bearer to draw sums in silver from Templar preceptories across Christendom – and which in some quarters are deemed to be as good as coin itself, perhaps even better, as they are easier to carry through dangerous lands. Anyway, the thief or thieves had possession of one of these letters, and they had copied it and used the copy to draw funds – five hundred pounds! – from the Paris Temple. The canny Knights of the Temple of Solomon handed over five hundred pounds of silver. Can you imagine? They gave a hoard of silver to a plausible thief who came to them bearing nothing more than a letter written in their code. He'd have needed a train of packhorses to carry it away, though I doubt he could sit his own horse for laughing.'

There was a little pause and I felt that Sir Nicholas was waiting for me to say something. So I said blandly, 'That seems a little foolish, to hand over such a huge quantity of silver to an unknown man on the strength of a little piece of parchment.'

'Doesn't it,' said Nicholas. He gave me an odd, penetrating look.

'Did I mention that the letter was an almost perfect copy of a genuine promissory note? Save for the sum involved. The original note, the genuine one, was made out for a little over two English pounds. The false note had been rewritten, copied almost exactly by someone who knew the Templar codes, and only the sum involved had been changed.'

Once more Sir Nicholas paused and gave me that strange look, as if he were trying to see inside my soul. I said nothing, so he continued: 'The Templars are, understandably, extremely angry about this theft. They plan to have their vengeance on the miscreant, and, if possible, to recover their money. In any case, they plan to make an example of the man – to deter others from attempting a similar crime. Harsh words have been spoken, and ugly sentiments have been expressed about the prolonged torture and summary execution of the thief. They plan to move against him, to take him up for trial before the next full moon.'

Again he paused, and again I stayed mute. Sir Nicholas de Scras sighed. 'The Templars believe that this bold thief was the man for whom the original note, the one for two pounds, was made out. And that man is listed in their records as one Alan Dale, the knight of Westbury in the English county of Nottingham.'

Chapter Three

After these words, Sir Nicholas put down his wine cup and looked at me levelly. 'Alan,' he said, 'tell me truthfully, as an old friend, was it you who stole the Templars' silver?'

I looked him straight in the eye and said, 'No, it was not. I swear by my faith that I am innocent. But it is true that I was the man with the original, the genuine note. And I must shoulder a small part of the blame for the theft. It was not of my doing and, indeed, I did not know about it until afterwards, but I did benefit from it.'

My friend looked puzzled. I carried on. 'But Nicholas, I am afraid that I cannot say more about this matter. I am bound to silence. It is a matter of personal honour.'

The former Hospitaller nodded slowly. 'I believe you are innocent of the crime,' he said. 'And that makes me easier in my conscience; but it does not materially affect what I am planning to do. If you will have me, I plan to remain here for a week or so until the Templars come: I am your man until then. If you choose to resist them, my sword is yours; if you wish to submit, I will stand beside you at your trial and testify to your good character – and ensure that you suffer no maltreatment at their hands.'

I felt a lump forming in my throat, and I was almost too moved to speak. Sir Nicholas was a formidable fighter: I had seen his silent savagery, his peerless killing efficiency on the battlefield and off it. I could hardly think of a better man to have at my shoulder in a hard fight; but he was also a much-respected knight, a man of influence and family. He could ensure, were I to surrender myself to the mercy of the Knights, that I did not end up screaming in a dungeon under the red-hot knives of the Templar sergeants. It was a noble offer, and I was grateful for it.

'It would be my great pleasure if you would consent to spend a few weeks here at Westbury,' I said. 'The guest hall is at your disposal, and though I must be off tomorrow morning on some private business, we can perhaps enjoy a little sport on my land with hawk and hounds when I return.'

And we clasped hands.

I met Robin the next day at noon by an oak tree half a dozen miles south of Welbeck Abbey. It was an old meeting place for Robin's men: a vast hollow oak in thick woodland at the edge of the manor of Edwinstowe, the lands belonging to his brother William. The tree was sometimes used to store poached venison carcasses and high up on the inside iron hooks had been hammered in from which to hang the meat.

Robin was not alone when we met, which was fortunate because, without the sight of Little John's massive form beside him, I cannot be certain that I would have recognized him. His light-brown hair had been made grey by the application of hearth ash, as had his sparse facial hair, which had grown into a disreputable straggling beard and moustache, and he had deepened the laughter creases in his face with the application of charcoal from the same fireplace. He wore a long ragged robe, with a deep hood, and stood so that his back appeared stooped and bent. He was leaning on a long staff, with a scallop shell tied to the end, and had even gone so far as to colour his teeth with resin so that he appeared to have only one or two remaining. I had to look at him twice to see that it was indeed my friend Robin – at first I saw nothing but a bent elderly pilgrim, weary beyond imagining by the long years of his life and with one foot already sunk in the grave.

When I slipped from my horse and took him by the arms to stare into his face, he straightened up and smiled at me and I could see for the first time, from a distance of no more than a foot or so, the skilful artifice that had gone into ageing him.

I greeted Little John and waved a hand at three hooded figures standing by the base of the tree, carrying long yew bows and holding the horses' heads. One of them I saw was Gavin, the curly-haired outlaw who had so coveted my sword. While Robin and John peered into my face and complimented me on my own disguise – John advising with a guffaw that I stay away from hungry horses which might wish to make a meal of me – I untied my sword belt and handed the weapon over to Gavin. 'Take very good care of that, my friend; I shall most certainly be needing it later,' I said with a friendly grin.

Gavin ducked his head and took Fidelity with both hands, almost reverently. Robin vaulted on to his horse, in an energetic bound that belied his old-man's costume, and we all mounted in turn and headed north towards Welbeck.

A couple of hours later, around the middle of the afternoon, we stopped at the edge of a patch of thick woodland, dismounted and stared out at the high walls of the Abbey that rose forbiddingly three hundred yards to the west across a stretch of marshy low-lying ground and a shallow, meandering stream.

'This is the meeting place,' said Robin, looking at Little John and the other three outlaws. 'Alan and I will do our best to be here before midnight tonight. If we have not come by then, we are likely either dead or captured. And you must ride for it

37

immediately in case the Abbey's men come seeking you. But until midnight stay silent, stay hidden, stay watchful. Understood?'

Leaving our friends, our horses and our swords in a thick stand of trees, we walked south, with Robin leading the way, his back stooped, a hobble in his stride. We planned to loop round the Abbey and approach it from the other side – the west – presenting ourselves at the main entrance as pilgrims and asking shelter for the night. While I had surrendered my sword to Gavin, I was by no means unarmed, and I doubted that Robin was either. A few weeks earlier I had been in Nottingham looking at jewellers, hoping to find a small gift for Goody and I had walked past the workshop of a saddler in the English part of the town. He was engaged in creating a rather unusual item and I paused for a few moments to watch. The man was making a small breast-and-back plate from cuir bouilli – very tough boiled leather – two thick, square slabs of leather each about a foot wide, connected by strong leather shoulder straps. It would be worn over the head, under a suit of mail, the thick leather flaps providing extra protection to the chest and back. But I noticed that the saddler was also sewing strips of iron into a series of pouches in the chest plate to strengthen it further – and this gave me an ingenious idea.

A week later, the saddler had made me a similar item: a pair of thick leather protectors for my chest and back that could be worn under clothing or mail; in the front, the square of leather was bolstered by three two-inch-wide iron strips, and at the back, the tough flap held a narrow, vertical holster for a peculiar weapon that I had acquired during the wars in France.

It was an old lance blade, sharp and well cared for, but rather than being joined to a twelve-foot-long spear shaft, it was mounted on a short T-shaped handle. It was a stabbing weapon, less than a foot long, held in the fist with the crossbar in the palm of the hand and the lance blade protruding between the second and third fingers. Punched very hard into a man's chest, it could smash through the cage of the ribs and pierce the heart, and I had discovered, at no little personal cost, that it was a most efficient tool for swift, silent killing. But it was also, I had been told, much more than that. The enemy from whom I had taken it had believed that this blade was the very lance that had pierced the side of Our Saviour Jesus Christ as he suffered on the Cross. I did not know whether or not this was true, indeed I doubted it, but I treasured the unusual weapon nonetheless, as much as if it were that wondrous relic.

And so, as Robin and I walked south, skirting an apple orchard and making our way round towards the Abbey's main gate, under my beggar's rags I wore the square cuir bouilli chest and back armour, and I could feel the T-bar of the lance-dagger, which was secure in its holster on my back, nudging my shoulder blades with every stride. At the bottom of the rough cloth bag that I carried over my shoulder, buried beneath an old chemise and a dirty pair of hose, was a flanged mace that Goody had given me some years ago: a two-foot-long shaft of oak topped with a heavy iron head to which six flat, triangular pieces of iron were welded in a circle. That, too, was a fearsome weapon capable, in the right hands, of smashing limbs and cracking skulls. And I had one final piece of killing equipment: a long, thin but very strong stabbing dagger, triangular in section, known as a misericorde. This weapon, sheathed in leather, hung from my belt at the back, above my right buttock. It was hidden from sight by the raggedy cloak that I wore – but I was not too concerned about it being detected. Even a beggar might choose to carry a dagger for his own defence while walking through outlaw-infested Sherwood.

Although I had made Robin promise that we would not hurt any of the Abbey folk unless it was absolutely necessary, I was not prepared to be captured by the canons and tried and hanged as a thief. If a man's life stood between me and freedom, I was quite prepared to take his life and repent of it most sincerely afterwards.

As we approached the main entrance in the outer wall of Welbeck Abbey, the sun was already low in the western sky and we joined a thin line of poorly dressed folk filing through a small wooden judas gate set in a much larger double gate. As Robin and I shuffled up to the narrow oblong door, and stepped through over the wooden lip and into the Abbey, we kept our heads down and our eyes lowered. We were greeted at the door by a canon in the white robes of the Premonstratensian Order, and asked our names and our business. Robin replied in a muffled old-man's croak that we were two pilgrims from Oakham in the county of Rutland travelling to Durham to pray at the shrine of St Cuthbert there.

'My brother Edgar here is much afflicted with boils and foul diseases of the skin, Your Holiness, and St Cuthbert came to me in a dream and promised that if we journeyed there and prayed with pure hearts before his image, and washed all over with holy water, he might be cured . . .'

The canon, a glossy-looking man of middle years, peered under my hood at my broad eye-patch and dirty, bloody, oatmeal-encrusted face and visibly flinched.

'Wa-ugh! Yes, yes, I see. Well, you are welcome, my brothers, the dormitory is yonder' – he pointed at a large building on the far side of the courtyard – 'and supper will be served in the refectory after Vespers. God be with you.' He ushered us into the Abbey with a flap of his hand and a shudder, being careful not to make contact with our noisome rags, and turned his shiny, well-scrubbed face to the next bedraggled wretch who sought entrance.

The Abbey buildings were laid out around that square courtyard. Looking back, I noticed that the main door was reinforced with strips of iron and barred by a great plank of oak that rested in two iron brackets fixed to the walls on either side, about ten feet off the ground. The little judas gate opened outwards, I saw, and was fitted with bolts at head and ankle height and a stout brass lock. It was the obvious weak spot and would be targeted by any attacking

40

force, and so the canons had made it doubly secure. To the north, on my left as we entered, was the Church of St James the Great, a massive construction of creamy limestone that occupied the whole of that side of the yard, and a part of the eastern side too, as the transept thrust out at right angles to the main body of the church and formed the first part of the eastern boundary of the courtyard. Beside the transept, on the far side of the square, was a cluster of low buildings that appeared to be the refectory, kitchen and wine cellars. And south of them a long building that the canon had pointed out as the dormitory. In the south-eastern corner stood the cloisters that accommodated the canons and I could just glimpse the pillared interior of a chapterhouse. On the south wall was a small stable block, housing about a dozen horses, and a tall store-house on two floors. Directly to our right, beside the main gate, stood a large wooden crane in the shape of an upside down letter L, and a group of young canons were unloading heavy barrels from a wagon. They rolled them off, allowing them to fall on a straw pallet, and then rolled them into a large hemp net, which the crane winched upwards by a system of ropes and pulleys attached to its horizontal arm, to the second floor of the storehouse, fifteen feet up in the air. The half dozen men looked fit and strong – unafraid of hard work, many stripped to the waist to display their pale muscular bodies. I hoped I would not have to tangle with any of them, either armed or unarmed; I did not think I could best these strong men without killing them. They were not the only formidable-looking folk in that courtyard: as Robin and I limped towards the dormitory, my lord affecting to breathe with great labour and leaning on his staff a good deal, I noticed a dozen men-at-arms, in hauberks and helmets, with swords strapped to their waists, lounging at a table by the refectory drinking ale and throwing dice to pass the hours. And staring discreetly around the Abbey, I could see a handful of other fighting men, some in mail, some in leather armour, all apparently well armed, sitting here and there.

41

And just then a knight came striding out of the door at the western end of the church, and marched briskly, diagonally across the courtyard, cutting in front of us, heading for the cloisters on the opposite side. The man, who was in his middle years, dark-haired, square-faced and competent-looking with a large prominent nose, was dressed in a long purple robe of fine wool trimmed with squirrel fur. He wore a sword at his waist and a matching dagger; silver spurs were strapped to his riding boots and he passed close enough for me to notice a small mole just below his mouth on the right side.

In the cool space of the dormitory, a long low room with a double line of wooden cots on either wall, Robin and I chose two beds by the door and hunkered down for a brief conference. 'Well, so far, so good,' murmured Robin, too low for any of the other inhabitants to hear. Apart from us, it housed half a dozen mangy wretches – men and women of varying ages, who all looked as if they badly needed a hot meal and a dry night's sleep – and three lean, sun-darkened men in a huddle on the far side, each bearing scallop-shell-adorned staffs and the kind of cloth shoulder bag known as a scrip, that marked them out as pilgrims. A very fat man-at-arms in a torn mail coat was snoring drunkenly on a cot midway down the left-hand row, about a dozen yards from us.

'I don't like it,' I said to Robin in a similarly low tone. 'There are too many soldiers here for my liking.'

'The Abbot needs to protect himself, just like anyone else,' countered Robin. 'Sherwood is a dangerous place.' His silver-grey eyes twinkled. 'I should know.'

I said no more. I did not want Robin to think that my courage had failed, but I was truly uneasy in myself. I had never seen quite so many armed men doing quite so little in a peaceful House of God before. I told myself that it was merely nerves at the prospect of action and I surreptitiously brushed a hand behind my neck along the crossbar of the lance-dagger. But when one

42

of the pilgrims dropped his staff with a clatter, I nearly jumped out of my skin.

Robin and I rested for an hour or so on the narrow straw-filled cots in the dormitory, my lord appearing to sleep like a newborn. I was too tightly wound to rest, and in whatever position I tried I found the handles of either the lance-dagger or the misericorde sticking into my spine and the eye-patch seemed overly tight and itchy. We were roused by the ringing of the church bell, summoning us and the other guests of the Abbey to Vespers, and trooped across the courtyard with almost the entire population of the place, more than a hundred souls. We all moved solemnly through the western doors into the large nave. I smelled the familiar holy stench of stale incense and candle smoke, hot wax and human sweat, and Robin and I pushed our way to the front, stationing ourselves beside a large pillar: as we waited for the senior canons and the Abbot to arrive, I looked at the faces around me: ordinary men and women of all ages, from stick-thin crones to boisterous children, chatting and coughing, and a few men standing with their heads bowed in prayer. But something was awry, something did not sit right. I saw glimpses of iron mail, and here and there the gleam of a sword hilt – yet it was more than the large number of men-at-arms in the congregation, there was an air of something else: expectation, a collective holding of breath. Was I imagining it? Was my skittish mind causing me to see enemies where there were truly none? I could not tell.

Abbot Richard, a short, fattish, stern-featured man, strode into the church, using his tall elaborately carved crosier as a walking staff. His mouth was tight with disapproval – but of what I could not tell. Behind him hurried a dozen of the senior canons and they all took up their places in the choir of the church. As the canons began to chant the opening words of the service – *Deus, in adiutorium meum intende. Domine, ad adiuvandum me festina* . . . O God, come to my assistance. O Lord, make haste to help me – I bowed my head and added a similar request to the Almighty that He might protect Robin and myself in this coming task.

'O Lord,' I said silently in my heart, 'I do not seek to profit from this enterprise; I do not look for personal gain: I beg you to shield my master and myself in our hour of danger and make us worthy instruments of your justice. I ask this in the name of your son Our Lord Jesus Christ.'

As I finished my private prayer, I opened my uncovered eye and my gaze reached out to the altar. A young canon holding a rush taper was in the act of lighting the wicks of a dozen candles, fixed in a glorious golden candelabrum on the right-hand side of that holy table. A similar candelabrum on the left was already ablaze.

I caught my breath in wonder.

Between the two sources of light, glowing warmly, reflecting the glory of God magnificently in the drab interior of the church, lay Malloch's hoard of gold. The centrepiece was a tall crucifix nearly two feet high, the surface of the buttery metal worked with intricate geometrical shapes and patterns. A silver figure of Our Lord was fixed to the golden Tree of Calvary, beautifully wrought, each muscle of Our Saviour's body clear and distinct, the thorns of his Crown needle sharp, the cheeks of his beloved face as hollow as those of any beggar, and yet that grave, suffering, silver face seemed to be filled with compassion for the world. Before the crucifix and a little to the right blazed a large golden cup – the chalice. Its thick rim, long stem and broad stand were embedded with cut jewels of blue and green, amber and red – each as large as hazelnuts. To the right of the chalice, a broad smooth golden plate, the paten, reflected the candlelight like the sun. And placed around on the snowy altar cloth were half a dozen other pieces of wondrous work: a fine monstrance in the shape of a bright star; a lustrous round pyx like a nugget of pure bullion; a tiny bell with a wooden handle, like a drop of molten sunshine; an elegant long-handled wine jug radiating warmth like a hearth fire . . .

I was not the only one to be gazing in awe at this display of wealth. Almost every eye there was fixed on the magnificence of the altar. Even if we set aside Malloch Baruch's exquisite craft-work – and I had truly never seen its equal before – I was staring at a rich man's ransom in precious metal alone.

I turned to look at Robin and noticed that he had a curious expression on his face. One eye was tightly closed and he had his head cocked to one side. He looked exactly like a goodwife at the market, eyeing up a cut of pork or mutton and, ignoring the patter of the eager-to-sell butcher, trying to guess its true value.

For an obviously wealthy Abbey, the meal served out in the refectory to the bedraggled travellers housed in the dormitory was woefully bad: a watery soup of turnips and bitter herbs; stale bread and powdery, tasteless cheese. As I choked down the last spoonful of soup, I reflected that I had eaten worse meals than this on campaign, but not for a good long while: had I grown soft in the past few months at Westbury? After the meagre meal, Robin and I took to our cots, and while my lord appeared to be enjoying a restful sleep, I struggled once again with the discomfort caused by my disguise and my assorted weaponry as our fellow travellers snuffled and snored and farted all around us.

The eye-patch was itching my brow badly, and I seriously considered taking it off – in that dark dormitory, who would see that I had two good eyes? But I resisted the temptation. I did not want to spoil my disguise just because of a little discomfort. We waited for two interminable hours after the last of the Abbey's guests had retired, and at, perhaps, an hour before midnight, I felt a hand on my shoulder and saw Robin's pale face looming beside mine. I rose swiftly and we crept out of the sleeping room as quiet as velvet-shod mice. The door creaked alarmingly, but nobody stirred, and once outside, we paused with our backs to the dormitory wall and silently observed the courtyard: deserted, still and utterly silent. A fat, waxing moon, yellow as a buttercup, hung above the stables on the southern side of the yard, but there was precious little other light, except for a faint glow coming from the stained-glass windows of the church. Robin touched my arm and we walked across to the door of the church on the western side. This one opened with only the tiniest squeak, and we were inside that cool, sacred space. I saw that a single thick candle had been left burning in the centre of the nave, a symbol of the eternal light of Our Lord Jesus Christ – and by that light Robin and I approached the altar where we had so recently admired the shining hoard that rightly belonged to Malloch the goldsmith.

The altar was bare, and for a wild moment, I wondered if some thief had beaten us to the reward. But Robin ignored the altar without comment and made his way to the north transept, and to a small door in a wooden panel that marked off the sacristy. I cursed my own stupidity: of course, the canons would not leave a fortune in plain view of the altar, with the church door unlocked, and the Abbey full of vagrants.

Robin fumbled in his robe and knelt before the door handle; I saw that he had in his hands two pieces of wrought iron bent into right-angles, like square hooks, and he was inserting them gingerly into the big lock on the door. He seemed to be having some difficulty, rattling the hooks in the lock and cursing quietly under his breath. I had not known that my lord possessed this skill; the power to unseal locks without the proper key – and it seemed that, in truth, he did not. Thirty heartbeats passed and still, Robin struggled with the door. Then my lord caught my eye; he looked irritated. 'Do something useful, Alan, and bring me that candle,' he said crossly, indicating the eternal flame with a sideways jerk of his head.

There was something deeply wrong, I felt, in the act of removing that thick candle from its spiked stand. It occurred to me, in a sudden burst of clarity, that we were robbing a church. A church!

Was there any act more contemptible, any sin more vile? But more than that – something in the very air, in the stink of wax and sweat, of people and old prayers, that spoke to me of grave danger. All my senses were telling me that I should grab Robin and run from this place. I am not, I think, a coward, but I felt the cold breath of fear on my neck and I was within a whisker in that moment of turning on my heel and heading for the church door. I took several deep breaths, and with my heart beating like a drum, I managed to master my terror. I forced myself to lay hands on the cool wax of the candle and pull it free from its stand with a jerk. And, just as I approached my lord with the wavering light held in both hands, Robin gave a grunt of satisfaction, the lock clicked, and the sacristy door swung open.

Robin grinned at me, his good humour restored, his silver eyes reflecting the candlelight. 'Young Gavin taught me that trick: he used to be an apprentice locksmith before his light fingers led him beyond the law.'

I nodded but said nothing – the eye-patch was making the whole of my head itch, it seemed. To take my mind off it, I held the candle high and looked keenly about me as we advanced into that dark room. The candlelight showed me a small square space, with a table and stool immediately to the left, a pole slung at head height from the roof for robes, and an X-shaped chair on the right – but it was clear where the golden hoard must be hidden: in the large chest that squatted near the back wall, secured with a solid iron padlock.

Robin walked forward, bent down and examined the chest, humming very faintly under his breath. He looked at the front of the wooden box, fingered the heavy padlock, and then peered at the lid's hinges. I expected him to produce his hooks and begin fiddling with the padlock, but he merely whispered, 'Alan, lend me a hand, will you?' And I found myself, crouched down by the side of the chest, with the candle on the floor beside me, helping

Robin to heave the strongbox away from the wall. It was extremely heavy, and only with some difficulty did my lord and I manage to move it six inches. Then he said, 'Give me your misericorde, please, just for a moment.'

I handed it over, hilt first, and he inserted the sharp tip of the strong blade between the hinge-plate and the wood at the back of the chest and gave a small shove. The hinge squealed like a scorched cat, and Robin stopped. 'Shut the door, Alan.' And when I turned and pulled the sacristy door to, I heard another loud cry of pain from the ancient wood of the chest, then, swiftly afterwards, another. The hinges prised loose, Robin lifted the lid up and over from the back and left it sagging open against the front of the box.

Its contents were now ours.

I picked up the candle and set it on the table and bent down to retrieve my misericorde, which had been casually discarded by my lord, and slid it back into its sheath at my back. I tried to see into the chest, but Robin's shoulders, head and hands were already deep inside blocking my view. I saw him dip down an arm and emerge with the golden plate, the paten, which he quickly stuffed into a rough woollen sack at his feet; a golden jug followed it in there a few moments later, and the little round pyx, and the star-shaped monstrance. And then Robin had the chalice in his hands – and he looked up and paused, smiling happily at me over the bejewelled golden rim, as if making a toast to my good health. 'Does this put you in mind of anything, Alan?' he said, chuckling with satisfaction.

I frowned. The eye-patch was itching like the plague.

'No?' said Robin. 'I had always imagined that this is what the Grail would look like,' he continued. I knew that ever since he had first heard of the Holy Grail several years before, Robin had wanted to possess it, but this was no time to indulge his madcap fantasies. 'Hurry up,' I whispered, 'we need to be getting out of here.'

And just then, I heard a noise, an unmistakable noise, out there in the dark, beyond the sacristy door. It was a tinny clattering sound, only heard once and unrepeated. But it was the sound of something metallic, a knife or sword perhaps, being dropped on a stone floor.

Chapter Four

Almost faster than thought, Robin was beside the candle at the table, and had pinched it dark. In the sudden blackness, my uncovered eye retained an image of my lord: the lumpy woollen sack bunched in one fist, the fingers of his other on the candlewick, his head questing forwards, his mouth a grim line.

We both stood silent and waited.

There were more gentle noises coming from outside: the sounds of men, several of them, trying to be stealthy. Cloth whispering on cloth, the shuffle of leather boots, tiny clicks as metal touched other metal, muffled coughs and even a damned idiot attempting to quieten his fellows with a sibilant: 'Shhh!'

I felt the heat of Robin's face close to mine; he breathed in my ear: 'We *must* not be trapped in here. Out, to the main gate, then into the woods, fast as you can.'

Then the door opened and the pitch-dark sacristy was filled with a glare of yellow light. A figure entered, a lantern in one hand, a sword in his other: a man-at-arms in hauberk and helm, and not alone. Behind him there were other figures bearing candles, swords and spears. There were men-at-arms crowded in the doorway and behind in the church, a dozen of them or more, their faces glowing with excited triumph.

The lantern man, a scarred sergeant of thirty years or so, advanced into the sacristy, taking cautious half-steps forward, his sword held out before him, the tip stopping a foot from my face. Two more men with drawn swords, and two men with candles, came in behind him. In the doorway lingered a knot of men-at-arms gazing at us from beneath half a dozen raised spear-points, and behind them I saw the face of the dark square-faced knight with the mole on his cheek, looking on and smiling. I lifted my hands in the air, my palms level with my ears, in a gesture of surrender. Out of the corner of my eye I noticed that Robin hadn't stirred so much as an eyebrow.

'I've got them; I got them, sir,' said the sergeant, the foremost lantern man, the man holding a sword up to my chin. And he looked quickly over his shoulder for approval from the square-faced knight behind him. 'Shall I kill them now?'

I moved.

With my left forearm I swept the sword-point away from my face and my right hand dipped behind my neck to grasp the T-bar of my lance-dagger. The blade slipped from its greased holster, came up and over my head and I stepped in and punched forward, hard, with the weight of my shoulder behind the blade, plunging it deep into the throat of the foremost man-at-arms. He dropped both lantern and sword, uttering a gurgling scream, both hands fluttering at his neck as I ripped the blade free in a spray of crimson gore. The band of newcomers to the sacristy seemed to be frozen in horrified shock, as I took a long step past the dying sergeant and surged forward, bloody lance-dagger leaping out to plunge into the chest of the next man holding a candle, my left hand groping awkwardly for the handle of my misericorde behind my back. The second man went down, his dropped candle went out, and Robin was there beside me, a long dagger in his hand. He shoulder-charged

51

a mail-clad swordsman, knocking him out of the way, dodged a jabbing spear-point, and twisting his whole body slammed the point of his weapon in a scything overhand into the eye of the second candle-holder. The man screamed, dropped his light and we were all of us plunged into utter darkness.

I knew Robin was to my right, and so I fell to my knees and struck left with the misericorde at groin level, plunging it randomly into the darkness, once, twice. I heard a howl, and somebody blundered against my shoulder, kneeing me in the bicep and deadening the arm. I came up fast and charged forward blindly, heading for where I remembered the door to be, and crashed into a mailhard body, the blade of my lance-dagger snagging on loose cloth. I tumbled to the floor, I took a hard kick to my ribs, rolled and came up again. In the nave of the church the moonlight coming through the coloured glass of the windows lit the room only very dimly. Yet it was enough to see the black forms of half a dozen struggling men. I heard the thuds and cracks and shouts and hisses of pain, but I was well clear of that blind mêlée. A voice with a strong French accent was shouting in English: 'Get that lantern lit, sergeant, now. Strike tinder and flint. For the love of God give us some light!'

And a dark form, a familiar shape in a raggedy hooded cloak, was running for the door at the western end of the nave. I was treading on his heels. Robin and I burst out into the courtyard, turned left and raced for the big double doors of the Abbey's main gate, skidding to a halt in front of their barred might. In less than a dozen heartbeats, the men inside would realize that we were gone, and they would be upon us once more with spear and sword. Worse, the noise of the fight must have awakened the whole community, for I could see lights blooming in the dark cloisters and refectory; the canons would be coming to investigate the disturbance. We needed to run, and now. But Robin was standing by the judas gate, staring at the lock, examining it closely. I could see by the moonlight that he had already slid back the bolts at the top and bottom of the little door; but the big brass lock had stalled him.

'For God's sake, Robin, you are not going to try and pick that, are you? We simply don't have time!'

'You have to hold them for me, Alan. Hold them off, come what may, just for a little while and I will get us out. I will get us out, I swear.'

Years of habit, years of obeying Robin's commands made me turn my back to my lord and prepare for battle. I trusted him, you see, although it was sheer madness. But there was nothing else to do. We were trapped by the main gate, locked inside the Abbey with scores of enemies coming for our blood. A picture of Goody came into my head and I felt a sudden wrenching sadness that I would never hold her again. I slid the lance-dagger back into its sheath between my shoulder blades, and quickly searched in my shoulder bag for the flanged mace my darling had given me.

'Goodbye, my sweet love,' I whispered to the image of my beloved, 'until we meet again in Heaven,' as the men-at-arms tumbled out of the door of the church in the north of the court-yard, to my left, and advanced towards me. They did not run, but came on slowly, eight of them, I counted, the mole-faced older knight in the lead, his face a picture of frustrated fury. The lantern had been retrieved from the floor of the sacristy and someone had taken the time to relight it.

I had the mace cocked in my right hand, two feet of iron-hard oak with that wicked, bone-crushing, flanged metal head; and the misericorde in my left fist – a weapon designed to punch straight though iron mail and into the soft flesh beneath. I stood equally balanced on both feet, as the men-at-arms advanced, and waited to meet my doom. I had once promised Robin, long ago when I was just a stripling, that I would be loyal to him until death; and now my lord had ordered me to hold off his enemies, so that is what I was determined to do.

53

I could hear Robin behind me swearing foully; and I snatched a glance at him. He stood by the southern side of the main gate, by the tall crane, and through the gloom I could just make out that he seemed to be tugging on the hemp netting underneath a large barrel, a stout rope in his other hand stretching up into the darkness. But I had no time to concern myself with Robin's pastimes: the men-at-arms were three paces from me, spread in a half-circle. I turned to face them. To my left was the forbidding black wall of the gate; in front of me were the enemy, between me and the church; behind me Robin was fooling about with God knew what. If I had wanted to run, the only way to go would have been to my right, into the centre of the square courtyard.

But I was not planning to run.

The knight, in the centre of the men-at-arms, said in a reasonable French-accented tone, 'Surrender your arms, thief, and you shall have a fair trial in a court of law – there is no need for more bloodshed. Hand over your weapons.'

I felt the weight of the mace in my right hand and the misericorde in my left. But my eye was fixed on the knight.

'Why don't you come take them yourself?' I said.

He merely snorted in derision.

Then I said, 'I'll fight you, sir, man to man, me and you. Winner goes scot-free.' Despite my bold words, my eye-patch was driving me to madness: I longed to tear it off, not least because I'd then have two eyes to use in the coming battle. And, oddly, I did not want to die with an itchy face.

The knight made an impatient hissing noise. 'I do not duel with creatures such as you.' Then, flapping his hand at the line of soldiers, he said, 'Kill them now.'

And they rushed at me all at once.

While I had been speaking with the knight, I had heard a curious creaking noise behind me, like the sound of a tree troubled by a

54

gale; and just as the men-at-arms came hurtling at me, I heard Robin shout, 'Down, now, Alan, get down.'

I instantly dropped to the floor as a huge black shape in the grey night, suspended in a hempen net, and attached by long ropes to the high horizontal arm of the crane, came sweeping through the air at just below head height in a wide semi-circle. The vast swinging object – a mighty barrel of pickled fish, I soon discovered – crashed into the leading man-at-arms, snapping bone and knocking him into the man behind him, and continued its unstoppable looping path to smack dead centre into the judas gate. The barrel, which must have weighed at least two hundred pounds, hauled five feet up into the air and propelled with all of Robin's considerable strength, smashed itself to kindling against the gate in a gush of brine and silver herring, wet barrel staves and clattering round iron hoops – and, in doing so, neatly popped the little gate open, like a stopper coming out of a bottle. I was on my feet in an instant, smashing the heavy mace overhand into the skull of a dazed and staggering man-at-arms directly between me and the narrow little door, and dropping him like a stone. Then I was out the broken gate, and running as fast as I could to my right, along the line of the Abbey's western wall. Without slackening my pace, I jerked my head around and saw that Robin was a mere two paces behind, but struggling with his wind. He seemed to be laughing wildly, almost hysterically, and running for his life all at the same time.

Beyond my lord, twenty yards away, the first helmeted heads were appearing through the wreckage of the gate. And there were white robes and tonsures too, and men bearing torches, spilling out with shouts and oaths, pointing at our retreating backs.

Robin and I ducked around the north-western corner of St James Church, which formed the outside wall of the Abbey and paused for a heartbeat, our backs against the stone wall, panting madly, trying to get our bearings. I sheathed my misericorde and tucked the mace securely in my belt; and pulled the irritating leather eye patch off my face and hurled it into the darkness. We turned and looked east. There was just enough moonlight to make out the bulk of the church to our right-hand side, and a dark smear of forest in front of us. To our left nothing but deep blackness. But the shouted commands and indignant rage were coming closer behind us, and we pushed off the wall and sprinted onwards, due east, following the line of the church wall towards the forest and our friends.

We had not run thirty yards when the torches erupted around the corner of the church; a horde of men, many scores of them, mostly white-garbed canons brandishing simple wooden staves, but a few men-at-arms mixed in too, with swords and spears; a couple of men had crossbows, I noticed. We ran, Robin and I, we ran for our lives. A hundred yards, two hundred, and I tripped and fell headlong into a patch of boggy grass, my face splashing down into foulness. Robin who was a few yards ahead of me came back and grabbed me by the scruff of the neck and hauled me upright. It was then that I noticed that he still had the woollen sack in his right hand, the sack containing a rich man's ransom in gold.

'This is no time to be taking a nap, Alan,' said my lord, chuck-ling, dragging me by the elbow as we splashed through a shallow stream and up on to the bank on the other side. 'We have an appointment to keep.' And I coughed up a little foul marsh water with my own near-hysterical laughter.

Our pursuers were only fifty yards behind us, and the tree line a scant thirty yards away, when the first arrows began to fly out of the forest. And good shooting it was, too, for night-time. The shafts arced over our heads, fine grey lines in the blackness, and lanced mercilessly into our pursuers, thudding into white-robed canon and man-at-arms alike, and dropping both in moaning, bleeding heaps on the dark grass. The yard-long shafts, mounted with man-killing bodkin tips, skimmed out of the trees as fast as Robin's men could loose them and thunked relentlessly into human flesh, with the sound of a butcher's cleaver on a slab of pork, transfixing limbs and piercing mail and thick wool habits with equal ease. The night was alive with the desperate yells of the wounded. One man-at-arms screamed a foul insult and loosed a crossbow bolt at the black wall of the forest in defiance – then the Abbey folk fled, back to the safety of their walls, dragging their hurt with them, and pursued by the pale killing shafts of the outlaws' barrage.

Little John and Robin's three bowmen might have seen off the Abbey folk for the moment but we did not assume that Abbot Richard would fail to rally his troops, roust out more armed men and attempt to follow us. So we saddled up, as soon as we made it to the tree line and joined our friends, and threaded our way south through the dark forest as quickly as we dared.

And it was not long before we heard the sounds of horsemen and the fear-emboldened calls of pursuers, and saw through the black trees the red blossoming of scores of torches. We could not move fast, a low hanging branch, unseen in the darkness, might crack a skull or sweep one of us from the saddle. And neither could we make light to see by. Instead we slowly walked our horses forward between the pillars of the trees, heads ducked low against their warm necks, and prayed that our pursuers might soon become lost or disheartened.

They did not.

Over the next quarter of an hour, the number of torches seemed to multiply until there was almost a sea of bobbing, ruddy flashes behind us, and the noise of our oncoming enemies had risen to the rumble of a multitude, with the occasional high shout breaking out against the background hubbub. We were being hunted like beasts by a huge pack of enemies. The Abbot appeared to have mustered more than a hundred horse and footmen for the pursuit, and very swiftly too, and against that number of foes we would have no chance in a fight. They were determined, well organized and seemingly unafraid of the wild forest in the depths of a midsummer midnight. And so the tide of fire-bearing hunters came on swiftly, more swiftly than we could progress. And soon, it seemed almost to be lapping at our heels and, as I nervously snatched another glance behind me, I could by now make out the silhouettes of the Abbot's hired men-at-arms and catch brief glimpses of others in white robes with tonsured heads.

I told myself that their burning torches would ruin their night-vision and that while I could make out their forms they would surely not be able to see us. But the ice snake of fear slithered in my stomach and I tried not to imagine our fate if we were taken: humiliation, disgrace and a long agonizing dance at the end of a rope.

Finally, Robin gave a low order and we urged our horses into a nervous trot, but after no more than a dozen heartbeats, my left knee cracked agonizingly against a protruding branch, and it was only with great difficulty that I avoided yelling out in surprised pain. I heard the sound of ripping cloth and a stifled oath ahead of me. Then came the unmistakable sharp thump of wood on bone – and my horse's nose was bumping on the rump of Little John's beast ahead of me.

'It's no good running,' whispered the blond giant. 'Dismount and pass the order on.' I turned to Gavin behind me and relayed the message, and then I found myself leading my horse by the bridle along a narrow track away to the left, almost at right angles to our original path, and heading roughly eastwards, as far as I could tell. We stopped after no more than forty paces, and Robin's face was right by mine, and whispering, 'We stay here, and let them pass. For all our sakes, keep your horse quiet.' Then he was past me and speaking to Gavin, who stood at his mount's head a pace or two away.

Robin had chosen an excellent hiding place. By luck? Or from his knowledge of these woods? I could not tell. We were grouped together below a stand of half a dozen skinny ash trees, growing close together, their thin branches swooping and curling around our bodies, the thick black foliage hiding us from sight even a few yards away. Even in daylight I think we six fugitives might have been well cloaked. I had my right hand clamped over the nostrils of my horse, willing her not to make a sound as the horrible red sea of firelight advanced towards us. At one point, I could clearly make out a helmeted horseman, twenty paces away, a tall man on a big horse, a blazing torch in his right hand, a white shield slung across his back. And when I heard him call out loudly to his fellow man-hunters, I confess my whole torso was sweat-slick and my heart was clogging my throat.

'Stay alert, men. Stay alert! A gold bezant for the first man to see the dogs.' It was the French knight, the man with the mole. And my thought was, oddly: That man has fought in the Holy Land. Who else has bezants to give away?

And then he was past me, still riding on the original line of march that Robin had taken, and the shouts and noise of excited men and horses was diminishing and the sea of bobbing lights beyond him was flowing away south into the ink-black forest, extinguished one by one by the bulk of the trees.

We waited a half hour in the safety of our clump of ash trees before remounting and heading on further east at a very cautious walk. After a mile or so we turned south again but we saw no more sign of our pursuers that night; and at the first light of dawn Robin led us to an abandoned hunting lodge on his brother's lands. We dismounted gratefully in the roofless space, rubbed down our horses, fed and watered them, and sat down ourselves for a bite of bread, cheese and ale, all of us exhausted but grateful to be alive and at liberty. I felt more wrung-out than I had in an age and I was just rolling myself into a heavy cloak for a few hours of blissful sleep, when I heard Little John quietly ask Robin what he thought had gone wrong, and I levered my sleepy lids open once more.

'They were waiting for us, John,' my lord said. He had an ugly purple-red bruise on his forehead and a smear of green lichen across it that made him look unusually wicked in that cold dawn. 'They obviously knew we were coming and had recruited scores of fighting men in the hope of taking us. A not-very-subtle trap was set and, I am ashamed to say, we walked straight into it.'

I reflected tiredly that I'd tried to warn Robin that something was wrong, but there seemed little point in reminding him.

'We should ride over to Lincoln and pay our good friend Malloch Baruch a little visit one of these days,' growled John. And just from his tone, an icy trickle of fear slid down my spine.

I told Goody what had happened at Welbeck and, predictably, she was furious at our narrow escape from an ignominious death. But I did not mention it to Sir Nicholas de Scras – it was not that I did not trust him to be silent about the matter, it was merely from a sense of delicacy. I did not want to admit to him that I had been undertaking larcenous adventures in search of an abbot's gold when I had only just convinced him that I had not, in fact, stolen a hoard of silver from the Templars. Better that he should not know.

Sir Nicholas and I enjoyed several days hunting red deer together across my lands in the next few weeks. The right to hunt beasts of venery, as these fleet creatures are called, came with the manor, and had been confirmed by William the Bastard himself as a favour to a comrade after he and his ferocious Norman knights had conquered this land. I had been much away at the wars since I had taken possession of Westbury a decade ago, and, as one of my huntsmen put it, the deer had multiplied and were now as thick as fleas on a dog's back. It was only a slight exaggeration: Sir Nicholas approached hunting with all the ruthless skill and determination that he brought to war and we killed half a dozen fat bucks with my pack of hounds in a fortnight. Some of the meat we salted and smoked for the winter, some I gave to the villagers of Westbury, to my tenants and to Arnold the priest, a funny little man who had a nervous habit of blinking his huge eyes constantly like a sleepy owl – but we did not stint ourselves in the hall either. Many a day we feasted on venison from noon till dusk – Goody, myself, Thomas my squire, Baldwin the steward, and Nicholas de Scras – regaling ourselves like royalty at their ease.

The weather was golden and a nagging fear that I might have been identified after the botched robbery at Welbeck Abbey receded with day after day of scrambling exhilaration in the woods and fields around Westbury as we chased down the nimble deer with our dogs and our spears, and nights drinking good red wine and playing backgammon by the hearth with Sir Nicholas or remembering old friends and refighting old battles of the Great Pilgrimage. I was happy in that time, perhaps as happy as I have been before or since. And when we retired to bed, Goody and I made the most of our married state, and tried energetically night and morn to put a baby in her womb.

It was a joyous, warm, sun-filled season, but not without its dark clouds. It was a week past Lammas Day – and the main summer wheat crop had been gathered in and the sheaves were drying safely in a dozen barns across the manor – when a woman in the village went mad. She was found naked at noon in one of the wheat barns at the eastern edge of the village, covered in blood and scratches and preaching a sermon to the sheaves on the wiles of the Devil.

It was Father Arnold who came to me with the news.

'Katelyn the alewife has been possessed by an evil spirit!' the priest told me, his mouth slightly open with excitement and his large owl eyes blinking rapidly. He found me in the stables with

Shaitan, where I had been inspecting the healed scar on my destrier's back with the head groom and discussing whether he was ready to take the weight of a saddle and rider.

The story came tumbling out. The day before, Katelyn – a woman who was as famous for the strength of the ale she brewed as she was for her frequent violent drunkenness – had been gathering herbs for the ale vats, alone, in the little copse on the knoll a mile or so north of the village, when she had come face to face with a demon: a ghastly creature, dressed all in black, leaning on a great staff, with a skull for a face and burning coals for eyes. The demon had cursed her in the vilest terms in some foul, Satanic language, had stolen her food, a parcel of bread and cheese and a leather bottle of strong ale, and had flown into the wood on great flapping black wings, cackling insanely.

Katelyn had been badly shaken by the encounter, but worse, that very night the demon or witch, or whatever the fell creature was, had come to her in her cottage, entered her bed and taken away her reason. The poor woman had arisen at dawn, naked as a babe, and run three times around the church, laughing and shouting wild curses and taunts, before falling into a patch of brambles and then staggering, scratched and bleeding, to the nearest shelter – a barn, where she had begun to lecture the stalks of grain on abstinence as a means of avoiding the snares of the Evil One.

Father Arnold related this tale with a good deal of relish, lingering on the fact that the woman was naked, and then proudly informing me that he had personally exorcised the demon with a bucket of Holy Water, drawn from the well, blessed and then cast over the woman's plump white body.

'She is sleeping now, thanks be to God,' said Father Arnold, 'but I have high hopes that in time she may recover her wits and do a penance for her sins.'

There seemed to be nothing that I was required to do for the unfortunate alewife Katelyn, and so I dismissed the priest with praise and thanks for his efforts and went back to examining Shaitan's long pink scar. However, this episode – although I was convinced it was largely a fantasy born of a surfeit of ale – made me deeply uneasy. Goody and I had been troubled by a witch, or a crazy woman who claimed to be one, for some years now – and the 'demon' discovered by Katelyn put me in mind of her. Her name was Nur and she hailed from Outremer.

I must confess that I had loved Nur once, when I was a callow youngster taking part in the Great Pilgrimage to the Holy Land. I had met her in Sicily and taken her with me to Outremer but, at Acre, a great fortress in the north, my enemies had taken her, abused her foully and mutilated her face, cutting off her lips and nose and ears, and I had found to my shame that I did not love her once her beauty had been sheared away. When I first saw her after her humiliation, I cried out in fear, and she fled immediately. I still pray that God will forgive me for that moment of weakness.

When I left Outremer and returned to England, she followed me in secret, a young woman alone and on foot, through all the wild lands of Europe, and her sufferings on that terrible journey, I believe, twisted her mind towards evil. On the day that Goody and I became betrothed, at the celebration feast in Robin's castle at Kirkton, Nur had made a terrifying appearance and cursed Goody and myself in front of all the guests. 'I curse you, Alan Dale,' Nur had said, in a voice rich with hatred. 'I curse you and your milky whore!' She pointed at Goody. 'Your sour-cream bride will die a year and a day after you take her to your marriage bed . . .'

That poor wretch had repeated her curse since that day; and, in a killing rage at this and other gross provocations, I had taken men-at-arms and attacked the place where she lived in the deep woods and, I earnestly prayed, driven her for ever from my lands with fire and steel. She was an enemy that I had believed was long gone from Westbury: a sad, mad woman with no real unearthly powers, just a hideous face and a savage hatred of all men – and of me in particular. But from Father Arnold's tale about poor drunken Katelyn, I feared Nur might once again be in our midst.

I told Goody that I suspected that our old antagonist had returned, and she took the news calmly, with a slow nod. 'Her hatred for us is a lure: it ever draws her, like a moth to a candle, back to Westbury,' said my wife, who was as wise as she was lovely.

'I am not afraid of her,' she continued. 'I do not believe in her so-called magic. She may try to harm us in many ways, but she will not succeed not through unnatural powers, and we are now forewarned. But, more important than that, I know for certain that our love is stronger than her hatred.'

Our love might indeed have been very powerful, but I like to put my trust in iron and steel. That afternoon I had Shaitan saddled, dressed in a full suit of mail, strapped on my sword Fidelity, and with Thomas and the half dozen men-at-arms who formed the tiny garrison at Westbury, I paid a visit to the copse on the knoll where Nur had appeared before Katelyn. I was determined that I would kill the unhappy woman on sight: I would not wait for her malice to be inflicted on Goody or myself or anyone at the manor. You may think me harsh – but I knew Nur, I knew the rage that drove her, and I knew that she would never cease in her attempts to harm us until she were dead.

In any case, we found nothing that afternoon of Nur or any other soul. And while I ordered Thomas to lead daily patrols around the countryside to search for signs of her presence, we found none. After a week or two had passed, I began to relax. Perhaps the black-clad, skull-faced demon that Katelyn claimed to have seen had been no more than a spectre conjured up by her drink-sodden imagination. Perhaps I'd responded to a threat that did not exist. I prayed that it might be so.

In any case, the threat of witchcraft, real or imagined, was driven from my head at the beginning of September by the arrival at Westbury of a powerful contingent of Templar knights.

Chapter Five

The arrival of the Templars, though most unwelcome, was not unheralded. Two days beforehand, Robin himself had ridden up to the gate in the Westbury palisade in broad daylight and demanded entrance. He brought with him Little John, Gavin and a dozen other scruffy-looking ruffians all armed to the teeth.

'The Templars are coming for you, Alan,' my lord said casually as we took our ease in the hall with a pot of ale apiece. 'There is a force of them at Nottingham, my people in the castle tell me; they want to arrest you and take you in for questioning.'

Sir Nicholas de Scras joined us at the table – he nodded at Robin and said coldly, 'My lord', and Robin replied with an equally chilly, 'Sir Nicholas.'

There was an awkward pause, in which I bustled around finding and filling a pot of ale for Sir Nicholas and relaying Robin's news. These two hard men would never be friends, I realized. Robin considered Sir Nicholas to have been a traitor to King Richard – and, indeed, the former Hospitaller had foolishly sided with Prince John, as he then was, while the Lionheart had been imprisoned. Sir Nicholas, in turn, loathed Robin for his lack of respect for the law and the Church.

'The Knights Templar are coming here to arrest Sir Alan,' said Robin unnecessarily, perhaps just to fill the void in the air.

'Indeed,' said Sir Nicholas. 'They suspect him of being a dirty thief. I believe there is a matter of some stolen silver in Paris that they wish to discuss with him.'

Robin straightened his spine, his eyes like flakes of flint. 'They do not call him a traitor, though, unlike—'

'I swear I am innocent of this crime,' I said quickly, looking at both men in turn, and willing them with all my soul to keep the peace with each other, 'and I will take any oath to that effect. Should I surrender myself to them, do you think?'

Robin laughed. An ugly grating noise. 'Have you gone soft in the head, Alan? Do you think these God-grovelling hypocrites are interested in justice? They've been made to look foolish and they need to show the world that they can punish those who cross them. They would tear away your innocence with red-hot pincers and leave you begging for death. Surrender? Ha!'

I feigned a coughing fit to hide my irritation.

'I fear the Earl of Locksley is right, Alan,' said Sir Nicholas, with a sigh. 'I do not think the Order is looking for the truth; they seek to make an example of you. If you wish, I will ride to Nottingham and speak on your behalf. Perhaps we can talk the matter through peacefully and come to some arrangement.'

Robin cut him off brusquely: 'They will be here tomorrow or the next day. We can do all the *talking*' – he gave this word a heavily sardonic emphasis – 'we want to when they get here. From the safety of the battlements of Westbury.'

Robin was right. We might as well wait for the Templars to come to us. But, if I could possibly help it, I did not want their visit to end in violence. Things were at a bad enough pass with the Order believing that I had stolen their money, without me being responsible as well for the slaughter of a squadron of their men. The Templars were a power in the land, very close to King John. Indeed, he was rumoured to have gone to them for ready money when he came to the throne.

'We will wait for them here,' I pronounced. 'I will not allow them admittance inside these walls; I will speak to them from the gate. And we will fight, if necessary. But I want you to promise me, Robin, that you will not attack them unless I give the order. I do not want a bloodbath on my doorstep.'

'This is your manor,' my lord said smiling grimly. 'You have dominion here. My men and I are entirely at your disposal.'

As so often with Robin, my feelings towards him were several and contradictory. On the one hand, he had arrived with a timely warning about the Templars and with reinforcements for my small garrison at a moment of urgent need, and for that I was most grateful. On the other hand, I knew that he had been the very man who had robbed the Templars of their silver in Paris – and so he was the one who had brought this trouble down on my head. Yet the contradictions ran deeper. He had indeed used a letter of credit made out in my name to rob the Paris Temple, but a good deal of the money he had stolen, he spent on ransoming my French cousin Roland from a brutal mercenary captain called Mercadier, who had taken him prisoner in battle and threatened to blind him.

Robin was as good as his word about ceding authority to me: he dressed himself in rough peasant garb and a shabby hood, and later that afternoon leaning on his tall yew bow and chatting to the other outlaws in the sun-lit courtyard of Westbury, he seemed the very image of an ordinary archer. Sir Nicholas de Scras kept himself busy with Thomas and Westbury's few men-at-arms, exercising them with sword and shield around the tall paling set in the centre of the courtyard. I looked at my troops: seven reasonably competent men-at-arms, twelve archers, Robin, Little John, Thomas and Sir Nicholas. And me. Twenty-four men. Not much of an army but we were not a company that it would be easy to beat.

The Templars were spotted a good mile off by Kit, one of my steadier men-at-arms, who was on sentry duty. It was a single *conroi*; a score or so of horsemen in the black surcoats of Templar sergeants, and two knights in white mantles at the head of the column. Even at that distance, I could make out the glint of iron mail beneath the surcoats, and each man bore shield and spear as well as a long sword. I sent Little John, Robin and his archers to sit up on the walkway behind the palisade on the left-hand side of the main gate. The Sherwood men had their backs to the wall of stout pinewood poles that made up the outer defence of Westbury, their legs stretched out on the walkway. They were hidden from the approaching Templars; and I hoped they would keep silent until I called for them.

My own men-at-arms I placed on the right-hand side of the main gate, also screened from view. I stood upright and visible from the chest upwards above the centre of it, with Sir Nicholas on my right and Thomas on my left and we watched impassively as the column approached. I could feel the first stirrings of rage in my stomach. These violent men were coming for me, seeking to snatch me from my wife and home and imprison me and torture me in unspeakable ways for a crime I had not committed . . . I deliberately dampened the glow of anger – uncontrolled rage would not help matters today.

They came towards us slowly, walking their horses, looking like peaceful visitors rather than an attacking force. And I was glad; angry as I was, I truly did not want to spill any blood that sunny afternoon. As they came nearer, I began to be able to pick out the individual features of the riders and recognize them. At the head of the column was a man I had known for several years – as both friend and foe – a decent man, I believed, a good Christian and a renowned warrior. His name was Sir Aymeric de St Maur, and he was one of the most senior Templar knights in England, second only to the Master of their Order, Sir William de Newenham. The other knight's appearance came as something of a shock: he was the French knight from Welbeck. I could even make out the mole below his mouth.

They reined in their mounts before the gate, the white knights in front, the black-clad sergeants ranged behind them, and Sir Aymeric looked up at me, shading his face with his hand against the low sun.

'Greetings, Sir Alan,' he said, 'may the blessings of Almighty God and his only son Jesus Christ be upon you.'

'God's blessings on you, too, Sir Aymeric,' I replied, with as much courtesy as I could manage, 'and what, may I humbly ask, brings you to my door on this day, armed, mounted and mailed for war?'

It was the French knight who answered: 'We come with a warrant for your arrest, Sir Alan, signed by the Master of the English Temple Sir William de Newenham himself. He orders us to remove you from this place and deliver your person to London to answer before a special court the charge of a grave felony.'

I remembered his French tones well from our meeting by the gate at Welbeck, and from the close encounter in the forest, but it seemed he did not recognize me as the beggar who had challenged him to fight man to man in the darkness that night.

'You appear to know my name, sir,' I replied, coolly. 'Be so kind as to identify yourself.'

'I am Gilles de Mauchamps, a knight of France and a member of the Poor Fellow-Soldiers of Christ and the Temple of Solomon, and I belong to the Paris preceptory of our sacred Order. I come to this land to bring you to justice for your crimes by order of our exalted Grand Master, Sir Gilbert Horal.'

'What crimes?'

I could see that Sir Aymeric was unhappy. 'Perhaps, Sir Alan, it might be better if we discussed all this calmly in your hall,' he said. 'If you would be so good as to order the gate opened . . .'

I ignored the English Templar. 'What crimes?' I repeated, looking down at Gilles de Mauchamps, the fingers of my left hand flexing rhythmically on my sword hilt.

The Frenchman turned in his saddle and plucked a parchment scroll from his saddlebags. He unrolled it carefully and leaning the parchment on the high pommel of his saddle read aloud in a dull, clerkly voice: 'We know that you, Alan Dale, knight of Westbury in the English county of Nottinghamshire, did visit the Paris Temple on the twenty-eighth day of August in the Year of the Incarnation eleven hundred and ninety-four and on that day you did deposit the sum in coin of three livres of one-tenth debased silver, issued by the mint of Count Bouchard of Vendôme. And on that same day you did receive a letter accrediting you with two pounds one shilling and sixteen pence. And we know that on the second day of September in the Year of the Incarnation eleven hundred and ninety-eight – almost exactly four years later – you did present what purported to be a letter of accreditation to the Paris Temple, but which was in fact a forged copy of the original letter, and you did receive from the knights the sum of five hundred and two pounds, one shilling and sixteen pence in silver coin. We therefore accuse you of the theft of five hundred pounds of silver, and charge you to open your gates and submit to—'

'Did you say September second, eleven hundred and ninety-eight?' Sir Nicholas de Scras spoke for the first time, interrupting the French knight in mid-flow.

Gilles de Mauchamps looked down quickly at the scroll on the pommel of his saddle. 'I did, yes. That is correct. The second day of September, Year of the Incarnation—'

'Sir Alan was not in Paris on that day,' said Sir Nicholas. 'I can vouch for him. He was in fact in Normandy at the Château-Gaillard, where he held the position of Constable under his sovereign lord King Richard of England. I can vouch for him because I was with him at the Château at the time and for several weeks before and afterwards. He could not possibly have been in Paris.'

'Who are you, sir?' said the Frenchman.

'I am Sir Nicholas de Scras, formerly of the Knights Hospitaller and now of the manor of Horsham in Sussex.'

'I too can vouch for Sir Alan,' said a calm, humble voice from my left. 'I am named Thomas ap Lloyd, I have the honour of serving as Sir Alan's squire, and I was also with him at Château-Gaillard on this day.'

Gilles de Mauchamps was speechless for a dozen heartbeats. He tugged at his large nose with his left hand, then he said, 'You are his friends, you stand beside him on his walls; you would naturally say anything . . .'

Sir Nicholas said icily, 'You doubt my word? You would call me a liar? Well, no matter. I am not the only man who can attest to this. In fact, several hundred English and Norman men-at-arms were there at Château-Gaillard and they could all swear to Sir Alan's presence at that time. Your charges are absurd, Sir Alan could not have stolen your silver. And I will swear in any court in Christendom that you have the wrong man.'

I could not help noticing that Sir Nicholas, although acting as if he were grossly offended by the Frenchman's implications, also had a tone of great relief in his voice. Though he had loyally supported me before that moment, he now knew beyond doubt that I had not been the man who robbed the Temple.

But Gilles de Mauchamps was clearly a stubborn fellow: 'I still believe Sir Alan of Westbury has a good deal of explaining to do. The code for the forged note that was used in this shameful crime was based on the original note issued to him—'

'Enough,' I said. 'You came to my hall garbed for war and threatened me with arrest. And I have listened patiently to your ridiculous charges. They are false and we have proved them to be so. Now I ask you to leave me and my household in peace.'

'Perhaps, Gilles, we should heed what Sir Alan says,' said Sir Aymeric de St Maur. 'He has too many witnesses . . .' He, also, seemed to be relieved that I could so easily prove my innocence. He had once asked me, I believe quite seriously, if I would consider joining the Templar ranks, and I liked to think he had a high regard, perhaps even some little affection, for me.

But Gilles was still not defeated. 'The matter will be decided in a Templar court,' he declared. 'I have my instructions from the Master of the English Templars and from the Grand Master of the entire Order – and so I command you, Sir Alan, to open these gates and render yourself to me. In the light of what has been claimed by your men, I will allow you to retain your sword until the trial – where this matter will be investigated and your innocence or guilt will be determined beyond doubt.'

'I don't think so,' I said.

'If you prefer to be stubborn, if you do not open these gates instantly and give yourself over to me, I must warn you that I am quite prepared to use force. I will not hesitate to attack this manor, to overrun the walls, to seize you as a prisoner, to bind you and drag you to London at the tail of my horse.'

'I don't think so,' I said. And made a gesture with my left hand. Robin and his men stood. More than a dozen powerful war bows were drawn back with a loud creaking noise like a gigantic wooden door being opened – and the Templar *conroi* was looking up at their sure destruction. My own men, on my right-hand side, stood too, hefting spears and javelins. It was clear that while our sides were closely matched in numbers, we had the unanswerable advantage of the shelter of the high walls of Westbury. If I gave the word, I could annihilate half of the Templar force in moments. The horses of the Templar *conroi* were moving about in agitation: it was clear to the sergeants at least that they stood on the brink of disaster. Yet Gilles would still not submit to the inevitability of the situation. He lifted the scroll, waved it gently at me, and said, 'I have the authority to arrest you here in my hand from my lord, a man anointed by God to wield power on Earth. This cowardly rabble with their contemptible peasant weapons do not frighten me—'

A single bowstring thrummed. An arrow flashed and struck, piercing the scroll of parchment and the hand holding it, pinning both to the wood of the pommel with two inches of needle-sharp steel and a yard of ash. Gilles looked down in astonishment at his left hand, bloody and nailed by the shaft to his own saddle. The *conroi* exploded into movement; the sergeants were shouting warnings and hauling out swords, lifting shields against anticipated missiles and sawing reins to control their startled mounts; the horses were jostling and shoving as twenty men sought to move, either out of danger or into an attack position. One or two of the black-clad men now had crossbows in their hands . . .

'Stop! Hold right there,' Sir Aymeric was shouting. 'Stop this right now! No bloodshed, no bloodshed!'

'Stand fast,' I bellowed at Robin's men, 'do not loose your shafts. Stand fast, I say.'

Gilles looked down at the slim arrow transfixing his hand and then up at the row of bowmen on the battlements. There was only one archer who did not have a shaft nocked and a string drawn back to the ear. It was Robin. He smiled mockingly down at the Templar.

I said loudly, 'It is time for you to go. Your charges are false and I will not surrender my person to you without a fight. Take yourselves away from my walls and off my lands immediately or you will suffer the consequences.'

My eyes locked with Sir Aymeric's. We stared at each other for a moment or two, and then he nodded and lifted a commanding hand to his men. 'Form up, form up,' he shouted. And reaching over a hand, he plucked the arrow from the pommel of Gilles's saddle, freeing his fellow knight's bloody hand.

The French knight turned and looked back at us only once as the *conroi* cantered away. Yet, even at thirty yards, the heat in that glare could have melted iron.

The Templars did not return with greater numbers, as I had feared they might, but I asked Sir Nicholas to stay another week just to be sure. It seemed that the combination of armed might and two witnesses to my innocence had accomplished a happy result, though I was irritated that Robin had nearly precipitated a bloody battle, despite my request that he allow me to control the encounter on my own lands.

'I didn't kill the arrogant fellow,' said the Earl of Locksley, when I confronted him about piercing Gilles's hand. 'I merely gave him a slap on the wrist.' He grinned at his own sanguinary wit. 'Besides, he called my men a cowardly rabble. And it all ended well, did it not? I don't know what you are making such a fuss about.'

In truth, I could not complain. The exchange had ended satis-factorily in the main part due to the presence of Robin and his bowmen. I changed the subject. 'Was that not a rather strange coincidence – the knight being the same one who was at Welbeck Abbey?' I said, hoping for conciliation.

'I do not think it was a coincidence at all,' said Robin. 'I have an inkling about it, about that man, and I mean to make a few enquiries of my own. It may well turn out that I should have aimed for the heart rather than the hand.'

Towards the end of September, Sir Nicholas de Scras made his departure. He was returning to Sussex to spend the autumn and winter with his nephews at the family manor at Horsham, and he wanted to travel before the weather turned cold and wet, and the roads became almost impassable. Robin had remained at Westbury for only three days after the affair with the Templars – he had several paid spies in Nottingham Castle and he promised that he would have advance warning once again if the Templars were minded to return for a second bout.

I was busy with my lands that autumn, and the worry of another visit from the Templars, perhaps this time in overwhelming force, was soon replaced by concerns about more mundane matters. We ploughed the fields for the winter crop of wheat, oats and barley with my two teams of oxen, and sowed them, and kept gangs of the youngsters from Westbury village employed in banging pots and running around screaming to scare the birds from the freshly broadcast seed until it could be harrowed under. The pears and apples from the orchard were gathered in, too, that October, some of which Goody and her maid Ada made into preserves and some of which were stored in straw for next spring. The pigs were driven out to the woodland dens to fatten on beechmast and acorns; and the honey was collected from the hives and stored in big round earthenware jars. It was a time of bounty when we gathered the plenty of the Earth with one eye on the hard winter that lurked just over the horizon.

In early November, when driving rainstorms lashed the manor, and it was almost time to slaughter the pigs, a rider appeared at the gate of Westbury, soaked to the skin and shivering with cold. He was a courier in the service of the Archbishop of York newly returned from Paris and he had a letter from my cousin Roland d'Alle. We fed the man and dried him and offered him a bed for the night, and while he warmed his bones before our hearth, I read the letter from the French branch of the family.

Roland and his mother, the beautiful Adele, were both in fine health but, while Thibault, the Seigneur d'Alle, my late father's brother, was in good spirits and had been much at court of late – indeed, he had been granted a pair of plump manors by King Philip of France – he was suffering from an attack of gout in his right toe brought on by a surfeit of royal hospitality. I was happy to read that my cousin's family were moving in royal circles. In his letter, Roland stated that he planned to visit at the beginning of December and he begged that he might be allowed to remain at Westbury for the season of the Nativity of Our Lord. I was very pleased that he was coming to visit. I was fond of him and his whole family and they had been very kind to me while I had been staying in Paris some five years ago.

I rushed to Goody who was standing over the Archbishop's courier by the hearth, ladling out a bowl of soup for him, and told her the news. 'Then we will have another reason to be joyful this Christmastide,' she said, with a mysterious smile. It took me a few moments to absorb the look on her face and then I burst out, 'Is it true? Are you sure?'

Goody nodded at me. 'Yes, my dearest love. I went to the wise woman this morning. The signs are all there – I am with child. The old woman says we will have a baby in June.'

I felt breathless and lightheaded; my chest was buzzing like a hive of contented bees; my stomach hollow. The colours of the hall seemed brighter, more vibrant, more real, in a strange way. It seemed that the whole world was subtly changed, somehow shifted, everything was exactly the same but also different, as if God had just moved the Earth a quarter turn to the right. My first concern was for Goody – should she not be sitting down? Perhaps she should drink some strengthening posset with eggs and ale and spices? Was she warm enough? I could easily fetch a blanket or fur from our bed. And where was Ada? She should be attending her mistress, surely.

Goody kissed me. 'Alan, my dear,' she said, 'you must calm yourself or we will never manage this successfully. I am only a few weeks gone, a little more than a month and a half, and I am fine. I shall go mad if you turn into one of those husbands who coddles his pregnant wife like a mother duck mooning over her ducklings.

Let us continue as normal for as long as we can. There will be plenty of time to coddle me when I am huge and unable even to waddle like a duck. We must relax and be calm for months yet. After all, I am only doing what women have been doing since Eve. If you want to be helpful, say a prayer to the Virgin for an easy birth.'

Although we tried to maintain our equilibrium, the whole manor was infected with our joy. Women from the village visited Goody almost daily bringing little presents, or pieces of fruit or honey cakes. I had had no idea of quite how popular my wife was with our tenants, but it seemed that every female in the neighbourhood wanted to share in our happiness and show their liking and esteem for my lady.

Even Robin's wife, the Countess of Locksley, heard the news somehow in far off Poitiers, where she was attending her mistress Queen Eleanor. She sent a canvas-wrapped bundle all the way to Westbury containing her love, a letter for Robin and a thick black bear's pelt, a pair of silver rattles and two dozen fine linen napkins for Goody. The package arrived in early December, on a crisp frosty morning while Goody and I were breaking our fast with bread and butter and a blackberry preserve, and Goody's immediate reaction to her gift was to run to the door of the hall and vomit into the mud of the courtyard just outside.

'It is merely *nausea gravidarum*,' said the apothecary, a man who went by the absurd name of Silvanus, and who I brought to Westbury at the point of my sword from Nottingham the next day.

He had been reluctant to leave his shop at first – indeed he would not budge until I had drawn Fidelity and told him that if he did not come with me immediately, he would very soon have sore need of his own stock of bandages and medicines. I paid the man handsomely for his time, of course, and he sold me a small bag of his own ground ginger at an absurdly high price, which I was to mix with honey and hot water and give Goody to drink whenever she felt queasy.

But I was not easy in my mind over Goody's condition. All the women of Westbury assured me that it was perfectly normal for a mother-to-be to feel a little sick in the first twelve weeks of a pregnancy, but I wished that my friend Reuben were with me. He had a rare skill with all manner of illnesses, and I would have taken his wise reassurances in much better part than those of simple country goodwives.

And, at the back of my mind, while Goody groaned and vomited of a morning was one fell name: Nur. Could this malaise be anything to do with her curse? She had predicted that Goody would die one year and one day after we were wed. But I told myself sternly that I did not believe that her wild maledictions had power – they were the rantings of a woman crazed with hardship and misery. Nevertheless, each time I heard Goody retch and spew, I could not suppress a shudder of superstitious fear.

Chapter Six

Roland arrived at Westbury just as the first gentle snowflakes of the season were beginning to fall, a week before the first day of Christmas. My cousin came with half a dozen attendants, well armed and mounted, and brought with him two large, heavy boxes, each strapped to a mule's sturdy back. These were filled with silver *deniers*. And every penny of it was for Robin.

As I looked at my cousin, my mind travelled back to a time a little more than a year ago, to the small castle of Dangu in eastern Normandy, to the aftermath of the bloody battle of Gisors. Roland, a subject of King Philip and consequently fighting in the enemy ranks, had been captured by Mercadier, the Lionheart's savage *routier* captain. And such was the hatred between the English and the French at that stage in the war that each side was going so far as to blind the enemy who fell into their hands. Roland had been about to undergo this torment, by means of a burning coal pressed to his naked eyes, when I had come across him by chance and had bargained for his sight and his freedom with the mercenary.

The loathsome Mercadier had sensed that I was vulnerable and had pushed up the ransom price to two hundred pounds, an absurd sum far beyond my reach. I watched helplessly as his laughing men-at-arms made to burn out my cousin's eyes, when Robin had stepped in suddenly and paid the ransom, in cash, right there and then, astounding everyone and freeing Roland with his sight intact. The money, heavy boxes of silver that Robin had magically produced in the nick of time, I discovered later, had been part of that huge haul stolen from the Templars.

'Well met, cousin,' said my relative as he stepped down from a fine grey stallion in the courtyard of Westbury, and he clasped my hand. I pulled him into my chest and hugged him, and then leaned back and looked into his face. A cheerful, healthy visage of roughly my own age looked back at me, blue eyes above a long nose, a mop of yellow-blond hair and a wide smile. He was almost a handsome man, my cousin Roland, his looks only marred by a large patch of shiny pink scar tissue on the lower half of his left cheek and extending down to his neck.

He greeted Goody and presented her with a long, rolled bolt of silk the colour of new bluebells. The gift came from Adele, his mother, and although they had never met, by some strange female alchemy the shade of the rich cloth that Lady d'Alle had selected matched Goody's eyes exactly. For me, he had brought a pair of well-schooled greyhounds that had been bred on the Alle lands and, he boasted, were the fastest hunting beasts of their kind in France, and yet the most docile in the hall. 'They can even be trusted around babies,' Roland said with a grin.

We celebrated the arrival of my cousin and his men with a lavish feast, seating all the visitors and inhabitants of Westbury at long trestle tables in the hall and serving course after course of roast meats with rich sauces, pies, pastries and stews. The meats were carved at table and set before each diner on flat rounds of bread called trenchers. The bread soaked up the meat juices and the servants broke the trenchers apart after the meal and distributed them to the poorest of Westbury as alms, with the rest of the scraps of the meal, and a barrel of new ale. Thus the whole village was able to share in our joy at my cousin's arrival.

Roland was seated at my right hand during the feast, with Goody on my left, and while we ate, he told me of the doings of my French family. 'The Seigneur is well at court,' Roland said, 'and he has the King's ear in most military matters. He has encouraged Philip to continue his support of Arthur of Brittany's claim to the throne of England, the dukedom of Normandy and all the Angevin lands in France. Father thinks John is weak and that he will almost certainly lose in a long war against Philip – saving your presence, Alan, but your new king is certainly no Lionheart.'

'He is my king in name only,' I replied. 'I have no love for him, and I will not willingly serve him in battle.'

'That will please Father,' said Roland with a wry smile, 'and me too.'

When he smiled, only three-quarters of his face moved. The shiny burn scar stayed immobile and gave him a strange mask-like look. I felt a stab of guilt. Roland had received that burn in a battle at Verneuil Castle in Normandy six years before. And I had been responsible for the wound. When it looked as if we might be overwhelmed, I had ordered boiling oil to be poured on to the French forces that were attacking the castle walls I was defending. Although I did not know it at the time, Roland was one of the French knights making that determined assault. And we had faced each other again over drawn blades at the Battle of Gisors four years later. Mercifully, that time neither of us had been hurt. But it was likely that if I should choose to serve King John in his war against King Philip and his protégé Duke Arthur of Brittany – by all accounts a rather stupid twelve-year-old lad – we would be forced to face each other in battle once more, and I knew that neither of us relished that prospect.

'If you will not serve King John,' said Roland, 'there would be a place for you in the ranks of King Philip's men, and much honour to go with it. Father could easily arrange it, and doubtless the King would provide you with lands and titles, should you so wish. Would you serve with us?'

'I have had my fill of war and the bloody squabbling of greedy princes,' I said. 'My heart's desire is only to remain here at Westbury with Goody, left in peace to compose my music, and grow fat and happy raising my children.'

'I understand what you say,' said Roland. 'And I honour you for your pursuit of a peaceful life, but I have not yet lost my love for adventure. Things are different for you: you have Goody, and the baby to come, and lands of your own, while I must live my life perpetually in the shadow of my father. He is the Seigneur, he is the master of our House and always will be – and I will be nobody until he is dead. And, although God forbid that his death should come soon, I cannot but think that I will remain only half a man until he is called to Heaven. No, I must seek my own path, Alan, away from the loving stranglehold of family. I cannot be happy until I have carved my own place in this world with gold and glory in equal measure won by my sword.'

'Talking of treasure,' I said, 'when would you like to deliver your silver hoard to the Earl of Locksley?'

'As soon as possible,' said my cousin, with a strange writhe of his damaged features. 'I have been in mortal fear of thieves ever since I left Paris. I could not bear to return to my father and say that I had been robbed on the way to paying my debt, and humbly ask for him to hand over another fortune. I did think of going to the Templars and exchanging the coin for a promissory note, but the fees that they demand for their services are extortionate. And in the end, I decided to risk it, but vowed that I would die rather than allow the silver to be stolen by bandits on the journey.'

I kept my face deliberately straight, but inside I was laughing like a lunatic at full moon. It would have been a sublime pleasure for me to see Robin receiving his payment in the form of a letter of credit drawn on the Templars.

'We may go to his winter camp tomorrow, if you wish,' I said. 'But I must warn you that I will have to bind your eyes with a cloth as we approach the place. It is a secret, and its location must not be revealed, even to a friend such as you. I swore a mighty oath to this effect many years ago, and I will not break it.'

'That seems oddly fitting,' said Roland. 'I must be blinded temporarily in order to pay the price for the salvation of my sight.'

Sherwood shivered under a thick blanket of snow as Roland and I walked our horses down the narrow deer tracks that took us towards Robin's winter den – a well-hidden complex of caves that he had used years ago when he first became an outlaw. Roland had been accompanied by his protective men-at-arms a good part of the way, and then at my command he had dismissed them and submitted to the blindfold, and alone, I had led him and the two heavily laden pack mules through the secret paths towards the hidden caves of my lord.

The wood was bright with reflected light from the snow banks, and silent, the trees appearing as huddled, frosted skeletons under ragged white mantles, and we walked our horses through a cloud of our own frozen breath. Robin greeted us by the entrance to the main cave, wearing a bearskin cloak and standing beside a roaring campfire with a broad grin lighting his face and his hands resting comfortably on his hips. His beard had continued to grow since our escapade at Welbeck Abbey, and his hair was long and unkempt. He looked the very picture of an outlaw: shabby, wild and decked in animal skins. And while Little John and Gavin unloaded the silver from the mules, he poured cups of hot spiced wine and led us to the big table at the back of the largest cave.

It was delightfully warm in that wide space, kept so by the roaring fire, and the cave had an air of comfortable male clutter:

swords, spears and shields were piled around the walls, and riding gear, saddles and bridles heaped in confusion; half a deer carcass hung from a hook by the entrance next to a box of apples and a large round of cheese. Half a dozen dirty, hairy men lounged about the cave, largely ignoring our intrusion, some sleeping, some drinking, some merely doing very little in a lazily, contented way. This was clearly a place of ease and comfort for men on the run from the law, with plentiful food and few rules and obligations. And yet, I could not help noticing how different it was from the early days of Robin's outlawry. There was an aimlessness about the place that I had not seen ten years ago, and a lack of order: then, Robin had had a plan – he had been raising an army of outcasts, training them, disciplining them, forging them into a company that could take on his enemy the Sheriff of Nottingham's forces in pitched battle. Then Robin had a goal – to be reinstated as a member of lawful society. Now, it seemed, he did not.

Little John and Gavin joined us at the table, helping themselves to cups of hot wine and pulling up wooden stools. I noticed that they sat unnaturally close to each other, their thighs almost touching. 'Well, it's all there,' said Little John, nodding in appreciation at Roland. Gavin beamed at the whole table.

'And I must thank you for such a speedy repayment,' said Robin, smiling at my cousin. 'Please pay my respects to your father the Seigneur when you see him.'

'It is I who must thank you, my lord,' said Roland. 'I owe the fact that I can see you today to your kindness.'

Though Roland's words were most courteous and polished, I could sense that he was uncomfortable in this fire-lit den of thieves and outlaws in the depths of the wilderness. He was more used to the cobbled streets of Paris and the grand halls of powerful nobles, and so when Robin invited us to stay and feast with him on fresh venison that night, I refused and said we had to return to Westbury before dark to keep an eye on Goody who had been particularly queasy that morning.

'There is just one little thing I would like to show you before you leave,' said Robin. I looked out at the winter gloom of early afternoon, saw that the snow was softly falling again, and I nodded absently, expecting some bauble, a golden or silver trinket to be produced for me to marvel over. Instead, Robin turned to Little John and said in a soft voice as cool as a breeze on the back of the neck, 'Bring him in here, and bring the shears with you too.' And Little John and Gavin got up from the table and went out into the grey, swirling snow.

A few moments later they returned dragging a wretched figure by the arms between them. The man was about forty years old, pale, filthy and dressed in the rags of what looked as if they had once been rich town clothes but which were now stained with sweat and dirt and a good deal of pus and blood, old and new. His skin was waxy, and a yellow-grey colour, and he was weeping freely from large brown bloodshot eyes. He had matted, curly brown hair in a fringe around his bald pate, like a monk's tonsure. But this man was no Christian monk: he was a Jew.

'This is Malloch Baruch, once a goldsmith of Lincoln,' said Robin in an empty voice. 'He accepted money from a mysterious knight to spin me a tale about the cruel Abbot of Welbeck refusing to pay for his golden altar ornaments. He came to me pretending to ask for my help but secretly helping those who plotted to have me trapped and murdered. It took some while, and no little trouble to coax the full, the true story from him but we managed it in the end . . . Show them, John.'

The pathetic man was slumped on his knees by the table, his hands together in front of him. John reached down with a meaty fist and pulled Malloch's wrists up on to the table – and my mind reeled in horror.

The prisoner's arms were tightly bound at the wrists from the heel of the palm to the elbow, but it was his crossed hands that drew the eye. He had but three digits remaining, two on the right hand, the thumb and middle finger, and a single finger on the left, the little one. Where the other six fingers and his left thumb had been there were now merely bloody stumps, some less than half an inch long, crusted and scabbed over, some festering and some half-healed, and some with a glimpse of bone poking through the dried cap of black blood. The digits had clearly been severed individually, and over a considerable length of time.

'No, no, not again, please God, please God. I've already told you everything . . . No, please, noooooooooo!' The man's voice rose to a howling scream as John pulled a large pair of sheep shears from his belt. These were ordinary farm implements; two long triangles of steel linked by a U-shaped springy metal rod, the inner edges of the blades as sharp as a barber's razor. With this tool, a farm hand could cut the fleece from a struggling ewe in a hundred heartbeats. Gavin stepped behind Malloch and grasped him firmly by the shoulders. John held the poor man's arms fast on the table and placed the cutting edges of the shears over the man's remaining thumb – and looked at Robin.

Malloch's screaming was at a near-deafening volume by now, a wailing assault on our ears, and he was writhing and thrashing, trying to break from Gavin's grip.

'Be quiet now and stay still or you will lose the thumb,' said Robin quietly and the man stopped his awful noise immediately.

Robin looked at me, his eyes like chips of mountain ice. 'When I heard you were coming, Alan, I kept this fellow to hand. I want you to hear this from his own lips so that you will know that it is true. So, are you listening?'

I nodded, my eyes fastened to the prisoner's poor mutilated hands.

'You will remember how this works, Baruch, I'm sure,' said Robin, looking down at the wretch trembling with fear, his eyes round and dark as ale cups.

'You answer my questions quickly; do not lie, do not prevaricate, do not try to mislead – otherwise . . .' Robin clicked his own fingers and thumb together, making a dry, cracking noise.

The man was nodding jerkily, pathetically trying to please, holding Robin's grey eyes with his huge brown ones, pleading silently for a little mercy. I felt an almost overpowering urge to vomit; my cousin Roland's face was as pale as the snow in the deep drifts outside the cave; his mouth was clamped shut.

'Who was it who paid you to set the trap for me?' said Robin.

Malloch answered in a high, fast, gabbling voice. 'It was a French knight who goes by the name of Mauchamps; he paid me ten pounds in silver to set the snare for you.' He took a huge breath. 'Good sir, I beg you, I beg you . . . please forgive me; you must know that I am truly sorry . . .'

'Be quiet,' said Robin in a low voice. 'Just answer the questions slowly and clearly, nothing more. Now, which Order does this false knight serve?'

'He is a Templar, sir; he wore their white surcoat with the red cross on the breast when first he came to me.'

'And what else?' said Robin.

'And he belongs to another Order as well, but I do not know its name. Their device is . . . their shields bear a blue cross on a white field inside a black border.'

'How do you know this?'

'The boy, my only living son, he followed the knight at my orders after he made me the offer of the money. I wanted to see where he went, with whom he spoke after me. Shimon followed him to a mean lodging in the poorest part of Lincoln and when he went out that night, the boy searched his room. He found a shield with a blue cross, and a white surcoat also with this same device on it . . . but, sir, you already know this, I've told you many times, please sir—'

'Silence!'

Robin looked at me. 'So, Alan, what do you think?' he said.

'I think you are the cruellest man I have ever met. How can you do this?'

Robin frowned. 'It's not about this treacherous piece of slime; he doesn't signify. I mean about the knights of the blue cross, or as we know them, the Knights of Our Lady . . . and their Master.'

He looked at me, eyebrows raised expectantly.

I said nothing, collecting my horror-bruised thoughts.

Robin waved a hand at the kneeling prisoner, who was now silently weeping. 'John, take this foul thing away, would you. I think we're done with it . . . for now.'

'So,' said my lord again, when Malloch had been dragged, still whimpering, from the cave. 'What do you think?'

The Knights of Our Lady. I had not thought about them for many months. Nor had I thought about their leader – a man who called himself simply the Master. I had believed that I had managed to block them from my mind – but now, here they were, their spectral image conjured up before me in this smoky, fire-lit cave in the wilds of Sherwood by a mutilated, sobbing wreck of a Jewish goldsmith.

The Master was a Templar turned monk who had led this secret organization of knights sworn to serve the Virgin Mary. He was a man who appeared to exude holiness and yet was truly one of the most evil men I had ever encountered. Some even said that he had the mark of the Devil upon him – for he had a curious deformity, an extra thumb on his left hand, or rather two tiny twin digits growing from the same root. Robin and I had fought the Master and his Knights of Our Lady in France during Richard the Lionheart's long wars against Philip. The Master had been responsible for the death of my father, and the murder of a loyal friend of mine called Hanno. I'd tracked him down in Paris, and Robin had ousted him from his privileged and powerful life there as the Bishop's amanuensis by exposing his wickedness to the world. I had assumed that the Master was a fugitive somewhere in France, in hiding, powerless.

This was clearly not the case.

'If Gilles de Mauchamps is a Knight of Our Lady,' I said slowly, 'and that much is clear from that poor fellow's confession, then we must assume that the Master was behind the attempt to trap you at Welbeck.'

'What happened at Welbeck?' asked Roland.

'That's not important,' I said, catching Robin's slight shake of the head. 'What is important is that now we know the Master is coming after Robin, presumably seeking revenge. I thought he was finished but he clearly still has the desire – and the power – to strike out at us.'

'That was my conclusion as well,' said Robin. 'Do you think he still has the Grail with him?'

Robin had hunted the Master halfway across France trying to take possession of that legendary relic.

'I suspect that while he has one trickle of breath in his lungs he would try to keep possession of the Grail.'

'Good,' said Robin. 'I think so, too. So let us go and get him, Alan. Together. Let us find him, kill him and steal that last trickle of breath from his body – and the Grail, too, of course. Come on, Alan; for Hanno, for your father – and if they mean nothing to you, for your own safety and the safety of your family. Let us track down the Master and end this threat to ourselves. What do you say, old friend?'

Robin's eyes were shining like polished silver; he was using the whole force of his personality on me, willing me to take up this challenge. I realized now why he had subjected me to the sight of the poor Jew. He had wanted to be sure that I truly believed the Master was back in our lives.

He wanted me to join him in this mad quest.

'Tell me about the Holy Grail,' said Roland.

'It's a mysterious vessel from a long romantic poem by a *trou-vère* from Troyes in Champagne – have you never heard of it?' I said.

'I have heard its name but I have never heard it spoken of in a serious manner. Is it real? Does it truly exist? What is it like?'

'It is the most costly, most fabulous object in the world, my friend,' said Robin in a reverent tone. 'A golden treasure of surpassing beauty, set with the finest gem stones, and worth a dukedom at the very least, a kingdom, perhaps. And, for men of faith, it is much more than that – and that makes it even more valuable. The Grail, they say, can cure any hurt, any wound; it is said to be able to hold back Death itself. Some say it is the vessel that was used by Jesus Christ himself at the Last Supper, and it was used again by Joseph of Arimathea to collect his blood as it spilled from the wound in his side on the Cross . . .'

'We don't know that,' I said grumpily. I was irked by Robin's attempts to manipulate me into joining his mad treasure hunt. 'These could be merely the extravagant claims of a few drunken poets trying to make a name for themselves—'

This time Robin interrupted me. 'The Master believes it to be the most sacred, the most valuable object in the world – and he is prepared to kill again and again, to slaughter churchman or churl, anyone, absolutely anyone, in the name of the Grail.'

Both Roland and Robin had a slight pink flush on their cheeks.

'I should like to see this Holy Grail one day,' said Roland. 'I believe that would be a noble quest worthy of my mettle.'

'Well, good luck to you,' I said crossly. 'But on this day I am going home to Westbury to care for Goody; while my wife is unwell nothing on earth will induce me to leave Nottinghamshire and to head off on some silly chase after something that may be no more than a myth.'

And with those intemperate words, I made a farewell to my lord and, with some difficulty, steered Roland outside. Leaving the warm, masculine fug of Robin's Caves behind us, we both rode into the cleansing, snowy wastes of Sherwood.

Christmas should have been a time of joy – we decked the hall with evergreen boughs and sprigs of holly bright with berries; we set a giant yule log to smoulder in the hearth for the full twelve days; we drank and danced and feasted; I sang and made music on my vielle to amuse my cousin and the household. And yet I could find no joy. The blight on the season was Goody's health. She was by then a little past twelve weeks of the pregnancy but she still continued to vomit up her breakfast most mornings and added to that she developed a low, hacking cough that would not yield to the infusions of honey and herbs that my wife drank several times a day in an attempt to tame it. At night, she would lie beside me, both of us sleepless, and bark quietly long into the early hours, her chest convulsing painfully. Sometimes I knew that she had been unable to catch a wink of sleep until dawn. And I was sick myself – with worry for her and the baby. At the back of my mind loomed Nur's curse.

By early January, Goody's cough had not improved and she developed a fever as well, her body alternately raging hot and icy cold. She took to her bed and despite being plied with all the delicacies that Westbury could muster – honey cakes, fatty salt pork, preserved berries from autumn – she began to lose weight. She soon found that she could not lie flat without feeling suffocated and could only breathe shallowly and with some difficulty propped up in a nest of pillows. I was badly scared by this point, and summoned the apothecary once again from Nottingham. The man spoke at length about evil humours and noxious airs, balancing the black bile and yellow bile in her body; he felt her brow, took her pulse and demanded a sample of her urine. To my disgust, he examined it closely in the light from the shutter in our bedchamber, sniffed it deeply like a lover of fine wine and then took a sip. He prescribed a greyish powder that cost me three shillings for a pound – he claimed it was ground unicorn's horn – and Goody took it with a little warm milk that Ada brought her morning and night. But she did not recover. Indeed, she told me that it merely made her feel more nauseated.

The wise woman from the village came to see her almost daily and she clucked and bustled around the bedside but although she managed to calm the fever with her steaming, foul-smelling herbal infusions, the wrenching cough and the nausea persisted. And one day the old biddy came to me and told me with much sadness in her rheumy eyes that she feared the baby might be lost if Goody did not recover soon. This had also occurred to me – indeed I prayed to God most earnestly that if He must take a life, it should be mine – but if it came to a choice between Goody and the baby, He should take the baby, so long as He let my beloved live. We were young, we would be able to have other children.

If Goody lived.

In a black fog of desperation, I had Father Arnold come to the bedchamber and try to counter the curse, if curse it was, with holy water and prayer. He came and dutifully mumbled away in bad Latin and splashed my beloved with a few freezing drops – but once again it had no effect. Goody coughed and hacked, day after day, and vomited up all that we gave her to eat. She did not complain, but she sometimes wept a little from the frustration of her constant ill-health. Yet she did not curse God nor the Devil nor even Nur for her condition, and she always wore a thin, brave smile on her wan face when I came to sit with her.

The nights were the worst. By day, Goody would sometimes force herself to rise and go about the hall, and even occasionally into the courtyard if the weather was mild, and she would sit by the hearth for an hour or so, if she felt strong enough, and talk to Ada a little about the doings of the village or chat with Roland about his family. But at night – lying in our big sweat-soaked bed, cough-cough-coughing her life away with myself beside her, sitting on a stool, holding her pale hand and feeding her spoonfuls of honeyed water – I think she must have had a taste of what Hell might be like.

But God moves in mysterious ways, as my old friend Father Tuck always used to tell me – for it was Goody's illness that saved my life and hers. Indeed, it saved a good few souls at Westbury. For one dark night in mid-February, I was fully dressed and wide awake, even though it was long past midnight, and reading a poem about King Arthur and Queen Guinevere aloud to her, when the Knight of Our Lady, Gilles de Mauchamps, returned to Westbury.

Chapter Seven

The first I heard of the attack was a scream and a thump. The sentry who patrolled the palisade of Westbury had been shot from the darkness below by a crossbowman, I was told later. The man, whose name was Rinc, God rest his soul, must have been gathering wool in his mind as he paced up and down the windswept walkway – either that or the attackers were particularly skilled at making a silent, unseen approach – for he apparently saw nothing and gave no warning of the assault.

However, Rinc did his duty with his death cry. Swept off the walkway and back into the courtyard by a bolt to the chest, he had enough time to give a wild howl of pain before he smashed to the floor ten feet below and never made another sound in this world. And that was enough to give me warning. By God's grace, I was fully dressed in tunic and hose, and well shod in a pair of stout riding boots, and when I heard Rinc's scream, I jumped up from the stool beside Goody's bed and snatched up my sword from the corner of the room. I ran out of the bedchamber at the eastern end of the hall, through the main living space, leaping over the now stirring bodies of sleeping servants, and burst out of the main hall door into the courtyard. It was a freezing night with a clear, starry sky and there was enough light from a sliver of moon to make out the humped black shapes of men coming over the top of the palisade, and to see a knot of indistinct figures by the main gate lifting the massive locking bar from its brackets. A cold hand gripped my heart and I thought: *God save us, they are already inside the walls. We are lost!* But I had no time for fearful thoughts or useless recriminations.

'Westbury! To arms, to arms!' I bellowed and rushed forward across the courtyard. But I was far, far too late, the big double gates, our doughty defences, were swinging slowly open and I could see the red light of torches and a press of armed, mounted men outside. As the gates swung open, the enemy outside it gave a roar and surged forward. I felt a bloody glow of unthinking, bestial rage bloom behind my eyes, as if I was seeing the world through red-tinted glass – these filthy creatures were invading my home; these invaders were threatening Goody, they were threatening my *family*. They must be destroyed – all of them – right now. And I charged towards the gates alone, all caution abandoned, my long sword whirling around my head, a scream of furious wordless defiance on my lips. But before I could throw myself, undoubtedly to my doom, on the incoming tide of foemen, a man-at-arms already inside the courtyard rushed to intercept me and we met in a bone-jarring crash of steel on steel. He knew his business, my enemy, and he skilfully parried my furious blows as I tried to cut him down and reach the gate in time to stem the flow of attackers. But he blocked my blizzard of sword blows with a rare skill and even made me duck under a lightning lunge to my face. But that was his downfall. It unbalanced him and, even as I ducked, I took out his knee with a simple low sweep and left him crouched, shouting in pain as I pushed past and hurtled towards the gate.

It was wide open by now, and there were mounted men spurring their destriers through the gap, the huge beasts' warm breath pluming like dragon's smoke in the cold air, and a pack of yelling footmen following in their wake. Westbury had come abruptly to life: there was a light showing in the guest hall where Roland was lodged, and I heard running footsteps behind me, and a young voice crying, 'Westbury! Westbury! Come to Sir Alan's aid, men. Rally to our lord!' And Thomas was at my shoulder, half-dressed but with a sword in his fist.

There were two big fellows before me now: one wielding a large axe, the other a spearman. The axeman was slow, so very slow; he pulled back his weapon in a mighty backswing ready to cut me in half – and I danced forward and flicked the razor tip of Fidelity under his chin, slicing open his throat and leaving him stumbling, jetting blood, and toppling backwards with the weight of his own swung blade. The spearman jabbed at me in the same moment, but I twisted my body and he missed, the spear shaft sliding over my shoulder – and Thomas stepped in and half-severed his neck with a vicious backhand.

A man with a blazing torch swung its fiery end at my face and I rocked back out of reach, came forward again and with Fidelity grasped in both hands hacked down hard, splitting his helmeted skull. There were strange men-at-arms all around by now and enemy horsemen galloping across the courtyard towards the store-houses against the eastern wall. I saw one of my dairy maids running in panic, her skirts bunched up in her hands; then a rider gave chase, caught her and with a low looping sword blow, sheared off the top of her head. I saw one of my greyhounds, the bitch of the pair, speared through her skinny ribs by a laughing enemy horseman. But I had my own concerns: I attacked a man to my left with a pair of swinging lateral cuts, then disembowelled him with a straight lunge into his belly and savage twist of Fidelity. A molten rage seethed through my veins: these men had come to burn my hall and kill and maim the people – and the animals – that I loved. I realized that I was roaring foul curses and shouting, 'Die, you filth,

97

die, die, you sons of swine', as I swung my sword almost blindly into the wall of men that seemed to spring up from nowhere before me. Two men went down to two huge sweeps of the sword, like corn before the scythe. I killed another, and another; blood sprayed warm on my face, something knocked hard against my leg, and I killed again with a lunge. I was the deadly whirlwind, slaying all in my path. I was dimly aware that Thomas was fighting close by with two of my men-at-arms, and that Roland was beside me, sword in his hand, barefoot and clad in nothing but a dirty chemise, pale and ghostly in the night. He exchanged cuts with a man-at-arms, killed him with the second stroke, but he was yelling madly at me between sword blows.

'Alan, Alan, we must retreat to the hall. Alan, the hall – we cannot fight them all here.' A crossbow bolt flickered between us. The yelling crowd of men-at-arms in front of me suddenly dispersed and revealed a horseman, a sergeant in a dark surcoat with a white cross on the breast, mailed, steel-helmeted, with a couched lance. And he was charging towards me. He held the lance in his right hand and tucked under his elbow. I could feel the hoofbeats of his heavy horse vibrating the ground through my boot soles, and he bore down on me, the long weapon's killing-tip winking in the moonlight and aimed straight at my chest. There was no point in running – I could not outdistance that huge beast and its metal-masked rider. At the last moment I took a fast, desperate leap to my right, to his shield side, across his line of attack, rolled, rose and hacked down with Fidelity at the horse's left hind leg as it swept past, snapping through the brittle bone with my blade. The animal's muscular hindquarter caught me a glancing blow as it passed and spun me back to the ground, but a moment later horse and mount somersaulted and smashed into the dirt with a rattling crash of metal on wood amid a cacophony of shouted human oaths and equine screams of pain. The rider had one leg trapped beneath the horse's bulk and was trying to wriggle free, but Roland jumped forward and buried his sword edge in the struggling man's helmet, and even while he was tugging the blade free from the limp and jiggling corpse, he was still yelling at me, 'Alan, Alan, we must get back to the hall. We must get to Goody and the others.'

His words snapped me out of my rage; I felt the red mist before my eyes dissolve and the night was filled with hellish screaming, and the clang of steel and dancing flickers of yellow torchlight. I parried a cut at my head from a stocky sword-wielding man-at-arms who ran at me out of the darkness, kicked him hard in the stomach, and he went down; I stamped on his chest, feeling his ribs crack like kindling, then I fled for the safety of the hall, with Roland panting at my back.

Enemy men-at-arms, on foot and mounted, swarmed all over the place, scores of them; I could see a dozen corpses lying in the dirt, some of them recognizable as my own people; most of the scatter of buildings on the eastern side, the wine store, the blacksmith's forge and the pigsty, were already smashed open and ablaze. The dim, freezing courtyard rang with the victorious shouts of the enemy, the squeals of escaped pigs and the crackle of burning thatch. There were men, strangers all around me, but they kept their distance from Fidelity's gory blade, and in a few moments I was hammering on the door with the silver pommel ring, with Thomas and Roland at either shoulder, and screaming through the wood for entry.

We tumbled through the door of the hall and slammed it behind us, right in the faces of a pack of yelling pursuers. I slid the locking bar home and leaned with my back to the stout door, catching my breath and feeling the buffets transmitted through the oak as our enemies hurled themselves against it and hacked futilely at the seasoned planks. I found I was looking at a dozen terrified faces, wide eyes and open mouths, gathered by the door and staring at me as if they had never seen me before. I realized that I was slathered in blood, from crown to toe, with a naked blade in my right hand. Some of the Westbury folk were weeping, some were shocked into silence. All looked to me to save them. Baldwin was in the front rank, his hands grasped together in front of his chest as if he were pleading for something. Thomas was kneeling beside him strapping a sword belt on my steward's slim middle and speaking low, lying words of encouragement. 'Everything will be all right, Dwin. Sir Alan is here now. Everything will be fine. You'll see.'

'No time to lose,' I said to Roland. 'I want everybody armed, dressed and ready to go as quickly as possible.'

'Where will we go?' quavered Baldwin. He was clearly very frightened; and who could blame him. He was no warrior and his home was now overflowing with a horde of brutal enemy soldiery intent on rape, loot and slaughter.

'We cannot stay here,' I said briskly, my words accompanied by a furious bout of hammering on the door. 'They will burn us out in less than half an hour. We must make our way to the stables, if we can, find ourselves mounts and break out of Westbury. We will shelter in the forest – I know a place where we will be safe.'

I tried to sound confident but my heart was in my boots: our chances of survival were very slim indeed. There must have been more than fifty enemies running riot in the courtyard – and I had no doubt in my mind at all that they were Gilles de Mauchamps's men – and we no more than four or five fighting men and a gaggle of terrified women and servants.

Still, no good ever comes of despair.

'Thomas,' I said, 'be so good as to help Sir Roland get everybody ready. Warm clothes and weapons only – no personal possessions.' And I slapped my squire on the shoulder and went into the solar to fetch Goody.

As I walked through the door, a long, wicked blade lanced towards my face, and it was only by God's grace, that I managed to rock my head an inch or two out of its path and avoid losing an eye. I seized my attacker, throwing my arms around a slim torso, and struggling to subdue its manic writhing – and found myself face to face with my beautiful beloved who was clenching my own misericorde in her small white fist and still trying to stab me with it.

Goody was already dressed. She had heard the awful clamour of battle in the courtyard, the screams and shouts and the clash of steel, and had drawn conclusions.

'I thought you were dead, Alan,' she sobbed, her face as pale as milk. 'I thought you were one of them. Oh God . . .'

I kissed her and released her, and told her that we had to leave, right now, and she asked no questions and made no comments – she was a woman in ten thousand – just busied herself finding a warm woollen gown and changing her light slippers to outdoor shoes. I knew I would not have time to dress in full mail but I slung the cuir bouilli chest-and-back plates over my neck, with the lance dagger in its sheath, and struggled unaided into my knee-length hauberk. I found Fidelity's sheath, strapped it over the top and slipped my blade home, and tucked my mace into the belt at the back. I plucked two cloaks from the back of the solar door, draped one around Goody and slung the other from my shoulders.

Time to go.

I led my wife by the hand back into the hall. Between them, Roland and Thomas seemed to have wrought some calm from the frightened chaos. Half a dozen servants, including Baldwin and Ada and three men-at-arms, were dressed and the men had been issued with whatever weapons and armour we could find, from one or two of my old swords and a kindling axe to a long kitchen carving knife. One man, a kitchen servant known as Alfie, had only two heavy, round-bellied cooking pots, one in each hand. I caught his eye and he grinned. 'I'll give 'em Hell with these two ladies, sir,' he said, lightly tapping the two iron pots together with a clang. 'Don't you worry, sir, we'll make 'em rightly sorry they disturbed our sleep.'

I was about to applaud his attitude with some bold jest or other, when I heard a commanding voice shouting in French outside the wall, the chunk of axes and the splintering of wood at the main door. So I saved my breath and, keeping Goody close by, I led my little band to the western end of the hall to the wide screen that hid the scullery and servants' work benches, cupboards, buckets of water and so on from view at feasts. Behind the screen was the hall's other door, which allowed cooked food from the kitchens just beyond to be brought to table while it was still hot. It was barred shut at night, and as I pressed my ear to it, I could hear nothing from outside. But I could smell smoke, and the wood felt horribly warm against my cheek.

It was then, I believe, that I truly realized that I was going to lose Westbury – and that it was entirely due to my lack of vigilance and my underestimation of the threat the French Templars represented to my happiness. I knew we were going to have to abandon our home – but I had not understood till then that I would never see the hall and the buildings as they now were again. To shut out this dolorous image, I drew my sword and cautiously unbarred the door. Opening it and thrusting my head through the gap, I peered out on to an inferno. The flimsy kitchen hut and the square brick oven beside it where we baked our bread each day were both raging with flame. The heat, even five yards away inside the hall, was like a physical blow. But there were no enemies to be seen. Perhaps they did not know about this back door, or perhaps they were so engaged in battering down the front one – or more likely in looting the wine store – that they were indifferent to us.

I herded everyone outside into the roaring heat, keeping Goody by my far side, and we hustled to the narrow scorching space behind the burning kitchen by the southern wall of Westbury. I could feel the flames roasting my face. But so far we had been lucky. I counted heads: twelve souls and me. To our left, forty yards away, was the stable block, the broad door open and a light coming from the inside – likely not a light made by a friend, I thought grimly. Across on the other side, the north side, was Roland's guest hall, its thatched roof merrily burning, the wattle and daub walls smoking and blistering in the heat. I gave the word and we ran towards the stable, a crowd of frightened people tripping over their own feet, bumping into each other in the darkness, with myself in the rear, holding Goody's hand, trying to urge greater speed without making a sound.

And at that point our luck ran out.

Six enemy spearmen in pursuit of a pair of squealing shoats raced around the corner of the stables, saw us in the firelight and charged into our terrified little party. The pigs escaped unharmed. We did not. A moment later four of our folk were curled on the ground screaming, bellies punctured, faces hacked and bleeding their lives away; although Thomas with a deft bit of sword work had crippled one of the men-at-arms and dropped another with a savage kick to the groin. Roland faced off against a spearman in helmet and mail. He attacked instantly, two quick half-steps then he swept the man's spear contemptuously out of his way and skewered him through the neck with a classic lunge.

As he pulled his blade free with the help of a boot on the dying man's chest, he turned to me: 'Alan, we must leave very soon. Very soon. We cannot kill them all.'

I released Goody's hand and pushed her towards the stable. And I joined Roland and Thomas in a loose line, guarding the door and facing the three remaining spearmen. They dithered, not wishing to attack, turning to search the night behind them and yelling in French for their comrades to come to their aid.

A tall dark figure on a dark horse trotted out into the centre of the courtyard by the well; he was shouting something to a group of unseen men over in the west of the compound and gesturing with his drawn sword. I only made out half of it: '. . . and make

103

sure you search every hut – and thoroughly – before you burn it. It must be here somewhere. It must be!'

He had no shield on his left arm, and no weapon either, his arm ended in the white swaddling of a bandage. He heard the commotion outside the stable caused by our brief fight and turned in the saddle and a sudden flare of light from the burning kitchen illuminated his face: it was Gilles de Mauchamps. He saw us at the same moment and shouted gleeful orders behind him, and many more men came running out of the darkness.

Gilles pointed his sword at me like a spear and shouted in French, 'I want him – it is Dale; take that man now; take him.' Then he jabbed back his spurs. His horse leaped towards me, but by then we were all running as fast as we could for the stable door just a few yards away. Roland got there first, then Thomas, and as they tumbled inside I heard shouting and the crash of steel blades, but I stupidly slipped on an unseen frozen puddle, skidding and only just managing to stay upright. And then Gilles and his horse were upon me.

His destrier's iron-shod hooves fanned the air above me, his sword hammered down on my head, and I had to block the blow double-handed with my own blade held at hilt and tip; and then he was past and wheeling his mount in a tight circle and coming at me again, snarling like the beast he was. An enemy soldier, unseen, pelted out of the night and blundered into me from the left knocking me to the floor. I dropped Fidelity. Alfie, the kitchen boy, came yelling back out from the stables, and with wild swinging blows from right and left he crunched the two iron pots into the head of the man-at-arms who was just now raising an axe to carve through my head. But Gilles, on horseback, towered over the boy and hacked into the brave lad's unprotected skull, cleaving it open with one tearing blow. Something wet and warm splattered on my bare hands, but I was busy scrambling under Mauchamps's horse's hooves trying to recover my sword. My clutching fingers closed around the hilt and I twisted and flung the blade upwards, by sheer chance managing to deflect Gilles's next downward strike. He turned his horse again but I did not stand to face him. Instead, I scuttled for the stable and dived inside, while the surviving men of Westbury stopped the door with swords, spears and knives – a bristling hedge of sharp steel.

Inside, I saw how few of us had made it there intact. One of our men-at-arms, a good man named Joseph, sat by the wall bleeding from a huge gash in his stomach – I knew he would not live long. Alfie the pot boy was surely dead. That left myself, Roland, Thomas, Goody, Ada, Baldwin and two men-at-arms who had gone with me to Normandy named Kit and Ox-head.

Two enemy warriors lay in a gory puddle on the floor but, praise God, I saw that four of the horses were still in their stalls. Three of them, two bay mares and a roan gelding, were clearly very frightened by the noise and smoke of battle, stamping and fidgeting, and rolling their eyes. But Shaitan, the horse nearest to me, looked calmly over and merely whickered a soft greeting.

I said, 'Mount up, everyone, two to a horse, and head for the gate. Once we are out, ride like hell for Sherwood and Robin.'

Everyone nodded. We were all a-horse in a few heartbeats, Goody up behind me on Shaitan, gripping my waist firmly. We had no time to saddle or even bridle our mounts – at any moment the enemy, whose shouts outside seemed to be growing in volume, could charge in and overwhelm us – so we merely untied their halters and swung our legs up and over their backs. I gripped tight with my knees and ordered Shaitan onwards with my heels, sword in my right hand, mace in my left, Goody snug behind my back, her left arm tight around my middle, when the first man cautiously stepped through the stable door, a spear extended in his shaking hand. I put my heels hard into Shaitan's sides and my destrier jumped forward. I flipped the wavering spear-point out of our path with my sword and a moment later Shaitan's huge glossy black shoulder smashed into the unfortunate fellow, hurling him to the floor, and I heard the snapping of bone and shrill cries as half a tun of iron-shod horseflesh churned over his body.

We came out of the stable at a dead run and barrelled straight into a loose crowd of men-at-arms, scattering them like chickens. I managed to catch one man on the cheek with a flick of my mace as I passed him, and he flopped to the ground, and then we were through them. The whole of Westbury was ablaze now, and I saw that Gilles de Mauchamps had been gathering his horsemen in the centre of the courtyard – fewer of them than I had expected. I counted six mounted men in the surcoats of Templar sergeants, but the place was still thick with unmounted men-at-arms, mostly spearmen. Gilles's horsemen were directly between us and the gate. I glanced behind me and saw that the other three horses had emerged from the stable, and Roland on a bay, with my man-at-arms Kit behind him, was besieged by a scrum of enemy foot soldiers jabbing up at them with sword and spear. But not for long. Roland laid about him efficiently, left and right with his sword, and Kit killed with equal ferocity, and their foes fell away, gashed and bloody, as they urged their mount towards me. Beyond them came Thomas on the roan, with plump little Ada clinging to his shoulders; and last of all Ox-head, an experienced and very tough soldier on the second bay, with Baldwin's thin, frightened face peeking over his shoulder.

A squad of men-at-arms was running straight at me from the right, but I ignored them and urged Shaitan straight at Gilles and his knot of mounted black-clad sergeants. My destrier bounded forward and in half a moment I was slicing Fidelity hard at my enemy's skull. He blocked the blow with his sword and broke away, circling his charger out of range. And I heard the yelling behind me of the footmen; I nudged Shaitan with my right foot in a special signal, and my black friend dipped his head, pecked forward and shot out both hind hooves at the same time with the force of a pair of battering rams. There was a crack and a scream and the leading man-at-arms who had been racing towards me was cata-pulted backwards, into his following comrades, bringing a second and third man tumbling to the ground. But I had not time to praise Shaitan's skill, for Gilles was upon me again, scything his blade down at my shoulder. I blocked with Fidelity, pushed his blade away and guiding Shaitan's shoulder into his horse's haunches, I smashed the mace into the back of his helmet and saw his dark eyes flutter at the blow.

I heard Goody give a gasp of fright and turned to see a mounted Templar sergeant swiping his sword at us, by God's mercy, but we both ducked just in time and the blade whistled half an inch over our heads. Goody's thin left arm jabbed out like a striking snake and I saw the misericorde sink deeply into his inner thigh, and then we were past him and clear through the enemy horsemen. The gate, still wide open, was but twenty yards away. It was time to run.

I pointed Shaitan's head towards the gate with my knees, slammed back both heels and he took off like a frisky young roebuck. Goody's arms gripped me tightly, but we both somehow kept our balance on his saddle-less back. Before we raced through that portal and into the welcoming darkness beyond, I just had time to snatch a look behind: Roland and Kit were clear and only five yards away; Thomas's face was a mask of blood and fury but he and Ada charged straight through a pair of spear-wielding men-at-arms as I watched, Thomas dropping the two with short vicious sword strikes.

But of Ox-head and Baldwin there was no sign at all.

We covered a mile at a fast canter, across the dark flat sheep pasture outside the walls of the manor, and up to the wooded knoll where poor drunken Katelyn believed she had met the demon; but with six folk on only three horses, I dared not push the beasts too hard, and it seemed that there was no pursuit. We stopped at the knoll and looked back at Westbury – and I admit that I wept then at the sight. The whole compound was alight, with the flames leaping highest from the hall itself. The village of Westbury, a few hundred yards to the east of the manor, a straggle of homes of varying degrees of prosperity gathered round the stone church, was burning too, and I could see horsemen in groups of two or three riding up and down its only street. I prayed that the villagers might escape the wrath of Gilles de Mauchamps, but feared that his men would loot the place as savagely as the manor and slaughter anyone who stood in their way. Then I looked back at my home, tears blurring my eyes. I could see the tiny black stick-like figures of men crossing the courtyard, some running, some moving slowly, some bearing burdens, others unencumbered. And in the centre, surrounded by the orange glow of a settlement put to fire and sword, was a tall dark shape on a dark horse, and I fancied, even at that distance, that I could make out the white flash of the bandage on his arm.

Chapter Eight

'I told you I should have aimed for his heart not his hand,' said Robin. We were in the main cave of Robin's hideout, deep in Sherwood, in the grey light just before true dawn, and all the surviving members of my band of escapees were now sleeping, fed, warmed and wrapped in blankets and furs by the central hearth fire. It had been a gruelling ride through the forest from the high copse to Robin's Caves; a freezing rain had soaked us to the skin, the horses became so fatigued with carrying their double loads that they nearly collapsed from exhaustion and the roan had to be whipped to get him to move at all; and to make matters worse, I had lost my way twice on the tangled deer tracks and secret pathways in the utter darkness of the forest, and it was only by the grace of God, and the fact that we stumbled into a pair of Robin's alert sentries, that we were now in the safety of my outlaw lord's limestone demesne.

'You should have killed him, yes,' I admitted. 'And you have my permission to do so next time you see him – I would even ask it as a favour,' I said with no little bitterness. 'Though I think there is little point dwelling on what might have been.'

I did not take too much offence at Robin's I-told-you-so attitude. To be honest, I was not paying much attention to the conversation. I was bone-tired myself and aching to crawl under a blanket by the fire and sleep, but more than that I was desperately worried about Goody. The freezing ride – thinly clad and soaking wet – as we fumbled our way through the forest had reduced her to a state close to insensibility, and she had nearly slipped from Shaitan's back twice during the journey. Eventually, we switched positions and I rode with her cradled in my arms. Her breathing was very shallow, and even her occasional coughs were merely feeble convulsions that produced only a dribble of sputum from her slack, bluish lips. At the caves, she responded very slowly and a little strangely to my questions and comments when I had prepared her for bed, wrapping her in a huge, thick bearskin that Robin provided and feeding her hot broth with a horn spoon. I clawed my heart to ribbons over her and the baby – indeed, I was almost certain that they could not both survive her illness. As I sat on the straw-covered ground of the main cave beside her, a great fur-wrapped bundle by the hearth, still as a stone, her face as white as a swan's wing, I realized that she already resembled a corpse. I closed my eyes and prayed then: 'Dear God, please, I beg You of Your infinite mercy spare my woman, and my unborn child – I do not think that I can live without her. But if, in Your wisdom, You must take a life, let it be mine, O Lord. I offer my life for hers. I ask this in the name of Your Son, Jesus Christ. Amen.'

Robin took me by the arm. 'You must sleep for an hour or so, Alan. She will need your strength. I will watch over her until morning. Sleep! That is an order from your liege lord.'

I slept, fitfully, for a few hours and when I awoke it was full morning, though a grey day of drizzly showers and sullen clouds. Thomas – that prince among squires – brought me hot water to wash my face and a clean towel, and a breakfast of bread, dried venison and ale. Goody slept on, as white and motionless as before, and I left her in her fur by the fire and went to find Robin.

The Earl of Locksley was with Roland d'Alle in a large, crudely constructed wooden shed where the horses were stabled, looking at a pony with a split off-hind hoof. A villainous-looking outlaw-groom was saddling a grey mare two stalls along and obviously listening to their conversation.

'How is Goody this morning?' asked Robin. He looked tired; it was clear that he had not slept. 'She did not stir once in the night and I left her in Thomas's care just after dawn, with instructions to wake you if she awoke.'

'She is still sleeping, but her skin is cold. And . . . I fear for her, Robin, I think . . .'

He gripped my shoulder. 'I have sent for Brigid, she will come swiftly and cure whatever ails her. I am sure of it.'

'I think it is Nur's curse,' I blurted. I hated to sound credulous or weak-minded in any way around Robin for fear that he'd laugh at me; but I was not fully in control of my heart on that bleak day.

'We will see what Brigid has to say on the matter,' said Robin. 'This is her corner of the battlefield.'

Brigid was a strange woman: a hermit, a healer and, some whispered, a witch, who lived not far from Robin's Caves. She had cured me once, long ago, of an infected wolf bite but since then I had avoided her – for there was another side of her, apart from her apparent ability to cure almost any hurt, illness or wound, that I was wary of. She was also a priestess of the Old Religion, as she called it – a heretic who shunned God and who worshipped instead a collection of foul pagan woodland spirits that clamoured for the sacrifice of living flesh.

I was half-glad that she was coming to treat Goody for she undoubtedly had great powers of healing but, for the sake of my immortal soul, I did not want to have any further dealings with Brigid than were absolutely necessary.

111

'I'm going to Westbury this afternoon – alone,' I told Robin, and he nodded sympathetically. 'I need to borrow a fresh horse.'

'Of course,' said Robin, and he jerked his head at the groom. 'Are you done with the grey, Andrew?' Then he looked back at me. 'You know that you won't like what you see there?' he said.

I nodded. I could well imagine the devastation and how it must look in full, bleak daylight.

Robin continued, 'Nevertheless, you can tell any of your people who survived last night that they can come to me if they are in need. Food, clothing, shelter, beasts of burden, whatever they wish. And from what you have told me about the fire, we will need to think about rebuilding the whole place from the ground up.'

'I don't have the money for that; I'd be much surprised if a single silver penny survived the looting unscathed.'

'Don't worry about that for now. I have plenty of money at the moment, thanks to your honest cousin here.' Robin smiled at Roland.

I felt a vast swell of affection for the man. He was truly a generous lord, whatever other sins he was guilty of – and they were legion. He was a true friend. 'Thank you, Robin, for that offer – for taking us in last night, for seeing to Goody, for everything. I don't know how I will ever be able to repay you . . .'

'Well, I'm glad you mentioned that,' said Robin with a mischievous grin that I knew well and did not relish. 'I've something to discuss with you when you return.'

I frowned and took the bridle of the grey horse from the groom's hand. As I stepped up into the saddle, a most unpleasant thought struck me. 'What did you do with the poor goldsmith? He had surely told you everything. What became of him?'

Robin said nothing. He merely stared at me, his face blank, as I sat on his grey horse, my belly full of his food and drink, my sick wife and unborn baby under his care. 'Have a safe journey,' he said. 'We have much to talk about when you return.'

'What did you do with him, Robin?' I insisted foolishly. 'What became of Malloch Baruch, the Jew of Lincoln?'

Robin looked at me levelly for a few moments. 'I gave him to Brigid – I gave him to Brigid for the ritual,' he said with nothing in his voice. 'He is the price of Goody's care.'

The journey was safe – and very nearly uneventful. The deer paths and woodland tracks were narrow but clear to follow. I could not understand how I had lost my way so easily the night before: and yet I knew that darkness can make even the simplest task a dozen times more difficult.

As I approached Westbury and rode towards the high knoll with the little copse, a thin figure burst out of the stand of trees and came running towards me calling my name. I released my sword hilt and stepped down from my horse to embrace Baldwin: dirty, his robe damp and torn, his face grey with fatigue and fear, but it was truly my steward, more or less whole and hale. My joy at discovering him alive leavened the deep sadness I felt at the sight of Westbury in the daylight. As we stood by the copse and looked down at the charred ruin a little over a mile away, Baldwin told me his story in short, excited bursts.

My steward had ridden out of the stable behind Ox-head with the rest of us, but the surprise of our eruption from the building on horseback had lessened by the time he and his riding companion emerged. While we had ridden to safety out of the gates, they had been surrounded by a crowd of enemy men-at-arms and pulled from the horse near the gate. While Ox-head had battled manfully for his life, killing at least two of his enemies before he succumbed, Baldwin, perhaps less gloriously though more prudently, had wriggled free of the press and run as fast as his legs would carry him to the well in the middle of the courtyard and had jumped inside. He had remained there somehow undetected for several hours and towards dawn, when the soldiers had all departed, he climbed out with the aid of the rope that was attached to the bucket. Fearing that Gilles de Mauchamps' men might return, he had left Westbury and hidden himself in the undergrowth in the copse on the knoll until he had seen me approaching.

I congratulated him on his survival and told him that he had done exactly the right thing in the circumstances.

I was very glad that he yet lived, but I was drowning in a sense of shame and failure. The primary duty of a lord is to protect his people. Yet a great many of those who had looked to me for their protection were now dead. As we walked slowly together down the slope towards my now blackened and smoke-stinking property, I pictured the faces of the fallen, so many fallen. My servants, my soldiers, my friends . . . For of the thirty-two people who had once called the manor home, only seven now remained on this earth.

As a place of human habitation, Westbury was no more. The hall, the stables, Roland's guest hall, the store rooms – every structure had been deliberately torched and was no more than a collection of half-burned blackened timbers that had collapsed in on themselves. Our dead lay where they had fallen: men-at-arms, the women of Westbury, even a couple of innocent children lay in the pathetic attitudes of death, their bodies blackened with soot and sprawled like discarded dolls on the hoof-churned, blood-soaked earth. Baldwin wept openly as we bent together to the task of gathering the corpses of our friends and companions, many cruelly burned or mutilated, and carried them out of the reeking compound and on to the green turf of the sheep-pasture to line them up in rows for a Christian burial.

We were joined after an hour or so by Father Arnold, who popped up, a little soot-blackened but apparently otherwise unharmed, and told me blinking his owlish eyes a little more madly than usual that the village too had been ravaged by the marauders. However, only two or three houses had been destroyed, and, while several folk had suffered slight injuries at the hands of the enemy, only one man had been killed. Many of the village folk had seen Westbury burning and overrun by enemy soldiers, and had escaped by hiding in the woods nearby.

I passed on Robin's offer of help to the little priest and gave instructions for a Mass for the dead as soon as it was possible. I also charged Baldwin with beginning the rebuilding of the manor, as Robin had so accurately put it, from the ground up. Father Arnold assured me that the village men would be only too glad to help with the reconstruction of my home under Baldwin's supervision, and I promised that suitable payment would be forthcoming for their efforts.

It was a desperately sad day, but a busy one. There was so much to do that I felt that I was drowning in decisions. But, even while giving dozens of detailed instructions to Baldwin and Arnold, and greeting villagers who emerged from a wide variety of hiding places to offer their condolences and help with the clearing up, I was distracted by grief and worry. I found it hard to focus on my labours, many and onerous as they were, for one most urgent question hammered away in my heart: did Goody yet live?

It was late in the evening when I returned to Robin's Caves, more tired than I had been for months, and I discovered that my beloved's condition had not changed. She appeared still to be in a deep unnatural sleep, her breathing only the faintest whiff of air, her pulse feeble and uneven. She had been moved from her bearskin by the fire into a small cave all of her own and Ada was tending to her, feeding an iron brazier with billets of wood and sitting beside her lest she wake.

Ada told me in a hushed voice that the notorious witch Brigid of the Wood had been to visit and had examined her closely all over and declared that the malaise that Goody was suffering from was magical in its nature – and furthermore that it was a powerful spell that could not easily be countered. Brigid feared for Goody's life, Ada told me, and even more for the life of the baby inside her. However, the witch had agreed that she would use all her skill to cure my girl, and that she had returned to her home in the forest to brew up the most powerful medicines at her disposal.

'It will be tongue of toad, and a hanged man's member, all boiled together in a cauldron of fresh baby's blood, I expect,' said Ada, with a good deal of relish. She was a devoted servant to Goody, and had nursed her tenderly, but I could not help but feel that she seemed to be enjoying the drama of her mistress's illness a little too much. I did not like to dwell on what witchy charms and cures Brigid might be concocting. An image of the finger-cropped goldsmith Malloch leaped into my mind; and I shuddered at the knowledge that he was in Brigid's blood-stained hands. But I was too worn out for true outrage at Robin's hellish exchange. Would I have killed Malloch to save Goody's life? Would I allow an enemy, a man who had tried to have me killed, a treacherous fellow who had asked for my help, and been generously offered it, and then had tried to trap me – would I allow this man to be murdered by a pagan priestess to save my beloved and my unborn baby? I could make that decision in a single heartbeat. There was no question about it at all.

I sat beside Goody in her cave for an hour or so, holding her hand and staring at her still white face in the flickering light of the brazier while Ada bustled about making a broth. I prayed silently once again: offering myself to God if he would allow her to live. But I took little comfort from my attempt to commune with the Almighty. My thoughts turned to Nur – the foul bitch who, I was truly beginning to believe, had somehow caused this vile sickness to come down on my beloved. If I could kill her, I thought, surely that would lift the curse on Goody. And if, God forbid, Goody should die, I would kill her anyway, slowly, for what she had done. Finally, I put away these dark thoughts and rose to my feet. I kissed Goody's cold brow, tucked the blankets tight around her unresponsive body and went in search of Robin.

My lord of Locksley took one look at me and sat me down at a stool by the table and poured me a large cup of wine, and moments later Thomas appeared with a hot bowl of venison stew and some bread. As I ate and drank, Robin looked hard at me. Then he spoke. 'If you will permit me, Alan,' he began, 'I would like to outline your position. May I do so in full honesty as an old and trusted friend?'

I was too tired to comment so merely nodded and spooned some more of the venison into my mouth; it had been a while since I had had anything so good to eat.

'Your wife is dying, and with her your unborn baby.'

I flinched but said nothing. It was the cold truth.

'Your home has been burned to the ground by an agent of the Master, our old enemy. And we can be certain that the Master, or minions such as Gilles de Mauchamps, will continue to attack you – and me – without warning whenever he can until he has destroyed us. Or until we have destroyed him.'

It was clear to me what Robin was aiming at; in fact I had known what he wanted from me since I rose that morning and I had already decided my answer – but, for reasons that I cannot fully express, I remained silent.

'We know also that the Master possesses a holy vessel, a sacred relic that many have claimed can cure all hurts, wipe away all disease, even hold back death itself.'

I nodded but I seemed to have lost the power of speech. I had washed down the stew with plenty of wine yet my tongue seemed glued to the roof of my mouth.

'Is your path not clear to you? You must come with me to the south. We will track the Master together, we will hunt him down and kill him and prise the Grail from his dead hands, and we will use it to cure Goody of her malaise, and save her and your baby.

Will you not come with me, my friend, and help me to accomplish this task? To help me and to save Goody's life.'

My tongue unstuck itself at last. 'Yes, my lord,' I said. 'I will come with you.'

A week later, I found myself once again seated at a table with friends and drinking wine. It was long past nightfall, and I was in the hall of a wine merchant's house – a grand place of black timber, white plaster and red tiles owned by one Ivo of Shoreham – a hundred yards to the east of the royal dockyard of Queen's Hythe in the City of London. The hall was large for a townhouse in a crowded port, even a little larger than my burned-out country hall at Westbury, and sumptuously decorated with brightly patterned wall hangings and tapestries. The long table at which we sat was two-inch-thick English oak polished to a high shine with beeswax; the wine was the clear ruby-coloured juice of ancient Aquitainian vines, fermented, casked and blended by masters in the art from the area around the city of Bordeaux, and shipped to England by Master Ivo. We had dined simply, for it was Lent, on fish and boiled vegetables with bread, and a fruit pudding to follow – but the wine, served in egg shell-thin, beautifully-engraved and gilded glasses, had been of the finest quality, a rich, smooth, crimson nectar. Beneath my feet I could feel the rumble of huge iron-hooped wooden barrels, each heavier than three men, being rolled around the stone floor of the undercroft. A delivery of fresh wine had arrived from Queen Eleanor's homeland that afternoon and it was being trundled only now into its storage position in the cellars by gangs of porters, servants of the wine merchant, our host.

Master Ivo had been presented to me the day before as an old friend of Robin's. But I did not believe he had much love for the Earl of Locksley – indeed, wealthy and powerful as he must be, he seemed to stand in fear of my lord, almost to go out of his way, without offending, to shun Robin's company. I did not ask what dealings Robin and Ivo of Shoreham had had in the past – but I could well imagine some sordid tale of black murder or brutal persuasion, of a crucial favour done and repayment subsequently demanded by Robin. Whatever had passed between them, Ivo clearly stood in Robin's debt – and urgently wished to redeem himself. The merchant – although he had excused himself gracefully shortly after our arrival – had indeed been more than generous with his wine and food. And, on this second day of our sojourn in his house, I had recovered some of my spirits.

Were it not for my stomach-grinding concern for Goody and the baby – I had left her still unconscious at Robin's Caves in the care of Ada and under the protection of Baldwin and Kit – I might have felt the embers of excitement. We were about to embark on a grand adventure, a quest to find the most fabulous object in Christendom.

The cup of Christ, the Holy Grail.

One voice in my head argued stridently, even a little shrilly, that this quest was futile; the Grail could not possibly be what some claimed it to be – it could not be the vessel that had been used at the Last Supper and that had held Our Saviour's holy blood at the Crucifixion – it just could not. How could an earthly object encapsulate the sacred life fluid of God Himself? Was it not far more likely that this object was merely some gaudy trinket, the focus of a collection of lies, half-truths and fables designed to enrich an unscrupulous seller of such sacred oddments? Was it not far more likely, the grating voice whined, that I was wasting precious time that could be spent with Goody, perhaps her last days on this earth? That this so-called Grail was no more than a tool for gulling the credulous?

But another voice, a calm, clear, soothing voice told me a different tale. Have faith, it said. Have faith in a loving and merciful God whose designs you cannot possibly fathom. This miraculous

cup of Christ will be given to you – and Goody will be cured by
its holy power, if only you have sufficient faith. Seek out this Grail,
said the voice; overcome the evil men who pollute it with their
touch and use its power for good; use its power to save Goody and
the baby.

I liked the second voice a good deal more than the first. It
reminded me of my mother's voice, calm, loving, reassuring. It was
how I imagined the voice of Mary, the Mother of God, would
sound – and then I checked that thought. I remembered that the
Master and his knights claimed to serve this same Queen of Heaven
– and the Master, too, had heard the voice of Our Lady, which
had told him to go forth and do murder in her holy name.

That notion snapped me out of my reverie. I took a sip of
wine and looked at the flushed, excited faces around the table.
These men would be my companions over the coming weeks as
we journeyed to far-off lands and braved unknown dangers. We
had all made an agreement that, while Robin would shoulder
the expenses of the journey, we would all share in any booty that
we accrued along the way, and that Robin would also have possession of the Grail, if we found it, to do with as he willed. We were
due to leave London the next day on a ship belonging to Ivo of
Shoreham and we would sail south to Aquitaine as his guests. In
the ancient city of Bordeaux we would begin our quest to discover
the Master and the Grail.

I did not expect it to be an easy task to find our enemy and
overcome him, but my companions were some of the best men I
had ever encountered, in battle and out of it. Seven men, seven
of the best men I had ever known; we seven bold men would
succeed in this quest for the Grail – or perish in the attempt.

To my left, at the head of the long table, sat my lord, my old
friend and benefactor, Robin of Locksley, bubbling with high spirits,
his eyes sparkling silver in the candlelight. He was joking with the
man on his left, Little John, who, with his big red mouth open in

his big red face, was roaring with mirth at some quip of my lord's. Beside John, Gavin – the only man at the table that I did not know well – gazed up at Little John's battered visage seemingly lost in admiration for his huge friend. Robin had vouched for Gavin and named him as a thief of uncommon skill, particularly when it came to defeating iron locks, but also praising him for his prowess as a bowman. He had mentioned, too, that John had said that he would not come without him. I caught Gavin's eye and he smiled happily at me, inclining his handsome curly head and lifting his exquisite wine glass towards me. I had no doubt that if I were to fall in battle, he would be the first to claim ownership of my sword Fidelity – for I had seen an unmistakably larcenous look whenever he eyed my blade – but if Robin and Little John trusted him, then I was content to do so, too.

To Gavin's left, at the other end of the table sat Sir Nicholas de Scras. It had not taken much persuading to entice the former Hospitaller to join us on this quest. When I had ridden to his lands at Horsham to suggest it, I had found him bored and feeling a little uncomfortable at his family hearth. He wished very much to see the Grail, he told me, and to hold it, if only once, in his hands. From what I'd told him of the Master, he seemed to think that destroying him was a task sanctioned by God.

'It is a most worthy endeavour,' Sir Nicholas had said. 'This Master and his knights have perverted the True Faith with their crimes and their false worship of the Virgin. It is our Christian duty to stamp these heretics out.'

At the end of long table, there was an empty place, but I saw that Sir Nicholas, ignoring this position at the head of the board, was deep in conversation directly across the polished oak with Roland d'Alle who was seated on my side of the wood. It had not been difficult to persuade my cousin to join us either – he had grown fond of Goody during his time at Westbury and was convinced that the Grail would save her life. That was reason enough, he said, to join our number, but I knew, too, that his acceptance of my offer had as much to do with his own urge for adventure and his lust to win gold and glory, as it had to do with saving the life of my lady.

The final member of our company of seven sat beside me, directly to my right: Thomas ap Lloyd, my faithful squire, a young man of extraordinary courage and skill, and seemingly unlimited devotion to me. I had not needed to ask him whether he wished to come on this quest: when I had told him that I would be accompanying Robin overseas, he had merely nodded and begun to gather our few remaining possessions together at the caves, and the only question he asked was about the horses. After a short discussion with Robin, we decided that it was impractical to take them with us on the long sea journey. And so, reluctantly, I left Shaitan and the other two beasts – the only cattle I now possessed – in the care of Baldwin and Kit and Robin's men in Sherwood.

Seven men, seven friends, seven bold warriors, sat around that long table in the wine merchant's house on the night before our departure for Aquitaine. I pushed back my stool and came to my feet. I rapped on the table with my knuckles to capture the attention of everyone present and said, 'My friends, if I may, I would like to say a few words before we embark on the arduous journey that lies ahead.'

There was a general rumble of assent, and every eye on the room was on me. 'My friends, we are gathered here with a common purpose to seek out the murderous villain who calls himself the Master and crush him. It is true that I seek vengeance for the burning of my home – and also for the provocations that have been given to my lord, the Earl of Locksley – but our primary goal is to take from him the sacred vessel that once cradled the lifeblood of Our Saviour. We are all equal companions in that noble endeavour; we are indeed a fellowship in this quest – this quest for the Holy Grail. I therefore propose that we swear an

122

oath as Companions of the Grail that we will be loyal and true to each other, that we will honour each other and protect each other in battle, that we will never leave a wounded man to his fate, nor turn our backs on a comrade in danger, until that task is done . . .'

There was another general murmur of assent, which was broken by a loud knock at the door. We all turned to look and, through the arched panelled door behind Robin's back, the head of a servant appeared. He looked nervously at Robin and said, 'Sir, I beg your pardon, sir, for this intrusion, but that . . . er, woman . . . the, er . . . the lady you mentioned is here to see you. May I show her in directly?'

'Please do,' said Robin. And I felt a flash of irritation. Why did he have to bring his guests into the hall at this very moment? Couldn't she wait? I wished to make it a solemn affair among men, among warriors, with powerful oaths and the forging of a bond. I could not do that if Robin introduced some passing London slattern into our company.

'We seven men,' I said loudly, 'we seven Companions of the Grail shall make a mighty vow this night. We shall . . .'

But I had lost the attention of my audience. Robin had risen from his throne-like chair at the head of the table and was walking towards the door. For it had opened and a short figure dressed in a long black robe had entered the room. Her hair was covered by a black headdress, her face by a heavy veil. The only visible features were a pair of liquid brown eyes that seemed to glow with a strange inner fire.

Robin said, 'I beg your pardon, Alan' – he had taken the woman's white hand on his arm and was leading her towards the far end of the table to the empty place between Sir Nicholas and Roland – 'but you are mistaken. We shall not be seven *men* embarking on this quest. We shall not be *seven* Companions undertaking this perilous journey. We shall be eight.'

Robin seated the black-clad figure on the stool at the end of the table.

I looked into the blazing eyes above the veil, and with a volcanic upwelling of rage and fear and hatred and plain dumbfounded disbelief, I recognized the new arrival.

It was Nur.

Part Two

Chapter Nine

Father Anselm must believe that I am a particularly wealthy man – or a particularly gullible one: he has asked me to purchase a golden casket with a clear glass top to house the Flask of St Luke the Evangelist, so that the faithful may flock to see this holy relic, and pray before it, but will not be tempted to sully its saintly leather with the touch of their hands.

I told him no, and had some difficulty in keeping my temper. I am not a pauper, it is true, and Westbury has been bountiful in the past few years, but I will not throw good money away on this ridiculous form of ostentation – and for a fake as well.

By God's mercy, I managed to restrain myself from telling him the true base nature of his absurd 'relic' – but I sent him away from my hall with a few choice expressions of my wrath ringing in his ears.

However, yesterday, on All Saints' Day, that bouncing tonsured puppy preached a long homily in church all about the flask and the blessed St Luke and the power of prayer. He exhorted the villagers to pray before it and ask for whatever they wished and, he said, if they had sufficient faith in miracles, St Luke would help them.

Then he had the God-damned effrontery to lead the congregation in a prayer for a casket to house the flask. He said that God would surely grant us this gaudy trinket – which would cost no more than twelve pounds – if we prayed hard enough and believed with all our hearts that the miracle would occur. I was standing there right in front of him, blushing in my best clothes, and thankfully unarmed, while he begged St Luke to intercede with the Almighty and persuade Him to send us a suitable container for the flask. If I'd had a sword with me, I might have run him through. If he had made some slighting mention of my refusal to pay for this golden extravagance, I might well have slaughtered him. No, I tell a lie, I would not have done that – my killing days are undoubtedly over – but I was tempted to duck his head in his own font, and I could certainly do that, I warrant, even at my advanced age.

Worse, the villagers have taken his words to heart. When I returned to the church this very evening to pray for the soul of my wife Godifa – as the day after All Saints, it is, of course, All Souls' Day, and I come each year to light a candle for her and sit quietly alone and remember the happiness we once shared – I was greeted by a piteous sight. Two of my tenants from the village, a devoted couple called Martha and Geoffrey, were praying before the altar where the flask is displayed. These two had found each other late in life – she is a plain, hard-working woman who will never see forty again and he is almost as old as I am – and yet they seem to be as enamoured of each other as a pair of giggling twenty-year-olds. Martha and Geoffrey had been there since the service the day before, on their knees at the altar, taking neither food nor drink, never moving, and praying continuously for St Luke to grant them a child. At their age! That would indeed be a miracle.

I lit a candle for Goody, and said a prayer, but I did not linger.

I leaped on to the wine merchant's table in a single bound and took three fast steps down its full length, heedlessly crushing costly glasses, and scattering dirty plates, fish bones, scraps of bread and jugs of good red wine. I hurled myself at Nur, my fifteen stones of muscle and bone smashing her slight form from the stool and on to the reed-strewn floor. I had no weapon – all my war gear was in the sleeping chamber on the first storey of the house – and I had not paused for a moment. I saw her; I flung myself at her. We crashed to the floor and I reached for her throat, gripped, locked my hands and began to squeeze . . .

I think that if there had been lesser men seated at the table that evening, the witch would have died there and then. I could feel her tiny neck like a twig beneath my palms, and the swordsman's muscles in my heavy arms writhed – a few more moments and I would have snapped her spine as easily as a farmer dispatches a dove. But Nicholas and Thomas were on me almost as soon as I had Nur in my grasp and with their considerable combined strength pulling my wrists away from the woman, and with Robin on my back, choking my neck with his left forearm and shouting in my ear that I must release her immediately or I would suffer the consequences, I soon found myself separated from the woman in black, my vision blurring and helplessly pinned by three friends against the solid edge of the table. Roland swam into my field of view; he was saying, 'Alan, give the Earl your word that you will not attack this lady and you will be released. Alan, you *must* give your word.'

I mumbled something through a clogged and swollen throat, and Robin released his grip a fraction. 'Do you swear on your soul that if I release you, you will not attack the lady Nur again? Do you swear on Goody's life?'

I struggled futilely for a moment or two, growling like a mastiff in my half-crushed throat.

'Do you swear that you will not harm her?'

I managed to cough out the word: 'Swear.'

'I am serious, Alan – do *not* attack Nur again tonight.' Robin removed his forearm from my neck, allowing me to take a ragged breath, but Nicholas and Thomas still had my arms in their grip.

I stared at my victim. My sudden assault had ripped the veil from her face and I looked into a gaunt visage that would have terrified the Devil himself. The lip-less mouth seemed to be permanently grinning, mocking me, the nose was a truncated snout, no more than two gaping red-rimmed holes in the centre of her face. I caught a glimpse of the mass of scarring where her right ear had been and a frill of remaining earlobe – and her eyes burned with an unquenchable demonic hatred as she hastily rearranged her headdress to cover her ugliness from the world.

'I swear that I will not kill that Hell-spawned hag this night – but I make no promises about the morrow and there had better be a God-damned good reason why you sprung her on me like that, Robin, and why you seem to be inviting her to join our sacred quest. And I want to know that reason right now – or *you* will suffer the fucking consequences.'

It hurt me a good deal to speak but I do not remember when I have been so angry. The sight of Nur, that vile agent of Goody's illness, seemed to have ignited something powerful inside me. I was fully prepared in that instant to make an enemy of Robin – and my lord must have sensed this.

'First of all let us sit down and compose ourselves, and take a deep breath,' Robin said. 'Gavin, would you kindly run through to the servant's quarters and ask them to bring us some more wine.'

I found myself sitting back at my place, staring at my twitching hands, my blood still simmering, my bruised windpipe on fire, while Thomas fussed about mopping up spilled wine and gathering the shards of broken glass. After a very short time, order had been regained and I looked up. For some reason I could hardly bring myself to look directly at the small dark figure, now fully veiled again and sitting as still as a statue at the far end of the table.

Robin spoke: 'I must apologize to you all, and to my friend Alan here most of all, for the events of this evening. I had anticipated having a chance to explain why I asked the lady Nur to join us before you were all presented with the fact of it. Alan – I am truly sorry.'

I said nothing. I looked down at my big hands again.

Robin continued. 'There are certain things that you should know, Alan; certain things that the lady has sworn to me, and which I have accepted as the truth. Firstly, while Nur admits that she did place a curse on yourself and Goody, she swears that she would now lift it if she could; but she tells me that this kind of magic cannot be undone, and that this curse would continue in its malevolence even in the event of her death. Is this not true?' He directed the question down the table to the witch.

Nur spoke. 'It is true, lord,' she said, her voice, though now a little hoarse and scratchy, had the same weird, sing-song quality that had long haunted my nightmares. 'I made this curse from a male mandrake root boiled in dew from a dead man's grave in a virgin's pelvis bone. I buried it in the earth and drowned it in a waterfall, and burned it on a fire made from a murdered woman's dry bones, before scattering it to the four winds. It is the most powerful curse of all. It cannot be unmade, not by my art – not even if I wished it so. I have pledged my soul to this curse: my death would merely make it stronger.'

She paused then, and I sensed that she was looking directly at me. 'If I were to die at your hands, my beloved, your pale Godifa, your milky whore-wife, would live not one hour longer. As it is: she will live until the curse claims her. One year and one day after you wed, she will pay.'

I lifted my head and stared at Nur just then, hating her from the depths of my soul, and remembered that she had often called me her beloved when we had been lovers, in a faraway land, long, long ago. Goody and I had married on the first day of July the year before. It was now mid-March. If the curse were to prove true, my beloved would be gone in a few short months. I thought of Goody as I'd last seen her, cold, still; my eyes filled with tears and I could make no sound more than a sob.

'Well, yes, be that as it may,' said Robin. Even his customary assurance seemed to have deserted him. 'But, you see, Alan, killing Nur can have no good effect on Goody's well-being – and perhaps, if you believe in this business of curses, it may have the opposite effect. But tell him, Nur, tell him why you are here.'

'I alone know where the cup of Christ may be found,' said the witch calmly. 'I alone know its resting place. Its magic calls to my magic. Its power calls to mine.'

Every face at the table was watching her keenly; not a man fidgeted, not a cough or a sniff was to be heard.

'Your sour-cream bitch can be saved only by the strongest magic in the world, Alan – by the power of the Christ God,' said Nur. 'And none other. If she were to drink a draught of ordinary water from the vessel that is called the Grail, into which had been mingled three drops of my own blood, the curse would be shattered and she would surely regain her strength. This is her only chance to escape her doom.'

When Nur finished, the silence continued among the assembled company for a dozen heartbeats. It was broken by Robin. 'Nur knows where the Grail is, Alan,' said my lord, a little too loudly, as if I were either stone deaf or very stupid, 'and she has agreed to take us there. So if you want your Goody to live, I am afraid you must suffer Nur's presence with us on our journey.'

We boarded *The Goose* the next day, on a sour, pewter-coloured morning, a little before noon. The ship, moored at Queen's Hythe dock, a mere bowshot to the west of Ivo the merchant's house, was an ugly, fat-bellied craft, sixty feet long and twenty-four feet across at the beam. I hated *The Goose* from the moment I saw her – although it must be acknowledged that I was in a mood to hate the whole world that day.

The night before, Robin had dismissed everybody to bed, including the witch, but had kept me back for a few words when the hall had emptied. I was angry and hurt that he had arranged all this behind my back and I ranted a good deal and behaved more than a little childishly towards my lord. His response was blunt: 'Do you want to save Goody's life or not?'

I had no reply to that, and no move to make except to take myself off to bed in an angry, sulky silence.

At the top of the stairs, I saw that Sir Nicholas was waiting for me. He put two hands on my shoulders and looked intently into my face. 'Know that I stand with you on this, Alan,' he said. 'It seems that we must endure the company of this vile sorceress for a little while, for the sake of the Grail. But I shall watch her every move, I promise you, and if she tries any devilment, any of her foul Satanic practices, I shall take her life in a single heartbeat. I will gladly slay her for you, Alan, whenever you give me the word, and we shall put our trust in the Lord God for Goody's recovery.'

I knew that the former Hospitaller meant this kindly but I shook my head. 'We have no choice but to suffer the witch to live, Nicholas,' I said. 'But I thank you from the depths of my soul for your generous intent.'

While *The Goose* was not spacious, we seven warriors, the seven Companions of the Grail, as I thought of us, managed to find shelter from the spitting rain under the aft-castle, a crenellated walkway that ran around the ship's square rear as a fighting platform. *The Goose* had a similar defensive position at the bow called the fore-castle, square and crenellated as well, and it was underneath this smaller platform that Nur made her nest. Our spirits were subdued that afternoon as the six sailors who manned the ship slipped the moorings, hoisted the square sail on the single mast and under the gentlest of breezes and a fine drizzle, we wafted downstream. We tacked around the end of the great stone bridge of London – which was then nearly two-thirds built, and which ran from St Botolph's in Billingsgate almost all the way across the water to the stews of Southwark – and once past that obstacle we took the centre of the greasy brownish stream and glided along the Thames, at about the speed of a walking horse, towards the sea.

The river traffic was light, and the passage was calm, but the vision of that small black-clad figure sitting alone in the bows made my stomach churn with frustrated rage and despair. We sat glumly on our baggage – mainly weapons and armour, some sacks holding a little food, bundles of spare clothes, and Robin's strong box, which contained silver coin and a few valuables – and munched dry bread and onions as the falling damp soaked into our clothing; I contemplated weeks of this experience with a shudder.

Before long, the captain of the ship came aft to bid us a formal welcome. He was a short, sturdy, muscular man named Samuel, with a wide, square face and cropped pitch-black hair and, in contrast to his master, Ivo the merchant, he was apparently a fearless soul.

'Welcome aboard my ship, gentlemen,' he said looking at Robin. 'As you know, Ivo of Shoreham owns her, and he tells me what is to be carried in her holds,' he said jerking a thumb over his shoulder at the main deck which was packed with hundreds of coarse lumpy grey sacks holding Staffordshire coal for the busy forges of Aquitaine. 'But once *The Goose* leaves the dock, she is entirely my bird, and I have dominion over her and anyone she carries. We will make you as comfortable as we can, but this is a working ship and, Earl or churl, you are merely passengers on it. Keep out of the way of the sailors, and obey any command you are given by myself and we shall get along fine. We'll be landing before dusk each day, wherever we can, and setting off again at dawn – in between times, under here is as good a place as any to roost. If we encounter pirates, you'll be expected to fight – but by the looks of you that should not be too outlandish an experience.' And he was rewarded with seven grins from the Companions. Then he frowned, and glanced at the huddled figure under the fore-castle: 'The lady, well, she makes the crew a little nervous, so just keep her out of the way, agreed?'

Robin stood. 'Captain Samuel—' he began.

But the man cut him short: 'You call me Governor or Samuel, one or the other, nothing else.'

'Very well, ah, Samuel, I would just like to thank you for allowing us on board your fine vessel and to assure you that we accept your authority and while under your care we shall be as meek and obedient as a troop of novice nuns.'

'That's good,' said Samuel. 'See that you are. We sleep tonight at Gravesend and, wave and weather permitting, we should make the mouth of the Gironde by the middle of Holy Week or there-abouts – in about twenty days, give or take.' He nodded at Robin, turned and strode away towards the bow.

For the next few weeks we submitted to the queasy tedium of travelling by sea. As the Governor had promised, we stopped at Gravesend that evening, and we passed the night in a stinking tavern that overcharged for its lodgings and for a vile eel stew and a few crusts of stale bread. The next day we took to the open sea and after a rough crossing, with a good deal of grey-faced vomiting from even the seasoned voyagers, we arrived in Calais, and dragged our drenched and aching bones off the ship in search of warm wine and a place that did not heave and creak and shift and splash quite as much as the deck of *The Goose*.

And so we proceeded down the coast of northern France – surging past the wide beaches of Picardy and Normandy and along beside the rock-bound coast of Brittany. The days merged into one another, each dull, damp and long; aboard we ate bread and vegetables boiled with pungent dried fish, and drank watered ale or the rough, sour cider of the region; we told stories to pass the time, taking it in turns to recount the adventures we had had in far flung corners of the world. I sang for the company my entire repertoire of *cansos*, *sirventes* and *tensos* and as many bawdy fabliaux as I could remember – unaccompanied by any musical instrument, for my well-loved applewood vielle had been consumed in the fire at Westbury and I had no money to replace it.

Robin sang with me, from time to time, and recounted comic, and occasionally hair-raising, incidents from his days as a young outlaw in Sherwood. On two occasions Samuel warned us that he suspected another ship in the vicinity of being a pirate, and we donned our mail coats and helmets and slung our swords and shields, and with any of the sailors who could be spared from driving the ship forward, we lined the wooden aft-castle and watched as the suspected ship came closer up behind to inspect us. By that point I was so bored that I would genuinely have welcomed a good, bloody sea-fight and, off the coast of the Ile d'Ouessant, at the furthest western tip of the Brittany peninsula, Little John went so far as to roar a foul-mouthed challenge at the approaching vessel, a red-and-white-sailed sinuous snake-boat from the northern lands, by the look of it, packed with a dozen fair-haired warriors. But the sight of so many fighting men in hauberk and helm lined up at the rail and all eager for battle, seemed to discourage any would-be pirates and, to Little John's chagrin, they put over their helm and headed north, and we were left unmolested as we began the long journey south towards the warm lands of Aquitaine.

From the first day of the voyage Nur seemed determined to stay apart. And I believe that none of us, except perhaps Robin, were entirely comfortable with having an avowed witch in our company – I saw the hostile glances that Sir Nicholas de Scras gave her as she perched up at the bow, an unmoving black bundle seemingly impervious to the discomforts of the journey.

She remained as still as a statue for hours at a time, but, very occasionally, she would withdraw a small dark-grey leather bag from within her robe, where it was attached by a thong around her neck. She would shake the contents of the bag, a collection of what looked like little grey-white splinters of wood, on to the deck and peer closely at the pile, poking at it with one skinny finger. Then she would gather the pieces up carefully and pour them back into the bag, which she would return to its place deep within her clothing.

Her behaviour was puzzling, and I feared it was some demonic ritual and crossed myself whenever I saw her perform it. But most of the time she sat, still and silent, and I, and most of the rest of the Companions, ignored her. By the second day, I had mastered my white-hot rage at her presence among us. But I still had every intention of cutting her scrawny throat, as soon as possible after we had accomplished our quest and taken possession of the Grail – I vowed to myself silently that I would take a good deal more than three drops of her blood once Goody had been cured.

From the first day on board, it became apparent that the witch had brought nothing with her in the way of nourishment. Each night, when we stopped and made our way gratefully on to dry land, we most often went without food. It was Lent, and while Robin cared little for this season of self-denial, Sir Nicholas insisted that we observe its strictures. How could we even hope to be worthy of finding the Grail, he pointed out, if we ignored God's will and flouted His holy laws? So, reluctantly, we restricted ourselves to one meal a day, consumed at noon aboard ship. As *The Goose* shouldered her way through the tall grey waves, and we chewed our dull Lenten fare beneath the aft-castle, Nur remained in the bow and apparently neither ate nor drank. She did not attempt to join us, nor did she ask for anything, she merely sat hour after hour, twenty yards away with the heap of dirty coal sacks between us. And while we chatted idly, told stories and swapped jests, and consumed our meagre daily meal, she stared out at the passing coast as if deep in a trance, or as if she were the only soul in the world.

On the fourth day of the voyage, at noon, Roland, who seemed to be oddly fascinated by the witch, took a thick slice of bread and a handful of radishes and a leather cup of ale and made his way carefully along the deck of the tossing ship. He called out something jovial to Nur as he approached, but his words were scattered by the wind, and anyway the witch ignored him. After a few moments of standing behind her, Roland placed the food and drink on the deck, and returned with a rueful shrug. For an hour or more Nur disdained the vittles, but when I happened to glance over towards the end of the afternoon, when a gory sun hung low in the sky, and the Governor was instructing one of the crew to steer for a stretch of grey-black shore where our flat-bottomed craft would beach for the night, I noticed that the food had disappeared. Nur remained in exactly the same position as before, and for a while I wondered if a freak wave had washed the meal overboard. Roland, too, noticed that the food had gone, and the next day at noon, he once again brought her some sustenance, this time pickled cabbage and an oatcake. Once again she took no notice, and refused to respond to his pleasantries. Once again the food vanished when nobody was looking.

For a week, Roland brought food to the witch, and slowly, very slowly, as if she were a wild animal being bred to the hand by my cousin's kindness, Nur began to respond. At first, it was a few muttered words of thanks, and a dip of the head, then Roland began to have very short conversations with her about the weather, and what the piece of land we were passing might be called. One day, a little after noon, when Roland was late in bringing her food up to the bow, I noticed her looking back at us with an unmistakable air of expectation. And twelve days into the voyage, miracle of miracles, Roland took Nur by the hand and led her slowly back to the aft-castle to join in our noon-time meal. She did not speak, and ate quickly and nervously, and crept away without a word of thanks after she had had her fill. But the next day she returned once again on her own. And from that day forward she shared the Companions' meagre repast as if by right.

One day, after we had been discussing the Master and his activities in Paris, Robin turned to Nur quite casually, as if she had long been an accepted member of the group, and said, 'Would you be so kind as to tell us what you know of the Master and the Grail and the company of knights who guard it.'

Nur, who had a hand under her veil at the time and was stuffing a piece of salted cod-fish in her mouth, registered a flash of panic in her dark eyes. But I saw that Roland was smiling at her and nodding encouragement.

The witch swallowed hurriedly, and looked around the circle of expectant men. She coughed, and Roland passed her the leather ale bottle, from which she took a small sip, sliding it under the heavy veil and jerking her chin upwards. No one else spoke, every eye was on her and, at last, in a small, almost timid voice she said, 'Some of you men here know my story' – she looked at Little John and the big man nodded. He had known her in Sicily, Cyprus and the Holy Land when she was young and beautiful and had been my lover. Robin said kindly, 'Take your time, Nur, we are in no hurry, no hurry at all.' And he gestured at the rolling blue-grey waves beyond the ship's rail and at the far distant smear of land.

Nur nodded at him, her black headdress bobbing on her shoulders. Then she began her tale, in the traditional Arabic manner, from the very beginning.

Chapter Ten

'I was born in a small village in the land you call Syria, a dozen miles outside the Christian citadel of Tyre,' said Nur, in her odd sing-song voice, 'and my people were farmers, growing vines, figs and melons. We were neither very rich nor very poor, but we were very happy,' she said. 'The days of my youth were filled with sunshine and joy; I played with my brother and helped my parents around the farm at harvest time; I even had my own pony to ride. All was well, all was indeed well, and I imagined that I would spend my days in that village, marry, have many children, and expire one golden afternoon as an old woman surrounded by those who loved me. I believed the world was a place of peace and happiness. I was a fool.

'One day, when I had just turned thirteen years old, the raiders came. They were rough, cruel men in steel and leather, stinking of onions and old sweat and speaking in the strange tongue of the Turks. They killed everyone who did not run from them, except for the children; those of us who were not yet fifteen, they kept in a wooden pen that they had built on the beach as if we were animals. The ugly and malformed children, they separated from the rest, including my brother Salim, who was eleven, and had an eye that did not look straight. They dragged Salim away and I watched him be raped, by ten, twenty men, perhaps. He fought, but they clubbed him down and took their turns, laughing, until he was not more than an unmoving bag of bruised and bloody flesh. I did not know if he was dead or alive. I hoped he was dead. I truly believed that they would do the same to me, but no. I was valuable merchandise, I learned, not to be lightly despoiled.'

Nur laughed at this point, a dry grating sound that made all the hairs on my neck stand up. Not a man in that rapt circle moved a muscle as she spoke. Robin's face was as grim as death and I saw that two of the crew had drawn closer to hear her words, finding simple tasks that brought them within earshot.

'I was taken aboard a large boat with the others, perhaps a dozen children from my village, and locked in the hold. There were perhaps about two score already there, boys and girls, and many had been there for days and were already weak. I told myself that a terrible fate, a fate far, far worse than death, awaited me and that I must be strong. But I was afraid. I prayed to Allah – but he did not listen to me. I prayed to the Christ God that I knew that the knights of Tyre worshipped. He was deaf, as well. I despaired.

'We spent three days in that small hold without air, tossed constantly by the sea, and we were all ill, and very, very frightened. One of the girls became particularly sick in the stinking belly of that ship with a fever of some kind, not just from the movement of the boat. She turned very cold and then very hot and sometimes she raved and screamed for her mother. But when we called to our captors, and begged for at least some fresh, clean water for her to drink, they laughed. She soon died, all of a sudden, just like the snapping of a twig. She fell asleep' – Nur softly clicked her fingers – 'and her spirit just left her. Like that. It was the first time I had seen someone die. And then the men came down among the sick children in the lapping filth of the hold, and they took her away. I heard the tiny splash as they threw her over the side.

'After only four days, although it seemed a month, the boat stopped at a little harbour with high cliffs and a castle. The harbour was filled with ships, vessels from across the whole of the world, it seemed: Moslem and Christian and Jew. I was told later that we were in Cilicia, in the mountain realm of the King of Armenia. To me it was the stinking crotch of the world. They took us from that foul hold, sick, bewildered, frightened, and herded us with their spears to a large house behind the harbour with a high stone wall. I prepared myself for the worst horror I could imagine – for a Hell even worse than that ship's belly, for the fate of my brother Salim. I looked about for ways to end my life. Instead, I found myself in paradise.'

Nur laughed again, the same awful grating rasp.

'The girls were separated from the boys on the quayside and we were taken into the care of a very fat man, a slave like us, but an important creature, too. We were washed and well fed and given three days just to sleep and restore ourselves to health, and then we were washed again and dressed in fine clothes and allowed to try on perfumes and run about in the beautiful gardens of that palace and play. We were told that we were members of a harem, a women's enclosure, the property of a great sea lord, and that our duty was to learn how to be pleasurable to men. If we did well, if we behaved ourselves and were obedient, we would be treated gently, like little princesses and fed the finest foods, and allowed to lounge all day on cushions of silks and eat curds and honey, but if we behaved badly, we would be whipped, and sold on to be used by the common sailors, or worked to death in the mines. There were scores of girls in that high-walled enclosure, and some of them had been there for several years – and seeing that they were, for the most part, content with their lot, my mind was greatly eased.

142

'I said a prayer for the soul of Salim, and prepared to learn and make the most of my new life. And while we were closely guarded by the fat slave and his men, eunuchs all, and never allowed to leave the compound, we were not mistreated. Indeed, I was well cared for. I had no freedom, except to run about in that delightful garden, or to sleep till noon, if I chose, but I was fed fresh fruit and honey and iced sherbets every day, and allowed to exercise and play with the other girls as much as I wished. It was there, in that place, that I began to be taught, very gently over a dozen languid weeks, how to please a man. I learned how to please in many different ways, with a look, a smile, a tilt of the head, with a song or by reciting poetry, with my fingers, and lips and breasts, with my whole body – but for one part of me. I was a virgin then and nobody had tried to lie with me, except for one of the older girls who claimed that she had fallen in love with me and would die unless she could have me. But I laughed at her ridiculous notions and she went away weeping and saying that I was cruel. But after that, she left me in peace.'

As I watched Nur tell her story, I remembered how beguiling she had been when I had first met her. Her hair so black and shiny that it was like a spill of rock oil, her lips red and plump and sweet as cherries, her full, jutting, bobbing breasts, and her skin so white and unmarked, like a marble carving from a pagan Greek temple: I had loved her deeply, with the whole of my boyish heart. She had seemed to me to be perfection in female form, as near an angel as I had ever seen . . . And now, all that was left of her beauty was her eyes. The eyes that I now found staring into mine, just for a moment, above her veil and below her headdress, just for a moment before she looked away. They were still lovely, deep and brown and, with the rest of her face covered by the swathes of cloth, I could almost picture the girl she had been.

I broke my reverie to find that Nur was continuing with her

tale: '. . . in truth, I was perfectly happy there; for four long months, I was in paradise. The ordeal of the raid on my village and the deaths of my parents and my brother faded from my mind. I spent the days making myself delightful to all the senses, with fine clothes, with oils and creams and powders and costly scents; or playing or talking with the other girls, or at my lessons in lovemaking. Some of the older girls whispered that there were secret ways that I could use to make a man fall in love with me, magical ways – for that was the great hope of almost all the women there, that a rich man would come and take them away to be his wife. But their magic was feeble, of little true power, much of it hardly more than childish nonsense, and I mastered it quickly – the tiny heart of a songbird, dried and crumbled into wine, water from the reflection of the moon in a pool at midnight, rhymes chanted over a burning candle – yet it was the beginning of my journey into the realm beyond this world. I did not then know the power that the spirit world wields over all mortals, and I could not imagine where the spirits would lead me in this earthly life. For I was young, and beautiful then, and for a little while, I was happy. I could have remained for my whole life in that garden of womanly delights, I think, and been content – but one day a tall man came to that secluded place, a Christian, a tall, bearded Frank. And although I had not misbehaved, although I had been an obedient girl in all the things that were asked of me, I was sold off to him like a fat-tailed sheep at the market. I had been a fool once again – I had forgotten for a time that I was a slave, of no more value than a fine kitchen pot or a silver bracelet.'

Nur paused and looked beyond the rail at the vast heaving surface of the sea. Still not a man in the circle around her spoke. She seemed to be summoning her courage before embarking on the next part of the story.

'The man who bought me was a knight in a long white mantle with a small red cross, here' – Nur drew the sign of the Templar cross with a gloved finger on her left breast – 'and a vast, thick black beard that stuck out, like so.' She made a gesture with her right hand, holding it under her chin, fingers extended to indicate the horizontal jut of the knight's beard. 'At first, I did not understand what he had come for; and in my foolishness, I did not know my happiness could be so easily shattered again.'

Nur coughed out another painfully dry laugh.

'The fat slave-master mustered us like soldiers and ordered some forty of us girls to form a line in the gardens. The knight and his companions, two other Franks who wore the same white mantles, and more men in black surcoats who served them, walked briskly down the line and pointed to ten of us. Including me, although I was the youngest by a year or so, being not quite fourteen at that time. We were taken from the garden that day, marched out under guard by the Franks, and I never saw that place or my friends there ever again.

'They took us by sea, a hundred miles east, to the port of Ayas – in more comfort than our previous journey . . . at least in some ways.

'On the first night at sea, the Frankish knight, whose name was Amanieu d'Albret, took me into his cabin and ripped away my innocence. He beat me with his fists and then he raped me, and afterwards he sobbed and prayed to the Christ God and begged my forgiveness for his sin. He said that I had bewitched him; that it was my own fault. For my beauty was a provocation, he said, a temptation no man could resist. Then he beat me again; this time with a riding whip, and then he raped me for a second time but in the other place, behind. And perhaps I had indeed bewitched him for, when we arrived at Ayas, the other girls were sold on but the knight, this Seigneur d'Albret, this cruel, weeping lecher, he chose to keep me for his own pleasures.'

The men listening to Nur's tale were spellbound and I could see that they were, to a man, utterly sympathetic to her plight.

Little John was even growling softly with rage under his breath and stroking the wooden haft of his axe.

However, the story was familiar to me and I noticed that Nur had left out certain things: for instance, she once told me that she had tried to escape from that paradisiacal garden of women and had been branded on the ankle for her pains when she was recaptured. I realized that she was altering her tale to make the listeners more amiable towards her. And I warned myself not to be seduced by Nur's sad history: I closed my eyes and pictured Goody, dying Goody, my beloved wife who had been cursed by this black witch before me now. Whatever evil Nur had suffered, it did not excuse her actions against my poor innocent girl.

'Although I hated the very sight of the knight Amanieu d'Albret, I submitted to his every whim; I pleasured him in all the ways that I had learned in the garden of women, night and noon, at daybreak and dusk; I gave my body to him in any way he wanted, whenever he wanted, and yet still he beat me. That, too, I discovered, was his pleasure. I thought of ways to kill him, a knife in the eye perhaps, while he slept, or maybe poison in his wine, but he was careful and quick of movement, and he slept like a cat and never in the same bed as me. And his guards, the hard-faced serving men in black, were ever watchful.

'But strangest of all to tell, this brutal man who ripped me and used me, who beat me and bruised me, this monster came to believe that he loved me. He told me so with tears in his eyes, after three months of our being together – as if that animal could even say love's name without defiling it. And I dissembled, I lied, I looked into his ugly face and I pretended that I too was in love with him. And sometimes, just sometimes, that filthy lie saved me from a beating.

'After he had taken his pleasure on me, of an evening, the knight liked to drink wine and talk. He talked of his family, the d'Albrets, who were a power in Gascony with wide lands and many castles.

He was a seigneur of his very own castle, he told me – the Jealous Castle, it was called, a town with a high tower and long walls, by a swift cold river on the edge of a vast pine forest that stretched all the way to the grey western sea. When he was drunk, he liked to indulge himself in a fantasy: that one day we should be married and live together in the Jealous Castle as lord and lady, and raise knightly sons. And, he once assured me with a kindly pat on the shoulder, I should not need to worry about being unworthy because of my low birth, my lack of Christian faith, for he knew of a magical bowl that could wash even the foulest stains from my heathen soul. Then he drank too much, and beat me for my presumption, and told me I was a worthless whore before he stumbled off to bed.'

In spite of myself, I did then feel pity for Nur and disgust for this barbarous knight. I hoped that she had found some way to punish him for his treatment of her.

'It was in Ayas that I first began to practise the craft,' Nur continued. She was by now tightly fenced in by a circle of staring eyes, captivated by her horrific tale; some were angry, some sad, but none was indifferent.

'In Ayas, in the household of Amanieu d'Albret and his fellow soldier-monks, there was an old slave woman, a woman of Africa called Kalisha, who tended my cuts when I had been beaten. She taught me the arts of her people, demonstrating them on my battered body; at first, she merely showed me how to use herbs and plants to mend sick and broken men and women of the house-hold, then she taught me the twelve spirit cures, how to channel the power of the dead to bring healing to the living; but later she also told me about other darker uses of her powers . . .

'I was interested in her wisdom, and she had much of it to give, for I longed to feed my master something deadly with his wine. But Kalisha persuaded me that poison was not the right path to take – it would be easily discovered, she said, and there were other ways, using the power of the spirit world, that would allow me to be revenged safely and in secret. In time, she became like a mother to me, big, warm Kalisha. She was kind and loving when I was weak and frightened. And I can hear her voice yet, like a trickle of honey – may the spirits guard her and keep her.

'A few nights later, d'Albret came to me. Again he was drunk, but I managed to avoid a beating by allowing him to swiftly satisfy his lust. Again he indulged himself in this moon-crazed fantasy that he would leave his Christian brothers and we would be married and live together happily as man and wife in his Jealous Castle. And, timidly, respectfully, I asked him to tell me about the magical bowl that could wash away all my sins. He was reluctant at first, but I cajoled him and flattered him, and after a little while he told me something that he considered to be a great secret. He said that, while he was a member of the Order of the Poor Fellow-Soldiers of Christ and the Temple of Solomon, and he was the preceptor of their house in Ayas, he was also a member of another order, this one within the Templars, which had miraculous knowledge that the ordinary Templars did not possess.'

I caught Robin's eye, and he raised his eyebrows as if to say, 'You see! Alan, I told you!' But I was still angry with him for springing the witch on me in the abrupt way that he had, so I ignored him and looked back to Nur.

'This secret order of Templars, inside the Templars, venerated the Mother of Christ,' Nur was saying, 'and their Master, a wise and powerful man, was the possessor of the cup of Christ, a vessel that had once held the Son of God's blood. It was the holiest, most powerful object in the world, d'Albret told me, and it had been housed for a while in an underground chapel within the walls of the Jealous Castle.'

Every man under that aft-castle was leaning forward, listening intently to Nur's words by now, even me. The black-clad witch held us all like raw potter's clay in her hands; hers to twist and mould and fashion as she liked.

'But this was all ten years or more ago,' I said grumpily, deliberately trying to break her hold over the Companions. 'The Grail may not be there now. It could be anywhere. It could be in Caen or Carcassonne . . . or even Constantinople. If this is the price of Nur's place among us – if this is all the meat she brings to our pot – then we have been thoroughly cheated.'

Robin scowled at me. 'Do try to think before you speak, Alan. Of course we cannot be certain that the Grail is at this Jealous Castle – but it is surely a good place to begin our search. I have ascertained from a friend in Aquitaine that the castle is still held by this Amanieu d'Albret, who left the ranks of the Templars in disgrace three years ago and has retired to a quiet life on his lands. With the right persuasion, I think he might be able to tell us the whereabouts of the Master – and the Grail. But you have interrupted the lady's flow, Alan. Please continue, my dear . . .'

'Thank you, lord,' said Nur. 'There is little more to tell. The Seigneur d'Albret tired of me quickly soon after that night in Ayas; a few short months after declaring his love, he grew indifferent to me, and he took his pleasure less and less often. I was pleased at first, and then I grew fearful and uncertain of my future. And one day, just after we had heard that a fresh shipment of slave girls had come into port, I was surprised while washing my body in my little cell by two of the Templar sergeants. They forced me to submit to them both at the same time, one at each end – and when I choked out that the Seigneur would punish them for their abuse of me, they merely laughed, and shackled me, and said that I would never see *him* again.

'I was taken to the dock and herded with several other girls on to a merchant ship, and thence I went to Messina and into the house of a spice trader there as one of his concubines. And it was there, in Messina, during the sack of the town by the Christian army, that I met Sir Alan and was kindly offered his protection.'

I looked at my boots. While I hated Nur for what she had done

149

to Goody, I knew that in our past relationship, I had not truly behaved in a chivalrous, gentlemanly fashion towards her. Indeed, my conduct had been shameful. When Richard's soldiers were unleashed on Messina, in a long, terrible night of fire and blood, I had rescued Nur and taken her under my wing. I had, of course, immediately fallen in love with her, and promised to cherish her and guard her for all time, in the reckless way that young men do. But, as I have said, in Acre she had been captured and mutilated by my enemy, and while I had been satisfactorily revenged on him afterwards, I had been unable to hide my disgust of her cruelly savaged face. I knew then that I could never love her again. And she had seen the disgust in my eyes when I first saw her after the mutilation and had fled from me – and, in my heart, I have never forgiven myself.

When I looked up again, I saw Roland's scarred face scowling at me. I was about to ask what ailed him, that he should glower at me like an ogre, when Nur began to speak again. It seemed she had a little more meat to add to the pot.

'I did visit the Jealous Castle once,' she said. 'I found myself in Gascony, heading for England and travelling on the road from Toulouse to Bordeaux. It was three years after I had last seen Amanieu d'Albret and I had not thought much about him since. But I was full of rage at the world and he came into my head as I trudged that dusty road under a brutal sun. I was hungry and a little feverish and in a strange and hostile land – but a beautiful idea came into my head as I walked: I would go to the Jealous Castle – or Casteljaloux as some call it – and confront this d'Albret with his cruelty and either demand recompense from him or have my vengeance for the insults I had suffered at his hands. I think my wits were scattered, at the time, and perhaps I was a little mad – I had been travelling for a long time, with little food and much hardship – for I wanted to see his expression when he saw my face; I wanted to bring fear to his house, as he had made me fear him when I was his slave.'

I was amused that Nur should consider that she had been a little mad, *at this time*, on the road in Gascony, as if at all other times she was as sane as anyone.

'Amanieu had told me where his castle lay and I found it easily, taking the road due south from Marmande for perhaps a dozen miles and keeping the deep pine forest on my right. When I arrived, footsore and still a little sick, I begged for my bread in the streets of his town for a few days, in the very shadow of the high tower of the Jealous Castle, hoping to catch a glimpse of Amanieu as he came and went. But the few folk in those parts who were prepared to speak to me said that the Seigneur was away in Paris, and after a week or so, the men-at-arms from the castle demanded to know my business there and, when I would not answer, they beat me with their spear butts and sent me on my way, back on to the road north.'

'Well, you shall see the Jealous Castle again, my dear,' said Robin. 'And no man will beat you. I swear it. You shall lead us there, and this time, perhaps you shall have the chance to pay that coward Amanieu d'Albret back in his own filthy coin.'

'Oh, aye,' said Little John, rumbling like a furious bear. 'I swear to you, lady, by God's great dangling gonads, that this Templar turd will pay in full. In full, I say.'

The rest of the voyage passed uneventfully – except for a violent storm in the Bay of Biscay when we were, unusually, out of sight of land. The tempest was short-lived, a matter of a few hours at most, and left us unharmed save for a few bruised limbs and sour empty stomachs – but it was still a terrifying experience for me. A purple-black sky rushed in from the west to blot out the sun, and the sea-world filled to the very brim with noise and fury. We clung to the poles that supported the fighting platform, and endured as best we could as the wind howled around the bucking ship, the rain lashed us and huge waves smashed over the deck and threatened to snap the spine of our frail craft.

A tempest at sea is far worse than any land battle, I believe, for the inactivity makes one prone to fear – one cannot do anything at all to reduce the risks, no amount of ferocity or determination or battle-skill can defeat a raging universe of wind and water. I have never felt comfortable sitting quietly to receive my doom and I have a peculiar horror of death at sea. I do not wish my corpse to end up as a sodden lump of pummelled flesh swept away by the waves to spend eternity in the deep. I would die on dry land with a sword in my hand; my body to be planted in the comfort of solid earth until the Day of Resurrection.

However, while I and the other Companions clung fearful, soaked to the bone and horribly nauseous to the aft-castle, our bodies smashed time and again by hard packets of spray, and hurled about recklessly, constantly in violent motion as if on the back of a wildly kicking horse, Nur reacted in her own special way to the rage of the elements. While we chattered teeth and shivered with cold, and prayed silently for an end to the torment, Nur suddenly stood on the capering deck and screamed, 'Enough – I will have no more of this. Spirit of the sea, spirit of the wind, I command you both to be still!'

She had clearly been driven mad by the storm, I thought, or rather, driven even madder.

Before anyone could stop her, Nur stripped off her sodden outer clothes, hopped to the middle of the ship and slowly began to climb the rigging. Dressed only in a thin, very dirty, linen shift, which clung to her skeletal form and became almost transparent in the wet, and with the little dark-grey leather bag swinging on its string against her flat chest, Nur seized hold of the rope ladder that hung from the main mast and slowly, painfully, she began to climb. The tempest tried its level best to pluck her from the slick ropeway, but she clung on, somehow, her wet shift now billowing with the wind, now flattened to her skin, and up she inched her way, up and up. After a few moments the rotten fabric ripped and the garment flowed horizontally like a thin flag, before being torn away. The sea-wise mariners gawped up at her as she continued to ascend, now baby-naked expect for the leather sack, seemingly crawling upwards like some gawky, white insect on a spindly twig into the heart of the storm. Miraculously, Nur did finally attain the top of the mast, a good fifty feet above the heaving deck, and clambered into the crow's nest and settled herself in place until all that could be seen over the bucket-rim of the look-out post was a pair of bony shoulders and an otter-sleek head. With her lofty perch rocking to and fro through an arc of twenty feet, I was convinced that the witch would soon be hurled free, catapulted like a rock from a mangonel and launched far out into the depths, to disappear in the raging spume.

Instead, Nur wrapped one arm tightly around the mast and began to curse the storm.

I could not hear exactly what threats and imprecations she uttered, the noise of the tempest drowned all but a few snatches of sound, nor could I tell in what language she damned the elements, but her mouth moved and her free arm waved, and her long bony fingers made intricate patterns in the air as she sang her songs and shrieked her threats. On and on, she cursed, seemingly filled with an energy, a demonic rage that was quite unquenchable; the wind howled, the witch howled back at it; the black rain thrashed her body, her long, white arm seemed to lash back at the deluge itself.

I believe that every man on that ship marvelled at her courage, as she raved and screamed at the sky, challenging the storm, riding it like a wild stallion, and seeking in her madness to make it submit to her will. A deafening crack of thunder overhead and a blue-white spear of lightning reminded me of the true risk she ran – she was defying God himself, begging him to strike her down. But the Almighty, in His wisdom, chose not to, and after less than an hour – incredibly – the tempest began to subside, cowed by the fearsome ranting of the witch.

I knew that it could not truly have been her power that brought the storm to heel yet I felt a touch of awe. And magical or not, it was a courageous performance – and when she finally climbed down from her high perch, mother naked, the ship by now rocked only by a gentle swell, and moistened by drizzle, every man on board cheered and applauded. And even I could not prevent myself from granting her a tight smile as she put her customary black robes back on. Before she reattached the veil that covered her face I looked at that poor ravaged head: the bone-white skin and pinky-yellow old scars, the cropped grey hair, and I felt a change within me. For the first time since I had seen her mutilation, I was not repulsed by it. She was still the ugliest woman I had ever laid eyes on, and evil too, I hastily reminded myself, responsible for poor Goody's plight, but I found that I could look upon her devastated features without the sense of disgust and horror that I had always felt before.

Just as Samuel had promised, we entered the mouth of the mighty Gironde Estuary in the middle of Holy Week, on the Wednesday before Easter, the fifth day of the month of April in the Year of the Incarnation twelve hundred. We had been some three weeks aboard *The Goose* by then, and I was heartily sick of her. I was sick of being damp, cramped and immobile all day long; I was sick of eating stale bread, salt fish and pickled vegetables – I could not wait for Easter Day, the end of Lenten restrictions, and the chance to eat meat and eggs and cheese once again – but most of all I was sick of the sight of so many of my comrades treating Nur as if she were a family member, a favourite sister or a beloved young aunt.

Since the day of her story, and more so since the day of the storm, the witch had been slyly working to capture the hearts of the men. Clearly she had been a good pupil in that delightful garden of women – for, even without her former beauty, she knew how to beguile and seduce a man. She made Little John a battle-charm for

154

his axe by holding it over a candle flame until a layer of soot had formed on the metal, and then scratching weird shapes and patterns with a seagull feather. She told Little John that he would be invincible in battle as a result. Was it true magic? I have no idea. But the big man seemed delighted by her charm and I saw him gazing at it for hours on end, twisting his axe so that the blade caught and reflected the watery sunlight.

Occasionally she would cast the contents of her little sack on to the deck near the men. As she squatted down beside it, I realized with horror that the fragments were not wooden, as I had supposed, but the bones from a tiny human hand. A baby's hand. The bones were grey-white and perfectly dry. Cleaned of all flesh. Immaculate. She would stare at the bones and mutter to herself for a while, before gathering them reverently and replacing them in her bag.

'What is she doing?' I asked Robin uneasily, the first time I saw this up close. I was having difficulty fighting down a growing sense of fear, a coldness around my shoulders.

'She is divining,' said my lord, who was watching her intently from my side. 'She is seeking out the Grail for us. I asked her to use all of her powers to locate the Master and his men.'

'She is using magic?' I was surprised at how much this act disturbed me. 'Do you believe she can really find it like that?'

'We shall see,' said Robin, 'we shall see.'

Nur used no magic at all to mend a tear in Gavin's tunic, just a plain needle and thread – but that handsome lad seemed pleased to have the motherly care of a woman, even one as hideous as Nur. And that was her scheme, I saw. By keeping on her veil all of the time – though it must have been irksome to her as we sailed south and the weather grew warmer – the Companions became used to her masked features and were rarely reminded of the ruin of her face.

The only man who seemed resistant to her wiles, apart from me, of course, was Sir Nicholas de Scras. He spoke seldom to her and then only if it was absolutely necessary. When he did choose to speak to her, he was abruptly formal, as if attempting through some notion of politeness to conceal a deep contempt and hatred for her. He prayed aloud each evening before bedtime – something that set Gavin and Little John to sniggering like boys – and on more than one occasion I heard him beseeching the Almighty to shine the light of his grace on Nur, to wash her clean of sin and bring her to the path of Our Lord Jesus Christ. But he and I were the only ones, by then, who did not seem to think of Nur as a welcome addition to the fellowship of the Companions.

She became especially close to Roland during those weeks on *The Goose*. She mixed a salve for his burn-scarred cheek from seaweed and fish oil that, rubbed in daily, was supposed to make the disfiguration grow less noticeable. To my disgust, my cousin was sickeningly grateful – I had not realized that he was so vain. For me, I noticed no change at all in the shiny pink patch on his cheek, despite his rubbing that foul-smelling goo into it day and night. And what are looks to a warrior? Nothing.

At a little before noon, on that Wednesday, the two of them were standing on the fore-castle – the slight witch and the tall blond warrior – as we glided past a series of daunting white cliffs off the larboard bow and turned in towards the harbour of Royan on the northern shore of the Gironde. Only just visible two miles in the distance on the starboard side was the southern lip of the estuary, a low barren marshland where a few scrawny sheep took their nourishment from the salty grasses. Samuel the Governor had told us that we must stop at Royan to pay a customs duty on the load of coal that he carried, and to find ourselves a pilot for the treacherous tidal waters of the estuary and to take us up the Garonne River to Bordeaux. As it happened, Royan's small stone harbour was crammed to overflowing with shipping when *The Goose* nosed around the point in the middle of the afternoon, and we were obliged to crunch the ship's bottom on the broad sandy expanse of the beach beside the harbour. As Robin and Samuel trudged across the strand, heading towards the castle high above the beach, the rest of us gratefully disembarked and were able, with a great sense of luxury, to stretch our legs properly for the first time in days.

We made a fire and Gavin set a pot near to the blaze to cook a thin fish stew for our daily meal. Then we passed an hour or so in weapons practice, happy to have the opportunity in full daylight to loosen our cramped muscles and raise a little healthy sweat. Little John set up a man-sized paling in the sand of the beach, hammering a driftwood pole deep with the flat of his axe blade, and we took turns to swing and jab our swords against it in the classic patterns, imagining that the length of vertical wood was an enemy knight, while the sailors watched us and applauded or jeered according to their whim. By mid-afternoon the food was ready and we were settling down to eat when Robin returned with Samuel.

The Earl of Locksley was beaming all over his long handsome face when he sat down next to me by the fire and accepted a bowl of stew from Gavin. But my lord said nothing for a good long while, blowing exaggeratedly on his brimming horn spoon to cool its contents and grinning like a madman.

'Did everything go well at the castle?' I asked. Clearly something had made Robin happy, and it cannot have been the task of handing over the toll of silver coins to the customs men.

'I picked up a little news,' he said, slurping down the spoonful and popping a hunk of bread in his mouth before chewing like a thoughtful cow. He looked at me out of the corner of his eye and smiled. 'It seems that Bordeaux will be rather crowded when we get there. Lot of visitors this time of year.'

I waited for him to elaborate on this statement, but he said nothing more for a long while. Finally, when he had swallowed the last of the stew and wiped his bowl with a crust, chewed and swallowed it, he said, 'It seems that no less a personage than Queen Eleanor, Duchess of Aquitaine, will be gracing her capital city when we arrive. She has been in Spain fetching her beauteous granddaughter Blanche – apparently she wants to marry the unfortunate chit off to Louis, Philip of France's idiot son – and she's on her way back up north to Poitiers with a mercenary force. But the Queen herself and the unlucky Princess will be spending Easter Week in Bordeaux.' He grinned at me. 'Which means—'

I finished Robin's sentence for him. 'That Marie-Anne and the boys will be there at Easter too.'

And I beamed at my lord. He smiled happily back at me. 'Is there any more of that stew? It really is delicious.'

Chapter Eleven

By noon on Good Friday, *The Goose* was moored at the docks in the deep bend in the River Garonne before the great walled city of Bordeaux. Although it was a holy day, the very day on which twelve hundred years ago Our Lord Jesus Christ out of love for this sinful world suffered crucifixion on the hill of Calvary, the quay was abustle with sailors and merchants securing their ships and cargos and preparing for the celebrations of Easter Week.

Robin's cheerful excitement at the prospect of seeing his Countess and his two sons had lifted the spirits of all of our party, and we wasted little time bidding farewell to Samuel and the sailors of *The Goose* and heading towards the Abbey of St Andrew, where we planned to seek lodgings for a few days.

We were warmly welcomed at the lovely old Abbey, although the place was filled almost to overflowing with visitors who had flocked to the city for the Easter celebrations at its cathedral, and the hosteller managed to find us seven cots in the men's dormitory, and a straw-filled corner for Nur in the women's quarters. Robin could, if he chose, have presented himself at the ducal palace and demanded that the servants of Queen Eleanor of Aquitaine find lodgings for himself and his party. But we wanted as little official notice as possible taken of our visit. There might have been a certain amount of awkwardness between the mother of the new King and the outlawed Earl who had so staunchly supported his dead brother. And while I knew that Eleanor was privately fond of Robin – indeed, she had provided a haven for his wife and children among her ladies-in-waiting – she was bound to support King John, her only living son, in public against any nobleman who, rightly or wrongly, had incurred his displeasure.

There was also the matter of our quest: we did not want to broadcast the objective of our journeying in these southern lands and wanted to keep our movements as quiet as possible. If questioned we had agreed to say that we were making for Montpellier to consult one of the learned doctors there about Goody's condition. It was a feeble lie, and anyone who looked closely at our party, seven oak-hard warriors and a deformed witch, would have questions to ask. But the story would serve as long as we remained in the guise of humble travellers. Staying at the ducal palace as Eleanor's guests would mean announcing Robin's rank to the world and that, he felt, would draw unwelcome attention. So we lodged as pilgrims in the dormitory of the abbey and were content to do so. Indeed I'd have been happy to roost anywhere – a pig sty or a palace – that was not the damp, cold heaving deck of a crowded, merchant's ship.

Once we were settled in the Abbey, Robin disappeared almost completely for the whole of Good Friday and Holy Saturday – we assumed he was spending his time with his wife and his two sons Miles and Hugh. The rest of us joined the throngs of people milling about the city on the last day of Lent or attended one of the many services in the vast cathedral.

I caught sight of Robin only once during that time, walking hand in hand on a path by the broad River Garonne with Marie-Anne, dark-haired Hugh who would then have been about ten,

160

running on ahead and then coming back to urge his parents on. Robin had Miles on his shoulders and the four-year-old blond lad was squawking excitedly at the assorted river craft that passed by. The sight of them squeezed my heart and I wondered if Goody and I and our unborn children would ever know such carefree happiness. England, home and Goody seemed so far away, the task ahead of me seemed so daunting, and I was conscious that I had already wasted nearly three weeks aboard that ship; when I thought about the little time I had in which to find the Grail and carry it back, my spirit quailed.

Sir Nicholas, Roland, Thomas and I attended Tenebrae in the cathedral at midnight on Holy Saturday. We were latecomers to this service of shadows – the most moving of all the holy rites – and stood at the back joining in the prayers and psalms with the rest. In the centre of the church, in the place of most honour, was the Tenebrae stand – a candelabrum holding fifteen candles, which were gradually extinguished, one by one, during the service. But despite the comfort of the presence of my friends, and the soothing familiarity of the Tenebrae, I felt an awful, creeping premonition there in that vast cathedral, one I could not shake from my mind: I felt that the candelabrum represented the life force of my lovely wife, growing dimmer and dimmer as the candles were extinguished and the rite ground on. I felt a cold lump grow in my throat – perhaps Goody was already dead, perhaps she had been dead for weeks. I muttered something along these lines to Sir Nicholas who was standing beside me in the gloom.

'But see, Alan,' he said, 'look there! A single candle remains burning – that is the hope of Jesus Christ, and tomorrow on Easter Day we shall celebrate the Resurrection of Our Lord. That is the omen you should take from the Tenebrae. The promise of Goody's resurrection to full health from her illness through Christ's love, and by the power of the sacred vessel that we seek.'

He was deliberately trying to bolster my courage, this I knew

161

perfectly well, but as I stared at the single candle burning like a bright hole in the total darkness, I was convinced by his analogy: *Goody still lives*, I thought, *and by the power of Christ she will be saved!*

On Easter morning, after a short night's sleep, we gathered again outside the cathedral in the chill hour before dawn, to await the rising of the sun, and to sing hymns to celebrate Our Saviour rising from the grave. And, as we sang those jubilant words with full hearts that radiant, freshly-scrubbed morning, and praised God for having overcome Death itself, I felt tears of joy flowing freely. *Goody lives*, I told myself with a sureness that could only have been inspired by the Son of God himself, *and she will be saved.*

There was a bustle at the far side of the crowd, and a festive burst of trumpets announced the arrival for Mass of the ducal party. The crowd parted and I saw Queen Eleanor herself, in a deep-red robe embroidered with golden threads, still slim and straight as an arrow after nearly four score years, striding towards the cathedral door with all the bounce of a young girl. Her fine silver hair was held in place under her elaborate white headdress by a circlet of gold and a jewelled crucifix glittered at the throat; her face was solemn but her crisp blue eyes twinkled with life. She was surrounded by a gaggle of high-born ladies, each in blood-red gowns that matched the Queen's – although my friend Marie-Anne, Countess of Locksley, was nowhere to be seen – and she was followed by a mass of noblemen and knights talking and jesting and laughing, proud as male peacocks in silks and satins of blue and green and scarlet.

But there was one man in that crowd of cheerful popinjays who stood out like a dog turd in a fruit bowl. He was dressed entirely in shabby black, with roughly cut black hair, dark eyes, and swarthy features bisected with a yellow scar from eyebrow to chin. It was a face that I knew of old – the face of a man whom I had encountered on more than a few unhappy occasions, and whom I thoroughly detested. It was the Lionheart's merciless old hunting-dog, a butcher

162

of men, women and children – it was the dark lord of war who called himself Mercadier.

I felt Roland, who was standing beside me, clutch at my arm, as he caught sight of the man in black. My cousin had clearly not forgotten his treatment at the hands of Mercadier and his men after the battle of Gisors. Then the mercenary was swallowed in the crowd of nobles, his drab weeds drowned in their gaudy plumage, his darkness extinguished by their light.

The Easter Mass was a joyous occasion, and I gave thanks to God for His blessed son's triumph over Death and for all the mercies that He had granted to me. I said a prayer, too, for Goody and our unborn child, and although I was not completely at peace – indeed, the worry was ever-present like a sickness in my stomach – I did feel the comfort of God's love and I reminded myself of Sir Nicholas's words of the night before.

After the Mass, we joined in a great and solemn procession around the city, with the Archbishop carrying the huge Easter candle around the inside of Bordeaux's tall walls, and the rest of us following and singing hosannahs. And then we all sat down to an enormous public feast in the market square, with food and drink provided for free by the bounty of Queen Eleanor and the wealthiest burgesses of that great trading city. Each guest at the feast, and there must at the very least have been five hundred at the rough-hewn plank tables, was given an egg, beautifully decorated with gold foil and painted with an image of Our Saviour, and we feasted on whole grilled lambs and vats of rabbit stew with bacon, and beef and pork in vast golden pies, and game birds roasted on spits, and cheeses and tansy pudding, and fruit and nuts and sweetmeats until we were close to bursting. Rose-coloured wine from the local vineyards flowed like a river all afternoon, and we were entertained by jongleurs, tumblers and beast-masters and magicians, fire-eaters and dancing dwarfs.

163

It was a glorious day, with much bawdy hilarity from Little John and Gavin, with Thomas quietly smiling and eating like a starving wolf – he was at the age when his belly seemed to have an infinite capacity and I knew that the strictures of Lent had been hard on him. Nur, too, put her face low to the table, lifted her veil and ate as if she might never eat again. Sir Nicholas ate sparingly, but drank a good deal of the delicious light red wine, and favoured me with a genial smile from time to time. Robin had absented himself again and was with his beloved Marie-Anne somewhere in the ducal palace, Little John told us, and we wished the reunited couple joy with many a cup. Only Roland seemed remote from the festivities, and he left us before we had finished our meal with a threadbare excuse about having to go and see a man about a horse.

That night, as I lay in my cot in the Abbey dormitory with a groaning belly and a head giddy from too much wine, my cousin sat down on a little stool by my bed and looked down at me.

'I must ask you for a service, Sir Alan,' said Roland formally, his face drawn and serious. I focused on his features with some difficulty. 'I do not like to ask it of you but I have no choice. There is a task that I must perform and I cannot do it alone – and I believe you are the best man to help me.'

I sat up in bed, suddenly sober. 'Of course, cousin, anything. What do you want me to do?'

'It is a grave matter. And you should not agree too readily; there may be a great deal of peril involved.'

'You want me to help you murder Mercadier,' I said.

Roland looked stunned. 'How did you know?'

'We are more alike than you might think, cousin.'

Roland dropped his eyes. 'When I think back to that night in Dangu, his men standing over me with the hot coals poised over my eyes, and your good self bargaining with that bastard for my sight . . . It was the most humiliating episode in my entire life, and the most shameful. I was in dread, I was in trembling terror

164

of the pain, and fearful for my eyes. I lost my courage that night; that man put me in fear and showed me to myself as a coward . . .'

'You are no coward,' I said. 'Any man alive would fear to lose his eyes – and in that horrible manner . . .'

'Nevertheless, I must kill him, don't you see? I must wipe out the foul stain on my honour caused by that night; and it can only be done with his death at my own hands. Will you help me, cousin? I humbly beg this service, this great boon of you.'

I did not consider his request for long. Roland was blood of my blood, and he was my loyal friend as well. Mercadier was one of the most unpleasant men I had ever encountered: cruel and utterly merciless. He had blinded a dozen or so knights and hundreds of men-at-arms who had surrendered to him during the wars with Philip Augustus; he and his *routiers* had ravaged vast territories – ours and theirs alike – with an almost demonic savagery, killing and mutilating women, children, priests and nuns – with no regard for the rules of war or even common decency. The world would be a far better place without Mercadier in it.

'How do you want to do this?' I said.

We left the Abbey at first light and made our way out of the city by the western gate. We told no one where we were going – I did not want to have to argue the case for a cold-blooded assassination to Sir Nicholas de Scras, who I was sure would disapprove, or to involve Thomas in a crime as black as this, or explain to Little John why he could not come along on this mission of revenge, which was a deeply personal one for Roland. Gavin I felt I did not yet know well enough to ask to commit a murder, and Robin was busy with Marie-Anne and his sons. We decided that we two would do it, alone. The fewer people involved, the easier it would be to keep secret, and for all his reputation, Mercadier was but one man, after all.

By casually questioning the revellers at the Easter feast in the market square, Roland had discovered that Mercadier's troops – fifty war-wise, hard-bitten *routiers* – were billeted out of Bordeaux a dozen miles to the south-west and their captain would be rejoining them after the Easter Day celebrations; then he and his men would escort Queen Eleanor and young Blanche of Castile north to Poitiers.

Accordingly, Roland and I set out as soon as the city gates were open on Easter Monday, having hired two riding horses from a sleepy groom at a livery stable nearby, and we rode half a dozen miles south-west on the narrow dusty road through neatly planted vineyards towards a small fortified manor known as the Château de Rouillac. We reined in long before reaching this place and stepped off our horses in a small but dense copse of yew trees beside the straight road that ran south-west out of Bordeaux at the edge of a neat vineyard filled with rows of thick, sinuous, waist-high vines. In the cool of the copse, we were out of sight to anyone travelling the highway, but we could see any horsemen approaching from the north-east.

We did not have long to wait. A fat clergyman on a mule heading towards Bordeaux trotted past without noticing us. A pair of vineyard labourers, gnarled sun-browned men with mattocks across their shoulders, trudged along the road without raising their heads. And then, a little before mid-morning, I nudged Roland – a swift moving cloud of dust approaching our stand of trees indicated a horseman. Or horsemen. For as it drew closer, I could see that it was not Mercadier travelling alone, as we had assumed it would be. I could make out five steeds.

Five riders.

It was the moment to make a hard decision. Five against two. Now this was no quietly efficient ambush, a sudden rush from our hiding place to take an outnumbered foe by surprise, followed by a cut or two with our swords and Mercadier lying dead in the dust. We were looking at a mêlée, and a far more uncertain outcome.

'We can still do this, Alan, I know we can,' pleaded Roland. 'You and I together – who can stand against us?' The desperate look in his eyes tugged at my heart. I weighed the odds. The sensible thing to do would be to sit tight and allow the more numerous enemy to ride past unmolested. The proper, the right thing to do would be to do nothing, to go home and make another, better plan. Recklessness, Robin had told me many times, is a grave failing for anyone who considers himself a serious soldier.

'Come on, then, cousin,' I said, a mad grin nearly splitting my face, and we swung up into the saddle, drew our swords, booted our horses in the ribs and charged out of that copse – straight into the path of the five startled mercenaries.

But our horses were not the destriers that we were used to riding into battle, merely hired hacks from a common stable and they refused to charge into the flanks of the enemy horses – in all fairness, they had not been trained to – instead, they shied away at the last moment and passed alongside at just over a sword's length away. My first strike from Fidelity, which had I been astride Shaitan would certainly have cut the head off the outermost mercenary on that side, whistled through the air a good two inches from his face as I thundered past.

I saw that Roland had been more skilful; he had managed to strike and wound a short, squat mercenary in the shoulder as he galloped by, but the man, bleeding and cursing foully, was still in the saddle. I heard Mercadier's familiar stony voice with its faint Gascon twang order his men to wheel, and engage us again, and then five hardened *routiers* were upon us.

And just like that, we were now the prey.

I exchanged a ringing cut with one very skinny man, whose gaunt, snarling face seemed familiar. But before I could remember where I had seen him last, Mercadier loomed to my left, bellowing something and hacking down at my head with his sword. I took the blow on my shield, but felt the manic force of it shudder through my upper arm. I could sense rather than see a third man behind me, and then a lance grazed past the waist of my hauberk, snagging and ripping my red surcoat, its vicious point thrusting out in the space between my hip bone and elbow. I blocked another sword swipe from the man on my right and desperately turned the horse – the animal was very frightened and confused, near panicked, by the shouting and the clash of steel – and spurred it off the road and into the vines. I did not seek to escape, to cravenly abandon Roland to his fate – I swear it on my honour – but I had to get out of that awkward triangle or I would have been a dead man. As I galloped into the rows of vines, I heard the urgent pounding of hoofbeats behind. I reached the end of the lane and turned the horse with some difficulty, and raced back down the next row, back towards the road, a line of thick stubby vines between me and the oncoming horseman. It was the lance-man, a long-haired villain with a flat-topped metal cap and a furious scowl – and I cursed my luck. His weapon, a twelve-foot spear, couched between his elbow and ribs and aimed at my chest, had a far longer reach than my sword. But I was committed. We closed, his lance seeming to stretch out towards me as if eager to pierce my heart. And at the last moment, I twitched my sword and flipped the lance aside, out of its line, and safely over my right shoulder, and as his horse flashed past me I hacked backwards with Fidelity, timing it perfectly, and crunching the long blade into the back of his neck, cutting through the long greasy hair below his helmet and seeing the blood spurt red. I snatched a quick look backwards and saw him flop in the saddle and then crumple slowly from his cantering mount. And then I was back on the road.

One body lay in the dust – a victim of Roland's skill. But my cousin was in the same position I had been, with three horsemen surrounding him and raining down blow upon blow. He was desperately fending them off with sword and shield.

I screamed, 'Westbury!' and spurred my horse forward into the mêlée. A squat horseman, alerted by my war cry, peeled away and came at me, yelling, whirling a long sword above his head. But I saw that his shield was drooping on his wounded shoulder. This was the man Roland had struck in our first disastrous attack. He was open, his guard was weak, and as our horses closed, Fidelity snaked out, a tongue of sharp steel, and skewered his throat before he could ever land his blow. He gave a despairing blood-choked cough and flopped back in his saddle. And now the battle was two against two.

Mercadier looked behind him, and I saw that he recognized me. He smiled grimly, and hauled the horse round, jerking viciously on its reins. Roland was exchanging blows with the remaining mercenary, the skinny, familiar-looking man; my cousin's shield was up, his blows were fast and precise, rhythmical and even elegant, but his right leg was sheeted with blood and his face under his helmet was bone white.

Mercadier trotted over to me. He lifted his sword and said, 'So you have sunk to murder and robbery on the Queen's highway, Sir Knight. I am not at all surprised. Your villein's blood was bound to come to the fore. And I shall enjoy seeing the colour of it.'

And his horse leaped towards mine.

I should have been concentrating on my enemy – for he was a truly formidable man – but my eye was dragged to Roland and his opponent, hammering at each other sword and shield, sword and shield. Then Roland mistimed his block, and the mercenary's sword clanged off his helmet. My friend reeled in the saddle. The thin man closed with Roland and launched a flurry of blows at his head and shoulders. My cousin just managed to parry and block them – but he was weakened by the blow to the head, and if I could see it from ten paces away, so could his opponent.

Yet Mercadier's sword was arcing down at my own head. I took the full force of the strike on my shield, and cut back at him laterally, aiming for his waist. But the dark mercenary captain had already spurred out of range and my long blade hissed through air.

I stole a quick glance at Roland, and to my surprise saw that he still lived. He was lolling in the saddle somewhat but his enemy had apparently decided to break off the engagement and flee. The familiar-looking mercenary was now fifty yards down the road, galloping towards the Château de Rouillac.

I had not time to ponder his prudence – or cowardice – for Mercadier's destrier barged into my horse's shoulder, and the scarred fighter cut left and right and right again at my upper body with astounding speed and strength and, to be honest, I was very hard-pressed to keep his steel from my flesh. I blocked with shield and sword, and even managed a low lunge that made him rein back and keep his distance. But he pressed back again, as fast as a cat. His horse peeled back its lips and snapped its huge yellow teeth at the muzzle of my mount, scaring the poor beast and causing him to rear alarmingly. And while I was busy merely keeping my seat, Mercadier launched a hacking blow that would have split my skull if it had landed. I just got my sword beneath it in time, catching his blade with my cross-guard. But a sideways slice came next, flowing seamlessly from Mercadier's first blow, and that chopped the corner from my shield, the small triangle of leather-covered wood striking me in the face. I cut back at Mercadier's shoulder, missed, and was very nearly skewered by his lightning counterstroke. I was going to lose this duel – I knew it in my heart. His warhorse was better trained, to be sure, and that gave him a huge advantage – but he was also, without a shred of doubt, a better swordsman than me.

However, I was not alone. And he was.

Roland recovered his battered wits, straightened in the saddle, jammed back his spurs. His horse bounded forward; my cousin hacked down once from behind – and sunk his blade deep into Mercadier's waist, hauling it free in a spray of red mist. The mercenary captain gave a short desperate bark of pain; and now the gore welled thick and dark from his opened side, drenching his leg and the horse's flank. He stared round at Roland, a look of almost comical indignation on his face. And he was down, slipping from his saddle to crumple into the dust of the road. Roland dismounted slowly, with great difficulty – his right leg was badly gashed – and he pulled a dagger from the sheath at his belt. He hobbled over to where Mercadier was lying, a dark pool spreading beneath his body.

'Remember me?' said Roland, his body casting a shadow over Mercadier's scarred face and staring, agonized eyes. The mercenary said nothing but I thought I saw him give the merest shake of his head.

'Let me remind you,' said my cousin quietly. And he bent down and flicked the blade of the dagger through Mercadier's right eyeball. The fallen man gave a grunt of pain, no more, as blood and pale jelly oozed from the eye socket.

'Still nothing?' said Roland. 'Well, you'll doubtless meet many men in Hell that you have wronged – men who, even if you do not recall them, I am certain will recall you. May the Devil allow their revenge to be slower and more painful than mine.'

And he stabbed down once with the dagger, squarely piercing Mercadier's remaining eye and driving the blade deep into his brain.

Chapter Twelve

While Nur salved and bandaged Roland's wounded leg in the infirmary of the Abbey of St Andrew, I went in search of an old friend, my former music teacher Bernard de Sezanne, who now served Queen Eleanor and whom I had bumped into the day before at the Easter feast.

I was experiencing the familiar flat, melancholic humour that I always had after a bout of bloody combat. Roland and I had barely spoken during our slow ride back to Bordeaux, and I had taken him directly to the Abbey's infirmary before carefully sponging the spatters of blood from the horses' hides and their saddles and returning them to the livery stable by the western gate. There were two things that greatly concerned me that afternoon: firstly, I could see that Roland's wound was deep, and I worried that our reckless revenge might result in the loss of his leg, or even his life; the second thing was the mercenary who had fled so abruptly from the fight and escaped down the road to Rouillac. If he was familiar to me, was I, too, familiar to him? And would his fellow mercenaries – knowing that I had been responsible for the death of their captain – come seeking their own revenge? Had I, in short, begun a dangerous, bloody feud with these *routiers*, these lawless killers-for-hire?

The death of Mercadier, Queen Eleanor's fighting man and her protector on the dangerous roads of France, would soon be reported in Bordeaux; the hue and cry would doubtless be raised and a culprit would be sought. And so I needed to find my old mentor Bernard. I did not need his advice, nor his music, nor yet one of his funny stories – I wanted his help with another of his special talents.

I found Bernard in a tavern in the least reputable part of the city, surrounded by a gang of oafish, drunken cronies, a brimming beaker before him, his silk-clad elbow in a small lake of spilled wine, his face blotched, his head already lolling on his shoulders, although it was only an hour or so past noon.

'The hour of day is entirely irrelevant, my dear boy,' slurred Bernard, when I pointed this out. 'A great artist such as myself must nourish his Muse with the fruit of the vine from dawn to dusk or it will surely wither and die. I drink to live, I live to drink, and I drink to you, my friend, my brother in art . . . once my most promising pupil, a musician of talent but now reduced to little more than an armed thug, a killer of men, the hallowed Muse long flown from his soul, her delicate sensibilities put to flight by the hideous screams of battle . . .'

Bernard drew a breath and sank the entire contents of his beaker before continuing. His cronies were grinning in anticipation. I had heard this refrain before: my friend believed I was squandering my talent by choosing the life of a knight, of a warrior, rather than that of a musician and poet.

'When was the last time you tuned your vielle? When did you last pluck a tender note?' he said, squinting at me out of one eye.

'I must confess, Bernard, that it has been a few weeks; my vielle was destroyed in a fire when Westbury was attacked . . .' And I told him briefly about that night.

'You see, you see – the wages of sin! Your chosen life of barbarism and brutality has laid you low. Now that sacred box, the heavenly machine that once allowed us to hear the very whispers of the voice of God, is no more – destroyed by beast-like killers, burned to ashes by uncouth men of the sword, violent men cut from the very same cloth as yourself.'

I was beginning to become irritated. 'I need your help, Bernard,' I said through my teeth. 'And I need it rather urgently.'

'Of course you do, my boy, of course you do. And it is not too late – oh no, no – it is not yet too late for you to turn aside from the red path of violence and rediscover your gentler, finer musical self. Even a gore-soaked slaughterman such as yourself can be saved. But first we must find you a new instrument. I know of a vielle-maker in Toulouse, a well-regarded man but expensive . . .'

The oafish cronies were hooting by now. And while I knew that Bernard was merely making sport with me for his own sodden amusement, I feared that I would do something rash, something I'd regret, if I did not shut off his teasing forthwith. So I grasped him by the elbow, my thumb digging into the soft point behind the knob of bone, and raised him up from the wine-stained table. He squawked a good deal but meekly allowed me to lead him to a table on the far side of the tavern away from his cackling friends.

'My wine . . .' he bleated.

'No more wine for the moment, Bernard. I need you as sober as possible – so that you can help your old pupil and friend.'

My former mentor sat forlornly at the empty table, staring at me with a sort of bemused aggrievement in his eyes, as I pulled up a stool and sat down opposite him.

'You've become just like him, you know,' he said miserably.

'Who?'

'Your master, the Earl of Locksley – you and he are quite a pair. Always in a hurry and always wanting something from me.'

'Bernard, I'm sorry, but I really do need your help urgently.'

'You know that you have fresh blood on your hose?' he asked.

'Yes, that is what I need to talk to you about.'

Robin's happiness was coming off him in a kind of glow, like Mediterranean sunshine reflecting from a white stone wall. All the Companions were gathered in the refectory of the Abbey of St Andrew, and were eating a supper of roasted mutton with wild garlic on trenchers of fine white bread – a rare treat for the refectory of a religious house, which was due to the fact that it was the evening of Easter Monday, a holy day. Roland, too, while he had an obvious limp, seemed to be inordinately cheerful, beaming at his fellows and calling out bawdy jests across the table to Little John. I believe that Nur, when she had finished treating the bloody gash in his leg, may have given him some powerful drug for the pain, but perhaps I am maligning my cousin – perhaps the joy of his successful revenge was the sole cause of his hectic spirits. He and Robin, who was joyful after two full days in his beloved's company, gave the whole gathering a festive spirit, and we were all, I think, even silent, black-shrouded Nur, enlivened by their exuberant gaiety.

We had only just started eating when Robin, who was beside me, gave a shout of happiness and leaped up from the bench. Then my lord was embracing a squat, fat figure in a black robe with thin hair the colour of rabbit fur cut in the tonsure. Then Robin was introducing him to the table: 'This, my friends, is Father Tuck! An old comrade and a very good man. Come, sit down here beside young Alan. Have some of this tender mutton . . .'

And I found myself smiling into a round, red face with a lumpy nose and kind, mellow eyes the colour of hazelnuts.

'Hello, Alan,' said Tuck, 'how have you been keeping?'

While my old friend and I exchanged our news, I took in the changes that time had wrought on the Countess of Locksley's personal chaplain. The former monk and follower of Robin in the old days in Sherwood seemed a little greyer and a little fatter than last time I had seen him – but for a man of more than fifty years he still seemed to be strong and tough enough for two men. Tuck might be a man of God but he was also a warrior to his fingertips – very skilled in the yew bow and with sword and quarterstaff. And while he might tend to the Countess of Locksley's spiritual needs, he also was quite capable of guarding her body against anyone who might wish to harm her. We had barely finished catching up with each other's lives, when Robin was on his feet once more.

'My friends, I have an announcement to make,' said my lord happily. 'I am very pleased to inform you that Father Tuck here will be joining us on our quest. He has long been interested in the particular object of our search and I believe that his knowledge of the Grail will prove invaluable to us all.'

There were universal calls of approval from those who knew Tuck, and polite smiles and nods from those who did not. Sir Nicholas de Scras called out, 'The blessing of Our Lord Jesus Christ be upon you, Father. And be welcome among us: we could sorely use a man of God in our company!'

'I'm so pleased you are coming with us,' I told my plump neighbour, who had helped himself to an enormous piece of succulent shoulder meat from the common dish and spooning about a pint of the garlic sauce over the top. With his mouth bulging with mutton, the grease running down his chin, Tuck told me that Robin had engaged a troop of the Queen's Gascon men-at-arms to act as his Countess's temporary protectors over the next few weeks while Tuck took leave of his mistress and joined the Companions in their quest. Tuck, it seemed, had been fascinated by the Grail ever since Robin had mentioned it to him some years ago in Yorkshire. And he had been making his own researches in his idle hours at Eleanor's court while it travelled about in her southern lands. Indeed, it was he who had confirmed to Robin that Amanieu d'Albret, Nur's brutal Templar, was in residence at the Jealous Castle. But that was not all he had to contribute to our fellowship.

'I have seen it, Alan,' he said to me with quiet but simmering excitement and a small belch. 'I have seen the Grail.'

His words jolted me. I knew, of course, that this wondrous object did truly exist in a physical form in the world – I had seen the Master carrying the very wooden box that contained it, and the purple cushion the box was set to rest upon, but I had never seen the Grail itself – and his words gave the holy vessel a reality that was in some way rather shocking.

'Have you truly laid your eyes on the cup of Christ?' I said, searching Tuck's face for the truth.

'Speak up, Tuck,' said Robin from the head of the table. 'I think we would all like to hear about this.'

An expectant hush fell over the company, as Tuck began his tale: 'It was not quite a year ago, a few weeks after the death of King Richard – may his soul swiftly find its way to Heaven – and Queen Eleanor asked me to undertake a discreet diplomatic mission on her son King John's behalf to Pedro, the King of Aragon, who was at that time holding his court at Barcelona. Ramon of Erill, a nobleman of ancient lineage and a vassal of the Spanish King, who had been visiting Eleanor in Aquitaine, was to accompany me with his knights from Bordeaux to Barcelona – as his family held a good deal of land in the Pyrenees. It was a long, cold, exhausting journey over the mountains that took many weeks – and the mission was ultimately fruitless – but as I was preparing to return to Queen Eleanor and the Countess of Locksley, the Lord of Erill invited me to break my return journey in his castle in the Valley of Boí, that I might admire the extraordinary adornments of the little Church of St Clement in the village of Taüll.

'I was reluctant – for I wished to return to my mistress as soon as possible – but Ramon of Erill was insistent. And he told a strange tale to entice me. Hundreds of years ago, Ramon said, an old man had come to the Roman city of Barcino, as Barcelona was then known. He was sick, ancient and a Jew, but also a gentleman who came from Arimathea in Judea. His name, he said, was Joseph. He was sheltered, fed and nursed on his arrival in the city by an ancestor of the Lord of Erill, a knight called Perillus. Every morning while the old Jew lay on his sickbed, Perillus would come to visit him, and they would talk. During these hours, the old man revealed he had travelled to the ends of the world, from England to Ethiopia, in his long life. He had seen wonders and miracles, and met monsters and saints. He claimed that he had known Our Saviour in person – indeed, he claimed he had been present at the Last Supper – and at the Crucifixion. He even said that it had been in his own family tomb that Our Lord had lain for three days. And he claimed to possess two wondrous objects, two items so holy and precious that they almost surpassed belief.'

Tuck speared a large chunk of garlicky mutton with his knife, popped it in his mouth and grinned at all of us as he chewed, deliberately letting the anticipation build. For five heartbeats he said nothing. Then he took pity on the silent table, swallowed his mouthful, chased it with a gulp of wine, and continued: 'These objects were the very lance wielded by a Roman centurion that had pierced Christ's side while he suffered on the Cross . . . and the Grail – the vessel used to mix the wine at the Last Supper and which he, Joseph, had later used to collect the blood of Our Lord after the Roman lance had wounded him. These two objects, both blessed by the touch of the sacred blood of Jesus Christ, had miraculous qualities, old Joseph insisted. The lance had the power to confer the gift of entry into the Kingdom of Heaven on anyone who was killed by it . . . but the blessed cup, the Holy Grail, as it became known, this wondrous object was by far the more precious of the two. The Grail could hold back Death itself, and cure any ill or hurt. All a man had to do was to fill the Grail with water, invoke the name of Our Lord over it and drink – and his life would be extended and his illness washed away.'

My right hand crept surreptitiously over my neck and I stroked the wooden handle of the lance-dagger in its leather sheath between my shoulder blades. It gave me a secret feeling of great warmth and joy to imagine that I might possess the very blade that had pierced the body of Our Lord. If this tale were true.

'When Joseph died, after calling out the name of Our Saviour in a loud voice, Perillus carried his body with great ceremony to his own private tomb and sealed the old Jew in it – for this man, he believed, had given up his own eternal resting place for Jesus Christ himself and so this was surely no more than his due.'

'And the Grail, Father, what happened to the Grail?' Sir Nicholas broke in – his lean face under his cropped grey hair was flushed with excitement, and he was thrusting his upper body forward over the table towards Tuck. I saw that the monks of the refectory were clearing the adjoining table of crusts of bread and scraps of food. And a few of the holy brothers were glancing disapprovingly over at the huddle of folk who lingered at our table where the meal was clearly done.

'Before his death, Joseph of Arimathea made a gift of the Holy Grail and the Holy Lance to the knight Perillus in gratitude for his care in his final days,' said Tuck. 'They remained in the knight's family for many, many generations.

'For centuries, while the family grew in power and became the lords of Erill, their possession of the Grail was kept a closely guarded secret. But my friend Ramon's grandfather, who held the Valley of Boí nearly a hundred years ago, felt differently. He was arrogant, very proud that his family were the guardians of the cup of Christ. Instead of keeping the Grail hidden from human eyes, this Lord of Erill decided to put it on display in the heart of his territory, in the new church that he was building, to be dedicated to St Clement, in the high village of Taüll. This proud lord ordered a local craftsman to construct a tableau of seven carved wooden statues, gilded, beautifully painted in rich colours and depicting the Descent of Our Lord from the Cross. In the background of this setting, affixed to their smaller crosses, were the wooden figures of the two thieves who were executed at the same time as Our Saviour; and the statues of St John and St Nicodemus looking on. In the centre, the figure of Joseph of Arimathea stood directly at the foot of the Cross; and he was shown as helping the dead body of Our Lord down from that dreadful Tree. The figure of Jesus himself, his thin body descending into Joseph's arms, had a long trailing arm, draped over Joseph's head and right shoulder. Below Christ's dangling arm stood the statue of the Virgin – the finest work of the whole set of figures, her right hand raised, pale palm facing outwards, her left hand held palm up and covered by her rich blue mantle. Here, in her covered left hand, the lord of Erill affixed the actual Grail, placed there as if to catch the drips of Our Lord's sacred blood as they trickled from his dead fingertips.

'This holy group of statues, by all accounts as beautiful as a perfect rose in bloom, was placed in the sun-lit northern nave of the church of St Clement of Taüll, and guarded by a stout, waist-high wooden paling to keep the figures from the common touch of the people. And I have no doubt that this sacred tableau caused all who saw it to shiver with a profound awe. Indeed, as the fame of the holy statues spread, men and women from all over the mountains came to view it, and they prayed before the tableau and made offerings – a silver penny, a sack of milled grain, a piece of dried fish or even as little as an egg or two – at the church for the good of their souls. But none were permitted to soil the Grail with the touch of their hands, even as the mere likeness of the Virgin had her hand protected from the Grail by the cloth of her mantle.'

Tuck paused for a moment and looked around the table. Not a

soul moved or spoke; all imagining the magnificent scene that the priest had just described. 'But, for the proud Lord of Erill, even this was not adornment rich enough for his new church, for he also commanded the master artists of Taüll to create a painting in the curve of the apse, behind the altar, a masterpiece depicting Christ in Majesty, surrounded by apostles, saints and angels. And in a small panel below the image of Our Saviour, he caused an image of the Virgin to be made, holding in her left, her mantle-covered hand, the Grail – in a pose that was a deliberate copy of her stance in the group of wooden statues a dozen paces away – and it was said to be even more awe-inspiring than the tableau of the Descent from the Cross.

'It was this image of the Grail that I was fortunate enough to see with my own eyes, less than a year ago, in Taüll. This little panel, this wonderful representation of a wondrous object, still blazes forth to this day beneath the image of Our Lord Jesus Christ in that little church, high in the snowy passes of the Pyrenees. And I will never forget its breath-stealing beauty.'

The Almoner was standing beside our table, and as Tuck paused, he said sternly, 'Good sirs, I must ask you to rise from this table, we need to clean the refectory before it is closed for the night, and anyway, it is high time that you made your way to the dormitories.'

There were groans of complaint from all around the table – as each of the Companions had been entranced by Tuck's tale and wished for him to continue in its telling.

Robin spoke: 'We shall have the rest of the story tomorrow – on the road. For I have decided that we must leave Bordeaux first thing in the morning.'

'Why such a sudden a departure?' asked Sir Nicholas.

Robin looked directly at me, his face devoid of expression, as he answered the former Hospitaller's question. 'It seems that one of Queen Eleanor's officers has been murdered on the road to

181

Rouillac a few miles outside the city. The dead man was a mercenary, quite a well-known ruffian named Mercadier, and he was killed, so the rumours have it, by two men-at-arms in the service of a rival mercenary captain called Brandin. If you can believe the gossip, these two reckless, mutton-headed idiots waylaid him and his friends on the road and killed four of them this morning – but then, these clumsy fools, these blundering, halfwitted morons, allowed one of Mercadier's men to escape. And the man who escaped, mark you, will soon be helping the Queen's provosts identify the miscreants. Although, of course, it *clearly* has nothing to do with us, I think it best if we leave Bordeaux forthwith. All armed strangers will be suspect. So we leave tomorrow at dawn.'

My lord finished his speech and turned his head to the left to stare casually at Roland's wounded leg.

'Rumours often prove to be true,' I said, blushing and hating the weakness of my own body for this tell-tale flow of heat. 'Brandin's men are said to be a murderous, unruly lot, to be sure,' I stumbled on. 'And Brandin and Mercadier have long hated each other . . .' I stopped, embarrassed by myself. But a part of me was blessing Bernard and his skill at spreading plausible scuttlebutt. Spending all day, as he did, in a variety of low taverns, he traded gossip with large numbers of drinkers almost every hour. But I was still surprised at how swiftly this false rumour he and I had confected a few hours ago had spread about the city.

I also knew that Robin was not so very angry with us for killing Mercadier – he understood the urge for revenge better than any man – but I think he was irritated that we had not consulted him first; and, of course, he was concerned that the man whom we had foolishly allowed to escape might identify us. I was quite content to quit Bordeaux, anyway, not just to avoid the Queen's provosts – but also because Tuck's tale had sparked a keen desire in my heart, like a vast hunger, to see the Holy Grail, and perhaps even to hold in my hand an object that might once have cradled Our Saviour's precious blood.

'We leave at dawn,' Robin repeated, standing up. And as we left the refectory, I heard him asking Roland with a voice dripping with false sympathy, just how he had hurt his poor little leg.

Roland, limping alongside Robin, offered up some fatuous excuse about sharpening a dagger on his lap and slipping. Nur was beside him, and he had his arm draped over her narrow shoulders as she mutely supported him through the low door of the eating hall.

'There is an important lesson to be learned here,' said Robin, standing in the threshold and once more looking directly at me while he ostensibly addressed another. 'We all need to be more careful in future. Carelessness with weapons can be very, very dangerous. It can quite often get you killed.'

Before the sun was a finger's breadth above the eastern horizon, we were on the road and heading south-east. Nine riders and three packhorses, following the north bank of the River Garonne as it meandered slowly towards Toulouse. Robin had purchased the twelve horses from a stables in Bordeaux the previous afternoon – and, to be honest, they were not the finest beasts in Christendom, indeed they were barely better than farmers' hacks. It occurred to me belatedly that Robin must have been obliged to dig deep into his coffers to pay for this expedition to Aquitaine, and he might well be nearing the end of his resources. He was no longer a mighty Earl with land and revenues at his command and the ear of the King. He was an outlaw, I remembered, and the silver that he spent on us came from a diminishing store. On the first evening after we left, when we stopped for the night at the village of Langon, perhaps twenty-five miles out of Bordeaux, I approached him when he was alone with the horses, talking to the stable boy about their feed and proper care while the rest of the Companions were already in the common room of the tavern, and ordering up jugs of wine, loaves of barley bread and the spicy grilled local sausages.

'This is for you,' I said, holding out a fat, black leather purse filled with silver pennies, which I had discovered in the saddlebags of Mercadier's warhorse.

'That is kind of you, Alan, but this is not how it works,' said Robin. 'As we agreed in London, I will cover all the expenses of the quest, and the Grail, if we ever find it, will rightfully belong to me. That is the agreement. Any loot that we gain along the way is to be shared equally. That looks a lot like loot, to me. It looks very much like the purse of a dead mercenary. I'll not say any more about how you got it, but according to our agreement that purse should be shared between the Companions, even Nur and Tuck.'

'I just want to help, Robin,' I said. 'I know that the cost of this expedition must be a heavy burden for you.'

'I'm not normally one for turning down gifts of cash, Alan,' said my lord, with a smile. 'But on this occasion, I will say no. If you don't want to share it with the others, keep it, I won't say anything and, who knows, one day we may be grateful for it.'

So I tucked the purse back under my belt inside my tunic, and made to rejoin the other Companions. But Robin stopped me, as I turned to go. 'I'm touched that you should worry about me, Alan,' he said, 'but do not be too concerned. Remember the robbery at Welbeck Abbey, and the hoard of golden altar furniture we took there? Well, I have brought some of those pieces with us – I paid for these horses here with just that little pyx. That little golden pot was worth the price of these twelve nags. Do not be concerned, Alan, we shall not be in want for a good while yet. Maybe never – once I have the Grail, I shall charge passers-by a shilling a go to drink from it!'

And he laughed, that carefree laugh that I knew of old.

I assumed he was joking about charging all and sundry to drink from the Grail – and hoping merely to shock me with his impiety – but with Robin, you never quite knew.

That night in the village of Langon, by the fire in the common room of the tavern, Tuck continued his tale.

'Word of the little church of St Clement and the wonders it contained spread far and wide in the mountains, and folk began to come to see these beautiful statues of Jesus, and Joseph of Arimathea and of Mary, the Mother of God, and the wondrous, magical vessel she bore in her hand. For fifty years, that little church was a place of pilgrimage – and scores of miracles were reported to have occurred there. Many folk claimed that the Virgin came to them in a vision as they prayed before her statue, and that the Grail cured them of their illnesses. The lame walked, the sick were healed, the blind were restored to sight, or so it was said. And Ramon's grandfather, the Lord of Erill, grew even more puffed up with pride, convinced that it was the awesome power of the Grail that lay behind these miracles. And he also enjoyed the revenues that the village of Taüll accrued from the flow of pilgrims.

'Ramon's grandfather filled the Grail with water from the font and allowed the pilgrims, for the price of a silver penny, to dip a finger in it and anoint themselves with its power. For another penny they were allowed to kiss the cold, dark metal of the Holy Lance, which was also on display in the church in a golden box in the southern nave. The miracles became common – indeed fantastical tales began to circulate about the power of the Grail of Taüll. Maimed men claimed that limbs lopped in war had actually grown back; a dead man brought over the mountain passes to this remote village was resurrected by the power of the holy water from the Grail. Many who prayed before the statue, and who kissed the lance, often heard the voice of the Holy Mother giving them wise advice and promising help. The trickle of pilgrims became a flood.

The Lord of Erill became richer and more powerful from the avalanche of silver pennies that the pilgrims brought to his church.

'The years passed and the old Lord of Erill died at a greatly advanced age, his life artificially prolonged, some dared to whisper, by the power of the Grail of Taüll. His lands were inherited by a new lord of Erill, Ramon's father. And, of course, as word of the Grail continued to spread, it came to the ears of the new Bishop of Roda, an ambitious young man from a wealthy family, who was fond of music and whose name was Heribert.'

I gave an involuntary start to hear that name – to be honest, I nearly fell off my stool – for suddenly this tale of generations past, of grandfathers and ancestors, had taken a giant stride towards the here and now. I had met Heribert briefly six years ago, when he was a fat, old Cardinal living in the city of Vendôme – and he had been murdered by the Master's men to prevent him from speaking to me about the Grail. Roland saw my agitation and gave me a curious glance but I merely held out my wine cup for him to fill with the jug by his boot. As a consequence, I missed Tuck's next few words.

'. . . when his demands were refused, Heribert and his men came in force, in the dead of winter, the cruel season of snow and ice, and they fell upon the village of Taüll like a wolf upon the flock. Ramon told me that he and his family are still very bitter about what happened next. Only a handful of Erill men-at-arms were in the village when Heribert struck with a large force of Spanish mercenaries, scores of them. Taüll was burned – and many peasants perished afterwards in the snows, driven from their homes by the marauders – and the Church of St Clement was broken into and ransacked for its hoard of silver. The Spanish captain of the mercenaries, a sacrilegious beast, may God curse him, took his sword to the wooden tableau of the Descent from the Cross. The figures were hacked and broken, and some thrown in the fires of the ravaged village, but this captain still feared to touch the Holy Grail

186

with his bare hands, so he cut off the whole arm of the statue of the Virgin with one blow of his sword and carried away the Grail wrapped in his cloak. He took the Holy Lance as well in its golden box, only the magnificent painting of Christ in Majesty, with its superb little panel depicting the Virgin and the Grail was spared – for how can you possibly carry away an image painted on a wall?'

Tuck paused at this point to refresh himself from his wine cup, and Robin threw a pair of dry logs on the fire.

'I think that is enough for tonight,' said the priest with a sigh. 'My old bones ache and I long to be snug in my bed.'

'May I take the story onwards from here, Tuck?' Robin asked. 'I will finish it swiftly, I swear.' And the fat priest nodded over the rim of his cup. 'Unless you would rather relate it, Alan?' Robin looked over at me. I shook my head. I knew the course of the tale from this point – it was to a certain extent my story, but I, too, was tired after a long day in the saddle; my head ached somewhat and I had little desire to recount it for the Companions.

'Very well,' said Robin. 'I will be brisk, for we must soon get to our beds; we have another hard ride tomorrow. So, this is what we know: Heribert, Bishop of Roda, now had in his possession the Holy Grail and the Holy Lance, and it sparked in him a lifelong obsession with relics of all kinds. About twenty-five years ago, Heribert paid a visit to Paris. He had heard that rare and precious relics were to be had for sale in that great city, if you knew the right people to ask. But he could not bear to be parted from the Grail and the Lance even for a few weeks and so, when the noble bishop travelled north, he took them with him. He had been blessed with good fortune all his life, wealthy parents, a fine bishopric, and now possession of that wonder of wonders, the Holy Grail – but in Paris his luck ran out. There, the Grail and the Lance and several other trinkets were stolen from him by a young chorister of the cathedral – a monk named Michel, who later became known as the Master, or the "man you cannot refuse", and who is our enemy.

'We believe that the Master is now at the Jealous Castle under the protection of its seigneur, Amanieu d'Albret, who so abused good Nur here, and that in his possession is the Grail. Tuck and I have made enquiries in Bordeaux – your musical friend Bernard was a mine of information, Alan. It seems that the Master was there a week ago and, as far as we know, is still there.'

'He is there,' Nur interrupted. 'The Grail is there, too. I have seen it in the bones.'

There was a short uncomfortable silence – nobody, it seemed, was inclined to question the witch's knowledge.

Robin spoke: 'We must assume that for now – we know that it is his recruiting base. For Bernard also told me that he has been summoning knights and men-at-arms to join him there from across Christendom.'

There was another heavy silence after Robin's words.

'How many men does he now have?' asked Roland.

'We can't know for sure,' said Robin, 'but it may be that he has already recruited as many as fifty or sixty to his banner.'

'Sixty men?' said Gavin. 'Against the nine of us?'

'It may not be as many as that. They may not all be there, all the time. The other snippet that I picked up from Bernard, is that the Master is building his own fortress on a mountaintop, a mighty keep, and the new knights he is inducting into his Order are to form a garrison of pious, dedicated men to protect the Grail from those who are unworthy of its sanctity.'

'Where is this mighty castle?' I asked. This was the first I'd heard of this. I'd thought of the Master as a fugitive, a hunted man, cowering from his enemies, under the protection of others. But the closer I came to him, the more puissant he seemed to become. Indeed, he now loomed in my mind as a potent, even daunting foe.

'Again, we don't exactly know,' said Robin. 'But right now he is most likely at the Jealous Castle – not two days' ride from here.

And it is there that we shall trap him, we shall kill him and we shall take possession of the Grail.'

Some of the Companions actually applauded. But, as we made up our straw pallets on the floor of the tavern, I thought about Robin's breezy assurance. Sixty men against us, and they tucked up inside a mighty castle – that did not seem an easy proposition to me. I slept badly and dreamed of Goody's death. She was carried away by angels, all singing in beautiful verse that this was the result of my failure in this quest. And, most painfully, as her face moved upwards, away from me, borne aloft by celestial wings, she said that she loved me and that she forgave my weakness.

Chapter Thirteen

The next day we rode a little north of east, following the looping course of the river, which was never more than a thousand yards from the road, and sometimes flowed within spitting distance of our horses' hooves. At a little before noon, Nur, who had been lagging perhaps a hundred yards behind at the rear of our column, raced forward to pull up, her farmer's hack snorting with effort, beside Robin, who was in the lead position. They conferred briefly – Robin scanned our back trail and then said crisply, 'Everyone off the road, right now.' And he urged his horse up a narrow path that headed northwards, away from the river, towards a small ruined church about half a mile distant. He took off at a full gallop and his turn of speed rather surprised me. But we all managed to scramble after him and a short while later we were sheltering behind tumbled-down walls, out of sight and trying to keep our horses from whickering.

And just in time.

We heard them before we saw them. A tight group of some fifty horsemen thundering along the road we had just forsaken. I do not know how Nur had detected them, whether it was her magic baby bones or just her keen mortal eyesight, but I was very glad that she had. For they were an evil-looking crew – tough, ragged, hungry men, well armed with lance and sword and armoured in leather and iron. They came past our hiding place at a fast canter, not bothering to spare their horses – and they seemed to travel in their own dark bubble of menace. For these were not regular troops, disciplined men-at-arms serving under a knight or a nobleman, these were *routiers*. These were mercenaries, the lowest scum of any army, willing to fight for pay and plunder against anyone, anywhere. These men, or men just like them, had burned their way across half of northern France in the long wars between King Richard and Philip Augustus, slaughtering everything in their path, desecrating churches, raping and ravaging the land with a near-lunatic fury, destroying what they could not carry away. They had no banners, and it was too far to see their faces, but I knew, without a doubt, that these were Mercadier's men.

They passed our hiding place in no more than a dozen heartbeats, riding as if driven on by the lash of whips or in pursuit of something or someone valuable.

I caught Robin's steely eye a moment after the horsemen had passed, leaving nothing but a billow of yellow dust and a faint smell of horse sweat.

'You let one of his men escape alive,' he said.

'I'm sorry,' I said. And I truly was.

His hard face relaxed a little and he half-smiled. 'Well, it is done now,' my lord said, swinging up into the saddle. 'Maybe we can manage to stay out of their path.'

'We can't know for sure that they were seeking us,' Roland said – though I could see that he did not believe it himself. Robin gave him a withering look, but said nothing.

'They were in an awful hurry to find somebody,' said Little John. 'And, by Christ's fetid foot-rags, it will not be good news for the folk they *are* seeking.'

That day we rode slowly and with great caution, each of us, except Tuck and Nur, taking it in turns to ride scout a mile ahead of the rest of our column. We camped outside Marmande, sleeping rough in a small dank wood not far from the river, and Robin forbade us to light fires on which to cook our supper, and ordered us to make as little noise as possible. But nobody complained – the Companions were all hardy campaigners used to cold, uncomfortable nights – and we chewed on leathery sticks of dried beef and dipped twice-baked bread in twice-watered wine to make it soft enough to squeeze down our throats. Then we scooped out a shallow hip-hole apiece, wrapped ourselves in our cloaks, and went swiftly to sleep on the hard ground.

The next day we rode along the western side of the newly built high stone walls of the town of Marmande, eyed warily by the sentries above us, but not challenged as we did not try to enter the place. We crossed the wide Garonne by a crumbling bridge of brick and stone that Tuck said must have been built by the Romans many hundreds of years before. The road on the other side of the water was as straight as an arrow, and ran due south, with a vast pine forest glowering on our right and more cheerful open fields to our left. Once we were on that arrow of a highway, Robin urged us to greater speed and we alternately galloped and trotted our horses as the sun rose high, bright and heavy before us.

By noon, Nur told us that we were nearing the Jealous Castle and we left the road and forced our way into the thick pine woods to the west. While the rest of us built a camp between the dense boughs, interweaving branches cut from the trees to make a large rain-proof roof, and piling other freshly cut feathery limbs to make comfortable beds, Little John and Gavin slipped away together into the gloom of the woods with their war bows. I watched them go and before they disappeared completely among the trees, I saw John take Gavin's smaller hand in his own. My jaw fell open.

I saw that Robin was watching me watching them, and he must

have noticed my shocked expression for he came over and drew me away from the other Companions.

'Did you not know about them?' he asked quietly.

I goggled at him. 'Are they . . . Is Little John really . . . How long have they been . . .' I belatedly pulled myself together and tried to sound worldly and matter-of-fact. 'They are lovers, yes? Ah, indeed, I had not realized that,' I said.

'It has been so almost since the first day they met three or four months ago.'

'You don't find this a bit, well, odd, or comical or just a little bit disgusting? Which one plays the part of the . . . oh, never mind.'

'John Nailor has been my most loyal follower for more than twenty years,' said Robin. 'He is still my most loyal man – along with you, of course, Alan. He has fought beside me on countless occasions, he has killed for me, and worse; and he has shed his own blood for me. For my part, he could bugger a whole den full of pigs, he could rape the Virgin Mary and every single one of the saints – all the women *and* all the men – and I would still love him.'

I considered this appalling, blasphemous statement in silence.

'He is still the same big, ugly, crude, bloodthirsty bastard he always was,' said Robin. 'He's still John.'

I thought about John then: he had been very kind to me over the years, and also, it must be said, unkind on a few occasions, but he'd always treated me with a rough brotherly camaraderie. He was my comrade, my friend.

'He's still John,' I said, nodding. And Robin smiled at me.

'I think it might be best if you didn't tell the others, Alan, particularly Sir Nicholas. He would say, I believe, that the Church considers it a mortal sin. And I don't want to foster any disharmony in our ranks.'

I nodded again, and Robin slapped me on the shoulder and walked away.

At dusk John and Gavin returned, quietly happy and with five good-sized hares strung on a broken arrow, which we skinned, gutted and roasted on the fire. I watched the pair of them covertly while we cooked and ate and saw clearly for the first time the tenderness between them. I could not believe that I had not noticed their love before, for it seemed to burn as brightly as the pine-wood fire. The Church might call it a mortal sin, Sir Nicholas might not approve, but I could see no wrongdoing.

When we had eaten and drank, and all the Companions were sitting around the crackling blaze, eight tough men and a half-mad witch, a light rain began to patter impotently on the branch roof above us and Robin outlined his plans for the Jealous Castle.

'Many of us here are known to the Master – and perhaps also to some of these Knights of Our Lady he commands,' Robin began. 'We dare not risk riding into the town in daylight. But three of us are unknown, at least by sight, to our enemies, and so they must undertake the reconnaissance.

'Tuck, Nur and Sir Nicholas will each enter Casteljaloux separately. These three will be our spearhead. Tuck, you will seek lodgings in the cloisters of the Benedictines – a small daughter-house of the Abbey of La Sauve-Majeure, which is in the east of the town near the river. You will claim to be a wandering preacher from Bordeaux who has been fired by a vision of the Virgin to save souls in these heretical southern lands, and you will search for news of the Grail. Sir Nicholas, under the name of Peter of Horsham, you will apply to join the ranks of the Knights of Our Lady – admitting to having been a Knight Hospitaller, which should make you an attractive recruit. Your task will be to get to the Master and his inner circle. And Nur – Nur, you have the most important task of all; you will gather information from both Tuck and Sir Nicholas and relay it back to us. By day, you will sit in the market square begging for alms, waiting for either Tuck or Sir Nicholas to pass on their news. At night, you will leave the town before curfew and, when you know what is needed for a successful attack, you will return here to pass on messages from Tuck and Sir Nicholas to us.

'It could take several days, I believe, until we have enough knowledge to make our assault – and when we do make it, I want everybody to be clear of our objectives. We are here to take the Grail from the Master. That is our goal. If we can kill the Master as well, that is excellent, and I know that some of us believe this would be a pleasure' – there was a bear-like growl of assent from Little John, but I remained silent – 'yet without the Grail, the Master is finished anyway. His power to recruit knights and men-at-arms and whatever other scum choose to serve him, is founded on his possession of the Grail. We take away the Grail; the Master is a broken reed. He can no longer hurt us.' Robin was looking hard at me. 'We are not here for revenge. We are here to take possession of the Grail. Is that clear?'

I nodded – for Robin's labouring of this simple point seemed to be entirely for my benefit. He didn't want another Mercadier.

'Does anyone have any questions?' asked Robin.

Thomas, who was normally silent during these conferences, raised a hand. 'Yes,' said Robin.

'Forgive me for asking a foolish question, sir,' said Thomas, 'but why is it called the Jealous Castle?'

It was Nur who answered him. 'These lands are the territories of the d'Albrets,' she said, waving a skinny arm in a wide circle above her head. 'The accursed son of that brood told me this long ago. From here all the way west to the great, grey sea, is d'Albret land. And they have many castles in them. But the Jealous Castle is right on the edge of their domain, away from the prying eyes of friends and family, and Amanieu told me that the d'Albret men had long used it as a place to conduct lustful liaisons with other men's wives. That is why it is called the Jealous Castle – from the feelings it arouses in all the cuckolded husbands.'

195

Tuck gave a discreet cough. 'That is a fascinating story, my dear Nur,' he began, 'and it may well be true in some ways, but I have heard a less romantic version of the naming of Casteljaloux. A learned friend of mine in Bordeaux, an elderly monk who has a particular interest in nomenclature, told me that the name came from the Latin "Castrum Gelo" – "Frozen Castle" – so named because the River Avance that runs by the castle is unusually cold.'

I saw a flicker of annoyance pass across Nur's brow, but before she could speak, Roland said, 'I think Nur's tale is more likely to be true. Frozen Castle: what an absurd name. Who would call their home that? No, I'm sure that Nur has it right.'

I was watching Nur's brown eyes above the veil as Roland said his piece, and I swear they glowed a little with gratitude.

The next morning at dawn Sir Nicholas left us, fully armed and mailed, and riding the best of the nags that Robin had bought in Bordeaux. Before he climbed on to his mount, he clasped my hand and said quietly to me, 'Never fear, Alan, we shall have our revenge on the Master, whatever Locksley says. From what I hear, he is a piece of heretical filth whose works are a foul stain on Christendom. We shall send the Master to face the judgment of God, soon enough, you have my word on it.'

An hour later, Tuck took his departure, bearing nothing but a tall staff of oak and a small linen bag of clothes and food. As I watched him walk away through the close-set trees towards the road, looking the very image of a poor, wandering monk, I noticed that there was a certain springiness to his step that I had not seen for some years. And it occurred to me that for a long time Tuck had lived a rather dull existence as the chaplain of a great lady – and he was relishing this chance to take part in a grand adventure. I was happy for him.

Nur, swathed in her customary black, though now much travel-stained by salt-water and dust, slipped away shortly after Tuck had gone. Roland called after her disappearing form, urging her not to take any unnecessary risks. And, to my surprise, she glanced back at him, just once, before vanishing quite suddenly among the thick trees only a dozen paces from the camp.

For two days we heard nothing. Thomas and I tended to our weapons and armour, scrubbing and scraping at rust spots on our hauberks, which had bloomed there during the long sea journey from England. We laid them all out on a cloak on the ground and sharpened and polished the blades, oiled my mace and the leather chest-plate and holster for the lance-dagger, and checked straps on our shields and repainted the surfaces to make my personal blazon, the image of a black wild boar, stand out afresh on the red background.

With my war gear spread out on a cloak on the ground, I was painfully aware of how little I owned. Much had been destroyed at Westbury during the fire – a decade of accumulated possessions – and many things that I had treasured were lost for ever. Apart from Shaitan, who was no doubt taking his ease in Sherwood and terrifying Robin's outlaw-grooms with his big teeth and lethal hooves, this motley collection of metal, wood and leather lying before me – all of which I could easily carry on my back – was my entire worldly goods. For a knight who had once been lord of a prosperous manor, and the companion of a great king, it was pitiful.

I had plenty of leisure to fret about Goody. Did she still live? She had been very close to death when I had left her. Would I be able to find the Grail in time to save her from Nur's curse? Would the Grail even be able to save her? I had no answers to any of these questions, and they chased themselves around and around in my head from dawn until dusk.

On the afternoon of the third day, a Sunday, Robin, Gavin and Little John went out into the wood with their war bows in search of fresh meat for the pot, and Roland, Thomas and I stirred ourselves to practise our swordplay. Anything, I thought, to take my mind off Goody. We took it in turns to pair up and fence, the third man acting as an umpire. Roland was recovering swiftly from his wound – whatever magic or medicine Nur was using was proving more than efficacious and, apart from a little stiffness in his movements, you could hardly tell that it was less than a week since he had been injured. But it was Thomas who truly impressed me with his skill – overcoming Roland's guard twice in a pair of lightning passes. He'd been with me as a squire for seven years, I realized, and it was time to begin thinking of making him a knight. Certainly he had all the prowess of one.

My thoughts were interrupted a little before dusk by the appearance of Nur. I do not believe it was witchcraft, just superior fieldcraft – she had, after all, spent many years living in the wild – but the woman was suddenly among us, as if she had popped up from beneath the soil, standing beside me as I watched Roland and Thomas exchange half-strength sword cuts. One moment she wasn't there, the next she was.

'Your boy Thomas is very nimble,' she said casually, in her sing-song voice, as if we had been in the midst of a long, intimate conversation, 'but my Roland would surely kill him swiftly in a real fight – he has the longer reach.'

I don't know if I was more surprised by her sudden appearance, or by her apparent expertise in the arts of war, or by the fact that she referred to the young blond French knight with the large burn-scar on his face as 'my Roland'. I found myself babbling something about the leverage possible for a shorter man with a low centre of his weight, if he moved his feet properly, when she interrupted me, cutting straight through my words with a brusqueness that bordered on insolence.

'Yes, most interesting, Alan,' she said. 'Now, where is Robin? I must speak with him urgently.'

As I was gaping, speechless with astonishment – for this was a wreck of a woman, an outcast witch, who only weeks before had called me 'my love' and now she was treating me as if I were an irritating child – I spied Robin, Little John and Gavin coming towards us through the trees, John bearing the limp form of a fallow deer carcass across his broad shoulders, and the three of them wearing expressions of deep satisfaction.

That satisfaction was instantly dispelled, like woodsmoke in a whirlwind, for the first thing that Nur said after Robin had greeted her was: 'Bad tidings, lord. Sir Nicholas has been taken.'

Chapter Fourteen

'The town of Jealous Castle is roughly square in shape,' said Nur, drawing with a stick in the pine needle-covered forest floor. The deer carcass had been slung from a stout branch and we were all gathered around by the fire as she told us what she had gleaned from her time spent begging in the main square.

'Here is the *freezing* River Avance to the east' – she drew a gently wiggling line in the pine needles – 'and here are the town walls.' She drew a rough square adjacent to and west of the river. 'The castle is here,' she said, stabbing in the centre of the square, roughly the middle of the town. 'And it is very strong – thick stone battlements three times as tall as a man and patrolled by many sentries, perhaps a dozen. A square tower on the north-west corner of the castle forms the keep, and look-out is kept up there at all times. This is where Sir Nicholas is being held.'

We all leaned forward to take in the layout of the castle, the lines in the dirt clear-cut in the flickering flames of the campfire, and Robin said gently, 'Tell us what happened, Nur.'

The witch nodded. 'Some of this I saw with my own eyes from my begging place. Some of this I was told by Father Tuck this afternoon, and some I had by asking a maiden at the market who wanted a love-charm.'

Nur pointed with her stick to the rough plan of the town and drew a small rectangle in front of the castle. 'Here is the square, and here I sat this morning', and she stabbed a spot on its eastern side.

'Sir Nicholas had met with the castle knights and had spent two days in their company but today he had evidently been asked to demonstrate his skills in the square – as an entertainment in front of the Seigneur d'Albret and his men—'

'D'Albret was there?' interrupted Robin. 'You saw him yourself?' Nur nodded. 'And he did not recognize you?'

Nur gave a short dry cackle. 'He would not know me as I look today. I am certain of that.' She laughed again. 'But I saw him today and spat in his shadow as it passed my begging place.'

'And the knights – what blazon did they wear?' asked Robin.

'Some wore the colours of Casteljaloux – black and gold. And some wore white surcoats with a blue cross inside a black border.

'Knights of Our Lady. Good,' said Robin. 'Go on.'

'The crowds gathered and around mid-morning they watched Sir Nicholas defeat three local men-at-arms, with the greatest of ease, one after the other. The Seigneur d'Albret congratulated him personally and embraced him. And they walked together towards the castle until stopped by a man-at-arms, a dusty, mailed man on horseback, a man who I believe had just arrived in the town. This man pointed at Sir Nicholas and began to shout angrily at him. I could not hear what was said but I was told afterwards that the name of Westbury was spoken. And also that of Sir Alan Dale. And then a large number of other knights fell on Sir Nicholas, and though he struggled like a hero, they subdued him and dragged him inside the castle. And I did not see him again.'

'This is a serious blow,' said Robin, he looked half-angry. 'But Westbury is so far away . . . Still, I should have considered the possibility that someone could recognize Sir Nicholas' – he was thinking furiously – 'a mistake. My mistake . . .' Robin gathered himself. 'Can you tell us more, Nur?'

'Father Tuck made some enquiries as soon as Sir Nicholas was taken. As a man of God, he has the freedom to go where he will in Casteljaloux. He talked to some of the guards there and this afternoon he told me that Sir Nicholas has been accused of being a spy in the pay of their enemies. He is being held in the castle, in the dungeon below the tower. And they have been questioning him.'

I felt a shudder ripple down my spine at that word and memories of my own time under 'questioning' came flooding back – a time when red-hot irons had been applied to my tenderest regions. The recollection of that agony made my gorge rise.

'We must get him out of there immediately,' I said. 'He is a Companion of the Grail and we cannot leave him to the mercy of the Master. It is our duty to rescue him as soon as we can.'

There was a growl of agreement from the gathered men.

'Yes,' said Robin. 'The sooner we rescue him, the less likely he is to reveal our presence here.'

'Sir Nicholas would never willingly give you away!' I was outraged by Robin's suggestion that our friend would betray us.

'Maybe. I do not think he cares for me overmuch,' said Robin. 'But, no matter, all men, even the very bravest, talk under torture. It is merely a question of time. It is my fault that he is in this predicament, and I must get him out. We go in tonight.'

Two hours after sunset, we were all crouched on the edge of the forest, a mere hundred yards from the walls of the town of Casteljaloux, each Companion more or less behind the trunk of a pine tree. The smell of resin was strong and clean in my nose, and a bead of sweat ran down my spine, but my belly felt hollow, light and cold, as it often does before an action.

The town itself lurked before us, a mass of darkness against the skyline, but with a faint orange-pinkish glow above it. Although most townsfolk would have retired to their homes at that hour, light from hearth fires, tapers and tallow candles leaked from the shutters of their windows to lighten the darkness ever so slightly above their habitations. I could just make out the square bulk of the high tower that stood guard over the castle courtyard – and wondered if the look-out was asleep or drunk, or wide wake and even now gazing in our direction, and frowning at the unusual humped shapes that he could see against the darkness of the forest. I shivered, ducked down further behind the tree trunk, and took a firm hold of my sword hilt.

We had left all the horses, our mounts and the three laden packhorses, securely fastened to a fallen tree about fifty yards behind us. And Little John had marked a path to them through the forest by stripping a small section of the bark from a dozen trees with his axe so that, even at night, if the bright three-quarter moon and the cloudless star-filled sky lasted, we'd be able to find our way by following the white flash of the naked wood.

Robin had little in the way of a plan, but the little he had he had explained concisely to us after we had packed up the camp. Tuck would let us in by a postern gate in the south-western corner of the wall of the town – that much had been arranged that afternoon between Tuck and Nur. We would cover our weapons and mail in the loose robes of Benedictine monks, which Tuck would provide for us having stolen them from the Abbey. We would then proceed, led by Tuck, to the castle where we would affect an entrance by guile, or if that failed, by brute force. We would then locate Sir Nicholas and free him. We would fire the castle, the keep and as many of the houses of the town as we could and, in the confusion, we would make our escape out of the same postern gate and back to our horses.

'If we encounter the Master or the Grail – we may change our plans accordingly,' said Robin. 'But the priority is to get Sir Nicholas out and safely away. We all need to stay together. If anybody becomes separated from the rest of us, he is to exit the town by the postern gate, or any other way he can, and make his way back to the horses. Does everybody understand?'

It was a threadbare plan, I privately noted. There was much that depended on chance and much that could easily go wrong. But if we all stayed together, there was a slim chance of success. And I had to admit that I could not think of a better plan at such short notice. The longer Sir Nicholas was in the hands of our enemies, the more dangerous our situation would become. We had to act, put our trust in our fighting skills and our lives in the hands of God.

Robin had also decreed that every Companion should accompany him on the rescue attempt. 'If we have to battle our way out, and I think we might, we'll need every blade we have,' he said grimly.

'What about Nur?' asked Roland. 'Surely the lady should not be exposed to the dangers of battle?'

Robin simply asked Nur if she wished to come with us, or remain in the forest with the horses, and when she said that she wished to come, he overruled Roland's objections. Later, in the last, low gleams of daylight, just before we left the campsite and started towards Casteljaloux, I noticed Little John offering her a choice of weapons, and saw the witch choose a vicious hatchet, which she fingered for a moment, feeling the edge of the wedge-shaped blade with her thumb, before tucking it in her belt.

Guided by Nur, we had made our way for two miles through the dim forest towards the western side of the town. She led us with total self-assurance through the tangled undergrowth and between the tall trees, and we followed in single file, on foot and leading our horses, all of us linked by a long rope and trying to be as quiet as possible. Even though it was not a pitch dark night, I never discovered exactly how Nur knew how to pick the right path through the trees like that – and I asked myself once again whether she might truly have some other-worldly power – but she did it, and by the time we had secured the horses, and that big three-quarter moon was high above the tree tops, we found ourselves peering out from the wall of scented pines at a dark, forbidding portion of the town walls.

We did not wait there long. At Robin's whispered command, we crept slowly forwards, first through some scrubland and then stumbling over a knee-high wattle fence into a large kitchen garden, freshly planted with tender shoots of leeks and onions. I tried my best not to break the delicate plants beneath my earth-clotted boots, for I reckoned that some poor husbandman and his family might be depending upon this very crop for survival – but, from time to time, the sharp, homely smell of crushed alliums wafted up, pungent in the darkness.

Then, a flare of light to the right of our line of march, a square candle-lantern, seeming to spring out from the blackness of the walls. I could see a squat round body and a large round head behind it, the features made weird and demonic by the guttering yellow light. It was Father Tuck, and we hurried towards him, greeted him in excited whispers, and he pulled us through a small, narrow door, the postern gate, and inside the walls of Casteljaloux.

As we passed through, Tuck handed each one of us a thick black woollen robe and a cowl from two soft heaps on the ground, and we all wrapped them around us as quickly as we could, tied them with a length of knotted rope and pulled the shapeless, scratchy cowls over our heads. We were in a small square with tall timbered houses on three sides and a narrow alleyway leading north. The square stank of ancient piss, and worse, but the houses were locked up dark and quiet and there was not a townsman or an enemy man-at-arms in sight. Nevertheless, I found that my pulse was banging loudly in my ears and my mouth was dry and chalky.

The robes were extremely voluminous, which was good fortune

for Little John and his vast frame but less so for Nur. She held the enormous garment up to her skinny chest and it still puddled around her feet on the cobblestones. So she contemptuously tossed it aside and simply pulled the cowl over her head and shoulders. Her own sombre everyday dress was close enough to our new clerkly attire to pass in the darkness of the streets.

Tuck bolted the door behind us and pushed us into in a double column, two files of four, the formation that genuine monks used while travelling. Just before we moved off, as we stood looking at each other in our new robes, I was able to catch a glimpse of the faces of all the Companions, and I can remember that brief glance at my friends quite vividly to this day – Robin looking stern and noble; Little John openly grinning with delight at the prospect of the battle; Gavin seeming apprehensive and thin-faced, but hiding his fears like a good soldier; Roland's visage grim and purposeful as befits a man with a hard task ahead; Thomas radiating a quiet calm and the unyielding solidity of an oak stump; Tuck's mien was eager, almost boyish; and Nur – her dark, blank eyes looked out at us with the implacability of an executioner.

The streets of Casteljaloux were deserted at that hour, perhaps nine of the clock, as we hurried north in our double column behind Tuck and Robin – the town eerily quiet save for the muffled tolling of a church bell and the lonely calls of a watchman some streets away, calling out to all the sleeping burghers that all was well.

After no more than a hundred paces, Tuck led us out of the narrow streets and we turned into a large market square. It was a vast black space, now empty of the myriad stalls and carts that must have filled it by day, and on its far side I could make out the block-like shape of the castle itself. There were a few slim, vertical lights showing through the arrows slits in the walls in the high tower and I could see the silhouette of a single man-at-arms walking on the battlements. As we approached the main gate, to my surprise, it opened and half a dozen men-at-arms in the white surcoats of the Knights of Our Lady came out striding purposefully, three of them carrying bright pine-wood torches. They did not wear mail but soft tunics of fine material under their surcoats, and each had a long sword hung around his waist. We were walking directly towards them, and I confess that my heart was pounding so wildly I almost missed my step – I did not know what to do. Should we pause and let them pass, or fumble through our robes and pull our weapons? I was walking directly behind Tuck, in the second rank, and I was utterly shocked by his loud hail of 'God bless you, good sirs, and keep you in His grace!' when the Knights of Our Lady were within only a few yards of us.

The men-at-arms returned with a chorus of 'God be with you, Brothers', and they briskly walked away without giving us a second glance. I began to relax – in our black robes and cowls, and with Tuck's utter self-confidence as our blazon, it was quite clear that we eight interlopers were easily accepted as rightful denizens of Casteljaloux.

And, better still, the gate of the castle was wide open before us. As we approached, I saw that another group of soldiers – four men this time, likewise also in the surcoats of our enemies – were about to leave the courtyard of the castle, striding out in their fine clothes with torches in their hands and swords on their hips, and a total disregard for the security of their citadel. Our black cowls pulled well forward, we crossed paths with them on the very threshold of the castle, Tuck calling out a jolly salutation as the two bodies of men passed each other, one going in and one going out. And we were inside. I could hardly believe it. If only the tower, looming on the far side, the north-eastern side of the castle, would prove as easy to penetrate.

Yet we were challenged, after a fashion, as we walked across the courtyard towards the keep, still in our double column. A man-at-arms, a small balding fellow in a red and gold tunic who was clearly drunk, stumbled into our path and, after greeting Tuck like an old and trusted friend, asked him in passable French if we had seen a big bastard of a sergeant called Fournier. Tuck greeted him in a friendly way and informed him courteously that he had not and, in turn, asked the man whether the Captain of the Tower was to be found at his post.

'Not him,' slurred the man in a reasonable approximation of Tuck's French. 'He's gone to St Mary's with all the other bigwigs. They're all there for the initiation ceremony – all those high and mighty foreign knights are there, along with our good Seigneur. It's not right, Father, not right at all. I've heard they get up to all manner of ungodly tricks at these initiations, blasphemy, trampling the Cross . . . begging your pardon, Father, but I think it's a sinful debauch that—'

'So who is holding the Tower, then?' Robin interrupted from inside his deep cowl.

'Oh, it's only old Guilhabert, the turnkey,' the man said.

'Would you be good enough to take us to him?' Tuck asked. 'We need to speak to him on a matter of the gravest importance.'

It really was that simple. We were a gaggle of harmless-looking Benedictine monks, led by a roly-poly, happy-faced priest who was personally known to one of the castle's men-at-arms. We were in.

The friendly and slightly drunken man-at-arms – Tuck called him Sabatier – happily escorted us to the base of the tower and hammered on an arched wooden door reinforced with iron studs.

'Hey, Guilhabert, wake up,' shouted the man. 'I have some mos' distinguished guests for you . . .' He winked at me in the second rank, and I smiled back at him in a suitably pious manner.

There was no response from inside, and our friend hammered again, and again, and bawled out the same message until, finally, the door opened a crack and a grizzled head poked out and I found I was looking into the face of an astoundingly ugly old man, who had evidently just been awakened.

208

'What do you want, Sabatier, you dog?' growled the man. 'I've had enough of your tomfoolery for today. Go away and sleep it off.' He caught sight of the eight cowled figures behind the man-at-arms and his eyes opened fully in surprise.

In half a heartbeat, Robin was through the door. He had the shocked old jailer in an armlock and was forcing him backwards into the dim interior of the tower. The man was beginning to squawk in alarm, when I stepped into him and seized his lean, unshaven jaw in my left hand, cutting off his attempts at speech. My right held my long misericorde with its needle tip pressed into the pouched, grey skin below his eye.

'Make another noise,' I hissed, 'and you die.'

The other dark-clad Companions were bundling into the tower. Sabatier was still on the lip of the doorway, staring at us in astonishment, and I saw Little John, at the end of our column, slap a hand over his gaping mouth and pick him up bodily and carry him inside. Roland slammed the door behind him, and we were all inside the keep.

And, so far, undetected.

It was ill-lit. A single candle stood on a table on the left-hand side of the square room. A three-legged stool bore a pair of iron manacles, a crust of bread and a leather cup of ale. A rumpled cot on the right indicated the place from which Guilhabert had been disturbed. And that was it. But the room was growing lighter, I suddenly realized – a man was coming down the stone staircase in the back left corner of the room bearing a wavering light and soon enough I heard him calling out: 'Guilhabert, who is that with you down there?'

The grizzled jailer, writhing suddenly in Robin's arms, tore his face from my hand before I could react, and bellowed, 'Roger! To arms . . .' And I twisted my wrist and whipped the round pommel of my misericorde hard into the side of his head There was a faint crack of bone and the man went limp and slipped to the floor.

But by then we were fighting. Men-at-arms were tumbling down the stairs from above; one . . . two . . . three . . .

We were hampered a little by our thick robes, but I managed to get the oak shaft of my flanged mace out from my belt and into my right hand and transfer the misericorde to my left. I broke the upper arm of the first man down the stair with a crushing strike from my right hand; he screamed once, a horrible high girlish sound, and his sword clattered on the steps. The second man, right on his heels, jumped down into the room, yelling madly and waving a long spear at Robin.

My lord said, 'Be silent, sir', dodged a vicious jab at his face from the spear, stepped past the haft and plunged his sword right through the man's throat. The next fellow in a black and gold surcoat who jumped into the room and blundered forward waving a sword was immediately seized around the chest by Roland, who neutralized him by wrapping both arms around him tightly and lifting him off his feet. Little John reached forward and grasped his skull with his two big hands and, with a sharp twist, broke his neck. Roland allowed him to flop to the floor. I crushed the skull of the man whose arm I had broken, who was sobbing on his knees before me, with a single downward swipe of the mace – and we were in silence, save for the ragged panting of some of the Companions and the shuffling limbs of my victim as he lay in the floor and twitched his last few moments away on this earth.

'Gavin,' said Robin. 'Quick now. Look outside and see if the alarm has been raised.'

Sabatier had been shocked into total stillness. He just stood by the door with his mouth open and his empty hands hanging loosely by his sides as Gavin pushed roughly past him and stuck his head out of the solid arched door. The fight had taken less than five heartbeats. Tuck went over to the terrified little soldier, all the cheap wine and good humour now flown from his body, and said kindly, 'Sabatier, you will not be harmed if you help us – and if you do not try to shout out for aid. Tell me now: where is the prisoner being held?'

The man dumbly shook his head.

'All quiet outside,' called Gavin from the door.

'Where is the knight who calls himself Peter of Horsham being held?' asked Tuck again. He shook Sabatier briefly by the shoulders. 'Is he being kept below?' Our stout priest gestured towards a set of stone steps in the far corner of the room that led down into darkness.

But Thomas was ahead of the rest of us. He'd found a stub of candle, ignited it from the one on the table and was halfway down the stair.

'I don't know, Father,' mumbled the frightened man. 'I honestly don't know. The foreign knights took him away this afternoon. They went to the Chapel of St Mary the Virgin, I think. I could not say for certain . . .'

'There is no one in the cells below,' said Thomas, emerging from the dark stairwell like a swimmer from the sea. At the same time, Little John's bulk stepped out from the stairs leading upwards, and he clumped towards Robin.

'He's not here,' the big man said flatly. 'Not anywhere.'

Robin stalked over to the little man-at-arms and stood looking down at him for a few moments without speaking. The poor man seemed to quail under Robin's blank metallic gaze.

'Where is the Chapel of St Mary the Virgin?' he asked quietly. 'Is it near here?'

'Yes, sir,' whimpered the little man. 'A few hundred yards, no more, at the end of the street of the parchment-makers, near the western wall. Not very far, sir . . .'

'I know it,' said Tuck. 'It's the chapel in the crypt below St Peter's Church. Though I have not been inside.'

'How many knights are there?' my lord said. His eyes were boring into Sabatier.

'I do not know, sir. Perhaps a dozen, a score . . . I cannot truly say . . . Please do not kill me, sir, I beg . . .'

Robin turned away. I caught a glimpse of his expression; he looked utterly serene, like a man on a peaceful Sunday stroll. But I knew he could not truly be that calm. 'Right, everyone,' he said. 'Back into robes and cowls; weapons out of sight. We're leaving.'

'Shall I silence this one, sir?' asked Gavin. He was standing behind the little man-at-arms with a long dagger in his hands.

Robin looked at him and, for a moment, I thought he would give the lethal order. Then he said, 'Tie him up and gag him.'

Outside the tower, we formed up again in our double column, with Tuck and Robin at the front. But, as we shuffled across the courtyard, I saw with a sinking heart that a pair of men-at-arms in the colours of Casteljaloux were in the process of swinging the gates closed. As we approached, the man on the right, a junior officer of some kind, ceased his labours with the door halfway closed and marched up to us, demanding to know who we were and what our business was in the castle.

'God be with you, good sir, on this fine evening,' said Tuck. 'My brothers and I have come from the Abbey and we have been visiting our honest friend Guilhabert in the tower . . .'

The man was suspicious. I saw him look at Nur, smaller than all the rest of us by some margin, and in the torchlight of the courtyard, it was easy to see that her black gown was not cut from the same cloth as our robes.

'Guilhabert is a Godless bastard; he has no friends at the Abbey. I'd be surprised to learn that he has any friends at all. Stay exactly where you are. Do not move.' He half-turned towards the other man. 'Pierre, go and fetch Sergeant Fournier from the—' And he got no further.

Tuck pulled back his big round head, went up on his toes and smashed his forehead into the bridge of the officer's nose, powering through skin, gristle and bone, dropping the man unconscious on the ground like a dropped sack of onions. It was a move that I frankly did not know the old priest had in him – and then we were all running for the half-open gate. The second man-at-arms ran towards us, and Little John planted a beautiful right-handed punch on his cheekbone as we passed him, hurling him backwards off his feet, and we were through the gates and sprinting for the darkness on the other side of the square.

We gathered panting, laughing, wheezing, all of us in a huddle, two streets and a couple of hundred paces away. There was no sound of pursuit, barely a sound at all in the quiet streets. But it could only be a matter of time; then every man in Casteljaloux would be on us like a swarm of wasps on a honeycomb.

'What now, Robin?' asked Roland. 'Do we cut and run? We can get out by the postern gate and be away before the castle troops get properly organized. We could come back and try again another day?'

'No, we are not leaving this town without Sir Nicholas. If the Knights of Our Lady are holding an initiation at the Chapel of St Mary, the Master will surely be there – and so will the Grail. We still have a little time, I am sure, before this town becomes too hot for us. Take us to the chapel, Tuck. Everybody fit? Everybody ready? Good. Come on!'

My lord, I realized, was thoroughly enjoying himself.

A little while later, we were standing in a line in the moon shadow cast by the overhang of the second floor of a grand house in the street of the parchment-makers. We had abandoned our cowls and robes, and I was glad once again to have free access to Fidelity. Robin, who was standing beside Tuck by the corner of the street, beckoned me forward. He put his face close to my ear and whispered, 'A single sentry. By the entrance to the crypt yonder. Can you take him down quietly?'

213

I peeped around the corner, looking to my left, and saw a small, plain stone church and a lone man in mail with a tall spear and a shield slung on his back standing at the head of a set of steps that could just be made out disappearing down into darkness. He wore a white surcoat with a blue cross on the chest and a black border around it, and I noticed that the man swayed slightly from foot to foot as if in some slight discomfort. But he was alert and armed, and blocking our path.

'Well, I can try,' I said, and reached for my boot top and slid the misericorde into the left sleeve of my mail hauberk.

Robin grinned, his teeth white in the darkness, and clapped me on the shoulder. I touched my sword pommel for luck, and on jelly legs I attempted to stride nonchalantly towards the tall man-at-arms by the entrance to the little Chapel of St Mary the Virgin. I had taken no more than five paces, and was still a good fifteen yards from the sentry, before I knew that I had already failed in my task.

'You, sir. Halt, sir. What is your business here?' called the soldier loudly, speaking French with the accent of Maine, his voice echoing around the empty space before the chapel.

I had an insane urge to make a shushing noise to quiet him but instead, I answered in the same language in a normal tone.

'Am I too late for the ceremony? My damned shield strap broke and I wasted time trying to find another. Then my squire spilled wine down my surcoat. I know I'm improperly dressed but the Seigneur will have my hide if I miss the service.'

These words were a feeble subterfuge, of course, but they were just enough to carry me across the space between the wall where my comrades lurked and the sentry. From his point of view – assuming that he had not yet heard about the fight in the tower – I was an incompetent idiot who only wanted to attend a church service. The sentry did not know me by sight, and yet he heard me speaking good French with a Norman accent, and saw that I

214

was dressed as a knight, and he naturally assumed that, like him, I had recently been recruited to the Master's banner from somewhere in the north. He smiled and relaxed.

'They have just started,' he said, 'but if you are quiet you could slip in and stand at the back, and I'm sure nobody would notice.' He turned side on to me and pointed to a dark opening in the cobbles of the street and I saw a set of steps leading downwards. 'The entrance is down there . . .'

I reached for my left sleeve and the handle of the misericorde slipped easily into my right fist. As he turned away to indicate the steps, the eight-inch long blade shot upwards behind his head and fell like an axe, driven by all the considerable power of my right arm, the needle point slamming into the place where his neck joined his shoulder. The weapon punched straight through his iron-link mail and down, down deeply into his chest until the narrow blade pierced his heart. It happened almost faster than thought; in fact, I truly felt as if another man were doing the deed, not myself – perhaps the spirit of my murderous old Bavarian friend Hanno, acting through me. The unfortunate man, a kindly soul I am sure, made a kind of choking gasp and I slapped my free hand over his mouth to stifle any further outcry, but I need hardly have bothered, he died almost silently as the long blade of the misericorde delved into his chest cavity, his legs spasming a little as his soul ebbed away with the merest trickle of blood that pooled in his collar bone and spilled down over his mailed chest. As I gently lowered the corpse to the floor, I heard the scuffle and stamp of running feet and then Companions were all around me.

'It's down there,' I said, pointing at the steps. 'The ceremony has already started but . . .'

By then Little John was already past me. There was a flash of silver in the moonlight from his axe blade, as the big man leaped down into the darkness. A noise of a heavy blade carving into living flesh, once, twice, and a sharp cry of agony abruptly cut off.

215

And the Companions were piling after John, like a river of mailed men flowing into a drain. I wiped my misericorde clean on the dead man's surcoat, muttering a brief prayer for God's forgiveness, and sheathed it once again in my boot. I stood upright, pulled Fidelity from its scabbard and made to follow my comrades down the stone steps into the crypt. Down the steps and into battle.

At the bottom of the stair was a wooden door, partly open, with yellow light spilling from it on to the gashed corpses of two mailed men in the white and blue surcoats of the Knights of Our Lady. From inside the crypt I could hear shouts of pain and the ring of steel on steel. I stepped over the bodies, went through the little door and into the underground chapel with my unsheathed sword in my hand and the blood thumping in my ears.

The crypt was a long, low stone room, with an altar at the far end, blazing with candles – but my first impression was of a scrum of men snarling like a pack of hounds around a wounded hart. The hart was not one beast but three men: Robin, Gavin and Little John, back to back, with a dozen armoured men in white and blue surcoats surrounding them, shouting insults and trading blows. To my left, Roland was fencing with a tall knight, and despite his wounded leg, I could see he had the upper hand; to my right, Thomas had his sword blade embedded in a man's throat, and as I stepped into the crypt, he ripped it out with a shout of triumph. Tuck was under siege from two swordsmen, and he was only fending them off with his long oak staff with some difficulty. Nur jumped nimbly on to the back of one of the men raining sword blows down on Tuck, put a skinny white arm around his neck and began to batter at his bare head with her hatchet.

At the far end of the chamber a man dressed only in off-white linen braies was trussed to a door-sized wooden board set vertically beside the altar; his chest was naked, well muscled and scarred like a galley-slave's and he was gagged and held firmly in place by thick ropes. It was Sir Nicholas – and two paces from him, standing stock still behind the candle-bearing altar and gazing calmly, even arrogantly over the bloody mêlée that had broken out in the chapel, was a tall knight of middle years, flanked by two terrified-looking priests. The man, who had a vast black beard jutting from his jaw, a thin filet of gold holding back his springy black hair, and who wore the gold and black surcoat of Casteljaloux, seemed unnaturally composed, considering the chaos that had engulfed his initiation ceremony. It was not hard to guess that this was Amanieu d'Albret, the Seigneur of the Jealous Castle, the man who had tormented Nur.

All this I took in in two or three fast heartbeats – and then I took a deep breath, stepped forward and began to kill.

Chapter Fifteen

I took a firm double grip on the handle of Fidelity and waded into the battle like a man charging into the sea. My first blow struck the head clean off the knight who was grappling with Tuck, and I saw then that I had intervened just in time; blood was shining wetly at my old friend's waist and there was a flapping rip in his robe. I killed a wounded man who blundered towards me with a bloody dagger in his fist – a straight-arm lunge to the throat – and stepped into the centre of the mêlée, trying to move towards the altar and the Seigneur d'Albret's place behind it. I took out one of the knights in the jostling ring around Robin and Little John – a simple downward hack that split his skull. And then dropped another knight who had his back to me with a strike to the calf that nearly severed the lower part of his leg.

And then I was fighting for my life.

Two Knights of Our Lady peeled away from Robin and John and came for me at the same time, one either side. I attacked them both – swinging Fidelity back and forth above me, crashing down heavy blows at their heads like a frenetic overhead pendulum, giving them no time to do anything but block, before changing rhythm abruptly and smashing the steel crosspiece of my sword in the right-hand man's mouth. He screamed and dropped, teeth scattering like spilled peas, and on the back swing I carved my blade deep into the other man's chest.

I saw Robin eviscerate a knight with a perfectly elegant stroke, and as he came staggering towards me with his guts in his hands I ended him with a double-handed slice that took his head.

Then, as if I were in a strange dream or nightmare, I found that Nur was beside me, her veil gone and her mutilated, horrible, anguished face looking up at mine. She was shrieking and pointing: 'Alan, Alan – there is d'Albret. There! Get him for me, go towards him, Alan. You must get him for me! I beg you!'

I saw that she was pointing at the far end of the chapel where the Seigneur d'Albret had deigned to join the battle. He was holding off both Roland and Gavin with a sword in one hand and a mace in the other. And, as I watched, he blocked a mighty cross blow from Roland and managed to kick my cousin in the chest and send him reeling away to crash into the wall of the chapel, and almost at the same time, his left hand licked out and caught Gavin a glancing blow on the crown of his head that dropped him boneless to the floor.

The man could fight.

I surged towards d'Albret, with Nur at my heels still shrieking encouragement. Out of nowhere, a Knight of Our Lady lunged at me with his sword and I ducked under the lancing blade, and shoulder-charged the man, knocking him to the floor, but just as I was about to finish him, I found Nur tugging at my sword arm, almost hanging on it.

'Not him, Alan, not him. Don't waste time. Get d'Albret!'

I left the fallen man alive and moved forward, stepping over the prone body of Gavin, and now I was within a sword's length of the Seigneur d'Albret. He saluted me briefly, lifting his hilt to his lips, then attacked faster than a hunting weasel.

His sword arced in from the left at my head and, as I blocked the blow with Fidelity, fist up, blade below, my body turned side on to his, his mace thudded into my back, just over the middle of my spine. It hurt like a kick from a fear-crazed horse. But the double protection of my mail coat and the square leather plate beneath it was enough to save me from harm. The man had given me a serious shock. He was fast. And he was very, very good.

I stepped back, and circled to the right. Wary, now.

'Kill him, Alan! Kill him, now!' Nur was still dancing around behind me, yapping like a lapdog.

A snatched glance to my left, and I saw that the floor was a gory carpet of reeking corpses, and feebly stirring bodies. One man was screaming horribly, then was suddenly silenced. Little John was crouched over Gavin, and I saw that the lad had his eyes open.

And d'Albret launched another devastatingly swift attack at me. A swing of his mace made me duck; then his sword speared straight forward and I scrambled right out of its path, and only just got my sword up in time to block his second mace strike, which would have smashed my skull to shards, had it landed.

Then I went on to the attack.

Two hard diagonal slices from right and then left forced him to block hurriedly and back up. I made as if to chop down hard vertically on the fancy gold-filet that adorned his black head and, as he automatically raised his sword to block, I kicked him hard in the fork of his crotch with my right boot, almost lifting him off his feet. He said something like 'Whuumph' and folded immediately, huddled on the floor like a newborn and clutching his belly. A jet of brown spew erupted from his mouth, and he was panting like a woman in childbirth.

Nur pushed past me, stood over the cowering man and lifted her hatchet. She said something in Arabic that I didn't catch, then smashed the axe down on to his back of his head. It was a relatively feeble blow, merely slicing off a flap of his scalp the size of my

220

hand. Gore spurted from severed vessels and immediately covered Amanieu's white face in a sheet of red. But Nur was nothing if not determined. She hacked down again and this time the wedge-shaped axe-blade stuck firmly into the Seigneur's red, glistening head-bone. Nur wrestled the hatchet loose with some difficulty and lifted the weapon and smashed it down again with a loud cry. The skull was penetrated this time and the little axe buried deep in the brain. He was surely dead. But Nur was still not satisfied. She levered the slick steel out of the wound and struck down again.

And again. And again.

I turned away and looked out over the chapel, trying to ignore the wet, rhythmical crunching noises behind me, and the joyous, wordless shrieks of a witch's bloody revenge.

There were no enemies still standing though I could see that a handful of our foes were alive, moaning and moving slowly on the floor. The place looked like an abattoir, blood spattered thickly on the whitewashed walls, the stink of fear and fresh shit heavy in the air. Robin was helping a dazed Roland to his feet and even Gavin seemed to able to sit up, with Little John's arm around his back. I caught Thomas's eye and he jerked a thumb silently at the door. I nodded, suddenly very weary. And Thomas slipped out of the crypt, pulling the door closed behind him.

'Thomas has gone to check outside,' I called over to Robin. 'It can't be long until the castle garrison comes for us.'

'He's not here. The bloody man is not here, and neither is the Grail!' Robin's face was a white mask. He rarely showed his anger, almost never. But raw fury was coming off him like smoke.

'Little John, stop fussing over Gavin and start dealing with the wounded,' said Robin. 'No quarter, absolutely none at all.'

I saw John give Robin a black look, but he said nothing and helped Gavin to his feet and went off to begin quietly murdering the few Knights of Our Lady who had survived.

I crossed over to Sir Nicholas, gagged and trussed to the wooden board by the altar, and began to cut him loose. He was shaken but largely unharmed – his face bore the marks of a beating but apart from those cuts and bruises he was perfectly whole. I took off my red surcoat and offered it to my friend to cover his nakedness, and he took it with gratitude. Robin came over to us as he was pulling the garment over his head; he handed Sir Nicholas a scabbarded sword with a belt.

'I thank you from the heart, my lord,' said Nicholas. He seemed embarrassed. 'I would have endured an unspeakable death but for your gallant rescue—'

Robin cut him off brusquely: 'Where is the Master? Where is the Grail? Why are they not here? They must have let something slip. You must have heard something in your time among them. It cannot all have been wasted.'

Sir Nicholas looked bemused at Robin's rudeness and then suddenly angry, but he answered civilly enough: 'The Master left this morning, a short time before I was imprisoned. I saw him ride off with a dozen men, all Knights of Our Lady, but I do not know where he went.'

Thomas put his head through the door of the crypt. 'They are coming, sir, a great crowd of them. Men-at-arms, knights, some militiamen from the town. Hundreds of them, sir.'

'Get in here, Thomas, and barricade the door,' I said. My weariness was gone, and in its place a cold terror. The words 'hundreds of them' were ringing in my ears.

'Where could he have gone to? Where would the Master go?' Robin was still speaking to Sir Nicholas.

'I don't know,' said Sir Nicholas. 'All I do know is that we need to get out of here right now. Or we will be caught and killed like rats in a trap. Did you not hear what young Thomas just said?'

I looked around that grim chapel, picturing it as I'd first seen it, and comparing it to now. There was something in the back of my mind that I was sure was important. What was it?

Thomas had bolted the door and was busy hauling the dead bodies of the Knights of Our Lady to pile against it. As a barricade, it would not hold long against a determined assault. They could burn the wooden door and burst through in less than half an hour, and then we would all be slaughtered.

'Where would he go?' Robin seemed to be talking to himself. 'Not north or west. No. East or maybe south.'

'Robin, we need to concentrate on this,' I said. 'The wrath of Casteljaloux, all of it, is about to fall on our heads.'

My lord looked at me and his eyes seemed to come into focus.

'Yes, we had better leave,' said Robin. 'There is clearly nothing for us here.'

'Robin,' I said, speaking slowly. 'We cannot get out of here, there are hundreds of armed men outside that door looking for vengeance. We are trapped. We're stuck in here and most likely we'll die in here.' I was very far from calm.

'Trapped?' said Robin. 'No, I don't think so. Take a look behind the altar. Go on, Alan, look behind the altar. You'll find something there to lift your spirits.'

And light dawned. The priests. When I had first seen the Seigneur d'Albret, he had been flanked by two priests. But when I looked again, they had disappeared.

I strode over to the altar and looked. There was nothing but empty space and a cheap, scruffy dun-coloured mat woven from bullrushes. I looked over at Robin, who was grinning at me like a demon, kicked angrily at the light mat . . . and it skidded away from its place to reveal a trapdoor set into the stone floor of the crypt.

'Thomas, help me here!' I shouted, and in moments my squire was standing beside me and we pulled open the flat, square door together and found ourselves peering into a black hole with a wooden ladder descending into darkness.

I grabbed a three-branched candelabrum from the altar and

lowered it into the hole. The air smelled musty and stale, and very strongly of raw earth and damp. But I could see very little. However, it seemed likely that there were no enemies waiting down there in the deep shadows to ambush us. Equally, there was no sign of the priests who had so suddenly disappeared, for by the wildly dancing light of the candles, I could just make out a narrow tunnel, man-height and broad enough for three men to walk abreast, that seemed to be leading to the west, stretching away into the darkness.

We did not tarry long in the crypt. Tuck, it seemed, could walk after a fashion. He had taken a sword cut that had sliced through the rolls of fat around his large belly. It was painful, to be sure, but Roland, who had strapped a clean pad of cloth over it, did not think that any vital organs had been punctured. He and Robin helped the old man to the trapdoor, and eased him down the ladder. Little John and Gavin followed them down – Gavin looking dazed, his head bandaged.

We only induced Nur to leave the crypt with a good deal of difficulty. She was bustling about from corpse to corpse, her hands, bloody to the wrist and wielding a small knife, busily engaged in lifting their clothing and rummaging around in the dead men's undergarments. I called to her urgently, told her that we must go but she ignored me and raised her hands with a yip of triumph and I saw she had a bloody lump of flesh in her fingers.

'What in God's name is she doing?' I asked Roland, who was beside me, about to climb down through the trapdoor.

'She says she is harvesting their manhood,' he said in a quiet tone, his face pale.

'What?'

'She says there is power in a fighting man's collops.' I stared at him in horror but he avoided my eyes.

Finally, we persuaded her to enter the trapdoor and I noticed an unmistakable air of satisfaction as she pushed past me and stepped on to the wooden ladder. A sodden linen bag hung from her shoulder bulging with her disgusting booty.

Behind me, Sir Nicholas, dressed in my red surcoat, with a stolen sword at his hip, was the last man to leave, closing the trapdoor behind him. And, as the square of light was snuffed out, I could hear the sounds of angry shouting from the crypt door, as the fighting men of Casteljaloux tried to heave it open against the bolt and the weight of half a dozen corpses. We hurried down the long tunnel, Robin leading the way, with an altar candelabrum lighting our way. I was at the end of the line and could hardly see anything ahead of me except the distant glow of Robin's candle some twenty yards ahead. At one point I tripped over the uneven earth floor and blundered into the back of Sir Nicholas, and he cursed mildly under his breath. But soon, I could see a grey circle of light beyond the bobbing candelabrum, and I knew with a huge sense of relief, like a vast burden being lifted from my shoulders, that we were very nearly free and clear.

The tunnel, we discovered, exited from the side of a high bank into a bramble thicket deep in the forest, far outside the walls of the town, and perhaps half a mile north of the place where we had left the horses. The forest was absolutely silent, the moon was still high and the sharp, pine-wood-perfumed air, which I sucked deep into my lungs, was as refreshing as a draught of mountain spring water. Looking back at the high walls of the town, some fifty yards behind us, it was difficult to imagine the scene of mutilation and carnage we had left in that small, underground House of God. There was no sight nor sound of pursuit – not yet – but our enemies were bound to know of the tunnel. It could not be long before a horde of men-at-arms came surging from that dark mouth in the bramble-covered bank.

Nur led us south, through the tall trees, to the place where we had left the horses, and we mounted immediately and moved off westwards, pushing deeper into the trackless wilderness of pine.

At dawn, we made camp in a small clearing, I would guess some six or seven miles from the town of Casteljaloux. I was exhausted – a night of combat and mortal fear had left me drained of all strength. I was ready to fall into my blankets and sleep for a year. Instead, we tended to the wounded as best we could and ate a few scraps of bread and dried meat, and drank watered wine from our flasks. And then we sat down in a circle to take counsel.

I was not the only one near the end of his strength. Gavin appeared to be in a deep stupor, with Little John trying from time to time to keep him awake by feeding him sips of wine; Tuck was huddled in his blankets with his eyes closed; Sir Nicholas's face, marked with overlapping bruises of blue and red, and black crusts of dried blood, looked some ten years older; while Roland and Thomas both had to stifle their yawns as Robin spoke. Nur sat apart, playing with her little bag of finger bones, casting them on to an old scrap of cloth and muttering over the patterns they made.

Only my lord of Locksley seemed unaffected by the rigours of the night before. Indeed, he looked indecently youthful and full of energy. 'Well, my friends, we have missed the Master, and the Grail,' he began. 'But we must not despair. We have slain a goodly number of our enemies and we are all still living.'

'We're not all exactly in prime condition,' growled John.

'No, that is true,' conceded Robin. 'And that is why we shall rest here for a full day, to give us time to tend our various hurts. But we are not beaten. No, my friends, we are very far from beaten. We have, indeed, achieved a victory of sorts. We have boldly entered the enemy's stronghold, rescued our comrade, slain his soldiers, and made our escape. We have won the first battle. In this war with the Master and his followers, we are winning!'

Winning? It did not feel like it. We were no closer to capturing the Grail, and time, I was conscious, was slipping away. In fact, we were worse off than we had been yesterday, for now, we did not know where the Master and the Grail were.

As he so often did, Robin seemed to be reading my thoughts: 'We all need to rest and recuperate, before we put our minds to whence the Master and his men might have fled . . .'

The bruised knight lifted a hand, and Robin stopped speaking and turned to him. 'Sir Nicholas?'

'I believe the Master has gone east,' he said.

'Indeed?' said Robin. 'And how do you know this? When I asked you last night—'

'Last night, last night I was not in my right mind . . .' Sir Nicholas cut straight through Robin's words. 'But I know this because the Seigneur d'Albret came to me after I was taken. His men stripped me and took turns to beat me with their fists while he watched and laughed, and asked me questions. All of which I refused to answer . . .' Sir Nicholas touched his battered face with a questing fingertip.

'They did not have the time for a more lengthy and sophisticated inquisition, praise God – and for your speedy rescue, my lord, I am eternally grateful – but, as he left me in that cell below the tower, d'Albret promised that in a few hours his newly initiated knights would dismember me as part of the ceremony – a blooding, he called it – and that my head would be cut off and set on a spike on the walls of the town, *facing east*, to greet the Master when he returned.'

'East,' said Robin. 'Thank you, Sir Nicholas.'

To my surprise, Tuck spoke then. His voice was stronger than I had expected, though I could tell he was in pain.

'East means Toulouse. The Master has gone there. Where else would he recruit knights to fight for his banner? The largest town to the east is Toulouse.'

'He could have gone further afield,' Roland said. 'Carcassonne or even Montpellier . . .'

227

'If he has gone further,' said Tuck, 'he would surely be obliged to pass through Toulouse and we might well get wind of him there.'

It was Nur who spoke next: 'The bones say eastwards. The Grail is to the east of here,' she said with extraordinary authority. 'The Grail is in Toulouse.'

Two days later, at midday, we found ourselves on the south bank of the Garonne, opposite a town that Tuck told us was called Tonneins. We were about to enter lands that for generations had been controlled by the Counts of Toulouse.

We had rested for a day at our temporary camp deep in the pine woods then packed up and headed east, looping far north around Casteljaloux and cutting through forest and farmland, avoiding all established roads, even drovers' tracks, which we were sure would be patrolled by armed men from the town, and eschewing all forms of human contact. Our mood was subdued, a little discouraged, by the time we reached the river, even though we now considered ourselves beyond the limit of the fury of the Jealous Castle.

Roland and Tuck were in considerable pain, even with their wounds tightly bound and travelling on horseback at a walking pace. Gavin was pale and ill but determined not to allow the crack to his pate to slow our pace, while John hovered around him like a vast, red-faced, mother hen. Only Nur was in a buoyant mood – after her revenge on d'Albret, she now carried his manhood, with a dozen or so others, in the sticky bag that banged against her hip as she rode along beside my cousin. As we paced the southern bank of the Garonne, she warbled a weird lilting Arabic song whose words I did not understand but which I assumed was some sort of bloodthirsty victory chant.

And Robin, as always, was determinedly cheerful.

'We have won a decisive battle, Alan,' insisted my lord of Locksley as we walked our horses beside the wide, slow-flowing expanse of brown water. 'The Master has been materially weakened.

He has lost many men – maybe as much as third of his total strength. And, after such a bloody defeat, his grip on his remaining followers must be loosened, perhaps fatally.'

'He also knows that we are coming for him. From now on, he will be on his guard,' I said gloomily. 'And he can still use the power and mystery of the Holy Grail to recruit more fighting men.'

'Maybe, maybe . . . but I feel it in my bones: we shall have him the next time, and the Grail, too. I am sure of it.'

The mighty trading city of Toulouse, set on a gentle bend of the Garonne, had high, well-defended walls and for the most part happy, healthy, wealthy inhabitants. But the first thing that struck us about that southern citadel was its colour. It was built, almost entirely it seemed, not from honest granite or limestone, but from slim, delicate orange-red bricks – and I swear to you that Toulouse glowed like a vast pink jewel on the horizon as we urged our tired horses towards it.

We approached from almost due west, having parted from the river near Agen. When we asked for news outside that little town, a frightened local villein tending a herd of pigs had told us that a party of *routiers* fifty strong had been raiding along the north bank of the Garonne and burning and looting like a pack of fiends from Hell – Mercadier's masterless men, I had no doubt. Out of the Casteljaloux frying pan and into a mercenary fire, I thought to myself. Robin, with a flinty glance at Roland, had decreed that to avoid the risk of encountering them, we should make our progress towards Toulouse by riding due south across forty miles of rich corn-growing land to Auch, then another forty miles due east through neat vineyards to enter the rose-bright city through its drab western suburb of Saint Cyprien.

And so we did.

As we crossed the river by the thoroughfare over the Pont Neuf, a little before noon on a bright Sunday, we heard all the church bells of the city ring prettily out in celebration – it was St George's Day, Tuck informed us – but although we knew it was in truth merely the jubilation customarily shown on a feast day, the place appeared to be happily welcoming us. The smooth pink walls of Toulouse stretched out before us like the widespread bare arms of a sun-kissed giantess, and when we had stated our business at the gatehouse to a jolly sergeant-at-arms and his men – we were pilgrims heading for Montpellier wishing to consult the learned doctors there – we were admitted to the narrow streets of the Cité. We asked the jovial warden if a party of knights, friends of ours, in white surcoats with a blue cross on the front, and commanded by a monk who called himself the Master, had passed through his gate. But the man merely shook his head and denied all knowledge of such a group. We pressed him to ask among his men-at-arms, and after a short delay, he returned from the guardhouse with a rueful shake of his head and some advice: 'If you seek tidings of your friends, go to the St George's Haberdashers' Fair in the big square by the Maison des Consuls in the heart of the Cité, and ask around. They sell more than fancy clothes and frilly folderols. They sell good wine and honest food – and information. Ask at the taverns. You might even be able to buy yourself a little love as well. Ha-ha. If you ask the right demoiselles!' And he roared with laughter as if his words were the drollest ever spoken.

Brick houses two or even three storeys high loomed over us on either side as we entered the Cité, glowing in the strong southern sunlight. Like the sergeant at the gate, even the lowliest denizens of Toulouse seemed to have a happy, ruddy light to their faces as they flowed with us in huge numbers towards the centre of the town, play-fighting, singing and calling jests loudly to their fellows in the Langue d'Oc, the musical tongue of that land. We decided that we would first seek information at the Haberdashers' Fair and then head for the northern area known as the Bourg, which housed the town's richer merchants, and also the cathedral of

St-Sernin, where the gatekeeper had told us that we might conceivably find lodgings in the dormitory.

We scarcely needed to touch spur to horse for the crowd was enough to carry us along like a great jostling tide. And, by good fortune, having shouted out a few questions to the throng, we knew we were being carried in the right direction. After a while, we found ourselves entering an enormous space in the centre of Toulouse that seemed to contain half the population of Christendom. Here, clearly, was the great St George's Day Haberdashers' Fair. Hundreds of carts filled the middle of the square, piled with thick woollen cloth dyed a homely rusty red or bolts of snowy linen, or mounds of fine lace, ribbons fluttering from poles like miniature pennants, and even a few rolls of bold silks in sky blue and grass-green. All the haberdashery carts were arranged in two rows. Around the outside, squeezed between bustling taverns, were the shopfronts of the permanent haberdashers', their counters displaying parti-coloured hose, and long robes of velvet, magnificent hats adorned with the long feathers of exotic birds, worked-leather jerkins – more than the eye could take in at once. The noise was enormous and continuous, bewildering after the peace of the countryside – a babbling, rainbow sea of humanity; the merchants crying their wares, the Toulousain men and women strolling about in their own saint's day finery, buying goods, fingering the fine cloth, arguing and laughing and shouting greetings to their friends. Long ago I had acquainted myself with the language of these southern lands, and, in truth, it was not so far removed from French as to seem utterly outlandish. Indeed, most of the Companions could make sense of it, but even so, the strange, twangy Toulousain accent occasionally defeated my ears – although that may have been partly the assault of the colour and noise and the sheer numbers of people. The heavenly smell of onions frying in pork fat broke in upon my senses just then, causing my stomach to give a start of joy. It had been many hours since we'd broken our fast.

231

We tethered our horses at a tavern on the northern side of the square and, while the rest of the Companions took their ease in the shade at a long communal table under the overhang of the upper storeys of the house and ordered up cool jugs of wine, Robin quietly asked Thomas and I to make a circuit of the square and ask at the taverns for news of the Master and his Knights of Our Lady.

I was not best pleased – I was hungry and, to be honest, the smell of well-spiced sausages cooking on the tavern's hot griddle was tormenting me. But I obeyed, and Thomas and I dutifully pushed our way through the crowds, stopping at each tavern and, trying to avoid drooling openly at the varied and delicious smells that we encountered, we asked each proprietor or serving man in turn if they had seen any men in the surcoats of the Knights of Our Lady or had had any word of someone who called himself the Master and had an extra thumb on his left hand. After half an hour, I returned to Robin, having nothing of any significance to tell him. In truth, I am surprised that my lord could hear me make my report over the growling of my stomach.

But the wondrous thing about being afflicted with hunger is that its cure, while never permanent, is so delightful. I munched on a vast pile of sausages laced with pepper, marjoram and sage, and eggs stirred in butter in a frying pan, and chewed good white bread and sank a cup or two of sweet red wine in the company of my friends and companions, and very soon my good humour was restored.

I sat back, replete, poured another cup of wine and began to take a proper, measured look at the bustle of the fair. To our left, perhaps twenty yards away, I noticed a well-dressed lad of no more than fourteen or fifteen in the act of climbing on to a brick mounting block. He was a jongleur, I assumed, by the old vielle he carried, and apprenticed to a rich music master judging by the quality of his clothes. I sat back and listened happily while he began to play and sing for the passers-by. I could not clearly make out what he was playing, but it sounded like a simple *canso* – a love song of the kind that these southern lands were famous for. Even at that distance, and over the bubbling noise of the market, I could tell that he was a musician with no vast store of talent, and worse, his old vielle was slightly out of tune.

I strained my ears to hear him nonetheless – I had not heard any music for some time and I swiftly realized that I had longed for it without quite knowing what it was that I longed for – and I was rewarded by the sound of him merrily butchering a piece by an old friend of mine, a Norman *trouvère* called Ambroise d'Evrecy who had been on the Great Pilgrimage with me. The lad clearly favoured the northern style of poetry and music, the style of Champagne, Normandy and England – which I remember thinking strange as so many in the north sought to emulate the music of the south. But these musings were driven from my mind when he began a new tune and sang, to my utter astonishment:

> My joy summons me
> To sing in this sweet season . . .

He was singing a *canso* that I had written. Or that had been partly written by me. Indeed, I had composed it together with King Richard en route to the Holy Land and I was astounded that this stripling jongleur should have knowledge of it, and should be performing here it so far from my homeland. I was entranced, even though I must admit he made a mess of the vielle fingering in the middle section somewhat, and he did not correctly hit the high sung note at the end of the third line of each verse. But here he was, a stranger, in this strange land, singing my own song.

I grabbed the shoulder of Little John who was sitting beside me, and shook it roughly. 'Listen to this, John, just listen to the lad over there. It's "My *joy summons me*." He's playing "My *joy*" . . .'

Little John looked up briefly from his wooden plate. 'Yes,' he said. 'That's nice . . . are you not going to finish those last couple of sausages?'

'Robin,' I called down the table, 'can you hear what that jongleur over there is playing?'

But my lord was engrossed in conversation with Tuck and waved his hand dismissively at me as if to say, Not now, Alan, I'm busy.

'Because, if you are not going to eat them,' said Little John staring at my plate, 'would you mind a great deal, Alan, if I did?'

I stood up and left my boorish companions and walked over to the jongleur. I was just in time to hear him sing the final verse:

> A knight who sings so sweetly
> Of obligation, to his noble lord
> Should consider the great virtue
> Of courtly manners, not discord

And with a final flourish of his bow, and a light smatter of applause from the indifferent crowd, he stepped off the mounting block and began to move away towards the other side of the square.

I took two fast steps and caught up with him: 'Good sir, please forgive this intrusion. But I wanted to congratulate you on your performance . . .' My command of Langue d'Oc was not perfect, I was sorely out of practice, but the lad caught my meaning and he swung round smartly with a beaming smile stretching his already generous mouth. Under his neat bowl of glossy black hair, his honey-brown eyes glowed with joy.

'Did you like it? Did you truly like it? My uncle says I have no talent in this field and I should punish the poor ears of the world no more. But you really liked it – you swear before God?'

'I did, sir, I have not been so pleased to hear a tune for many years,' I said, truthfully. The boy was brimming with happiness and I was instantly infected by his good humour.

234

'I am a musician myself,' I continued. 'Would you care to take a small cup of wine with me and my friends over there and discuss our shared interests in the Muse for a little while.'

'Nothing would give me greater pleasure,' said this agreeable fellow.

I introduced the young man to my friends, who received him with varying degrees of courtesy, from a 'God save you' from Tuck and a 'Welcome, friend' from Robin, to a blank, silent stare from Nur. Thomas busied himself fetching the lad a drink.

'. . . and I am Sir Alan Dale,' I said at last.

He nodded and said absently, 'My friends all call me Tronc.' Then, to my secret, prideful pleasure, his face suddenly changed. His eyes widened, his cheeks flushed. 'Did you say Alan Dale, as in Alan Dale, the troubadour, Alan Dale, the knight of the Great Pilgrimage, and companion of Richard of England?'

He was goggling at me.

'The same.'

'But I was just singing one of your *cansos* – it is my favourite, my absolute favourite, and you . . . you . . .'

'As I said, I have not been so pleased to hear a tune for many years, but if I may be so bold' – I reached over and picked up his old vielle from the table. I plucked at the second string, which was a little loose, listened to its voice and tightened its tuning peg. While I was engaged in this delicate act, Tronc was chattering away, almost babbling:

'I have written a few pieces myself – nothing to compare with your masterful works, of course, Sir Alan, but I think they may show a little promise . . .'

'So you are not content to be a jongleur,' I said, my fingers busy with the fine strings of the vielle, only half-listening to him, trying to get the tone of the middle note just right. 'You would wish to be a fully fledged troubadour?'

'A jongleur! No, no . . .' And he burst out laughing, as if what

235

I had said was the funniest thing imaginable. I looked at him a little oddly and wondered if things were different down here. In England and Normandy, a jongleur performed other men's music, as he just had, while a *trouvère*, or troubadour as the southern folk called them, composed his own works. It was a question of rank. A troubadour might take offence at being called a mere jongleur, but not the other way around.

'I can see how you might be mistaken,' Tronc said, and laughed merrily once again. 'I do not come to the market on a feast day to play pretty tunes for pennies – but for another reason. I know that I am not yet adept, so I come here, on my own, to hone and test my skill as a musician. It is my belief that, if I can please the crowds of people here just a little, then there is hope for me. But tell me, Sir Alan, do you know the works of Folquet de Marseilles? He too was a friend of King Richard?'

I admitted that I did not know the great man himself but said that I had admired his famous love song '*Amors, merce: no mueira tan soven*' for many years. And so began a long, intense conversation with this extraordinary young man, who, if he lacked a perfect ear and polished technique for fine music, had at least enough enthusiasm for a dozen would-be troubadours. An hour passed, and a second, and I was just about to call for more wine, when I saw that Robin was standing at my side. And looking down the table at my Companions, I saw that they were all on their feet as well, brushing crumbs from their laps and preparing to leave, and that Thomas and Roland were leading the horses to our table. I had been so lost in my talk with Tronc that I had completely forgotten our circumstances.

'It's time to go, Alan,' said Robin kindly. 'We have been waiting on you this half hour past. We must make our way to St-Sernin or all the places in the dormitory will be taken.'

He turned to Tronc. 'It has been a pleasure to meet you, young man. I am only sad that we did not all have the pleasure of more

236

of your conversation. I fear Alan here has enjoyed the lion's share of it.'

'You are going to St-Sernin?' said Tronc, with an air of surprise. 'You would seek lodgings there?'

I told him that we would.

'But you are far too late,' said my new friend. 'It is St George's Day and the day of the great fair – all Toulouse is filled with merchants and travellers, pilgrims, revellers and folk from the villages hereabouts. All the cots in the dormitory will have been taken long before now. You must stay with me.'

I looked uncertainly at Robin, who merely shrugged, and said, 'That is most kind of you, Master Tronc, but I am sure that we would be far too much of an inconvenience to your household.'

'Nonsense, masses of room, and of course the servants will see to everything – but it might be best if you did not call me Master Tronc. Just Tronc will do or, if you insist on being absurdly formal, you may call me my lord.'

'"My lord"?'

It was my turn to goggle at him.

'Well, um, yes, actually, didn't you know? I am Raymond-Roger de Trencavel, Viscount of Carcassonne, lord of Beziers, Albi and the Razès. But as practically everybody who is anybody around these parts is called Raymond or Roger or Raymond-Roger, all my friends call me by my family's name – Trencavel – or Tronc, for short.'

Chapter Sixteen

As we rode away from the tavern, with Tronc walking beside my horse's head, I discovered a little more about our noble friend. While he spent much of his time at his own court at Carcassonne, he told me that the Trencavel family had long maintained an inn in Toulouse for convenience when visiting the city. They were the vassals of the Count of Toulouse, Raymond, the sixth of that name, who also happened to be Tronc's uncle, and the family were frequently called upon to serve the Count at the Château Narbonnais, his fortress on the southern edge of the city. So Tronc led us through the crowded streets with the familiarity of a native Toulousain, through a guard post in the wall that divided the Cité from the Bourg, and north about five hundred yards towards the pink bulk of the cathedral of St-Sernin.

The oval space around the brick-built cathedral was almost as crowded as the market square where we had spent the afternoon, but this part of the town was mostly inhabited by travellers and pilgrims of the poorer kind, with a large proportion of the city's beggars taking refuge in the shade provided by the cathedral. I realized that Tronc had been right about St-Sernin – we would indeed have had a great deal of difficulty in finding even the meanest accommodation within its precincts.

Our new friend's rather grand inn was on a quiet street a mere fifty yards from the pink walls on the eastern side of the city, but before we reached it, I observed a curious sight. Not far from the inn's stout gate, a small crowd had formed around two women. They were dressed in rough black robes, belted at the waist with a thick leather-bound book dangling from the belt, their pale, thin faces seemingly shining with some inner goodness. As we approached, they spread their arms wide as if in benediction and almost all of the members of the crowd around them, some thirty people, prostrated themselves before the two dark figures and lay full length in the mud and filth of the street. The women began to recite the Pater Noster over the prone bodies of their followers:

Our Father, which art in Heaven,
Hallowed be thy name.
Thy kingdom come,
Thy will be done on Earth as it is in Heaven.
Give us this day our supplementary bread,
And remit our debts as we forgive our debtors.
And keep us from temptation and free us from evil.
Thine is the kingdom, the power and glory for ever and ever.
Amen.

The Lord's Prayer that these strange women spoke was subtly different from the Pater Noster that I am sure all of the Companions (save for Nur, of course) had been saying since we could first speak – but that was not what shocked me the most.

'Women priests?' I said to Tronc. 'You have women priests here?' I cannot remember when I have been so astonished.

'They are Good Women,' replied Tronc with a smile.

'No doubt, but are they also priests, in holy orders?'

'No, Sir Alan, that is what they call themselves: Good Women and Good Men, or sometimes Good Christians. We call them Perfects, and their followers are called Believers – and they are Christians too . . . after a fashion.'

I heard Sir Nicholas, who was directly behind me, mutter savagely, 'They bloody well are not. They're nothing but damned heretics.'

'And the Church – and the Count of Toulouse – they allow them to preach here quite freely?' I said.

'They do nobody any harm,' said Tronc. 'They are genuinely holy folk – they eschew meat and sexual coupling and oaths and money and . . . and, well, all worldly evils. Besides, they have many followers – even some of the lesser nobility are Believers. It would not be, ah, politic for the Church or the Count to act against them. We do things a little differently here in the Languedoc, Alan, as you will discover if you remain with us. Live and let live, we say, and let each man and woman find his or her own path to God.'

While I was still digesting this extraordinary laxity in matters of the Faith, we entered into the courtyard of the inn and my mind was diverted by the sight of a dozen servants in yellow and white livery who debouched from a large three-storey building to take our horses' bridles and lead us inside.

The hospitality of the Viscount of Carcassonne, the lord of Beziers, Albi and the Razès, was lavish. Servants were dispatched to fire the cauldrons in the bathhouse and for the first time in weeks I was able to soak in the luxury of a great wooden tub, with a sheet draped over the top to protect my modesty, while the male Companions made use of the half dozen other tubs. Nur disappeared temporarily and we men splashed and chatted and laughed at our good fortune – this was so much better than a flea-infested cath-edral dormitory – and allowed the gallons of hot soapy water to wash away the cares of the long journey.

Then, clean, refreshed, dressed in new clothes, and hungry once more, we met at dusk in the great hall where our host Raymond-Roger de Trencavel had caused a 'light' supper of pigeon pie, smoked ham, roasted capons, grilled trout, ragout of beef, coddled eggs, onion soup, five kinds of cheese and many bowls of fruit to be laid out for our delectation.

As we ate heartily, I gave Tronc a limited explanation for our presence in the Languedoc. I made no mention of the Grail, for Robin had told me privately to keep that part back, but I gave him a good deal of truth. We were seeking a former monk named Michel, who now called himself the Master, and who led a band of soldiers calling themselves the Knights of Our Lady. He could be easily identified because of the strange deformity that he had been born with: two thumbs on his left hand, twin miniature digits where only one should be. We sought him because he was a thief and a murderer, who had been responsible for the death or my father Henry and also of a good friend of mine called Hanno. We sought revenge, I said, on the Master and we suspected that he might even now be in Toulouse, perhaps staying with powerful friends in the Church or the nobility, or might have passed through in the past few days.

Tronc's young brow furrowed at my words. 'I believe I have heard rumours of this Master and his Knights of Our Lady – but I have not heard of his presence here in Toulouse.' He paused and looked keenly at me. 'I have also heard that he had some magical trinket, a golden cup studded with fabulous jewels, an object of enormous value, priceless indeed, that was supposed to be able to make a man immortal or perform other such wonders.'

I said nothing, not wanting to lie to him, but noting privately that this Trencavel, for all his youth and enthusiasm, was no fool.

'Well, no matter,' said Tronc. 'I shall make enquiries in the city tomorrow with a number of people and see if I can bring you any news of this evil fellow, this three-thumbed Master.'

We had all finished eating by this point and were lingering at the table over the wine, when Robin said, 'Those extraordinary women priests we saw outside this afternoon, the Perfects, I think you called them, and you named their followers Believers – what do they believe?'

'But where shall I begin,' said Tronc. 'I have several friends in Albi and Carcassonne who are Believers – indeed, a large proportion of the people in my own lands, perhaps a third of them, perhaps even as many as half, follow this path to God.'

I filled his wine cup from the jug on the table, and he smiled his thanks. Tuck was leaning forward from the end of the table in an attempt to hear Tronc's words more clearly.

'These people are commonly called Cathars, but they think of themselves as Christians, in that they believe that Christ was the son of God who was sent to Earth by his Father and appeared in the illusion of a fleshly form. However, they do not believe that God, the essence of Goodness, has total dominion over the universe; he shares it with another deity. The world, as they see it, was made by the Devil, or Rex Mundi, as they call him, the King of the World, and he has power over all material things; God, in contrast, is manifested in immaterial things, the holy, invisible things of the spirit, and so they reject all the things of the world, things of the flesh, as works of the Devil. They despise wealth, for example, and the eating of meat, and the making of oaths, and carnal relations between men and women, even married men and women desiring to procreate, of which the Church, of course, thoroughly approves.'

I was looking at Tuck's face as Tronc spoke and far from being offended by what he heard, he seemed fascinated. Robin too was absorbed by our host's lecture. But Sir Nicholas de Scras, his face flushed with wine, was scowling at the table in general. Then he spoke: 'How can they possibly believe that the Devil made the world and has dominion over it? What rubbish! We know that God made the world and everything in it – it says so in the Bible.'

242

He took a deep breath, seeming to make an effort of commanding himself. 'Surely these wretches are heretics of the vilest sort – a foul poison inside the community of Christians.'

'Yes, they are heretics – and they are condemned by the Church,' Tronc replied. 'Nonetheless there is a certain logic to their argument, I would say. If God made the world and He is omnipotent why does He allow evil to exist? Disease, war, famine, pain . . . Why does God stand idly by and allow wickedness to flourish? Is it not reasonable to suggest that the Devil rules the world and the body of a man or a woman – and that God rules the spirit, the soul that is imprisoned inside that body, and it therefore follows that the only way to God is through a renunciation of the evil world and all the corruption that our flesh contains?'

'It is not our place to question the actions of God,' said Tuck reproachfully. 'We cannot know His plan – if He allows evil to exist, it must be because of some ineffable scheme . . .'

But Sir Nicholas was clearly boiling with fury by this point, the dark bruises on his face making him seem inordinately ugly. He glared at our host and said, 'You seem to know a good deal about these God-damned heretics. Perhaps you are one yourself!'

Tronc looked steadily, coolly, at Sir Nicholas, a man seasoned by more than forty years of life. Our host said nothing, just looked at the former Hospitaller, apparently unperturbed by his extraordinary rudeness. But I could feel Robin gathering himself to rebuke Sir Nicholas. And then, to my great surprise, Sir Nicholas himself suddenly dropped his angry gaze to the table and said, 'Forgive me, my lord, for my gross and vile discourtesy. I believe I may have taken too much of your good Toulousain wine. I retract my boorish remarks and I beg your leave to retire from the board and seek my bed.'

'You have my leave to retire, certainly, but before you go I will answer your question. No, I am not a heretic. In my minority, after my father died, my tutor Bertrand de Saissac naturally instructed me in the theology of the Cathars, since he was a Believer himself.

But he left me free to choose my own religion – and I am a faithful son of Holy Mother Church. However, I cannot hate the Cathars, whatever the bishops might decree. While their beliefs do not coincide with my own, this is the Languedoc, and we know that there are good men and women to be found in all creeds. My father's senechal, for example, was a Jew, and a very fine man just the same. No, Sir Nicholas, I am no God-damned heretic, as you put it, but neither am I the enemy of heretics.'

'I will thank you, my lord, for this fine feast and bid you good night, then,' said Sir Nicholas rising from his seat. 'I apologise again for my discourtesy; I am deeply ashamed of my inexcusable behaviour.'

At Sir Nicholas's departure, most of the rest of the Companions also took their leave – trooping out of the hall and across the courtyard to the guest hall that had been prepared by Tronc's legion of servants. But Robin and Tuck and I remained at the table. 'If it does not tax your good nature, sir, may I enquire a little more about these strange Cathars,' said Robin. 'Do they have their own churches, sacrifices and rituals?'

I looked at my lord – I had long known that he had little love for the true Church, and that he had indulged in some unspeakable pagan rites in the past, but I had always believed that, at heart, he was largely indifferent to spiritual matters. Now he seemed to be burning with curiosity about these southern heretics. Tuck was also looking at Robin, with a worried frown wreathing his already wrinkled brow.

Tronc said, 'I will tell you a little more, but I do not wish this pleasant evening to be burdened with too much talk of faith. It divides men, I find, and leads to disharmony, even violence and unnecessary deaths. And, furthermore, my heart yearns to hear some of Alan's famous music before we sleep. But I shall tell you a little more about them, if you will it, so that you may come to a better understanding of these matters . . .

'So, you asked about Cathar churches – no, they do not have churches as such, merely houses where the Perfects gather and minister to their Believers. And as for rituals, there is but one main one, called the *consolamentum*, and roughly equivalent to our baptism, except that it occurs, usually, towards the end of a man's life and transforms a Believer into a Perfect. Before receiving the *consolamentum*, a Believer is not expected to follow the tenets of their faith: avoiding meat, milk and eggs, and so on. But, once a Believer is made into a Perfect, he or she must avoid the temptations of the world, fleshly love, for example, and the coveting of money. A Perfect must keep himself pure until the day of his death, when his immaculate soul can be taken up out of this evil world and into the arms of God.'

'And what if a Perfect were to die unclean?' asked Robin.

'There are some who say that an unclean soul of a Perfect will go into another body, of a newborn baby or perhaps even an animal, and so it is reincarnated again and again until the soul has been purified . . . But that is quite enough of these solemn matters – Sir Alan, I beg you, will you not take up my vielle and give us some of your wonderful music?'

For the rest of the evening and long into the night we sang and played and gave ourselves up to the pleasures of poetry. I found that my bowing skills were a little creaky from disuse, but I was surprised by Tronc's dexterity with words – for his own poems and *cansos*, though a little unsophisticated, were most pleasing to the ear. We even induced Robin to sing, some of the old English country songs, although Tuck declined to take any role except that of entranced listener, and so we played and sang and ended the night in good fellowship and perfect harmony.

Tronc left early in the morning with a small retinue of men-at-arms – and the Companions took the opportunity to wallow in the Viscount's lavish hospitality. We tended to our hurts, and slept,

245

and ate another huge meal at noon prepared by his many servants and, afterwards, I spent a few hours working on a tune that
I picked out on Tronc's old vielle, a eulogy to the lord of Trencavel
and his generosity, which I hoped to play for our kind host later.

I also stepped out to visit the cathedral of St-Sernin, a mere
hundred yards to the west, and there I prayed for Goody and asked
God to preserve her until I could take possession of the Grail.

Prayer is a strange thing. Sometimes, in a quiet and holy place,
a man can feel that he is genuinely speaking to God and that the
Almighty is listening to his every word. And sometimes a prayer,
no matter how heartfelt, can feel as if it is falling on empty space.
At the cathedral of St-Sernin, I had no sense at all that God was
attending to my entreaties. I stayed on my knees on the stone floor
for some hours, my eyes screwed shut, holding a picture of my
beloved in my mind, and earnestly beseeching the Lord to keep
her safe. But, the image of my lovely wife, her face white as bone,
her violet-blue eyes huge and infinitely sad, kept slipping away,
and I found my mind wandering without direction. Instead of
Goody, an image of the Grail came unbidden into my head – a
shining golden cup, lavishly bejewelled and glowing with holy
power. And then the image changed to that of the Master: I could
clearly see his thin pock-marked face and cloying eyes; I saw his
deformed thumb; I could actually hear his voice – he has mocking
me for my impotence to help Goody. He was laughing at me . . .

I pushed aside that evil image with some difficulty and opened
my eyes to see the monks of the cathedral file into their places in
the choir and begin to chant the service of Vespers. As I listened
to the grave, deep, familiar cadences, my mind was calmed and I
rose from my station, giving relief to my aching knees, and I made
my way out.

As I was leaving, I paused at a stall that offered a variety of
items to pilgrims – for the cathedral had long been a popular place
of pilgrimage. I fingered the little tin medals depicting images of

the saints, looked at roughly carved walking staffs and cheap linen shoulder bags, and finally made a purchase of a pear-shaped leather water bottle, the outside stamped with an image of the martyrdom of St Sernin – he was dragged to death by a bull through the streets of Toulouse many hundreds of years ago. I bought it, not because I harbour a particularly deep veneration for the saint, but merely because I thought an extra water container might be useful on our travels, and perhaps as a sort of money offering to the cathedral itself, perhaps even to God, in an effort to persuade him to hear my prayers.

Tronc returned a little after dark with bad news. He had spent the day visiting a good many of his friends – some of them from the noblest families in the Languedoc – and, once he had gathered us all in the hall of the inn, he told us that not one of his many and varied acquaintances had heard even a whisper that the Master was in Toulouse.

'You hinted that he might have powerful friends here,' Tronc said, 'but I do not believe that this Master could be in Toulouse and word of it not come to the ears of the people I know. I may be mistaken, but are you certain that this fellow is in the city?'

The bald truth was, we were not certain at all. All we had to go on was the Seigneur d'Albret's threat to Sir Nicholas that revealed the Master had gone east. And Nur's devilish hocus-pocus with a bag of old bones. But east could mean anywhere. And if the Master was not in Toulouse, we had absolutely no idea where he might be. Our quest was dead. My Goody was dead. No wonder the phantom of the Master, which had appeared in the cathedral, had laughed so heartily.

'Well, I will continue my enquires tomorrow,' said Tronc, 'but I am afraid that I may have alerted the authorities to your presence. I hope that is not a problem for you. I have been told that you must make an appearance before the Consuls at the Maison tomorrow at noon.'

247

'Who are the Consuls?' I asked.

Tronc smiled at me: 'It is they, not my uncle Count Raymond, who truly govern Toulouse. Although, of course, the Count is the nominal ruler in the eyes of God and the Church. The Count owns all the lands hereabouts but Toulouse's wealth comes from its merchants, and the twenty-four Consuls, the Chapter, as they are known, are elected by the guilds – they are, more or less, the twenty-four richest men in the city.'

'What do they want from us?' asked Robin.

'Officially, the Consuls say that they wish to welcome your esteemed selves to Toulouse – of course, in truth, they most probably just wish to cast an eye over you and will probably demand an accounting for your presence here. The Count himself is away – he left this very morning for his estates – but he left instructions that, in his absence, all armed strangers are to be scrutinized by the Chapter. There have been reports of lawless *routiers* raiding the lands west of here towards Agen, and the Consuls no doubt wish to reassure themselves that you have no ill intent in the Count's domains. It should be no more than a formality, an hour at most, and I will accompany you and tell them that you are my guests. There is nothing to fear, I assure you.'

I played my eulogy for Tronc after supper, a tale of his musical prowess and his generosity to strangers, and he was quite delighted by it, and insisted on learning it note for note that very night. And then he and I sat up till midnight, long after the others had gone to bed, telling tales of troubadours we had encountered and comparing those we admired or deplored and drinking a little too deeply of his rich red wine.

It was with an aching head and a leathery tongue, but a sense of deep satisfaction at the forging of a new friendship, that we set out on foot the next day a little before noon, dressed in the finest clean clothes we possessed, for the Maison des Consuls. Tronc had said that only the belted knights needed to wait upon the Chapter and the rest of us might remain at the inn – he said this with a wary eye on Nur, who had not spoken a word to him during the entire course of her stay. But Tuck, John, Gavin and Thomas seemed quite happy to spend another day in idleness.

As the hot sun towered above us, Tronc, and half a dozen of his liveried men-at-arms, Robin, Nicholas, Roland and myself left the inn and walked through the guarded city wall that separated the Bourg from the Cité, into the main square. Without the cheerful bustle of the Haberdashers' Fair, it seemed vast, drab and intimidating.

We marched across to the grand doors of the Maison des Consuls, which occupied a large part of the eastern side of the square, and were immediately granted admission. The inside was built in similar massive proportion to the square – a huge cool space built from thick timbers and the slim red bricks of the region and bustling with servants and lackeys of all kinds. We were told to wait in an anteroom until the Consuls were ready to receive us, and while we kicked our heels on a long pine bench, I admired an enormous fresco painted on the white plaster of the wall directly in front of us.

It was an image of a group of rich money changers or bankers of some sort standing by a long bench passing sacks filled with golden coins between them; one man in a strange square hat was recording the accounts in a ledger, and smiling broadly. All these men seemed to be very satisfied with themselves and their apparent wealth and I could see that this land was one of golden plenty. I wondered idly what it would be like to be very, very rich. An image of Westbury came into my head as I had last seen it – black, reeking and destroyed. What I could do with that manor if I had the kind of wealth that these men possessed, I mused. I could build my own castle, of fine dressed stone if I chose, and Goody and I need never be troubled by enemies again. Would I ever have wealth enough to build a castle? The answer to that questions was plain – and it was like a cold, wet blanket cast over my soul.

A servant in red-and-black livery broke my reverie and told us that the Consuls were ready, and we four knights rose as one man and filed into the grand audience hall, leaving Tronc's men-at-arms to wait in the anteroom.

We found ourselves in a large, long room panelled in dark wood, standing at the centre of a horse-shoe of tables that occupied three sides of a square and were covered with a snowy linen cloth. At this hollow square sat the twenty-four Consuls of Toulouse. They were all men of middling years, none of them younger than twenty-five, and they almost all had the plump, prosperous look of the golden men in the anteroom's fresco. Around the walls of the large chamber, every yard or so, was stationed a man-at-arms, with a red-and-black shield, a spear and a belted sword at his waist. A piggy little man with small eyes and an enormous paunch, who sat in the centre of the horse-shoe swathed in a fur-trimmed mantel, rapped the table with a gavel to call the Chapter to order, then he spoke in a slow, deep voice in Latin.

'Strangers to our city, I am Master Vital Barravi, the Senior Consul of this Chapter, be so good as to name yourselves and your business within our precincts.'

Robin stepped forward briskly. 'Master Consul, I am Robert Odo, Earl of Locksley, and these are my companions, the noble knights Sir Alan Dale, Sir Nicholas de Scras and Sir Roland d'Alle. We have journeyed from the north, by sea and by land, and we hope merely to pass through the County of Toulouse, staying at most two or three days in your city, with your gracious permission, then to continue east to visit the city of Montpellier, and consult the learned doctors of medicine there on a grave matter. We mean no harm to the Count of Toulouse nor to his city nor the lands that we must pass through to reach our destination.'

Robin's words were greeted by a general muttering among the Consuls, as each man turned to his neighbour and rumbled some comment, too quiet to make out.

It was not a welcoming sound.

'So you say,' said the Senior Consul, wrinkling his round, snout-like nose, 'but your personages are not known to the gentlemen of this Chapter, and I must inform you that we have heard ill tidings of you.'

The man rummaged on the white linen on the table in front of him and briefly picked up a large piece of parchment. Then he looked up, his reddish eyes glittering. 'It is my unfortunate duty to inform you that grave charges have been laid against you, by another outlander, but a person of birth and rank, and the Chapter must determine if these charges have any substance or merit before we may allow you to enjoy the freedom of our city.'

I felt as if a cold hand had been placed upon my bare neck – this meeting was no formality, as Tronc had promised; it seemed to me that, despite the Viscount of Carcassonne's reassuring words, there was plenty to fear. I glanced at the row of men-at-arms standing around the walls of the chamber and estimated forty men, and the fingers of my left hand brushed the hilt of my sword.

Robin spoke, his demeanour as cool as a trout in a mountain steam. 'Would the Senior Consul be so good as to enlighten us as to the nature of the charges that have been levelled against us? I'm sure there must have been some sort of silly misunderstanding.'

'The charges are not levelled against you all – they are directed only at you, Lord Locksley. You have been accused of the crime of theft – something we take very seriously. You have been accused of fraudulently depriving a most Christian institution in the city of Paris of a very large sum of money. I refer, of course, to the Order of the Poor Fellow-Knights of Christ and the Temple of Solomon – you have been accused of stealing the goodly sum of five hundred livres in silver from the Paris Temple.'

I quickly surveyed the room once again: Sir Nicholas de Scras's black and purple bruised face seemed almost pallid, Tronc looked bemused, Roland appeared to be quietly furious. I observed the company of standing soldiers, alert, ready to prevent any attempt at escape; the stern-faced Consuls seated on three sides of a square, the grave accusation of their leader lingering in the air like smoke above a battlefield. This gathering of smug, wealthy Toulousain dignitaries, I recognized with a sinking heart, was far from a kindly welcoming committee.

This gathering was, in fact, a trial.

It was a trial for Robin's life.

Chapter Seventeen

I do not think I have ever known a better man under pressure than my lord of Locksley. When the porcine Senior Consul Vital Barravi finished intoning the charge of theft against the Templars in his grave Latin, Robin just laughed, a deep, relaxed belly laugh that shocked the assembly more than any other response possibly could.

'You find this amusing?' Consul Barravi was on his feet, his chubby little fists clenched in anger. 'This is a jest for you?'

'Forgive me,' said Robin, wiping the apparently genuine tears of mirth from his eyes. 'I ask your pardon – all of you. But I have heard this absurd nonsense before. It is risible. I am the Earl of Locksley – I have lands stretching from Scotland to Normandy – why would I trouble myself to pilfer a paltry five hundred livres?'

A voice behind us spoke, the Latin crisp but tinged with the harsh tones of northern France: 'You are indeed the Earl of Locksley, no one here denies that,' the voice said. 'But you are the outlawed Earl of Locksley. Driven beyond the law and out of decent Christian society by King John of England for your many black crimes. Even these gentlemen of Toulouse will have heard of your infamous name, a *nom de guerre* that you commonly adopt while carrying out your vile crimes – the name of Robin Hood.'

I will not say that the assembled Consuls all gasped in awe at the mention of the name of Robin Hood, but a few straightened in their seats and the muttering arose once more around the tables as each man began to speak urgently with his neighbour.

I glanced behind me and saw two figures standing beside the grand door of the council chamber. I did not know who the man on the right was – he was a handsome young knight with a wide mouth, smiling eyes and reddish hair – but I knew *what* he was. He and his companion wore black caps, black robes and a white cloak over the top with a red cross marked on the left breast. They were Templars. And the second man, the one who had spoken, was Gilles de Mauchamps.

I had half-expected his presence here ever since I heard the nature of the charges levelled against Robin, ever since I first heard the word Templar spoken by these plump merchants. And with a slow dawning of hatred, mingled with a little fear, like a deadly poison gradually spreading through my body, I stared at the ugly features of the man who had burned Westbury and killed so many of my friends and my servants – and who was now grinning across the chamber at us with an unmistakable air of triumph.

Then Tronc spoke.

'Most noble Consuls. I trust that you know me and my family, and that my standing is good enough for me to speak a word or two before this august gathering.'

The was an eager chorus of assent from the lines of seated men, and the piggish Senior Consul said, 'By all means, my lord', with a flourish of his little trotter.

'This is not a court of law,' Tronc began. 'This is, as I understand it, an *ad hoc* meeting of the Chapter to determine whether the Earl of Locksley and his companions are decent, honest folk, fit to reside for a very short time in Toulouse.'

He paused and there were a few nods and mumbles from the Consuls. Nobody denied it.

'And so this is what I propose,' Tronc continued. 'Lord Locksley has been accused. Firstly, his accuser must present his case and his evidence. Then the Earl must be allowed to answer the charges. Does that not seem fair and reasonable?'

'Very good, my lord,' said Consul Barravi. 'It is a most reasonable suggestion. And marvellously well put, my lord, if I may say so. A worthy contribution. Bring forward the Frenchman – let the Templar make his case and demonstrate his proofs.'

Gilles de Mauchamps strode forward, giving us a spiteful smirk as he moved past us. I saw with a little flame of pleasure that his left hand – the hand Robin had pierced with the arrow – was missing. In its place was an empty sleeve. I truly hoped its amputation, presumably after the puncture wound had turned stinking and bad, had been exceedingly long and painful.

His fellow knight came forward as well and held up a scroll, which he unrolled slowly and held in front of de Mauchamps. Gilles began to read aloud from it. It was, as far as I could tell, much the same document as the one he had read out before my gates at Westbury earlier in the year, just as dull and filled with dates and numbers, but the chief difference being that my name had been changed for Robin's. When he finished, the Chapter was quiet for a few moments.

'You have made an accusation that on such and such a date this man did steal from the Paris Temple such and such a sum,' said Tronc, in a kindly voice, as if trying to be helpful to a small and rather backward infant. 'But, other than your say-so, do you have any proof that the Earl of Locksley was the culprit?'

'We know the Earl of Locksley is guilty,' Gilles said. 'He is the notorious thief Robin Hood. His very name and his reputation condemn him in the minds of all law-abiding folk. There is no doubt that he is guilty. The Grand Master of the Temple himself

255

has charged me with bringing him to justice. Look, his friend there, the man who calls himself Sir Alan Dale, he is the villain who took out the original promissory note for two pounds one shilling and sixteen pence. Sir Alan Dale does not trouble to deny it. The sum stolen was exactly that, plus five hundred pounds. Alan Dale serves Robin Hood. One must therefore assume that it was the Earl of Locksley who stole the money!'

'So, then . . . no actual, erm, proof?' said Tronc kindly. 'Just your assumptions. Hmm. What say you, my lord of Locksley.'

'The whole thing is a pack of lies,' Robin said softly, with a wonderful open-faced sincerity. He stood straight, he half-smiled – he seemed preternaturally honest. 'But I can explain something to the noble Consuls here. This man is my enemy – as, I'm grieved to say, are all the Knights Templar. I wounded him in battle not long ago' – Robin pointed at Gilles's empty sleeve. 'He has clearly concocted this ludicrous story of forged notes and fraudulent withdrawals to embarrass me as some cowardly form of revenge.'

'You call me a coward!' Gilles was red-faced and shouting.

'You *are* a coward – and a liar,' my lord responded coolly.

'You Godless outlaw bastard . . .'

I reached for my sword . . .

'Order, order! I will have good order in my chamber.' Consul Barravi was pounding furiously on the table with his wooden hammer, trying to wrest back control before a full pitched battle broke out.

The little man pounded the oak with his gavel on and on and gradually Gilles stopped roaring and a quiet descended. I noticed that the smiling red-haired knight looked embarrassed by the behaviour of his Brother Templar.

'May I speak, sir?' said Tronc.

The Consul Barravi nodded silently – he was now beetroot red in the face and I saw that his gavel had snapped in two.

'I do not think we can achieve much more here today,' Tronc

said. 'Tempers have grown hot; high, intemperate words have flown. I propose that, while the Chapter deliberates, and seeks further information from this noble gentleman of Paris' – here Tronc nodded at Gilles – 'these travellers should be remanded into my personal custody at the Maison Trencavel—'

'No, by God, I say, no!' Gilles's voice had grown loud again. 'The outlaw Robin Hood must be handed over to me and my men, immediately. This wet-behind-the-ears boy is their friend and ally – he cannot be trusted to keep them here.'

His fellow Templar was by now openly wincing.

'This young gentleman is the Viscount of Carcassonne,' said Consul Barravi in a shocked voice, 'and the lord of Beziers, Albi and the Razès . . . and the nephew of our own beloved Count Raymond of Toulouse. When you insult him with your foolish, unmannerly comments, you insult us all . . .' Barravi swallowed a breath. 'Indeed, I have had enough of your impertinence, sir. It shall be done as my lord Trencavel suggests: these travellers will be handed over to him forthwith and he will act as their custodian until the Chapter has completed its deliberations.'

'I must protest!' Gilles's voice had not lost any of its overbearing volume. 'The outlaw must be handed over to me. He will be secured in the dungeons of our preceptory until this matter is resolved. And then he will be hanged for the black thief that he is. And the Knights Templar will not be pleased if you try to thwart our just designs. I give you fair warning, sir!'

'Sir, your threats are as intolerable as they are absurd.' The Senior Consul was in a fine temper. 'This is Toulouse; this is the Languedoc' – he was very nearly ranting at Gilles, and waving one pudgy little finger at him. 'This is not France or England where they tremble at the name of the Order of the Temple; we have our own customs here and, if you cannot respect them, you shall be summarily ejected from the city. Kicked out today, if I have my way.'

The Consul was standing now, panting and glaring at Gilles like an angry, miniature bull. Then he turned towards Robin and said, 'Get out, get out of here, all of you and leave us to our own counsels. We will summon you in a day or two when we have reached a decision.'

And so we left that hot-blooded chamber and went back to the comfort of the inn with Tronc.

Over the noon day meal, the mood was tense. Tronc seemed to be deeply embarrassed, and, although our host was as generous and affable as always, I caught him giving Robin some strange looks across the board. I wondered fleetingly if he would tell his servants to count the silver spoons after the meal. When we had finished eating, the Viscount of Carcassonne addressed us all: 'My friends, I must be about the city. I need to speak with friends and relatives and see what can be done about these Templars and their accusations. While I am gone, I beg you to remain inside the precincts of the inn. I swear that you will not be molested here. You will be quite safe, on my honour.'

And he left us to stew in the lavish comfort of his home.

Robin gathered us after Tronc had left and said, 'I believe that we are safe for the moment under the Viscount's protection. But I do not know how long that will last. It may be that we shall have to leave Toulouse in a hurry. So, I say, eat as much as you can, pack your belongings and be ready to depart at a moment's notice.

'And go where?' asked Sir Nicholas.

Robin had no reply. He almost seemed embarrassed – and I realized that for once in his life he was unsure of his plans. Then he smiled broadly at us all, and gave a light chuckle and a shrug. 'Sometimes, Sir Nicholas, it is the going *from* that is the crucial element in a journey, not the going *to* . . .'

We kicked our heels in the inn all the rest of that day, our bags and baggage packed, our horses saddled, but when dusk fell, there was still no sign of Tronc. An hour or so after the bells had rung for Vespers, the servants brought out soup and bread and cheese and wine, but few of us had much of an appetite. We were keyed up for action, half-expecting to have a horde of angry Templars crashing through the gates at any moment, yet no enemy came, the night seemed utterly tranquil. Only Nur seemed to be calm, and with great gusto she set to a steaming bowl of leek soup with a fistful of bread and a lump of cheese.

At an hour or so after midnight, the gates of the inn creaked open and a lone horsemen entered the courtyard. It was Tronc.

Robin woke those who had been asleep and we gathered to hear what our host had learned.

'Well, my friends,' said the young lord, 'it has been a great pleasure to have you as my guests, but I fear that you must be gone as swiftly as you can. The Templars are coming at dawn, a *conroi* at the very least, perhaps thirty men; with or without the permission of the Chapter, they mean to take Robin and anyone who stands with him and hold them prisoner in their preceptory in the south of the city. I had this information from impeccable sources – from a friend who is himself a senior Templar knight, but who feels that his Order should not ride roughshod over the wishes of the Consuls.'

'We could fight them,' said Little John. 'This place looks very defensible, we could hold them off for days easily . . .'

Tronc, I noticed, looked pained but said nothing.

It was Robin who answered his huge lieutenant. 'We could fight them, John, yes, but what toll would that take on our host's house, and on his servants? I cannot ask the Viscount to risk the lives of his men or the destruction of his home for me. We will leave as soon as we are able, and take our chances on the road.'

'Thank you, my lord, I do not fear the Templars but—'

'This is not your fight,' Robin said. 'You have done more than enough for us and we will not forget your kindness.'

'I do have some information that may be of some little use for you,' said Tronc. 'My Templar friend told me that he has heard of the fellow that you seek, the man with three thumbs. He has heard that this Master has had some dealings with the Count of Foix recently. But I'm afraid that is all that he could tell . . .'

'It is enough, I think,' said Robin, 'and once again I thank you from the bottom of my heart. We shall pay the Count of Foix a call, I believe, and see if he can enlighten us any further.'

'I can at least give you an introduction to the Count,' said Tronc smiling. 'He has known my family for generations. He is a strange man, and not one I would care to trust very far, but perhaps he may be willing to help you. It is in God's hands. First, however, we must get you safely out of Toulouse . . .'

The Lord of Carcassonne, Beziers, Albi and the Razès made us generous gifts before we left less than an hour later. From his kitchens he gave us an ample supply of smoked hams and roasted ducks and chickens, dried meat and fish, fruit and cheeses, fresh and twice-baked bread; from his cellars two small barrels of new wine; and to each of the Companions he gave a fine grey woollen cloak, but to me alone he made a particularly fine gift. It was a vielle made in Toulouse by a master craftsman, the body carved from polished yellow pear wood, the neck a strip of ebony – in all a beautiful instrument engraved with images of leaves and fruit.

'But Tronc,' I protested, shocked and surprised, 'you badly need a new vielle yourself. That old tuneless one you have now is no instrument for a man with your musical taste.'

'Oh, it will serve well enough until I am a better player. In truth, I did buy this pear wood one for myself, but I would be honoured if you would accept it. It has been a great pleasure to have known you and to have heard your music – I adored my eulogy – and I will take great pride in knowing that, with my gift, you will bring pleasure to many, many people.'

Our parting was brusquely interrupted by a servant. He came

into the hall, breathless, red-faced. 'Horsemen sir, there are horsemen at the gates demanding entrance. They are Templars.'

'God be with you, Alan,' said Tronc and he grasped my hand. 'I will delay the Templars while my men escort you to the city gates in the eastern wall.'

It was a good two hours yet before dawn, by my reckoning. 'Surely the gates will be locked tight at this hour,' I said.

'A little silver makes a wonderful key, my old father used to tell me,' said Tronc with a smile. 'But you must all be away – Arnald here will lead you out through the back entrance. Go swiftly, and God keep you safe!'

I could hear the angry calls of the Templars from the street outside the inn, and a hammering on the main gate, as Tronc's servant Arnald led us speedily through a stone passage at the back of the stables barely wider than a horse and out via a low wooden door into a stinking alley. There was no sign of our enemies, and Arnald took us east into a broader street, without incident. We walked our horses no more than a hundred yards to a strong-looking tower in the city wall. The Viscount's servant spoke briefly with the sleepy sergeant in charge, then disappeared inside the gatehouse with him, while we waited, fidgeting in our saddles and looking up at the high brick walls and listening out for any sign of the *conroi* of Templars. I heard an angry exchange of words in the local dialect coming from inside the building, plainly a refusal, and then more soothing tones, and in a few moments Arnald emerged and nodded at us. Then the sergeant and one of his men-at-arms grumpily lifted the bar from the wide double gate, and allowed us to pass through. The Trencavel retainer wished us luck, and set us on a road that ran directly north-east towards Gaillac and Albi, before slipping away back to the gate and leaving us to our fate.

Mercifully, there was just enough moon and starlight to make out the road, and we put spurs to our horses and rode forth boldly into the darkness. I could not help feeling a deep regret that I had not been able to spend more time with Tronc, yet at the back of my mind I knew that we had wasted several more days, and we were still no nearer confronting the Master and taking possession of the Grail. While I had been enjoying myself and making music with my new friend, far to the north, my darling Goody was slowly slipping away.

A dozen miles later, the sky in the east had lightened into a beautiful milky grey and we turned south-east down a narrow farm track, eager to be off the road when and if the Templars gave chase. After a couple of miles, in the full light of morning, we stepped off our mounts in an abandoned grain barn, blackened with fire and with half the roof missing.

Despite my guilt about the time wasted there, my heart was full at having escaped the wrath of Gilles de Mauchamps and his Templars, but I was concerned that Tronc might suffer as a result.

'For all his tender years, he is one of the most powerful men in the Languedoc,' Robin told me. 'He has nothing to fear from a pack of Templars, nor from the Consuls; they would not risk offending him and they'll be pleased to see the back of us.'

'Do you think so?'

'Oh yes, despite their bombast, the Consuls merely seek a quiet life in which they can trade and prosper. They do not want strife and bloodshed, and private feuds on their doorstep. They will be quite content to see us gone, I guarantee you that.'

'How do you think that Gilles de Mauchamps happened to discover that you were in Toulouse?' I asked Robin. I had been pondering that question a good deal.

'Tronc's enquiries after the Master must have found their way to his ears. Our host mentioned having a friend who was a Templar – indeed, he said it was this man who warned him that they were coming for us. I think we can assume that Tronc spoke to this man when we arrived and it was he who revealed to Gilles de Mauchamps that we were in Toulouse.'

Robin stopped speaking, as if he had been listening to his own words with fresh ears, and frowned. 'Why do you ask this, Alan?'

'I have a strange feeling about all this; we have been manoeuvred out of Toulouse in a hurry, told that the Master is not there, and set on the road towards Foix. I feel a little as if I were being driven somewhere, like cattle.'

'You think Tronc has betrayed us? That he is a disciple of the Master?' Robin seemed genuinely shocked.

'I don't know. I think not. He had us in his inn for several days – if he meant to do us harm, we were completely in his power then. But there is something wrong – that performance by Gilles de Mauchamps, all that shouting and rudeness, the lack of evidence, that public disrespect of Tronc in front of the Consuls. Did it not seem out of character for a Templar? They are seldom clumsy, loudmouthed fools. Do you think he really wanted to take you into custody? Or was his true aim to drive us south towards Foix? Have we escaped, I wonder, or are we being subtly guided into a trap?'

Robin shrugged. 'Well, no doubt we shall find out – in time.'

The next day, we circled around Toulouse, keeping a respectful ten miles or so from the city, and then struck the main highway towards Foix. We made camp at mid-afternoon in a rare wooded hollow, but the moment we had dismounted, Nur came striding over to Robin and I and, rudely interrupting our conversation about the potential stamina of our second-class horses, she said bluntly that we were being pursued.

'Have you seen anybody?' asked my lord.

'No,' said the witch, 'but my thumbs were pricking as we rode, and I have cast the bones, too, since then. There are men behind us for certain, men of ill-will. We are being followed.'

Robin sent out Thomas and Sir Nicholas discreetly behind us. They came back after an hour and reported that they could see nobody on our back trail.

'There is nothing there,' said Sir Nicholas, his face now a rainbow of hues from the beating he had received in Casteljaloux. 'The witch is wrong; she may be merely lying to make herself seem important.'

'We will stop here this night,' said Robin.

The next morning we set off a little after dawn, and rode a mile or two without incident. Then Nur gave a harsh shriek and called out, 'They are coming, they are coming up behind us.' But nobody apart from the woman in black could make out anything, except for a few drifting shreds of dust that could have been made by the wind. However, after another dozen miles, I could make out a dense cloud on our back trail that could only be caused by a large body of horses – perhaps forty or more – being ridden hard.

We were in wide, open, rolling countryside, with scarcely a tree in sight. We were travelling almost due south by then, with the green foothills of Foix ahead, the wide River Ariège to our right and the shadowy forms of the snow-capped mountains of the Pyrenees in the far, far distance.

'Do you think it is the Templars?' I asked Robin.

'Maybe – I don't want to find out.'

We put our heels back and urged our horses into a raggedy gallop. But after a mile or so, the beasts began to show the signs of tiredness. Despite another hour of pounding our saddles, the sweat running in rivers from man and mount alike, it was clear that the horsemen were catching up – by now perhaps only a mile or two behind us. A mile later, Roland's horse went lame, while Gavin's mount was moving very oddly, weaving from side to side, and I could feel that mine was nearly finished, too.

'Enough!' panted Little John, hauling on his reins, his face scarlet with anger and exertion. 'Enough running. Let us fight them here. Let us stand on our own two feet and face them.'

'It would do us no good, John,' said Robin, wheeling his horse, 'we have four bowmen and four swordsmen, and they . . .' My lord made a gesture with his hand and we could all clearly see, a mass of horsemen, more than forty, perhaps even fifty strong, cantering down a gentle slope towards us no more than three-quarters of a mile away. It was clear by then that they were not disciplined Templars – it was worse than that. They were Mercadier's mercenaries, *routiers* now unchecked in their savagery by any lord. And they were plainly looking for us.

'I don't give an angel's pink, puckered hole how many they are,' growled John, 'fifty, a hundred, five hundred. This is just as good a place as any to die.'

'Let us go down by the river,' Sir Nicholas said. 'The water will make it harder for them to come at us and it never hurts to have something cool to drink in a hard fight.'

We guided our tired mounts down the steep slope to the river and found a shallow fordable place where we carefully led them over. Gavin and Thomas tethered them to a line of scrubby trees that fringed a large pool and Robin set us in a double line, with the river in front and facing the slope beyond it that led to the road: four swordsmen with shields to the front – myself, with Thomas at one shoulder and Roland at the other and beyond him Sir Nicholas de Scras, who was shaking his arms to loosen the muscles and whistling to himself happily as if he had not a care in the world.

The ground was marshy and littered with boulders, some the size of a prize Nottinghamshire bull. This would be good for men on foot fighting against mounted foes; the horses would have to negotiate the river – which could not be done at speed, and then fight us among the big, impeding stones with treacherous boggy ground beneath their hooves. But there were just too many of the enemy to make the outcome uncertain. This is where I would die, I reflected, here by this cold river, with my boots sunk up to the ankles in black mud, far away from Goody and Westbury. I felt a wave of frustrated fury flood my veins. It seemed such an absurd place in which to meet my end; such a silly death. I'd not even set eyes on the Master, nor glimpsed the Grail. I prayed that Goody and I would be reunited in Heaven.

Robin, who was lining up the four bowmen behind me – himself, John, Tuck and Gavin – saw my glum face and actually laughed.

'We are not quite dead yet, Alan,' he said. 'And with a band of fighting men such as ours – who can defeat us? Little John here has personally killed more men than the red plague; Sir Nicholas, once the pride of the Hospitallers, will not allow himself to fall to a pack of gutter-born, greasy mercenaries. Will you, sir? And Sir Roland – the flower of French chivalry; one of the finest knights that noble land has ever produced – he is not afraid of anything. Look at us – we eight, we eight men of war. We are such warriors that legends are made of – we cannot be killed. Not by a hundred enemies, not by a thousand. Indeed, I worry that we shall live for ever.'

I looked at my cousin and saw that Robin's absurd speech seemed to have cheered him and, to be honest, I felt better myself. Bring on the battle, I thought. Bring on the fight, you bastards, and I will show you how an Englishman fights and dies. I felt a warm glow at the top of my spine and down the length of my arms. And, I swear, the heavy shield and sword felt lighter in my hands.

'Where is Nur?' I asked Roland, who was fiddling with a strap at the top of his left chausse, his mail legging, that attached it to the belt under his mail shirt. I had lost my chausses at Westbury, and fought only in knee-length hauberk, helmet and thick leather riding boots – although I did have the reinforced breast-and-back plate under my mail, holding the lance-dagger between my shoulder blades.

'She's behind us in that little spinney, over there,' my cousin told me, 'brewing up a spell to bring a thick mist. Like a huge cloud coming down to earth, she says, that will shield us from the sight of our enemies and allow us to escape unseen.'

I looked up at the sky: it was a bowl of palest blue, with a few delicate wisps in the far south. *A magic mist?* I thought. *My chilly arse.*

'At least she'll be hidden,' I said, 'when the horsemen come.'

And at that moment, a lone rider, a thin raggedy man armed with spear and shield appeared on the lip of the slope above us. He was some fifty yards away, on the far side of the rushing river, but I recognized him. He had been the one who ran away from the fight with Mercadier outside Bordeaux. By some freak of the wind, I heard him shout in rough French as clearly as if he were standing next to me, 'Here they are, Vim! They are here! Down there by the river.'

I heard the wooden creaking sound of a war bow being drawn, and Robin's voice saying, 'Hold fast, Gavin; hold a little longer. Let's just see if these scum have anything worth saying before we start wasting our good arrows on them.'

A few moments later the eastern skyline was filled with the shapes of the massed horsemen – a long line of mounted men arrayed for war on the slope above, menacing as a storm, malevolent, dark and as bleakly immobile as statues. It felt as if we Companions were no more than a huddle of children standing under a vast black cliff, which at any moment would crumble, slide and crash down on our heads.

Mercadier's mercenaries had finally caught us.

Part Three

Chapter Eighteen

The Lord moves in mysterious ways, as my old friend Tuck never tired of telling me. Westbury has had its first miracle – and, of course, Father Anselm has given the credit for it solely to the power of the Flask of St Luke. Incredibly, the pious old couple of Westbury village that I mentioned before, Martha and Geoffrey, have found themselves with child. Happy Martha has all the signs of being pregnant. Three months ago, at the Feast of All Saints she and her husband prayed before the flask for three days and three nights without food, drink or rest, begging the Lord that they might be blessed with a baby despite their advanced age – and God Almighty, in His infinite wisdom, has heeded them.

A month after Christmas, my daughter-in-law Marie told me in wondering tones that Martha was expecting, and that she was planning to wrap up some of her old baby clothes and a few carved wooden toys as a gift for the newborn when it arrives.

I do not know what to think of this – I know for certain that the flask is the same one I purchased in the cathedral of St-Sernin, a perfectly ordinary piece of pilgrim's kit, and yet God has seen fit to grant a miracle in its name. Why? Does an old leather bottle hold the same power as a true relic? Is God indifferent to the authenticity of sacred objects blessed by the Church? I cannot understand it.

Alas, the fame of the Flask of St Luke is spreading; and people are coming from as far away as Sheffield to pray in front of it in our little church. For my part, I pray that the enthusiasm for this false relic will quickly die out – but I fear otherwise. I have encountered a dozen pilgrims on the paths around Westbury in the past few weeks, even in this inclement winter season. And when I stopped each of them and asked their business on my desmesne, I discovered that they were foreigners from other counties, women from Yorkshire and Derbyshire mostly, who had walked here to pray at our church for a child. Is the whole world planning to make a pilgrimage to my door? What if more miracles are announced? We would have no peace at all.

But I must confess there is another fear that lurks just beyond my thoughts. Was it truly God who sanctioned this miracle – or could it perhaps have been some other power? For the flask is not quite as ordinary an object as I often like to tell myself. In my most secret heart, I know that it once held a liquor that might well be a source of great power, but could also be a conduit for evil.

For that flask once held the blood of a witch.

There were forty-seven men and horses lined up above us – I know that because I had time to count each of them. Forty-seven iron-hard mercenaries – the scum of Christendom, men whose names were a byword for rapacity, cruelty and reckless slaughter. Our little group of eight Companions, standing straddle-foot in the rock-strewn valley of the River Ariège, grimly determined, gripping our weapons in sweat-damp hands, did not move: we waited for their attack.

Which did not come.

A lone man, gently waving a big, pale grubby rag – the closest they had to a white flag, I presumed – walked his horse slowly down the slope. He was a big-shouldered, brawny *routier*, square-faced and grey-blond, scarred and immensely tough-looking. His horse, a raw-boned bay with a black mane, seemed almost as exhausted as our own nags. The beast picked its way carefully, tiredly, through the boulders down to the opposite side of the river, some twenty paces from us, and there the rider halted it.

'I seek the Earl of Locksley,' said the man, in rough Norman French with, I swear, a touch of a Germanic accent.

Robin pushed his way past my shoulder and took a pace out in front of our little formation. He had a strung bow in his hands, an arrow bag at his hip, but his sword remained sheathed.

'I am Locksley,' he said, cool as morning dew, 'who are you and how may I serve you?'

'It is I – or rather we – who wish to serve you,' said the man, with a faint smile. 'I am Wilhelmus of Mechlin, though my men call me Vim, and we are a company of free lances, soldiers of the road, good men all and doughty fighters. But we have no lord, we are masterless men. We had a bold captain – and he was strong and wise in the ways of battle – but he is dead now. So we would take service with you, my lord, for a season and for a generous fee, and we will swear to accept all your commands faithfully and do your bidding in all things.'

'You are Mercadier's men?'

'We were. Now we are nobody's men.'

'What do you know of Mercadier's death?'

The blond mercenary laughed. 'We know how he died. Like a warrior, in battle, as we would all wish to die. And we know who killed him.' He inclined his head towards me. 'Olivier up there saw the fight; barely escaped with his own life.'

The familiar-looking man on the slope above lifted his left hand to me in a wary greeting. 'We do not seek vengeance, if that is what concerns you,' Vim said. 'There is no gain in it for us – as God above is my witness – we merely seek a lord, a captain under whose banner we can fight for pay and profit. Your name is known to us, as is your reputation – as a generous lord and man who knows the value of a bag of silver and how to get hold of one. We would serve you – Robin Hood. Would you have us?'

The mercenaries came down from the slope and one by one they each crossed the Ariège, bared their heads, put aside their many and varied weapons in a great, clanking pile by the river bank, and swore an oath of fealty to Robin, kneeling before him and placing their right hands on a tattered Bible that Tuck hastily produced from his baggage. They swore that they would never harm their lord and would faithfully serve him for a period of one year and one day from the day of the oath. Robin, in turn, gave each man a single silver penny as a token that he would, in due course, reward them richly for their service – although I knew that Robin must be running short of funds by then and wondered where the hoard of silver required to pay the mercenaries was to come from. Then, right there by the river side, not ten yards from the spot where I had believed a few hours earlier that I would be slaughtered, we sat down to break bread with these men.

We ate and drank from the stores that Tronc had furnished us with, cracking open a barrel of wine, and unwrapping whole hams and cold roast ducks and many cheeses, and I believe this impressed the hungry mercenaries. But I mused privately that their attitude might well change when the silver ran out and we were forced to eat rotten cabbage soup and drink rainwater.

As we ate, the Companions kept their distance from the *routiers* – Roland in particular seemed to be particularly suspicious of them, and he eyed them keenly as he ate. Nur crouched beside him, watching my cousin with a proprietorial air and, I noted to myself, perhaps rather meanly, that the weather remained glorious, the sun was shining, there was barely a cloud in the sky – no sign at all of the promised life-saving magic mist. But I was able – just – to restrain myself from asking her why this miraculous change in the weather had not occurred.

Robin had been making a round of the mercenaries, greeting them, making the odd jest and getting to know them by name, but he finally grabbed a piece of bread and a duck leg and came over to sit beside me.

We ate in contented silence for a while and then my lord said quietly, in a tone that would carry no further, 'Well, Alan, what do you make of them?'

I shrugged. 'They are a hard crew but I think we can trust them. They had us at their mercy and instead of slaughtering us they swore an oath of fealty to you. I think they genuinely do seek a lord. A mercenary must have a paymaster. The only thing that concerns me is the money. They *will* have to be paid handsomely. These kind of men do not fight for nothing. Can you afford it?'

'No,' said Robin. 'I can't. I have almost no silver left, and I must have coin for these men. No matter, a little money trouble is a good deal better than being dead.'

'What about Baruch's gold?' I asked.

'I pawned a good deal of it in London and Bordeaux to pay our expenses. I do have a couple of trinkets left but I cannot divide up, say, a tiny golden censer, with delicate silver filigree work, and share it out among fifty horny-handed men-at-arms. No, I must have silver coin, and plenty of it, before long.'

We camped by the river, mercenaries and Companions still keeping their distance, and at dusk Robin gathered all of us together and gave a speech. He told the *routiers* that we sought a three-thumbed monk who called himself the Master, who was our enemy, and who was somewhere in the County of Foix, and then told them that we aimed to take revenge on him. Robin did not mention the Grail at all; instead he implied that the Master had great riches in his possession and that, once he was dead, we'd all share in the loot. At that, the mercenaries gave a rousing cheer.

Once the Master was dead, Robin said, sounding as plausible as a courtroom cleric, we would ride north to Anjou and take up arms on the side of Arthur, Duke of Brittany, against the throne-stealing John of England, and when the usurper was dead or humbled, we would all be richly rewarded by the young, generous duke.

The mercenaries dutifully cheered once more. Then Robin gave his three rules of behaviour, the three unbreakable rules that I had heard him outline before on the Great Pilgrimage, as a measure to keep discipline in the ranks of his men. 'No man under my command steals so much as a penny, desecrates a church, or beds any woman without her consent – unless I give them my permission. And I will hang from the nearest tree any man who breaks these rules. No trial, no excuses, just a quick final dance at the end of a rope. Is that clear to everyone?'

The men looked sober at this but not one ventured to protest at the promise of such rough justice. They were, after all, veteran soldiers, men used to warfare with harsh rules.

As I washed my face in the river before bed that night, I found myself kneeling next to Olivier, who was making his own ablutions beside me. He smiled nervously, and I greeted him with a curt but civil 'God save you!'

An uncomfortable pause, then he said, 'So you did for old Mercadier, eh?'

I didn't know how to respond to that and so I said nothing.

'I knew you and he was enemies, like,' the man continued. 'He hated your guts, truth be told. Hated you from the first moment he saw you in Normandy, all those years ago – told me so himself. But you fixed him good and proper, sir, in the end.'

I felt obliged to say something; the man was trying to be friendly, but I was still struggling with an appropriate answer.

'It was not on my own account that we fought – it was for my cousin Roland, that blond man over there. Mercadier would have blinded him at Dangu – worse, my cousin was humiliated, and put in fear. In truth, we killed him for that humiliation.'

'Yes, I remember that night, after the battle near Gisors – we took a score of Frenchies prisoner, if I remember rightly. Blinded most of 'em. Would have done your cousin, too, if the Earl hadn't come in at the last minute with two dirty great chests of silver. I said to myself: that Earl, he's an open-handed gent, he's a lord who'd be generous to those who served him.'

'You were there? You blinded all those men?' I found that I had recoiled from the lean, grinning fellow. 'That is monstrous. A crime against God – you should be ashamed of yourself . . .'

'We don't make the rules,' said Olivier quickly. 'We're humble folk. We was just following orders. Mercadier's orders – do that, he says, and we do it. And old King Richard knew about it, too. Oh yes, the Lionheart turned a blind eye to all of it. Blind eye – ha-ha. But war's war, as old Mercadier often used to say to me; it's not a child's game. Our task is to win, and win any-which-way.'

I opened my mouth to rebuke him and then closed it. I did not want to debate the morality of the battlefield with a fellow who killed for pay and blinded his prisoners. I was about to tell him there would be none of that sort of disgusting and immoral behaviour under Robin's command, when I thought of Malloch, the Jew, and the bloody stumps of his severed fingers, and found I had nothing to say after all. So I stiffly bade him good night and went to join the Companions.

Roland came to me as I was preparing to bed down. 'I don't like it, Alan,' he said quietly. 'I don't trust these . . . people. They could murder us all in our sleep.'

'They could have killed us this afternoon, if they'd wished. But they did not. I think they will prove to be loyal – after all, a man must have a lord,' I said. 'Mustn't he? Besides, Robin seems to trust them.'

Roland grunted something rude, seemingly unmollified, and went back to his bedroll.

In spite of my words, I slept fitfully – the misericorde gripped in my hand.

We left just after dawn – riding south, through Pamiers and other villages, beside the rushing waters of the Ariège, and coming into the green hill country at the base of the mighty Pyrenees. Around mid-afternoon we rounded the shoulder of a mountain and saw the castle of the Counts of Foix standing proud on an isolated hilltop before us. Its sight drew a gasp from me.

It was a noble fortification: two square stone towers with a long, low stone hall joining them to each other, surrounded by a high curtain wall and all of it atop an almost sheer outcrop of grey rock that lunged upwards hundreds of feet above the surrounding river valley. At the foot of the mass of the castle rock, between that stark citadel and the place where the Arget river joined the Ariège, nestled the ancient Abbey of St Volusianus. The town, a stinking warren of craftsman's and tradesman's houses, was slightly to the south and squeezed between the abbey and the steep sides of the ancestral fortress of the Count of Foix.

We made our camp about five hundred yards to the south-east of the castle, in the water meadows by the Ariège, and we were not unobserved. Indeed, our passage along the banks of the river was punctuated by the brisk sound of slamming wooden shutters as the townsfolk began to barricade themselves into their dwellings. I could make out the figures of a dozen men-at-arms or knights in bright red-and-gold-striped surcoats on the battlements of the castle, and a stream of townsfolk making their way up the winding path to it, burdened with cloth-wrapped bundles. And no wonder, with the addition of the mercenaries, we were now a sizeable force – and when more than fifty dirty, raggedy, unshaven yet heavily armed men arrive unexpectedly in your town, you lock up your house, bury your coin and get your wife and children up to the castle as quick as your legs will carry you, if you are a wise man.

As the mercenaries set up camp in the water meadow, under the watchful gaze of the crowd on the battlements, I hunted out my best clothes and, with Thomas's help, managed to find a cleanish pair of grey hose and a blue tunic trimmed with silk that was only lightly stained. With my hair combed, my face more or less clean, my sword belted around my waist but without armour or shield, I accompanied Robin and Vim through the narrow streets of the town, past the locked gate of the abbey and up the steep, serpentine road to the castle and its main entrance, a barred double door set in a stone arch.

We were challenged fifty feet from the gate, and when Robin announced himself, the portal swung open and we were escorted by a dozen men-at-arms in their gaudy gold-and-red-striped attire, to the hall of the castle, and ushered into the august presence of Raymond-Roger, the fifth Count of Foix of that name.

We bowed and Robin handed over a letter from another Raymond-Roger, our friend Tronc, which briefly introduced us as peaceful travellers and commended us to his care. The Count – a fat, angry-looking man nearing fifty, with a weak, petulant mouth – read the letter quickly, standing by his hearth, and then scowled at us. He took a long pull from a jewelled goblet, wiped a trickle of wine from his lips with his embroidered sleeve and said, 'So you are the Earl of Locksley – the outlawed Earl of Locksley, if I'm not mistaken, also known as Robin Hood.'

'I am,' said Robin, smiling genially, though I saw a glint of steel in his gaze.

It was clear that the Count had his own sources of information.

'And you were chased out of Toulouse and have decided to come south to visit my lands – with a small army at your back; an army that I see is now encamped outside my peaceful little town.'

The Count gestured violently at a small barred window set high in the stone wall of his low-ceilinged hall. 'What am I to make of you? The infamous Robin Hood – here in my castle. How would you respond if I were to come to your lands in England – Yorkshire, isn't it? – under similar circumstances? Would you welcome me with open arms? Feast me, fall on my neck and rejoice to the heavens at my coming? I very much doubt it.'

'We mean no harm to you, my lord,' said Robin with a frank and winning smile. 'We seek a powerful man, a former monk, who goes by the name of the Master and who has an extra thumb on his left hand. We were told that you had had some dealings with him and we would be grateful for a little information. That is all.'

'And what would you do if you were to encounter this man, this Master?' asked the Count, tilting his head on one side and squeezing one eye shut. I realized then that the man was extremely drunk.

For a moment, Robin did not answer. He seemed to be weighing his words carefully. Then he said coldly, formally, like a man pronouncing a sentence in law, 'I would kill him; I would slit his belly, pull out his steaming entrails, roast them and feed them to him. I would cut off his head, but slowly, sawing through his neck with an old and rusty blade, and bear his ugly, severed poll, dripping, all the way back to Yorkshire on my spear-point. I would slaughter him, dismember him, turn him into fox-food – and I would destroy any man, *any man*, who seeks to protect him.'

The Count seemed rather taken aback by Robin's answer, and the naked threat that it contained. He was silent for several long moments. I wondered if he would order his men-at-arms to fall on us, and I readied myself. But he remained still and silent, and a range of expressions flickered across his wine-sodden face: outrage, anger, fear, calculation, wonderment – and was that last expression a look of relief? Then he gave Robin a sly smile, which broadened into a wide grin.

'That is a bold, warlike answer, my lord, one that I find gladdens my heart – perhaps you and your knights would be gracious enough to spend a few days here in the castle as my guests – although I would prefer your common men-at-arms to remain in the water meadow for the time being. I believe that we may have things of mutual benefit to discuss.'

The mercenaries stayed in the meadow, and ate and drank and slept, and more or less kept their discipline – Little John, Thomas, Nur and Gavin remained with them and Robin had repeated his three rules and even gone so far as to set up a semi-permanent makeshift gallows, a noose hung over the branch of an apple tree, as a reminder of the penalty for unruly behaviour. But Sir Nicholas, Roland, Robin, Tuck and myself – and Vim – were offered a floor to ourselves in the old, northernmost tower of the Castle of Foix, and the Count beamed and nodded at us and showed us the most lavish hospitality.

The square room we shared was three storeys up, at the top of three steep sets of ladders – and with six big men sleeping in there, it was not spacious – but I was very grateful to be indoors and not sleeping in the open or under canvas in the meadow. We discovered that the weather in late April and early May so near the high mountains was very swift to change – one moment bright sunshine, the next a deluge of stinging rain or a fog as thick as a fleece.

I was not present at the discussions of 'mutual benefit' that Robin had with the Count of Foix, but my lord related the gist of them to me, on the afternoon of the second day after our arrival, when we were standing on the flat roof of the tower, taking a little weak sunshine on our faces and admiring the view: to the south the snow-capped peaks of the Pyrenees, to the north the long valley of the Ariège, dotted with round green hills and crumbling rocky eminences. The Castle of Foix was a magnificent site for a fortification, one of the best I have seen, soaring high above the countryside and from which you could see a day's ride in all directions.

'The Master is now at a place called Montségur,' said Robin quietly. 'It is about twenty miles south-east of here, an old ruined castle on a mountaintop, which the previous count of Foix abandoned as too remote to bother with. Nine months ago, the Master came to Foix. He had only two retainers with him, a priest and a poor knight, and he begged the Count for permission to set up a retreat from the world at Montségur. He made it sound as if it would be a sort of hermitage – a place of contemplation for a handful of devout men who wished to venerate the Holy Mother of Our Lord, in their own quiet and humble way.

'Somehow – and the Count is not quite sure exactly what happened – he found himself setting his seal to a formal charter that granted Montségur to the Master. The Count cannot clearly remember why he was persuaded to sign over Montségur – it may be a surfeit of drink, or his own feeble will, but he believes that his mind was clouded by a kind of enchantment. I know what I think.'

Robin looked at me, but I looked away – I was embarrassed. I too had been susceptible to the Master's strange charisma when he had been our prisoner in the Limousin at Château Chalus-Chabrol around the time King Richard had died.

'But the Count was not too perturbed, at this point. He had deeded away a tiny tract of land to a religious institution – but his father had done something similar on a much grander scale, granting land for several abbeys to be built in Foix, where Masses for his soul are still being said. Montségur was little better than a ruin, and Raymond-Roger had given his word and set his seal on the document. What harm could a few devotees of the Virgin do down there on a remote mountaintop?

'For some months, the Count ignored his new neighbours, and carried on with his affairs here in Foix. He is a man, I think, who desires a quiet life. But he began to hear strange tales about the place. The Master was swiftly rebuilding the walls of the old castle, the Count was told, using forced peasant labour. And the Master was recruiting fighting men – knights and men-at-arms from all over Europe – in significant numbers. In the space of six months, the ruined castle had been repaired and turned into a fortress – and the Count began to be alarmed. But even more troubling were the stories coming out of Montségur, tales of Satanic ceremonies involving a magical relic, a relic so holy that its merest touch could cure all disease, even hold back Death itself. More warriors were recruited to serve at Montségur – and the castle soon became powerful, manned by scores of knights in white mantels with a blue cross on their chests.

'Our poor friend Raymond-Roger felt betrayed, he felt that he had been harbouring a cuckoo in his nest. A mighty castle had sprung up, almost overnight, in his own backyard, one that could even rival the Castle of Foix. Then it grew worse. Armed men rode out from Montségur and took what they wished from the local peasants; taxes, even tithes destined for the Church, all in the name of the Mother of God and this mysterious relic. They were acting more like bandits than men of the cloth. At this affront to his authority, and that of the Church, the Count of Foix was forced to act. About three weeks ago, he gathered his handful of knights and rode to Montségur to demand answers – indeed, he intended to rescind the charter and take back possession of the castle for himself.

'The mountainside was too steep for horsemen – the Count and his knights, a dozen or so of them, and about a score of men-at-arms, puffed and panted their way up a winding path to the top and demanded entrance and an immediate audience with the Master.

'Well, the Master defied the Count. He lined the battlements with his own blue-and-white-clad Knights of Our Lady – fifty of them, the Count saw, all armed and mailed and war-ready – and told the Count to depart at once and leave him in peace. This was his vassal, you understand, Alan, telling his own lord – a man who had granted him the castle in the first place – to get himself hence. And then, the oddest thing – the Count found himself retreating without a fight, without a murmur. He led his men all the way back to the foot of the mountain, without a blow being struck or an arrow loosed. Without even an angry word.

'Afterwards, the Count reasoned to himself that he could not have taken the castle with the men he had, not if he besieged it for ten years, but he still went home humiliated. He sees himself as the laughing stock of the Languedoc – a lord who gave away a castle to a passing beggar, on a whim, and who cannot get it back.'

'And then we arrived in Foix,' I said.

'Yes, then we came here with what the Count is pleased to call a small army.' Robin was grinning at me, that devilish look he often wore before a bloody fight or a piece of sinful larceny.

'And we have come to an accommodation, Count Raymond-Roger and myself. For a small consideration, a little something for Vim's men, we shall evict the Master from Montségur and deliver him, bound and chastened, to this very Castle of Foix for suitable punishment. As well as the money, the Count will supply us with arms and food and a guide and will allow us free, unmolested passage through his lands. The Count shall have Montségur back, we shall have the Grail, and the Master shall be put to a horrible death here in Foix. What do you think of that?'

'How much is he paying us?'

'Never you mind about that, Alan – your share will be quite enough to rebuild Westbury when we get home, let's leave it at that. Do you not like the arrangement?'

To be honest, I *was* impressed. Robin seemed to have made a most satisfactory deal. I could not see a flaw – except for the obvious one. 'If the Count was unable to take the castle from the Master – and you say it is a mighty fortress, a very tough nut – how are we going to manage it with fifty-odd men?'

'I don't know yet,' said Robin. 'One thing at a time – but we will manage it somehow, Alan. Trust me. We'll find a way.'

Raymond-Roger feasted us in his hall before we departed for Montségur. It was three days after my conversation with Robin and he had spent the intervening time seeing to the mercenaries – paying them a shilling a piece, money that he had promptly received from the Count, and checking that each man had adequate weapons, gear, clothing and five days' supply of food. This was not the first time that Robin had outfitted a small force in preparation for a campaign – and he did it with his usual speed and thoroughness. He hanged a man, too, a noisy braggart who broke into the wine barrels in the store tent during a long, hot dull afternoon, drank his fill and then rampaged through the town with a drawn sword, stealing anything he could lay hands on and terrifying the local inhabitants. Then, whooping, he chased down and raped the pretty daughter of the town's miller.

Robin did not bother with a trial – once the man had been identified by the outraged miller, Little John and Gavin bound him, cursed him and hauled him up by his neck over the apple bough. I did not attend the execution – I have a particular distaste for hangings – but Thomas told me that the rest of the mercenaries took the punishment of their comrade well, looking on in grim silence as he kicked out his last moments on earth at the end of a rope. As I have said, they were a hard crew of cut-throats and thieves, who had doubtless seen and done a lot worse themselves.

It was clear at the feast that Raymond-Roger loved his wine; he drank it beaker by beaker as a man who has fought a day-long battle drinks cool water. We were obliged to drink with him, for he was forever calling out toasts to the good health of Robin, Sir Roland and Sir Nicholas – whom he found the most respectable members of our Companions and so the most to his taste – and bidding us show our appreciation, too. The result, predictably, was that he became very drunk, very fast. None of us was sober by the time the last of the crumbs were swept away and his pages came by with ewers, bowls and towels to allow us to cleanse our fingers of grease. I had offered to play my vielle for the company, but the suggestion had been refused by the Count's steward and, instead, a Foix man – who, we were told, owned a particularly amusing dancing bear – was admitted to the dim hall.

The poor animal, moth-eaten and deprived of tooth and claw, shambled around the hall in evident terror of his master, who played a flute with scant regard to the laws of tone or rhythm while the animal shuffled about in a state of deep, agitated misery. I could hardly stand to watch the sad, capering beast and turned my attention to what the Count – now loose-limbed and garrulous with drink – was saying to Robin two places down from me.

'. . . I am sorry that I even considered it, my friend,' the Count was saying. 'I am so, so sorry. You are clearly a noble man of great honour, and renown . . . and honour, and I am ashamed that I even considered detaining you.'

My ears pricked up at this. But it was clear that Robin had heard it before. He nodded and laid a soothing hand on the Count's shoulder. 'My dear Raymond-Roger, think nothing of it. We are friends now. All's well that ends well.'

'It was despic-despicable of me to have even contemplated it. Despicable. You should despise me! You must despise me!'

Robin saw me listening and gave me a narrow, piercing glare that told me to mind my own damn business. 'I want you to despise me,' the Count wailed, his sodden words audible even over the shrill tones of the bear-master's execrable flute-playing. Robin soothed him with more wine. And, as soon as it was possible, I made my excuses and left the feast.

It was not until much later, in the cramped room where we all were sleeping, that Robin told me what was behind the Count's extraordinary words.

But I had to push Robin hard to get him to tell me what it was all about. 'If you must know,' said my lord crossly – he had been forced to take more wine than he liked and it made him irritable – 'you were right, oh wise Sir Alan. At the Maison des Consuls, Gilles de Mauchamps deliberately overplayed his hand with the Chapter. He knew that, with Tronc's friendship and protection, the Consuls would not hand us over to him. He meant for us to escape Toulouse and come south. You remember that Templar friend of Tronc's who told him that the Master had had dealings with Foix? Well, I think Tronc was fed that information deliberately. The Count here expected our visit – and he had orders to capture us and imprison us on our arrival. A Knight of Our Lady came to Foix a few days ago and told him, in unmistakable terms, that if he valued his life and his remaining lands, he should chain us up tightly and throw us into his deepest dungeon the moment we arrived. Happy now?'

'What – explain.'

Robin took a deep breath. 'If I do, will you let me get some sleep? Well, then. Apparently, the Master is particularly keen to have you, Alan, and all your possessions, in safe custody. The knight said exactly that: "Make sure the *trouvère* Alan Dale is seized, and all of his goods made fast." I don't know why and neither does the Count. There is no point asking either of us.'

'So why didn't he do it? Why didn't the Count seize us?'

'Damn you, Alan – will you ever let me close my eyes? It's quite simple. The Count saw the size of the force we brought with us – meeting the mercenaries on the road was a stroke of extremely good fortune, it seems – and he decided that here was his chance to rid himself of the Master once and for all.'

'Do you think he will keep faith with us?'

'I am certain he will not,' said Robin. 'The moment we leave he will send word to the Master that we are coming – the Count is a man who likes to play both ends against the middle, and then the middle against the middle. But I am too tired to worry about that now. I am going to sleep. And if you ask me any more questions tonight, Alan, I swear I'll gut you like a fish.'

Chapter Nineteen

We left the next morning on a cheerful day in early May when the world was green and bright and the sun was the rightful monarch of the clear blue heavens. Robin seemed oddly subdued, almost morose, as we rode along – he claimed that Vim's snoring had not allowed him to rest. But I was certain that, for all his bold front, he was worried about what awaited us.

The Count of Foix had provided a guide – an old shepherd from the area around Montségur called Maury, a surly, malodorous brute in greasy sheepskins on a mule that was as ill-tempered as its master – and had insisted on giving us a long speech before our departure about the deep friendships that had been forged between us and the gratitude that he felt at our taking his side in this world-shaking contest between him and the Master.

Nonetheless, we rode slowly, in full armour, our swords loose in their scabbards, each of us carrying a twelve-foot-long man-killing lance with a razor-keen leaf-shaped blade – gifts, selected by Robin from the Count's armouries. Robin had told us that we must expect to be attacked from the moment we left the town of Foix behind us. So, we were all at our most vigilant and rode south beside the Ariège for half a mile before taking a rough dusty farm track east, following the pungent local guide and his ambling mule. Vim had put out scouts before and behind us and two on each flank, and the mercenaries showed that they were masters of lesser but equally crucial arts of warfare by reporting in at regular intervals and changing over the sentries to make sure the men riding on the perimeter were always fresh and alert.

Robin was conferring with Little John at the column's head, and Thomas had just been sent out to relieve one of the forward scouts, when I found myself walking my horse beside Sir Nicholas de Scras's mount. The former Hospitaller did not look a happy man, his face was pinched and sour, although the cuts he had suffered at the Jealous Castle had healed and his bruises had faded to smears of yellow and brown. I asked him if he was quite well for he seemed to be sickening for something.

'I am perfectly healthy in my body, Alan,' he said in a low voice, a tone that would not be overheard by anyone nearby. 'It is my soul that I have been worrying about. I sometimes ask myself what I am doing in this strange land, surrounded by heretics, devil-worshippers, Sodomites and killers-for-hire. Is this my lot in life – to be no more than a squalid treasure-hunter? Sometimes I feel that I'm no better than these hirelings, these Godless *routiers*. Is this what I have become? A sword for sale?'

'The Grail is more than a treasure,' I said, 'and the quest to find it is a holy one, I think, blessed by God. Even if I did not need the Grail's power to save Goody, I would like to see the Master deprived of it – for he is unworthy of its virtues.'

'Yes, the Master is evil,' my friend replied, 'and even if we did not already know that, the unholy ceremony of initiation in the Jealous Castle proves it – did you know that the knights of his order planned to dismember me as part of it? God preserve us. But I fear that we have no moral advantage. Only those who are pure

289

in the eyes of God are fit to possess the Grail. And we are seeking to take the Holy Grail from the Master only to give it over to another who is no better.'

His words disturbed me. 'Surely you do not think that Robin is evil?' I said bristling and preparing to defend my lord.

'I do not know if he is evil,' said Sir Nicholas. 'But he is a thief – you cannot deny that. He stole that five hundred livres of silver from the Paris Temple, that much is now clear. And he is a murderer – he killed our friend Sir Richard at Lea in the Holy Land – surely you remember? – and many more besides. And he does not pray or respect the Church, far from it. He is a Godless, murdering thief. Tell me, Alan, can you honestly say that he is a good and decent Christian?'

I was feeling a little hot around the throat at Sir Nicholas's words. But I could not deny any of the things that he had said. I knew Robin well by then, and while I knew that he was unswervingly loyal to his circle – the friends and family who served him, and that he would offer his life for them without hesitation – I also knew that he was indeed a thief, and a murderer, and no lover at all of Holy Mother Church.

'Why then does a pure knight such as yourself continue to serve him?' I asked Sir Nicholas, somewhat icily.

'I did not come on this quest in order to serve him – I came for you,' said my friend, and I met his honest muddy-green eyes and saw that he spoke the truth. 'I came because your dear wife is sick and I truly believe that the Grail might save her.'

He gave a shy laugh, and broke our gaze. 'But that is not the whole truth, I must confess. I came because I was bored to death at home in Sussex, and I wanted, above all, to see the Grail. I wanted to behold the vessel that once held Our Saviour's sacred blood . . .'

'Are you talking about it?' Father Tuck had suddenly appeared on Sir Nicholas's flank and, although I knew that the wound in his side was still troubling him, his round face seemed to beam happiness like a tiny sun.

'We are talking about the Grail, yes,' I said, pleased that a difficult conversation with Sir Nicholas had been interrupted.

'I imagine it very often before I go to sleep,' Tuck said. 'It is my most sinful pleasure. In my mind, I see it as a huge golden cup, ten feet tall, and shining more brilliantly than a thousand fires, studded with bright jewels, diamonds, rubies and sapphires, and filled with a strong wine that tastes of honey and sunlight.'

I laughed at Tuck's words and I was relieved to see that even Sir Nicholas managed a smile.

We paused at midday and ate a simple meal of bread and cheese in the shade of a stand of pine trees. It was very warm; the big Languedoc sun seeming to think that it was a midsummer's day rather than spring – perhaps that was because we were so far south. I was reminded of my travels in the Mediterranean, the hot sun and the noise of cicadas buzzing in the trees, although the scrubby hill country that we passed through was far more lush than the parched hills of Sicily.

By mid-afternoon, we had turned off the eastern road and were heading more or less south, still following the haunches of the guide's mule. The track became thinner, less well trodden – indeed not much more than a footpath, and we began to climb. We were passing through a narrow valley between two great steep rocky hills when in a flurry of activity I saw Vim speaking urgently with Robin at the head of the column, and Robin turning in the saddle to shout something. That is when the noise hit me. A rumbling, rattling roar from my left, from the east, and I turned to see an avalanche of boulders, hundreds of them, some as big as houses, some the size of pigs, some no more than pebbles, sweeping down the mountainside towards us.

Robin was shouting 'Back, back, get back down the valley . . .' and gesturing with his left arm, urging us to retreat.

I wrenched my horse around – the animal was bucking and whinnying, clearly on the verge of panic – and urged it back the way we had come. And almost too late. A round boulder as big as a hay cart crashed across our path in a cloud of dust and as I laid my spurs in hard against my mount's sides and charged blindly into the gritty fog, I could hear the awful screams of men and horses crushed by the giant stones. I had to leap over a bloody tangle of a fallen mercenary and his mount. Another rock, even bigger than the first leaped out of the dust on my right and skipped across our path and my horse lost his head. He bucked and screamed, twisted and reared up on his hind legs, throwing me sideways out of the saddle. I crashed to earth, landing painfully on my shoulder, but bounced up in time to see the horse disappear into the clouds of dirt heading south. I blundered after him, cursing, and a rock that seemed almost square rolled slowly past my boots. Then I was out of the choking dust, and running downhill, free and clear.

After a hundred yards, I skidded to a halt and looked back at the swath of destruction in the valley behind me – I could see at least three humped shapes of horses or men, crushed by the tumbling boulders. I looked up at the mountainside to the east and saw the forms of men – some mounted, some on foot – more than a hundred fighters in all, streaming down the hillside to attack us in our confusion.

I was relieved to see that Robin had survived unscathed, he was no more than thirty yards away and I saw that he had a hand on my escaped horse's bridle and was shouting orders to the mercenaries to form a line in preparation of receiving the attack from the hillside. Thomas was unhurt too, and there was Roland drawing his sword – both of them still mounted. I ran to Robin and climbed back into the saddle, nodding thanks to my lord and trying to soothe the frightened animal with soft words and a gentling hand. But the beast was still skittish, prancing and crabbing under me.

And then the crossbow bolts began to fly – from behind us. A mercenary, trying to control his capering horse and get it into the battle line, gave a shout of pain and surprise, suddenly unstrung by a bolt in the spine. I saw that the quarrel had come from a small copse behind our loose crowd of frightened, milling, dust-streaked men, and out from the trees flitted more – black streaks in the sun-filled air. There must have been twenty crossbow men concealed in that small wood, invisible to us and undetected by the scouts as we rode past. The enemy were now emerging, their clothes merely brown and green rags, their faces smeared with mud and dust – but their weapons were clean and well-cared for. And deadly accurate. I saw another two mercenaries fall to their bolts, and a horse with a quarrel lodged in its haunch kicking out wildly as if to flick away the pain. We had enemies on both sides. The horsemen of the hillside were a scant fifty yards away, and I easily recognized them as the Knights of Our Lady by their flapping white surcoats. Behind them came a horde of shrieking foot men, bounding down the mountainside. And still the deadly quarrels flew from the little wood at the rear of our position. In our arrogance, we had walked straight into an elaborate trap – and it looked very much as if we would be swamped in a few heartbeats, crushed between the crossbowmen and the charging cavalry.

But Robin was nothing if not a superb battlefield commander. 'Alan,' he called out in his battle-voice, 'take a couple of good men and sort out those crossbows, will you. Be as quick as you like about it.' Then he turned away and I saw him marshalling the mercenaries into a rough line. I yelled, 'Thomas!' and was unsurprised to see that my squire was close at hand; he passed me his lance without a word and drew his sword.

'You and you are with me.' I pointed at two mercenaries within a few yards of me, one of whom was Olivier.

With Thomas on my left, and two mercenaries on my right, I lifted my shield, couched my lance, and we charged towards the clump of trees forty yards away and the cloud of grubby, ragged crossbowmen before it who were methodically loading their weapons and loosing, over and over again, their deadly bolts hissing and cracking into our disordered ranks.

Galloping into a hail of crossbow bolts is no merry task; but I did not allow myself time to think. I felt the wind of a bolt fan my cheek, another smashed against my shield, then the mercenary furthest from me gave a high wail like a smacked child, rose and slumped in his saddle, a quarrel jutting from his neck – and then we were on the enemy crossbowmen.

I took the first plumb on the point of my spear, driving the leaf-shaped blade in just below his sternum, and punching him back off his feet with the force of the impact. I released the spear and left it standing proud of his corpse but as I struggled to unsheathe Fidelity, my already terrified horse reared suddenly, its brown flank skimmed by the sharp iron tip of a passing quarrel, and I was almost unseated once again. Then there was a short, ugly crossbowman before me, his face one big battle snarl, his loaded weapon at his shoulder. As I stared at him helplessly, trying to cling on to my bucking horse with my knees and haul out my long sword at the same time, he raised the firing bar and loosed the bolt from a distance of less than five paces. A black blur, and the quarrel smashed into my chest like a strike from a stone-breaker's long hammer; I was rocked back in my saddle, my lower back crashing painfully against the high cantle. I looked down at my chest and saw that foot-long bolt sticking straight out from my mail coat. For a moment I was astounded to be alive – and then I gave thanks to St Michael for the leather chest-and-back plate reinforced with iron strips that had evidently just saved me from certain death. I had Fidelity free by this point and the crossbowman was still standing there like a mutton-headed oaf, gawping at me in plain disbelief, as if he had just witnessed a miracle. I urged the frightened horse forward a mere step or two and sliced the sword down into his shoulder, and he dropped. Wheeling, I saw Thomas ride down and behead a running man, and Olivier drive his spear into another's back. Half a dozen rag-clad corpses now littered the woodland floor. The crossbowmen were running, throwing away their big cumbersome T-shaped weapons and fleeing back into the safety of the deep woods. I pursued one, half-heartedly, clanging my sword tip against the top of his helmet as he ducked and scurried into the thick undergrowth. But we had performed our task; Robin's rear would be menaced by these bowmen no more.

I lifted my eyes to see what had become of my lord and was just in time to see a brave sight. Robin's thin line of mercenary cavalry had just charged the oncoming Knights of Our Lady. They were more numerous than we – perhaps fifty against our forty – and they had several score of infantry, spearmen mostly, in support who were coming down the hill at speed. But, as I watched, the two lines of horsemen smashed into each other with a tumult that I could clearly hear a hundred yards away: a screeching of metal scraped across metal, the sharp crack of wood and bone, the desperately yelled battle cries of 'For the Virgin' and 'A Locksley!' and the first horrible screams of stricken men.

'Thomas, Olivier, we are not done here. Come on, we must aid our lord!' I called my surviving comrades to my side and we spurred up the hill to join the fray.

Thomas, Olivier and I plunged into the wild mêlée on the mountainside. I cut down a Knight of Our Lady duelling with a mercenary with a huge sword blow from behind that snapped his spine. I exchanged cuts with another knight and killed him, I believe, with a savage chop from Fidelity into the back of his neck. Then I was defending myself desperately against a knight wielding a long lance. The spear drove towards my eyes, powered by all the man's strength and skill, but I managed to flick the lance-point above my right shoulder with Fidelity, just in time. The momentum of his charge forced him on to me and, as our horses passed each other less than a foot apart, I smashed the silver pommel of Fidelity into the side of his helm and was rewarded with a yell of pain.

There were footmen all about my horse's hooves by now and I slashed at them left and right, left and right, dealing out hideous wounds to faces and arms – sowing panic among them with the sheer momentum of blundering horse and snarling, hacking rider. A bearded foot soldier swung a long-handled axe at my horse's flank and I dropped my arm and took the heavy blow on my shield, which crumpled at the impact but saved the poor beast a grievous hurt. I killed the axe man with a cross-body chop, hurled away the broken shield and plucked the flanged mace from my belt with my left hand.

I smashed and sliced and tore my steel into the enemy on that lovely, sunny afternoon – I felt the surging God-given rage of battle fill my limbs with strength, and I bellowed like a bullock in a shambles smelling the blood for the first time as I carved through horsemen and infantry alike, splashing scarlet with every sweep of sword or strike of mace. The horse seemed to have recovered its courage and responded to the pressure of my knees, submitting to my will as I killed and battered and howled curses at our foes. Until the poor beast was killed under me, disembowelled by some evil, bastard footman with a long knife – I saw the man out of the corner of my eye plunge his blade deep into my mount's belly, and felt the animal's death shiver. I screamed a battle curse and managed to kick both feet free of the brave floundering beast as it went down, and released my rage upon his cowardly killer with one mighty blow of Fidelity that rent his body from shoulder to waist, his torso flopping open obscenely like a sliced plum.

I was dimly aware of Little John, also unhorsed, and laying about himself with his double-headed axe, dropping enemies with every

296

sweep, and Gavin in the lee of his friend's shield, skewering foes one after the other with his war bow. And Sir Nicholas was killing, and killing again, with a stony efficiency from the back of his mount, his shield and sword working together smoothly like a device designed for the harvesting of souls. But I was deep in some blood-drenched madness all of my own, and I slew with both left and right hands, thudding mace and whirling, dripping sword, killing and maiming, cutting and crushing, calling my foes to their deaths, until the broken bodies, still and writhing in pain, lay as thick as cut timber on the turf and there were no living men around me in a wide circle.

I came back to my true senses, surfacing like a man coming out of deep, drugged sleep, and saw that the battle was nearly over. My voice was painfully hoarse, my arms were like lead. Many of the Knights of Our Lady were pulling back, turning their horses and heading up the slope and away from the torn valley; their foot soldiers too were running for the hills. Except for a struggling knot some thirty yards up the hill: three men-at-arms were assailing a squat, strong figure in black, who was defending himself vigorously with a staff and a sword. It was Tuck, surrounded by a scrum of enemies. As I watched, dumb with exhaustion, I saw him neatly break the skull of one of his foes with the staff, and at almost the same time receive a vicious sword lunge from one of the men-at-arms deep into his generous belly. His mouth formed an 'O' of surprise and he dropped to his knees.

And I was running towards him, my tiredness forgotten, hurling myself up that slope at my greatest speed, my boots slipping on the gory grass.

Before I could reach him a Knight of Our Lady, one of the last on the field, cantered up to him and slashed at his tonsured head before spurring on past, a glancing blow that sliced across the top of his sun-browned scalp, but it knocked the stricken priest from his knees on to his back on the turf. One of the two remaining footmen looked about him, recognized that the day was lost, dropped his sword and sprinted after the departing knight. But the other man ran in and hacked down with his axe into Tuck's prone body, crunching the wide blade deep into his chest, then he too turned to flee . . .

Just as I reached him.

Fidelity cut through the air and slammed into the side of his neck, powering into the skin and through muscle, cartilage and sinew, severing interlocking bones and spinal cord, and flashing out the other side, splashing his life fluid through the clean air. His head jumped from his neck and thumped down on the turf beside my friend, and his body a few moments later, crumpled at the knees, folded and slid bonelessly to the earth.

I was on my knees beside Tuck by then, wiping the dribbling gore from his beloved face, pulling his robe together over his ripped body and calling his name over and over. He'd been badly wounded in head, chest and belly, but he heard me, praise God. His eyes fluttered, opened, looked into mine. And I gave thanks.

Tuck was not dead.

'Sir Alan, Sir Alan – are you hale? Have you been wounded?' A familiar voice broke into my thoughts, and I looked up and saw my Thomas, looking shaken and worried, peering down at me. I realized that I was slathered in blood, almost from head to foot. Other men's blood.

I got to my feet and ordered Thomas to fetch Robin. 'And water and bandages, too.' But, for once, my faithful squire hesitated; he stared down at my right leg. My calf muscle had been throbbing with pain for some time but now when I, too, looked down, I saw that it had a short, broad-bladed knife embedded in the flesh just above my boot top. I must have taken the wound while fighting a-horse and failed to notice in my frenzy. And the crossbow bolt was still protruding from my chest. I bent down and picked up Fidelity and saw that, like me, my sword was covered in blood all along its length. I gave my blade over to my squire and said, 'Fetch me Robin, Thomas, as quick as you can. Father Tuck has been gravely wounded and is likely to die.' And, looking down, with a suddenly shaking right hand, I tugged ineffectually at the quarrel protruding from my chest.

'Yes, Sir Alan, I will. But let me first attend to this,' said my squire. He knelt down beside me and plucked the knife from my calf in one swift jerk – and I swear I hardly felt a thing as the weapon slid out of the grip of my flesh. But I found that my body was swaying with fatigue, and my head was whirling like a drunkard's, as my squire stood and, with some difficulty, pulled the bolt from between the iron strips in my chest protector.

As Thomas jogged away, I slumped down on to the ground beside Tuck and took his big, soft hand in my blood-sticky one.

The enemy had all quit the battlefield, but they left a good number of their comrades behind – some forty foemen were dead or too badly wounded to run. Those wounded men did not live long. The surviving mercenaries paced among them, stooping down from time to time, relieving them permanently of their sufferings, and of any valuables on their persons.

I merely sat on the ground and held Tuck's hand, and looked over the dismal field of victory. I could count fourteen Knights of Our Lady among the slain – including one well-bred young Norman who lay not five yards away and whose dead face, turned towards me, I suddenly recognized. We had been slightly acquainted in the wars against King Philip of France in the north and I remembered him as a gentle aristocrat with fine manners, and an enviable sword-fighting style. What had brought that young man of good family so far from his home to die in a pointless skirmish in these southern hills, fighting for a man such as the Master? I knew that I would never know the true answer. Had I been the one to kill him? I did not know the answer to that either.

From time to time, I checked that Tuck was still alive. He had closed his eyes, but blood still pulsed from under the flap of cut skin on his scalp. However, I knew, by the slow bloody bubbling of his chest, where the last man-at-arms had crushed his thorax with an axe, and the great slippery gash in his belly from his first wound, that he was not long for this world.

As I looked at him, his large shapeless body sprawled on the torn, bloody grass, his hand grasped tightly in mine, I felt my eyes begin to burn. I thought of all the kindnesses he had shown me from the very first days after I had joined Robin's gang – long, long ago. I thought about his laughter, his courage – his vast love of food. I thought about how much I would miss his cheerful wisdom, his kindness and indomitable moral strength. The tears flowed like twin rivers down my cheeks.

'Do not weep, Alan,' said Roland, coming to my side, kneeling and putting an arm around my shoulders. 'Father Tuck yet has a chance to live, if we can get him to the Grail in time.'

My cousin's words shocked me out of my grief. Of course – I had been a fool! If the Grail could save Goody, it could save Tuck! The power of the Grail would surely cure him, no matter how sorely he was wounded – had we not been told that, by the loving power of Jesus Christ, the Grail could hold back Death itself?

I jumped to my feet even as Thomas arrived with Robin at his side. My lord stared down at Tuck, his face blank, emotionless.

'We must get the Grail and swiftly!' I blurted out.

Robin looked at me oddly, and frowned.

'We must get the Grail, and get it as soon as possible,' I repeated.

'Yes, that is the reason why we came down here. What are you trying to say?'

'To save Tuck – he will die if we cannot get him to drink from the Grail.'

Robin looked at the still body of his old friend, and he sighed, and said quietly, 'I have known Tuck for longer than you, and I

300

love him just as much, but, Alan, I think that it is already too late for our old friend. We need to bury our dead, bind our wounds, rest the horses, eat something, sleep, and accomplish a hundred other small things before we are ready to march.'

'No, no, if we can get him to the Grail, we can save him. We must save him, Robin.' I found I was shouting at my lord, my flushed, teary face inches from his. 'We must go now and capture this Montségur place, get the Grail and save Tuck. We must save Tuck, and then go home for Goody. Quickly. Now. We must get the Grail as soon as we possibly can. Are you listening?'

Robin took a step back, looking at me in a curious fashion, almost as one might observe a raving madman.

'I tell you what, Alan, you go on ahead. I'm told that the Castle of Montségur is less than four miles from here. Take the guide, and Thomas, and reconnoitre the place. Look it over, work out how we can take it, come back and report to me. Understand? Go and have a look, come back here and report by nightfall tomorrow night. I will care for Tuck in your absence.'

I realized that I had been ridiculous. We had just fought a hard battle – we could not charge off leaving our dead and wounded on the field; and the men were dog tired. I was exhausted myself. But the thought of resting and eating and sleeping comfortably all through the night while Tuck's life drained away was intolerable. We had to get the Grail – and quickly.

'Yes, I'll go,' I said. 'I'll go now – back before nightfall tomorrow.' I turned aside to seek out Thomas and the guide.

'Alan,' Robin called softly from behind me.

I turned quickly.

'Be careful,' said my lord. 'Don't throw your life away. We need you, all of us, we all need you – understand?'

I found Maury the surly guide in the care of two mercenaries. He was under guard: our men were convinced that he had led us directly into the trap at the orders of the Count of Foix, and I got the impression that they had been telling the shepherd a few horrible stories about Robin's vengeance on others who had betrayed him. The man was obviously terrified.

I squatted down beside him, and trying to make myself understood in my rough version of Langue d'Oc, I looked him in the face and said, 'Did you deliberately lead us into this ambush?'

The man shook his head wildly.

'Did you know that we would be attacked by these Knights of Our Lady?' I gestured towards a nearby white-mantled corpse.

'No, no, sir – truly I did not, but . . .'

'But what?'

I heard a spattering sound and looked down between the man's splayed grubby knees. The sheepskin there was wet and glistening and a small puddle was forming by his bare feet.

'But what?' I repeated.

Maury's answer came out as a whisper: 'But my lord told me that I must be certain that I came by this road. There is another way just as good, but the Count insisted we take this one . . .'

I stood. The two mercenaries were grinning all over their faces, the younger one, a squat ugly fellow, was licking his fat lips. I was suddenly disgusted by all of this. Treachery and revenge; blood spilled and yet more blood spilled in the name of vengeance. My wounded right calf was burning like fire, but I steeled my mind to ignore it.

'Give him to me,' I said to the older mercenary.

'Yes sir,' he replied. 'Do you need any help with him, sir? Jehan and myself would be more than happy to lend a—'

'That won't be necessary, but thank you.'

I grabbed a handful of the guide's sheepskin and hauled him bodily over to where Thomas was transferring my saddle and baggage from the dead horse to a new beast, captured in the fight.

I threw the guide at Thomas's feet and briefly explained to my squire why we were not finished for the day. Thomas, as usual, made not a word of complaint, he just nodded and said, 'Well, sir, we'd better have a bite of something before we go.'

I squatted down next to Maury, who was looking at me with great cow-like eyes, and said, 'Will you be a true and faithful guide, henceforth? Will you take me and my squire to Montségur, by discreet ways, unseen by the garrison of the castle there?'

Maury nodded. 'Oh yes, sir. I will be your loyal man, I swear it, sir. Please believe me, I did not know . . .'

I shushed him. 'If you play us false, our vengeance will be more terrible than you can possibly imagine. The infernal regions, when you finally reach them, will be a blessed relief compared to the agonies that I shall inflict on you if you are not true.'

I silenced his babbling protestations of fidelity.

'And do not tell anyone, particularly the Earl of Locksley, or John Nailor, him over there, what you just told me: that the Count made you lead us by this road. Others will not be nearly as under-standing as I am.'

Chapter Twenty

Maury the guide, now soothed and fed, took Thomas and I out of the valley, and we had ridden no more than half a mile up the winding road that led more or less south, when I was surprised to see Nur cantering towards us, her tattered black robe flapping in the breeze as she rode. 'I will come with you,' she said imperiously, when she reined in beside Thomas's horse. 'I shall view this Grail castle and mayhap I shall unlock its secrets.'

My first instinct was to order her back to the camp – but I doubted that she would obey. So I shrugged, nodded, remembering that she was adept at silent movement in rough country and that she'd be unlikely to give us away as we made our reconnaissance.

An hour later we four found ourselves in a patch of scrubby woodland, under the cover of a large bushy hazel tree, and looking up at Montségur through the broad leaves. For an attacker, it made for a truly daunting site: a great, rocky peak – or *pog* in the local dialect – like an upturned cup that towered above the surrounding countryside; its sides were sheer, almost vertical barriers of jagged grey stone, with only a few hardy shrubs managing to cling stubbornly to the dark cracks and crevices. At the very top, more than a thousand feet above where we stood, I could see the square lines of the castle, a tiny blue-and-white flag flapping over the high keep at the northern end of the structure, and a few ant-like men moving about on the walls. I must admit that my heart quailed at the very thought of assaulting this fortress. It was too sheer to easily ride a horse to the summit, and by the time we had climbed it on foot in our heavy armour, we would be quite exhausted before we were in range to strike the first sword blow. And then to carry an attack over those high walls in the face of fanatical resistance from the Knights of Our Lady . . . I could not even imagine our succeeding – this was truly an impossible task.

I thought about my rash words to Robin in the bright heat of my sorrow over Tuck, and blushed for such foolishness. But both Tuck and Goody would die unless we could overcome that high mountain and scale those forbidding walls at the summit.

As it was nearly dusk, I decided that we should sleep on the problem and make a full examination of the mountain the next morning. My leg, which had been growing increasingly painful during the ride, was bleeding freely and my right boot was now filled with blood. That was no matter but the pain was making it hard to concentrate on the problem at hand. I told Thomas to begin making camp in that patch of woodland, when Maury the guide approached, and very humbly said, 'Sir, if it would please you, I know of a cave not two hundred paces from here. Underneath the *pog*. We could make our camp there. It is used by the shepherds on cold winter nights, but I'm sure that we would be very unlikely to be disturbed at this time of year.'

I looked at the man, cringing before me in his filthy sheepskin rags, bobbing and ducking his head to try to appease any possible anger that I might show – could I trust him? I found I was too tired to make that decision and so merely nodded, and muttered to Thomas, 'Be on your guard', and we followed the man into the thickening woodland a little way up the steep slope of the mountain, through a patch of thick, and I would have sworn virgin, foliage until he proudly swept away a curtain of drooping willow branches and showed me two massive stones, grey and partially covered with yellow and grey lichen, with a narrow, cobweb-draped gap between them. I stepped forward, tore away the cobwebs and poked my head into the gap between the two monoliths, and found that my broad shoulders were no more than a foot from the stone on either side. Inside was a vast black space – though I could see almost nothing, somehow I could tell it was huge – and there was a smell of old wood ash and a hint of candlewax, but no wild animal scents. I had had a sneaking fear that we might disturb a bear.

Once we had struck flint and tinder and lit a crude torch of oil-dipped rags wrapped around a stick, I led the way into the cave and saw that our accommodation, although narrow at the entrance, was indeed enormous. It was as big as a fine stone church in a decent-sized English market town, being some fifty paces long and thirty wide with a high ceiling that I could not make out in the light of the torch.

Thomas led the horses into the cave, and rummaged into the saddlebags and found a couple of candles, which he lit from the torch, and I was able to explore the space a little further. At the far end was a jumble of rocks, with a great flat stone on top that formed a natural table or altar. It was clear that the place had been used by men before – and not only by rough shepherds – but I judged that it had not been occupied for some time. A crude hearth, a circle of fire-blacked stones, was set near the entrance of the cave, and in various niches in the limestone walls, I found the greasy traces of ancient tallow candles.

Nur, who had followed us into the cave without a word, now began to make excited little squeaks. When I asked the witch what ailed her, she replied, 'Oh Alan, you cannot possibly understand – this is a place of the spirits. There is strong magic here. I can feel it. This is the womb of the mountain.'

I could feel no magic – but I did find the cave unsettling. It was too big and too empty and felt a little wrong to me; not like a cosy womb, not like a place where life began, but like an abandoned hall, a place of death and decay. Nevertheless, it was shelter, and hidden, and I knew that I would be more comfortable here than elsewhere on the mountain. The guide was looking at me beseechingly, like a kicked dog, to see if the cave had my approval. I said gruffly, 'Yes, we will sleep here tonight. Well done, Maury', and the old man beamed with pleasure.

With a fire crackling in the hearth, the place took on a more friendly air, and it was strange to think that we were burrowed into a hole in the ground with a thousand feet of rock between us and our enemies. After nightfall, and a meagre supper of dried wild boar meat and twice-baked bread, I allowed Thomas and Nur to look at my wound. The flesh around the deep puncture was red and sore and Nur smeared a poultice of some black and foul concoction into the cut and around the muscles. Thomas wrapped it tightly with a bandage made from a clean chemise ripped into strips. When I stood on it, I found that I could manage the pain. I felt certain it would serve until we had taken possession of the Grail. When Thomas and Nur had finished, I stepped out of the cave to get a breath of fresh air before taking to my blankets. The mountain was quiet and still, and after a few yards it was impossible to detect the presence of the cave or our occupancy of it. I found a small clearing and sat down with my back to a tree, and looked up at the castle – only a few pin-pricks of light in the blackness high above. I could not see how we could possibly capture this place with the handful of men that we possessed, now further weakened by the bloody battle in the valley. It would take a mighty army – tens of thousands of men – to surround the mountain and even then they would be forced to starve the inhabitants out. For the life of me I could not see how we might capture this perfect fortification. I simply could not see it. And if we did not take it, and soon, Tuck would die. And Goody would die. I could not bear to entertain either of those black thoughts.

My calf was throbbing like a Saracen war-drum as I sat under that tree in the darkness. Better to rest, I told myself, and take another look in the morning. With that, I hauled myself to my feet and limped back to the cave. I rolled myself up in my blankets near the banked fire and fell immediately into a deep sleep.

I awoke in the middle of the night to find the cave suffused with a strange greenish light. It seemed to be coming from the walls themselves, and I was seized with an unearthly terror. Had I inadvertently stepped into some fairy realm, some eldritch half-place where, as Nur had said, the spirits of the wild had dominion? I could see no sign of my companions. I was alone, alone except for a tall figure dressed in shining white at the far end of the cave by the stone altar. I tried to speak, to call out to the figure, but my mouth was sealed with some sticky, glue-like substance and I was rendered mute. The figure turned and I saw that it was a woman – and that the face above the plain, long white dress, framed by a pure white headdress, was Goody's. Her beautiful countenance was deathly pale, as it had been when I last saw her in Sherwood, but her violet-blue eyes sparkled with love and understanding. She walked towards me, gliding on unseen feet beneath her white garb, and stopped and looked down at me in my blankets. I tried to raise a hand to her, to touch her, but my outstretched limb was far too heavy to lift. Goody said nothing, but she pointed to the altar where I now saw a shining cup of gold, bigger and brighter than any vessel I had ever seen before and seeming to shoot out rays of power. The vast cup was so bright that it hurt my eyes and I took my gaze back to Goody. And saw to my horror that she was weeping.

'Goodbye, my dearest, goodbye,' she said in a whispering voice quite unlike her own true tones, and the image began to fade, her features becoming paler, becoming ghostly and wraith-like, as if she were dissolving into the air.

With a huge effort, I ripped open my lips and screamed, 'No, Goody, no, come back to me. Don't go!'

But the wraith merely whispered, 'Goodbye, my love', and vanished into the blackness of the cave.

I opened my eyes, and all was pitch dark, except for the merest glow of the few remaining coals of our campfire. Someone was beside me, and a light, cool soothing hand was resting on my naked shoulder. But it was not until Thomas had thrown a few sticks of kindling on the fire and poked it back into life that I realized Nur was kneeling beside my bedroll, and she was talking to me in a quiet and reassuring voice. 'You were dreaming, Alan. The spirits came to you, as they often do in these places. Tell me, what did you see? Did you see the Grail?'

It took me a few moments to recover myself, and then I answered her: 'Yes, yes, it was the Grail. And Goody came to me too. Is she dead? Tell me, Nur, is Goody dead?'

I had struggled out of my bedclothes and was standing over the woman dressed only in my braies with my fists clenched. Nur rose and prudently took a step backwards.

'Go to sleep, Alan. All is well, let us all go back to sleep.'

I dropped to my knees and fumbled around on the ground next to my blankets until I found my sword and, gripping its handle in one hand and the sheath in the other, I stood and said again, through gritted teeth, 'Tell me now, witch, does Goody yet live?'

My threat was quite explicit. I would have chopped Nur down in that moment had she not said to me, 'Alan, I swear to you, by the spirits, by the love that I once bore for you, that Goody yet lives. Have faith. My curse cannot be unmade – much as I wish it might be. And killing me would only make it stronger, as my soul is sworn to it. But now, on this night, Goody lives! I swear it. She is alive, and she will remain so until one year and one day have passed from the day of your wedding.'

I was comforted, just a little, by Nur's words. But not for long. As we all settled back down in our sleeping places, I began to reckon the days. Goody and I had wed on the first day of July the year before; it was now early May, perhaps the third day of the month – I was not certain. That meant that I had perhaps eight weeks until Goody was fated to die. The journey back to Westbury would take five weeks, indeed it might be six or even seven weeks if the weather was inclement or there were no ships bound for England at Bordeaux on my arrival in that city. I had two weeks, I calculated, or perhaps less, in which to capture the impregnable Castle of Montségur, slaughter the Master and all his knights, take possession of the Grail, save Tuck and begin the journey back to Goody. Two weeks.

I did not sleep again that night.

We spent the first part of the next day, another glorious one, making a circuit of Montségur, heading in a sunwise direction and being led by Maury who had the eagerness of a young goat over the steep rocks, despite his grizzled hair and the burden of his years. My calf pained me somewhat during that rough scramble, but I would not let an old man best me, and I kept pace as well as I could. Mercifully, it was not difficult to remain unobserved from the castle walls, for the lower slopes of the mountain were well covered by greenery – but I believe that the Master, knowing that Robin and his men were surely coming, and doubtless discouraged by his defeat the day before, was keeping his men locked up safe in the castle. Certainly we met no enemies that day as we made a complete slow, very painful circumnavigation of his fortress.

The reconnaissance, however, was less than fruitful. From the north face of the mountain, we looked up at the square keep of the castle, its highest point. There was no way to attack from this side: the mountainside was sheer, almost bare rock, and an army of battle-hardened Welsh mountaineers would have had trouble scaling it, let alone fighting a fierce battle once they reached the top. From the north-east the same, and perhaps even more difficult, for to attack from that direction would mean starting in a deep ravine filled with thorny scrub, which lay at the bottom. The eastern side, however, was more promising. A narrow spur of land extended down from the southernmost point of the castle directly towards the rising sun, a steep-sided but gently sloping spine of rock that wended down over half a mile to the treeline. An attack might have been possible from the east along this spur – except for two things. First, a twelve-foot-high stone rampart had been constructed at the top of the spur some thirty yards beyond the castle proper, as an extra defence on this weakest of sides, and I could see that it was manned by half a dozen alert men. Second, in broad daylight, an enemy could be seen coming for miles as they slogged up. Any half-awake garrison, seeing this attack coming, would have an hour or more to prepare their defences – which were already truly formidable. An army struggling up that way could be bombarded with a trebuchet set up inside the castle walls, and knocked off the single-file path like skittles, or if the defenders lacked stone-throwing machines, the attacking force could be simply mown down with a blizzard of crossbow bolts as they approached, forced by the landscape to advance slowly on such a narrow front. We could not attack from that direction, I concluded.

The south too was impossible: a sheer rock face leading up to a blank twenty-foot stone wall. Which left the west. This side housed the main gate and a steep winding path, no more than a goat track, that led up from the saddle of land where the road ran past Montségur to the north. This was the ordinary way that a peace-able traveller might approach, and the track the peasants who rebuilt the fortifications must have used, and I could clearly see that the stony path worn by many feet, and even with some crude

311

steps cut into the rock, ended at a round arched double door in the thick castle walls. Once again, on a beautiful cloudless May day such as that one, an enemy could be clearly seen slogging up to the front door and there would be plenty of time to roll rocks down on to his head, skewer him with an avalanche of crossbow bolts, or fry him alive with boiling oil.

We returned to the cave a little after noon, tired from the long unsuccessful scramble around that stark mountain and, I must admit, a little despondent that we had not found even a remotely suitable avenue of attack.

I reported back to Robin by mid-afternoon, having rewarded Maury with a silver penny from Mercadier's black leather purse and repeated my warning not to let anyone in our camp know that he had been ordered to take a particular road to Montségur by the treacherous Count of Foix.

Robin had brought discipline back to our thinned company, I saw, and a mound of freshly dug earth concealed the bodies of our fallen comrades. Sir Nicholas de Scras, I later learned, had said the holy words over the grave and led the mercenaries in prayer for the fallen.

Tuck still lived, praise God, and I found him lying in the small copse of trees where we had defeated the ambushing crossbowmen the day before. Someone had crudely stitched the flap of scalp back into position and washed the worst of the blood from his face, but he was still and quiet, in a profound state of slumber and his face was unnaturally waxy and pale. His stomach wound had been strapped and bandaged and his chest had been covered with a flap of blood-soaked cloth that trembled with every escaping breath of air from his punctured lungs.

I kissed the old man on his blood-streaked pate and went to report to Robin. My lord was conferring with Sir Nicholas by our horses – those we had brought to the field and those we had acquired by right of battle. I noticed, too, that Little John and

Gavin were wandering over the battlefield and collecting up the discarded swords of our enemies.

'Well, Alan, you seem to be in a calmer humour: tell me all about Montségur,' my lord said, after we had exchanged our greetings.

I described for my lord the various aspects of the castle, and of the landscape around it, and the advantages and disadvantages of an attack from each of the cardinal points. When I had finished, I looked down at the green turf, unsure of how to conclude my report. 'I cannot . . . I cannot see a way in. That is the truth. I cannot see a way in which with the few troops we have we can conquer a castle that is this well fortified by man and nature. Maybe with a mighty army and a year-long siege . . . But, we cannot do it. It bruises my heart to say this but it is impossible.'

I felt I was condemning both Tuck and Goody with my words. Yet I could only tell the truth, as I saw it, to my lord.

'Impossible?' said Robin, cocking an eyebrow. 'I very much doubt that. What you mean is that it is going to be rather difficult.'

Although this was no more than a well-worn platitude, I was encouraged by my lord's cheerfulness. A few well-chosen words and the world seemed a brighter place. He possessed this skill, Robin, one of his main talents, I believe, that enabled him to put fresh heart into a man when he was feeling at his lowest.

'Well, no point sitting around here,' said Robin, 'I think we'd better get the men off their fat behinds and go and look at this "impossible" castle of yours. Go and get them all saddled up, will you, Alan.'

I led the Companions and the surviving mercenaries to the cave under the mountain. We carried Tuck there in a litter made of spears and roughly stitched cloaks and placed him on the altar rocks at the back, where he would be out of the way of any careless boots. Robin took one look at the castle, high above us, and detached two of the lightly wounded mercenaries to take the horses back down the road to a stretch of pasture that we'd passed on the way.

'This is no task for cavalry,' my lord said, gripping my shoulder. 'We must see this business through on our own two feet.'

Despite his apparent confidence, I sensed that Robin was a little surprised at just how difficult it would be to take the Castle of Montségur. I saw him eyeing the battlements and looking for paths up the sheer rock face – in vain. Over the next few days, while the men idled in the cave, Robin scouted around the mountain with only Maury for company, spending hours each day staring up at the walls. But there were no attack points that were practicable – of that I was quite certain. And I noticed that we, in turn, were being observed by several score of tiny figures in blue-and-white surcoats on the ramparts, as we went about our business at the foot of the mountain.

Up there, I thought to myself, up there somewhere was the Master. Up there was the man who had killed my father, who was responsible for the murder of my friend Hanno. The man who had nearly killed me once in Paris and who had ordered Westbury burned to the ground. Up there was the man who stood between me and the Grail. His miserable life, I said to myself, was all that prevented me saving the lives of Goody and Tuck. The fury began to flow in my belly, like a river of fire.

On the third day after our arrival at Montségur, Robin came to me, fresh from one of his unsuccessful rambles on the slopes. 'We'd better go up and speak to him,' he said, with no preamble.

'The Master?'

'We need to find out what is in his mind,' my lord said. 'And I want to gauge his strength of will to resist us.'

I merely nodded.

Robin constructed himself an *ad hoc* white flag with a clean linen chemise from his saddlebag and one of the Count of Foix's long spear shafts, and accompanied by myself, Roland and Sir Nicholas de Scras, set off up the steep, well-worn track under its dubious protection. The climb, even taken slowly, was a taxing one, especially with my half-healed calf, and in the bright May sunshine. And in my armour and carrying a heavy shield, I was sweating rivers and panting like a broken bellows as we neared the top of the mountain. The closer we got, the more difficult the task of capturing the castle seemed.

We halted about thirty yards from the main gate: a vast double door of thick, dark-brown wood that looked as if it could withstand a dragon's fiery wrath. We stood stock still under the flapping white banner. Me, Robin, Roland and Sir Nicholas. Four knights, armed and armoured, standing in a line. Waiting.

I could see the helmeted heads of a dozen Knights of Our Lady as they passed between the crenellations, presumably moving along a walkway behind the walls. Occasionally, a man would pause and stare out at us, before disappearing again. But we were offered no hostility, although we were well within crossbow range. The flag of truce, it seemed, was being dutifully observed.

'I'm tempted to walk up there and just knock on the door,' said Robin after we had been standing there for perhaps the time it takes to say ten Hail Marys. 'He must have been told that we were coming. I think he's just being deliberately rude.' Robin grinned at me to tell me he was joking . . . and at that moment there was a blast of trumpets, at least three long brass instruments, shockingly loud, that seemed to split the sunshine.

And there was the Master, standing atop the ramparts, unarmed, his sandalled feet spread wide, his hands resting on his robe over his hips, and towering over the helmeted heads of the defenders on the walkway beneath him. He looked a little younger than the last time I had seen him, a bound captive awaiting torture outside the Château Chalus-Chabrol, a little more than a year ago. He was smiling indulgently at us, like a father watching over his unruly children. His face had been lightly tanned by the sun, but I could still make out the faint marks of the pox that had scarred him as a young man. He was clean-shaven, and his hair was neatly cut. His robe was clean – pure black – but of some fine and faintly shiny, rich material, perhaps silk, a silver crucifix hung from a chain around his neck. But he looked happy, fit and handsome, a holy man from whom wholesomeness and Christian kindness seemed to pour like light from a lamp.

I realized then that I had forgotten the power of his presence. In my mind he had been this dark monster, lurking in the shadows, striking viciously at me and my friends from concealment like a footpad in a darkened street. But, looking up at him framed by the pure blue sky, it was difficult to imagine that he was evil at all. Indeed, he looked like goodness personified. He even looked a little like the images I have seen of Our Lord Jesus Christ. I found I was smiling at him, and secretly hoping that he would greet me with a friendly word.

Disgusted with myself, I jerked my head to the right and looked at Robin. He too was staring at the Master, and smiling, but there was a curl of gentle contempt around his mouth that I had seen on his lips many times before.

For a long, long time, neither spoke, and neither moved. They seemed to be intently taking each other's measure and there was no sound but for the wind whistling over the battlements and the far-away cry of a hunting bird. It suddenly seemed to me that they were in some absurd competition, a contest to see who could remain silent the longest, and to determine who would lose by speaking first.

If it truly was a bout of wills, then Robin lost.

'We had an agreement once, you and I,' said Robin quietly, calmly, but in a carrying voice. 'We divided the world in two at the line of the English channel. I had dominion over England, and you over France – and we were at peace with each other for ten long years. We could have that once again . . .'

Robin stopped speaking. The Master slowly nodded his head.

'Yes, for ten years I allowed you to play your childish games in Sherwood. That is true. But you broke our accord when you sent your man' – the Master jerked his chin at me – 'to Paris to hunt me down. And, by your actions, I was hounded from that city, and away from my beautiful cathedral – my whole life's work.'

'You reached out your arm into my domain and killed Sir Alan's father,' said Robin. 'Was he supposed to meekly forgive that? Was I? And later you sent men to England – treacherous Templars and their creatures – to trap me by stealth and cunning and have me hanged as a—'

My lord's voice had not risen in volume but, nonetheless, he seemed to have lost a little of his composure. He stopped speaking abruptly and seemed to take a moment to regain his mastery of himself. Then he sighed with what might have been taken for regret: 'We have wronged each other, you and I, we must both acknowledge that. We have been at war. That is the truth. But we can mend our discord, restore our honour – a word or two and some small gesture of good faith, a little forgiveness, and we can have peace again, on the same terms if you wish, you in France, and I in England. Would that please you, my old friend?'

The Master laughed – a light, musical, happy sound. It lifted my heart just to hear it. But his words were anything but joyful.

'The Earl of Locksley talks of peace – the man whose name is a byword for dissimulation, deceit and knavery, a man who has murdered dozens of my knights, and slain scores of my men-at-arms, a man who has tricked and robbed half the magnates of Europe – he comes to me now, stands before my gates, calls me "old friend" and talks softly to me of peace and forgiveness!'

The mockery was thick as curd, but the Master's voice, to my ears anyway, sounded oddly gentle and entirely reasonable.

Neither man said anything for a few moments. The Master said meditatively, 'And how would we achieve this lasting peace, I wonder? What could this small good-faith gesture be?'

'You know what I desire, I believe,' said Robin, his tone calm and friendly. 'If you deliver it up to me, my men and I will ride away from here and return to our own lands and you need never be troubled by us again. Give me the Grail and I shall go – and there can be harmony between us for the rest of our lives.'

'Do you think I am in fear of you? I assure you, I am not.' The Master laughed again; this time it seemed with real mirth. 'You cannot hope to take this castle – ever – and a man such as you, a man who mocks God, shall never possess the Grail while I have strength. What I have in my possession is worth a thousand men-at-arms. I have the vessel that has been blessed by Our Lord's holy blood. There is no more precious object in all the world. None can prevail against me – not you, not your raggedy paid men, not even all the noblest knights of Christendom, were they ranged against me – for while I hold the Grail, God, His only son Jesus Christ and his Holy Virgin Mother stand at my side.'

The Master spread his arms wide, adopting the position suffered by Our Lord on the cross at Calvary, seeming to touch the sky on either side of him. And his voice changed when he spoke, becoming deeper, warmer, somehow golden – seeming to vibrate with a weird and powerful music all of its own.

'You will go from this place, now, Robert of Locksley, Prince of Deceivers, I command you! You will go from this place or it will become the place of your death. By the power of the Grail, by the power of God Himself, I command you to go!'

And, so help me, I felt an almost overpowering urge to obey him; I felt an actual force, like an invisible hand pushing me down the mountainside – and I swear I wanted, just then, to depart from Montségur and never to come back.

Incredibly, I heard Robin give a low chuckle. 'For goodness sake, Michel,' said my lord, 'we have known each other too long for this

318

sort of silly I-command-you nonsense – do you think we are all as feeble-willed as your deluded followers?'

Robin's words were a splash of icy water in my face, breaking the Master's spell like a hand through a cobweb. I glared up at my enemy, flushed with embarrassed rage at the weakness of my own will.

The imposing black-robed monk standing atop the battlements of Montségur lowered his arms; he looked a little hurt, disappointed by Robin's words.

But my lord was speaking again: 'It's really very simple, Michel, you give me the Grail and I will depart and leave you in peace. Otherwise, I will come over that wall and get it myself.'

'I would roast in Hell before I gave up such a holy treasure to a Godless killer such as you.'

'Is that your final answer?' asked Robin.

'No,' said the Master. 'This is.'

And two score of crossbowmen, all in the white surcoats of the Knights of Our Lady, appeared at the crenellations below the Master's feet, forty weapons aimed down at the four of us. They put the crossbows to their shoulders, and looked down the length of the iron-tipped wooden quarrels, ready to loose a black rain of death upon our heads in an instant.

'Go now,' said the Master, 'or die.'

Chapter Twenty-one

We were moving even before the Master spoke his final words – for none of us was unversed in war, and none of us had really trusted him to respect the flag of truce. I had my big, kite-shaped shield up and was scrambling down the rocky mountainside the moment the crossbowmen popped up on the battlements and aimed their loaded weapons down at us. And the others were just as quick to flee the place of parley.

But not a bolt flew, not a quarrel was loosed. We four brave, soldierly men re-met about a third of the way down, well out of crossbow range, each of us looking half-defiant, half-sheepish at having fled so quickly, and without being offered any real harm; although, in truth, there would have been no point in standing still and taking a bolt to the belly merely to prove our manhoods.

'Did you really expect him to hand over the Grail?' I asked Robin, when I caught my breath after the undignified rush down the hill.

'Not really,' he replied with a rueful grin. 'But I wanted to get a closer look at the gate and the walls. And to get a sense of the strength of the castle and number of men he has at his command.'

'He just showed us forty crossbowmen,' said Sir Nicholas, 'and he may well have as many knights again, and as many men-at-arms again, too.'

'That would seem about right,' said Robin.

'A hundred and twenty men?' I said. 'That is three times our number! We cannot possibly defeat such an army.'

'Yes, we will have to find a way to reduce their numbers a little,' said Robin. He was looking back up the slope at the castle, framed in blue above him, seemingly lost in thought. 'But we have learned one very interesting thing . . .' he said. 'He is still putting his faith in all that mystical power-of-the-mind drivel. He really believed he could order me away like a naughty boy, and that I would meekly go. That is worth knowing, I think.'

'From what you told me, his powers of persuasion seemed to work just fine on the Count of Foix,' I said.

'Him?' said Robin. 'A child could command Raymond-Roger to jump from his own battlements and he'd likely do it.'

I said nothing, embarrassed. The Master's strange power had indeed had an effect on me, if not on my lord. I would have obeyed his command. And that, I felt, was cause for shame.

Once we had returned to the cave, Robin sent out Gavin and Little John with their war bows, to harass the walls a little and let the occupants of Montségur know that we were serious.

'Don't expose yourself,' Robin told his giant friend, 'but the more you kill at a distance, the fewer we will face in the assault.'

But once those two had departed, there seemed little else that could be achieved. The men spent the afternoon sleeping in the cool of the cave or climbing about the foot of the mountain, staring up at the castle on the summit. Robin seemed totally unperturbed; even when Vim came and spoke seriously with him, voicing the mercenaries' unease at tackling such a fortress, defended by so many men, he never showed anything but total confidence. 'Do not trouble yourself, Vim, we will triumph against them. And rest assured that there will be treasure inside the castle beyond your wildest dreams – gold, silver, jewels – more wine than you could drink in a dozen lifetimes. And the fewer men we are, the bigger share of loot we shall each receive.'

While Robin spoke to the mercenaries, I saw that both Roland and Sir Nicholas were listening intently. I was struck by their utterly different expressions. When Robin spoke of gold and silver and jewels, Roland's eyes sparkled and a broad smile broke out on his lips. Sir Nicholas, in contrast, seemed almost physically sickened by such crude promises of vulgar worldly gain.

However, I was fairly sure that Robin was lying through his teeth to the mercenary captain and his men. He dangled the prospect of wealth because he had to keep them on his side to have even the remotest chance of attacking the castle.

I was unmoved by the talk of riches: I only wanted the Grail. It was so close – a few hundred yards away; and yet completely out of reach behind impregnable walls guarded by an army of enemies. My wounded right leg was paining me somewhat, and so I sat about the cave all afternoon, resting it, gnawing my fingernails and racking my brains for a way into Montségur. Nothing came.

But, worse than a lack of ideas, was the knowledge that time was slipping away – by my reckoning, if I were to get the Grail home to Goody in time to save her life, I had to begin the journey home within the next ten days. And then there was Tuck – how much longer could he maintain his feeble grip on life? A day? Two days?

At nightfall, Little John and Gavin returned in a state of mild elation: Gavin had killed one man and probably wounded another and after that the defenders had taken care not to show themselves on the walls for any length of time. But it was a paltry victory, and their strength was still overwhelming compared with ours.

Thomas made us all some hot soup that evening, a thin pottage of wild garlic, hyssop, onions and barley, in a huge cauldron collectively owned by the mercenaries, and we all sat around the edges of the cave to eat. Before I had a chance to even taste a spoonful of my soup, Roland came over and said that Tuck was awake, and urgently wished to speak to me.

The old priest was in a pitiable state: his eyes were open but fluttering madly, his skin was quite yellow and he was moaning almost constantly from the pain of his stomach wound. I thought at first that he was delirious, and after I had mopped his brow, and spooned a little water into his mouth, I was about to return to my cooling soup, when he grasped my hand with shocking force. His kind brown eyes opened and they stared at me with a feverish, almost demonic glitter that I had never seen in them before. Tuck was trying to speak through his agony, and I was dimly aware that Robin was standing quietly at my shoulder.

'Too late,' Tuck said, panting. 'Too late . . . for me . . .'

'Save your strength, my friend,' I said, moistening his dry lips with a little more water. Sir Nicholas had told me that I must not let him eat or drink, not with a stomach wound, but his mouth was so cracked that it was beginning to split and bleed. 'Rest yourself for a little while and save your strength to heal your wounds.'

'The Grail . . .' he said, the words jerking out through his gritted teeth. 'I only . . . wanted . . . to see it . . . to hold it . . . just once . . . in my hands.'

'You shall hold it yet, my friend,' said Robin and when I turned to look at him, I saw a glint of moisture in his grey eyes, and all the muscles of his jaw were bunched and hard as iron. 'And drink from it. And it shall heal you of all your hurts. I promise you, old friend, you shall yet hold the Grail.'

'Too late,' Tuck said in no more than a panting whisper. 'But it has been . . . good this . . . journey . . . with . . . you . . . Robin. One . . . last . . . adventure . . .'

He closed his eyes and became silent. For a moment I thought

323

that his soul had gone from his body – and there were tears blurring my eyes, too. But, when I bent my ear down towards his open mouth, I felt the faintest stir of breath against the wet skin of my cheek.

Robin was silent during supper; but when we had eaten and were making our preparations for bed, he gathered us all together in the centre of the cave and said, 'Tomorrow, at noon, we will assault the castle. Rest now, every one of you – sleep well, and be ready for battle tomorrow. Tomorrow we take Montségur.'

In the morning, I oversaw a squad of mercenaries as they gathered wood and chopped down a few scrubby trees and built themselves half a dozen ladders with which to assault the main entrance in the western wall of the Castle of Montségur. I did not feel at all happy in myself about the coming attack – and I have done this sort of thing many times and do not count myself a coward. It seemed to me a futile waste of lives to attack with the few people we had – thirty-five mercenaries, by my count, and seven Companions capable of swinging a sword. I did not believe it could be done. I could get nothing down for breakfast and all that morning my belly felt cold and hollow. But Robin was bright and breezily confident, coming around to each of the work parties of the mercenaries and encouraging them with words and a few crude jests, which were happily reciprocated – and I realized the men already had a liking and regard for the Earl of Locksley for all that he was about to plunge their lives into terrible danger.

When Robin came up to my group of men, he led me aside, out of earshot and said something very strange indeed. 'Alan,' he said. 'In the assault, I don't want you to take any risks with your life. Play it safe, understand?'

I stared at him. We were about to attack a formidable castle, well prepared and defended by three times our number. As a knight and a leader of men, it was my clear duty to set an example – in fact, to take risks. How could I play it safe? Before I could frame a question about Robin's extraordinary words, my lord had moved on.

We were watched closely from the ramparts all the while during our preparations by the Knights of Our Lady – while we gathered wood and shaped it with axes, and lashed it together with rawhide to make ladders – but, despite their overwhelming superiority, the defenders made no attempt to sally out and attack. Perhaps they were sensible: why risk a sally when they could sit behind their safe walls and wait for us to come to them and be slaughtered? They would have ample time to prepare for our coming; we had utterly forfeited the element of surprise.

Not all of us, however, were engaged in constructing the scaling ladders: Little John and Gavin spent the morning inside the cave setting up a rough-and-ready forge in the cooking hearth, using large quantities of scrap wood as fuel, a big leather bag as a bellows, and heating and hammering the discarded swords of the enemy that they had collected on a big round stone anvil. I was too engaged in my own works to discover what they were up to, but their efforts made the cave hellishly hot. However, that did not seem to disturb Nur, who was seated at the back of that big space muttering about mountain wombs over several large bowls of water, and fiddling with a mound of semi-rotten gobbets of human private parts that she had brought with her from the Jealous Castle. Occasionally, she would throw out her little bag of finger bones and indulge in a weird, high-pitched cackle. Throughout all this, Tuck lay quietly on his altar, in a deep, deep sleep that I knew was a only hair's breadth away from death.

A little before noon, we were ready. We massed our full strength, on foot, forty-odd hardened warriors, a hundred and fifty yards below the castle, just out of effective crossbow range. The men carrying the ladders were sent to the front, Robin took his position in the centre of the line, with Roland and Sir Nicholas at either side; Little John, with Gavin in his shadow, took the extreme left

325

of the line, and Thomas and I took the extreme right. My stomach was a tight knot of fear. This day would be my last, I was utterly certain. There was no way we would be able to surmount those high walls and conquer the castle. But I kept my mouth shut, my back straight and tried my best to look confident.

Robin stepped out in front of the line and said, very simply, 'There is gold in that castle, and silver, and other treasures, enough to make all of you rich for the rest of your lives. Let's go and fetch it. On my command the company will . . . advance!'

We raced up that steep slope like hares.

Have you ever tried to scramble a hundred and fifty yards up a slope that rises almost the height of a man in a single yard? And then, on reaching the summit, launch yourself into a full-pitched battle and attempt to overcome a twenty-foot-high wall bristling with scores of fanatical enemy soldiers? It cannot be done, I tell you. Well, it cannot be done by a company of thirty-odd mercenaries and a handful of dismounted knights. We climbed, we scrambled, we puffed and panted – and we arrived at the outer wall in a disorganized, milling mob, as fatigued as if we had just run several miles in full armour. Robin was shouting at the men, yelling, urging them to raise the ladders against the walls, and climb. But the confusion was too great for his will to be enforced. Ladders were abandoned; men cowered beneath their raised shields. The crossbow bolts cracked off the stones and whined about us. A man just in front of me was dropped in screaming agony by a flung spear; a boulder the size of a small pig thudded into the ground at my feet a moment later, narrowly avoiding crushing my toes. The mercenaries surged around below the walls like frightened peasants, picking up the ladders that had been dropped, taking hits from hurled missiles, dropping them again, being picked off one by one; some men were reduced to hacking impotently at the huge double door with their swords and axes or screaming insults at the defenders. One man was blinded, his face sloughing off like melting butter off a skillet when a cauldron of red-hot sand was dumped on him from above.

In the end, only two ladders were raised against the wall, both on the right-hand side, the southern side. My side. The first was dislodged by the defenders with very little effort, pushed off the wall with a forked stick to crash to earth amid screams of agony from the scaling party; the second, I had the honour of commanding. My fear had swelled and grown almost to the point of panic. But I could not run, I could not prove a coward: I forced myself to move. The ladder crashed against the wall, held steady by two mercenaries, and I grabbed a rung at shoulder height and shouted for the men to follow me. A deep breath and I bounded upwards, eager to get this moment of extreme danger over as soon as possible. Fear gave wings to my feet. I could feel the ladder bouncing beneath me as other men came up behind. As I neared the top, a man-at-arms wielding a pole axe loomed over me; he swung the long axe at my head, but I managed to spear him in the throat with Fidelity in time and absorb the weakened blow with my shield. Then the axeman was gone, replaced by a mob of furious knights, slicing, hacking and lunging with their swords at my head, shoulders and upheld shield. Thank God for decent armour. I received half a dozen blows on my mail coat and helmet in as many heartbeats. I tried to bring my sword fully in to play, but with no free hand to grip the rungs of the ladder, a powerful glancing blow that skidded off my helm and on to my shoulder threw off my balance and a second strike, an axe, I believe, taken full on my shield, dislodged me completely. I had the sensation, for just a moment, of emptiness below me, almost of floating, and then I hit the earth. By God's grace there was a stout bush beneath me to cushion my fall and, as I emerged scratched and slightly bleeding from its rough embrace, I heard Robin calling off the attack and urging us to get back, back out of range of their missiles. The men needed no

327

urging. We were running down that hill before the echoes of Robin's battle-voice died away.

We regrouped near the foot of the mountain, and carried our wounded back to the cave. Six good men had been killed in that farcical, ill-conceived attack, and another ten had been wounded, some badly – and we had achieved precisely nothing.

Back in the cave the mood was sour. The mercenaries sat about, tending to each other's lesser wounds, binding their cuts and bruises, drinking wine with little moderation. We had lost that fight, and lost a handful of good comrades – we were weaker than before the assault and there was nothing for us to do but try once again to scale that damn mountain and conquer those killing walls.

I felt the weight of despair settle around my shoulders. The fact that I had been right – that this was truly an impossible castle to capture – was no consolation. I would now never be able to place the Grail in Tuck's sleeping hands and watch its holy magic restore him to full strength. He and Goody, and my unborn child, were now all as good as dead.

In the late afternoon, Robin and I trudged up the mountain once more under the white flag of truce. It was hot; the southern sun beating down without mercy. We took eight of the mercenaries with us, all unarmed, and under instructions not to speak or communicate with the enemy under any circumstances. We paused a hundred yards from the main gate and watched as the white-clad men-at-arms on the battlements scurried about and eventually found an officer who would recognise our flag and beckon us forward.

As we slogged up the last few yards, to stand a stone's throw beyond the gate, I saw that the Master had climbed up once again to his place atop the battlements, and was smiling sadly down at us, once more with his hands nonchalantly on his hips.

The bodies of half a dozen of our men were scattered below the walls of the Castle of Montségur, their corpses twisted in the inhuman attitudes of death, and Robin began his message with a gesture of his right hand towards the slain.

'Under the time-honoured laws of combat, we seek a truce to recover the bodies of our fallen comrades, and to carry them away without fear of molestation,' said Robin, in a flat, angry voice.

The Master let out a long sigh of exasperation. 'Such a waste, such a terrible waste of life,' he said. His face was a picture of sorrow and concern. 'Why are we clawing at each other like this, Robert? What is the purpose of all this bloodshed? Look at your men down there – did they have wives, children? They must have had mothers, at least. Will you tell their grieving mothers their sons are dead? I wonder. Or will you shirk that dolorous duty?'

'May we have your leave to collect the bodies of our fallen comrades or not?' said Robin stiffly.

'Oh yes,' sighed the Master, 'you may gather up the grim harvest of the day; be my guest.' His voice was tinged with sadness, but there was also an unmistakable hint of something else in his tone. Triumph.

Robin gave the nod to the mercenaries who moved forward and gently began to lift the corpses of their comrades, fold them over their shoulders and carry them away down the hill. The Master, however, had not finished speaking.

'Take the bodies, my friend, take them away with my blessing and the blessing of Holy Mary, the Mother of God, who weeps bitter tears at their deaths, but consider this – we did not slay these poor men, my knights and I – you did. It was your pride that killed them. You came against us in a spirit of violence and anger and your good men died uselessly as the price for that folly.'

Robin lifted his head and looked right up at the Master; and with a flicker of spirit he said, 'We will come again, Michel, mark my words, and make you pay for their sacrifice. You have not seen the last of us.'

'Robin, Robin, why must you persist in this madness? You cannot take these walls. Look at our strength! You could not take them with ten thousand men. You know that; I know that; every man on this mountain knows that.'

Robin said nothing. He looked down at his boots.

'We are protected here by a power far, far greater than you can imagine. Not just by these high ramparts and the strong right arms of the brave men inside them. God protects us, and Holy Mary stands with us as well. You cannot prevail here. Robin, I beseech you, come to your senses. You cannot win. If you come again, your men will be slaughtered like these poor souls, they will be sacrificed on the altar of your stubbornness. Have pity on your own men and give up this foolish cause. It is futile.'

I knew the Master was right – this *was* a futile cause. I had known it ever since I had first seen the Castle of Montségur. It was an impossible dream to attempt to take it. The Master seemed to be speaking inside my head, filling it with his words, and driving out any other considerations. Yet his simple message made perfect sense . . .

'Do the right thing, the honourable thing – pack up your bags and your weapons, gather up your wounded men and simply ride away. I will not molest you as you depart – go from this place with my blessing, and you and your men shall live long and happy lives. Go now, I say to you, go now and live.'

I looked at Robin and saw that he was nodding his head, ever so slightly. His eyes were still fixed on the ground but he seemed to be agreeing silently with every word the Master uttered. How could he not? The Master's words were as true as the Gospels. We must go.

'We have no quarrel, Robin, you and I – we are not enemies. As you said yesterday, we once divided the world between us, each in his proper place, each living in peace. As you said, we can have all that again. There is no need for you to kill your men, to kill your dear friends in this struggle – what can blood accomplish? Let

330

us be sensible, let us behave like civilized men. You go your way, and I shall go mine, and we shall wish each other well. There is too much pain and sorrow in this world – let us not add to the sum of evil. Depart now, take your men and your weapons and ride away. And we shall both live in happiness and harmony.'

There was a breathtaking beauty and purity in the Master's words. I could see his vision of a happy, harmonious world in which men did not slaughter each other uselessly in the name of greed or religion or differences of opinion. Surely this beautiful world would be Heaven on Earth. And all we had to do now was to walk away from this sordid, impossible, foolish fight.

'You will not attack us on the road, if we depart this place?' asked Robin, very quietly; he was still staring at the ground by his feet. 'I must have your solemn word on that, Michel. I will not allow my men to be put in danger on the march.'

The mercenaries had finished gathering the bodies by then, and a couple of them were looking at Robin, awaiting his orders. Some appeared deeply puzzled by his words. My lord waved them off down the hill, bidding them to follow the line of men bearing corpses and step carefully down the slope.

'Do I have your word?' he said, finally looking up at the Master standing so high above us.

'You have my word, old friend. Go in peace.' The Master made the holy sign of the cross in the air above our heads.

Robin put a hand on my arm and turned me so that I was facing down the hill, and we departed, saying nothing to each other, and stumbling a little on the loose rocks and uneven footing.

At the base of the mountain, Robin paused and looked back up that steep slope. I looked too and saw that the Master had gone from his commanding position atop the battlements, although a pair of Knights of Our Lady had taken his place, and now were watching over us, shading their eyes against the bright sunlight.

Robin turned to me. 'That should do it,' he murmured, and

331

slapped me on the shoulder to urge me back along the path towards the cave.

The Earl of Locksley clapped his hands to attract the attention of everyone in the crowded cave, and said loudly, in an oddly cheerful tone of voice, 'We failed this afternoon to take the castle by frontal attack – which was to be expected. We are too weak, there are too few of us here to ram home a successful, conventional assault. We know that; the Master knows that; the whole mountain knows that, apparently. So we shall do what is expected of us, we shall do the only sensible thing. We shall run away, like whipped dogs with our tails between our legs!' And he grinned at the assembled company, a group of thirty-odd bone-weary men, many wounded, all fatigued, bruised and downcast.

Then something truly magical happened. A ripple of noise travelled around the room, like a murmur, and heads began to lift, backs to straighten, and mouths to smile. For suddenly it was clear that Robin had a deeper plan, a stratagem, a ruse – and all was not lost after all. Indeed, if you had looked at Robin's grinning face, and the sly smiles of Little John and Gavin, you might easily have been led to believe that all was going according to plan.

We mounted our horses in plain view of the ramparts and, with slumped shoulders and drooping heads, and with the occasional shouted insult wafting down to us from above, we formed up on the saddle of land to the west of the mountain and took the road north away from Montségur, slowly riding back the way we had come. A keen observer looking closely at the dirty faces of the tired mercenaries might have noticed a few secret smiles, and conspiratorial nudges, or whispered jests. But from the ramparts more than a thousand feet above, I am fairly sure it looked as Robin wished it to look, as if we were returning to Foix, or perhaps even further afield, to lick our wounds and think again.

Once out of sight of the castle, shielded by a small, parched hill and finding ourselves in thick, almost virgin woodland, we jumped from our saddles and began to organize ourselves for the night march. Weapons, wool cloaks and water only, was the order from Robin – the horses and baggage being returned to their pasture under the care of three lightly wounded men.

And an hour after nightfall, after we had eaten as much as we could, on foot, and all of us I believe filled with a boyish excitement, we took to a narrow, little-used track through the close-set trees heading due east, being led by Maury, the malodorous shepherd. I was ordered by Robin to take up a place at the rear of the line, which gave me an opportunity to count the men as they marched past through the trees in the last light of that day. With Vim at their head, I tallied twenty-six surviving mercenaries fit and ready for battle. We had left Tuck in the cave with one of the hurt younger men to care for him – but all the other Companions who had left England with me in March were more or less hale. However, nearly half of these tough *routiers* had fallen as a result of serving Robin for a few short days. Would they stay true, I wondered, in the coming fight? And if Robin's plan were to work and we got inside Montségur, and they subsequently discovered that there was no hoard of gold and silver – how would they react then? Perhaps, I told myself, I was worrying over much. Perhaps I should put my faith in God – and Robin.

As the last man in the marching column, I received an unpleasant shock only a few moments after we set off, when I heard a noise behind me, and a voice calling, 'My lord? My lord? It is me, André, the scout. I have to make my report to the captain.' It was one of the mercenaries we had sent to guard the horses. I sent him swiftly up the line to speak to Robin.

Under the cover of full night and the thick forest of this remote region, we trudged in single file along ancient hunting tracks, stumbling a little in the dark and bumping into each other but led by Maury through secret ways and circling round Montségur to the north and then east. As the crow flies, we were never more than a mile or two from our enemies, but it felt as if we were in another county. My wounded calf throbbed awfully during that march. The forest closed in around us, and the night-black world was reduced to the stunted trees looming on either side, and the back of the man in front of you.

After two hours, or perhaps three, we stopped and huddled around Robin in the darkness. Our leader told us that we were now directly to the east of the castle at the foot of the spur. Here we would rest for the remainder of the night, and a little before dawn, Maury would lead us up the spine where we would assault the castle, with any luck, achieving total surprise.

'I have good news, my friends,' said Robin. 'It seems that after we left the cave the Master dispatched a strong force of knights to follow us, I believe to ambush us on the march – some forty men. Our friend André here watched them ride past on the road heading north. Even now, they are riding hard towards Foix, some fifteen miles away. The Master has weakened himself by a third, my friends, and we shall take full advantage of that fact when we attack. But there is more: we shall have powerful sorcery on our side in this coming struggle,' announced my lord triumphantly. 'Our wise friend Nur here has been in communion with the spirits of the sky and they have promised to come to our aid in the morning.'

The reaction to this from the mercenaries was mixed – some of the men seemed cheered by the prospect of supernatural help; some muttered, looked fearfully out into the darkness and crossed themselves. Others just got on with making their beds.

I sought out Roland before making up my own bed and asked him what Robin had meant about Nur.

My cousin had the grace to look shamefaced at this open talk of demonic practices by a person under his protection. 'She is

334

making a magic mist that will hide us when we attack the castle again tomorrow morning,' he said. Then, trying for a little levity: 'She says that if she had the freshly severed head of a powerful man, she could be absolutely certain of her spell – but she lacks one. Ha-ha. So she had to make do with a pile of mouldy knights' testicles! Ha! She even asked me today if I would cut off the Master's head and give it to her as a gift. Oh, she is an odd one.'

'Do you really believe all this disgusting magical nonsense?' I said crossly. I did not appreciate Roland making light of these matters. It was a time for seriousness, I felt. I was also full of apprehensions about the attack. It seemed to me to have only a slightly greater chance of success than our botched assault on the main gate.

'Do *you* believe that the Grail will save Tuck's life? And Goody's – if we can get it back to her in time? Do you have faith in its magical power?' my cousin responded.

I did not answer him – for his question had turned my head around. I *hoped* that the Grail would cure Tuck and Goody, I truly hoped with all my heart that it would. But did I truly *believe* that it would cure them? Did I have faith that the Grail could cure all wounds? Peering into my secret heart, I knew that I had my doubts.

Before I could answer my cousin, I saw that Nur was now beside us and bit my tongue. She was laying out Roland's cloak as a bed and had stuffed fresh green leaves and grass into an old chemise to make a little pillow for him; I saw, too, that he had already laid out a little mess of blankets for her a few feet from his. In an instant, a pure truth leaped unbidden into my mind, and I knew what I was seeing in this little tableau. It was an act of love, a quiet, ordinary, everyday act of love given freely by one human being to another. Whatever sordid, Devil-spawned magical fantasies this woman entertained, there was some good in Nur. And whatever type of bond this odd pair had forged – the tall French

335

knight with the scarred face and the mutilated Syrian witch – it was a bond of love.

And love, as Tuck had often told me, came only from God.

I was awoken a little before dawn – from a nightmare in which I was being trampled by a herd of wild pigs – by shrieks of unholy glee. Something that felt like a pebble from a boy's catapult crashed painfully into my forehead, and in the next instant a dozen more pummelled my prone body. I jumped up and reached for my shield which was on the ground just beside my head, and saw that the forest floor was littered with round white objects the size of dove's eggs, and that more were hurtling down from the dark-grey sky. Hastily grabbing my weapons and mail, and holding the shield above my head, I scurried under the shelter of the nearest tree, and plumped down next to Thomas.

The gleeful shrieking was coming from Nur, but the sound of her joy was now almost drowned out by the drumming rattle of the hailstones on the leather-faced wooden shield above my head. The strange Arab woman was capering about in a kind of ecstasy – heedless of the hail bouncing off her black headdress and robes – cackling madly and calling on all of us to admire her magical powers.

In my sleep-fuddled state, it was several moments before I took in the scene but, in the half-light, I could make out little groups of mercenaries huddled, shields held aloft, around the base of almost every neighbouring tree, each looking in awe at the cavorting witch and occasionally glancing up through the leaves at the relentless falling hail. It was hard to believe after so many days of sunshine that we were now in a furious ice storm.

Robin was running across the open space, the hail bouncing off the hard ground as high as his knees, with his cloak held over his head. He came crashing down beside me, shoving Thomas aside and putting his back to the wide trunk, and I was obliged to share my shield with him. My lord was breathless, hectic with excitement: 'What did I tell you, Alan, what did I tell you? That Nur is a true miracle worker. She has brought the very weather to our aid, or the spirits of the air or whatever you want to call them. She's bloody magnificent!'

And I saw that as the barrage of hailstones lessened a fraction, a thick white mist was creeping through the trees, advancing in tendrils from the south like freezing smoke from a forest fire or the breath of a northern ice giant. I suddenly realized that I was very cold, shivering, in fact, and tugged Robin's cloak from his unresisting fingers and wrapped it around my shoulders.

My lord was oblivious to the cold, it seemed. 'This is a God-send, Alan, an absolute God-send!' His voice was alive with happiness. 'We will be invisible, quite invisible until we are right on top of them. We can do it, Alan, I know it. I think we can honestly take that damned impossible castle in this wonderful fog!'

The hailstorm lasted less than half an hour, but the mist that followed it swirled and thickened around us and became an almost-solid grey-white wall until we could barely see five paces away. Robin delayed the attack while the fog continued to thicken, keeping everyone together in a tight huddle, lest any man should wander off and become lost, and it was not until mid-morning that, fully armed and mailed, we began to climb the steep path that led westwards up the spur.

Robin demanded absolute silence from the men, and we advanced in single file with each man taking a hold of the belt of the man in front. Once more Maury led the way, and thank the Good Lord that he did, for a couple of wrong steps to the left or right in that white blindness would have meant falling off the spine and crashing down the steep mountainside to our doom. But Maury led us true, and while it was a slightly more gentle climb than the path on the western side that we had sprinted up the day before, it was longer and still no easy stroll and my calf made a serious protest. But on we forged, the whiteness all around us, our hands sweaty on the belt of the man in front, stepping slowly and carefully, and trying not to let shield and spear clunk together as we moved, or sword hilt chink against mail coat. But we were fortunate – or Nur's unholy spirits were truly with us – for that freezing fog cloaked sound as well as sight, and we marched on, ever upwards, into the heart of this earth-touching cloud. Our mood was buoyant, too. The men seemed to believe that Nur genuinely had conjured a mist to hide us from our enemies: and in my experience men fight far better when they think there are powers beyond nature on their side, be it God – or the Devil! It took two hours, by my reckoning, and when I finally blundered into the back of the mercenary in front of me, to a volley of whispered curses, I saw that we were all gathered together in a low hollow on the mountainside in a space that seemed like a round white room with nebulous, shifting, ghostly walls of mist. We were within a stone's throw of the castle, undetected. And all of us, even the most hardened mercenaries, were eager for the assault, pink of cheek and filled with a soaring, breathless excitement.

Robin addressed us in a low whisper: 'There is a wall fifty paces over there' – he held out an arm in a direction that I guessed was westwards – 'that guards the castle from attack along this spur. It is twelve feet high with a little postern gate set into it. This is the first defence, manned by no more than a handful of men, but it needs to be taken speedily and in silence, or as quietly and quickly as we can possibly manage. Eight men will attack initially, scaling the wall using four of these. Little John is calling them his "war hooks" for want of a better name.'

My lord reached into a rough fustian sack at his feet and pulled out a large, curious-looking metal object. It had been roughly fashioned by welding together three sword blades that had each been bent into a hook. The blades were bonded together at one end with strips of iron and attached to a length of knotted rope.

338

At the top, the three sharp hooks branched out in three different directions. The device was heavy, and only crudely put together, but it seemed solid enough to take the weight of an armoured man – and I finally knew what Little John and Gavin had been constructing at the forge in the hellishly hot cave while the mercenaries and I had been gathering wood on the mountain.

'You hurl these war hooks over the top of the wall,' said Robin in his quietest voice, 'whereupon they will, with any luck, catch hold, and then you use the rope to ascend. Once at the top, leave the rope dangling for the next man. Behind the eight initial attackers will be the bowmen – myself, John and Gavin with war bows, and Jehan there with his crossbow' – a burly mercenary ducked his head and grinned at us all – 'and our task is to kill any enemy who puts his head above the parapet. This part should go easily enough – we think there are only five or six men manning this wall – the next bit is the tricky part. The first attackers must silence the defenders, open the gate for the rest of us, then immediately go on to assault the main wall of the castle. If God – or the spirits' – a smile here for Nur – 'are with us, we should be attacking an enemy that believes us to be long gone and, in any case, will not be prepared for an attack from this direction. I know that we can do this – but if you will forgive me for repeating myself, speed and silence are the essence. Now who will volunteer to be one of the attackers?'

Robin looked at me, and I reluctantly nodded. I knew that this was the most dangerous role in the coming battle but, well, how could I say no to Robin? How could I refuse my lord? Thomas immediately volunteered to be second man on my war hook, and Roland stepped forward promptly too. In the end, the eight men were myself and Thomas, Vim and Olivier, and Roland and Sir Nicholas with two mercenaries whose names I did not know.

'Remember,' whispered Robin as a parting shot, 'speed and silence, and the rest of us will be right there on your heels.'

Maury took us the last few paces through the fog and, the heavy war hook in my hands, I found myself crouching behind a rock and looking out at the blank grey wall a mere ten paces away. I could not see anyone atop the battlements, and for one wild, craven moment, I dared to hope that the Knights of Our Lady had abandoned the castle and fled and that there would be no fight today. I pulled myself together, looked over to my right and left at Roland, Sir Nicholas and Vim, took a deep breath and began to run, as quietly as I could, towards the wall.

Chapter Twenty-two

I swung the heavy war hook once, twice and then hurled it with all my might up the face of the wall. It hit the top with a deafening clatter and thumped back down to earth – but I gathered it in by its rope and swung harder, hurled it once more and this time, God be praised, two of the bent sword-hooks fixed themselves over the top and I pulled the knotted rope taut. Thomas was by my side, crouching down with his shield up, ready to secure the rope's end as I climbed. To my left, I could see that Roland had his war hook attached and was beginning to climb, but to my right, neither Sir Nicholas nor Vim had managed to affix their hooks to the top, and were swinging the ungainly metal shapes again and again. Just then, a helmeted head peered over the wall, the man looked down at us and opened his mouth. Thunk! An arrow smashed into his open mouth, jolting his head back, and away from the parapet – but I feared that the element of surprise was lost. I put my boots on the wall and began to walk upwards as speedily as I could, my shield on its carrying strap banging painfully against my spine, my wounded calf protesting madly. Another head appeared, and a crossbow bolt clanged off his helmet, but the man stayed in position, shouted a curse and I narrowly ducked a sword swipe that would had stunned me had it landed. By God's mercy, he was swept away in the next instant by an arrow that socked into his eye. Then I was at the lip of the wall. My left hand twisted itself securely into the rope, my right snaked over my shoulder and seized the T-shaped handle of the lance-dagger, and as a third man-at-arms loomed above me, looking down over the wall, I plunged the blade up, hard, into his neck. He shrieked and jerked back, blood jetting from between the fingers of his left hand which was clapped over the gaping rip in his throat. But I was over the wall by then, and I silenced his noise with a thrust of the lance-dagger into his open mouth and out the back of his neck. I could see Roland too was on the walkway on the other side, and I could hear the grunting breath of Thomas behind me. The mist was still thick around us – you could see nothing beyond ten yards away. I sheathed the bloody lance-dagger, shoved the dying man out of my way, and leaped down seven feet to the soft earth behind the wall, landing heavily, and immediately hauling out Fidelity. A man came out of a crude lean-to shelter beside the postern gate holding nothing more threatening than a wooden bowl of pottage and a horn spoon – but I killed him nonetheless, snapping my sword down two-handed into his bare head. Another man ran out of the fog on the far side of the wall – an untrained man, I believe, certainly un-armoured, perhaps a servant. He shouted something and jabbed at me clumsily with a spear, but I parried with Fidelity and dropped him with a counter stroke that ripped across his belly like a razor. Eviscerated, gasping, shocked beyond words, he goggled at me, gushing blood, and sank to his knees.

Miraculously, it seemed that the alarm had not yet been raised. I killed the servant before me with a merciful sword thrust under the chin, and he died with a quiet sigh. I watched Roland drop a man on the walkway with a single sword thrust to the chest, and the man gave a gargled cry before he fell, muffled by the fog.

342

Thomas was visible by now on the wall, looking grim with a sword in his fist, but no foeman before him. Sir Nicholas and Vim had also emerged from over the top. No more enemies came, so I jumped towards the postern gate, hauling back the locking bar and admitting Robin, who tumbled through the entrance as if he had been leaning on the outside of the door with all his weight. Little John was with him, axe in hand, and Gavin, and beyond them a score of madly grinning mercenaries emerging like joyful demons from the mist and running full pelt towards the open postern.

'On, on to the ramparts,' Robin said, trying to keep his voice pitched low, but failing in the excitement of battle. I saw that Thomas had collected the war hook from the top of the wall on his way down and was already pelting towards the castle a mere forty paces away. I sprinted after him, part of a swarm of thirty mercenaries and Companions, and as I reached the foot of the sheer stone wall I heard the cry above us: 'Alarm – they're coming, the Devils are coming. To arms, brothers. To the eastern wall!'

We no longer had surprise. But Vim was there swinging his war hook, and another man too beyond him, and Thomas had already secured his to the top of the wall and was climbing the rope like a monkey, a dagger clenched between his teeth. Twenty yards to my right, Sir Nicholas, too, had fixed his hook to the ramparts and was hauling himself upwards. Thomas had disappeared over the top of the wall and I heard him shout 'Westbury!' and another voice screaming in pain. I sheathed Fidelity, grasped the rope and pulled myself up, hand over hand, arm-muscles creaking with the strain, heart banging, the fire of combat coursing through my body like scalding spiced wine. I plunged up, unchallenged, got a hand on the stone crenellation, and a boot, and leaped over the rampart.

I was inside the impossible Castle of Montségur.

Next I knew, I was dodging a mace blow aimed at my head from a blue and white knight. I grabbed his swinging arm, pulled him towards me, off balance, and smashed my helmeted forehead into his face. He flew backwards, yelling, and plunged down into the courtyard. I did not stop to watch him fall – there were men running at me from both sides. I ripped Fidelity from the scabbard and took its edge to the enemy on my left. A flurry of blows and he was clutching the stump of his arm, bleeding, screaming. I fended off the man on my right, drove him back with a series of fast lunges and, as he retreated along the walkway, he met Little John rolling over the wall, who straightened, swung and hacked off his head with one blow from his axe. A crossbow bolt clattered on the stone of the walls by my shoulder. I got my shield off its carrying strap on my back and on to my free arm, just in time to stop a strike from a man-at-arms who ran in from the left – and felled him with my riposte, Fidelity ripping an extra, bloody mouth under his chin. There were enemies all around, now, and more coming my way. But more of my friends were on the walkway, too.

We boiled over that wall – all of us – in a less than a hundred heartbeats. I saw Vim stepping over the ramparts and immediately begin slaying men with great sweeps of his sword, snarling like a bear. There was André the scout cutting down a cowering cross-bowman who had spent his bolt.

I saw Thomas ten paces further along the walkway, facing down a mob of charging enemy knights. I raced to his side, stopped a sword strike at his head, and threw off his attacker with a shield-punch – and we held them, and blocked them and forced them back. Thomas killed the foremost man and I took the next. Then we fought our way forward, heading towards the keep, holding off a swarm of enemies with sword and shield, cutting, killing and maiming. Keeping their vicious blades out of our bodies. And behind us, in a space cleared of enemies, good man after good man came tumbling over that wall behind and screamed into the fight. Then Robin was behind me. He shouted in my ear just as Thomas was finishing off a big fellow with a twisted lip. My lord clapped me on the shoulder and pulled me away from my squire.

344

'I need you now, Alan,' he bellowed – for the din was terrific: the clash and scrape of steel on steel, the screams of pain, the yells of fury, a trumpet calling over and over for the Knights of Our Lady to come to arms. And they did – score upon score of them, erupting out of the barracks in the courtyard like ants from a kicked nest, and charging up onto the walkway via the stone stairs at the southern end. A crossbow quarrel slashed past my face, but I paid it no heed. Robin and I drove south, sprinting along the walkway, chopping down anything in our path, with Thomas following in our wake. Robin's blade was like a deadly serpent's tongue flicking to take the life of any man who foolishly stood before him. We slipped in gory puddles but somehow managed to keep our footing; we stumbled over corpses and the writhing bodies of the wounded, and Thomas, who was a pace behind me, killed any that he found alive beneath his feet. A group of four knights tried to form a loose shield wall in front of us, but Robin and I charged straight into it, shields up, swords pounding down, battering relentlessly. Thomas pressed in close behind, I could feel his breath on my neck, his sword arching over the top of my shoulder to stab at enemy faces – and we soon swept them backwards with our momentum, tumbling two of them off the walkway to thump down on the sandy floor twenty feet below. I remember thinking that these Knights of Our Lady would never have made the ranks of the Templars – they were soft, and slow, and unused to fighting in close concert with their brother knights.

We killed them.

I heard a great roar behind me, and stole a half-glance, as Little John, war hook in his right hand, double-headed axe in his left, jumped straight down on to the red-tiled roof of a stables below the parapet, smashing terracotta, and then kicking free of the broken shards to jump down a further ten feet to the courtyard. Gavin followed in his wake, sword and shield in his hands, a reckless grin on his handsome face.

345

At a set of stone stairs in the south-eastern corner, a fresh surge of enemies, led by two Knights of Our Lady and with half a dozen men-at-arms behind them, rushed up to confront us, and Robin and I met our first serious resistance. I took a pace forward and my right leg failed me – I felt the wound tear open and a lightning bolt of pain in my calf and, at the same time, the knight on the right, on my side, sliced forward with a long sword, driving for my face. I took the blow on the cross-guard of Fidelity, shook it aside, and, trying to keep the weight on my left leg, cut at his neck with my counter stroke, which he blocked easily with his shield. Robin was duelling with the knight on my left, a flurry of clashing steel and the dull cracks of metal on leather-covered wood. A crossbow bolt, loosed from the courtyard smashed into my shield, rocking me back. My opponent lunged again, this time for my belly, and I twisted out of the blade's path at the last instant, my calf screaming, and chopped down on his extended right arm with my shield, and dislocated the elbow.

Then he was mine.

I dispatched him with a feinted lunge to unbalance him, and a powerful strike at his throat. My blade smashed into the mail of his coif that protected his neck. The blade did not pierce the iron links but he stumbled and fell to his knees, and I cracked Fidelity down on his helmeted head, stunning him. His place on the stair was immediately taken by a wildly yelling man-at-arms, who stepped over the prone knight and began hacking at me with a sword in one hand and an axe in the other. I hobbled back out of range and something big and glinting blurred through the air between our bodies, and I saw with shock, and not a little horror, that it was a war hook, hurled up by Little John from the courtyard floor. The sword blades snatched deep into the man-at-arms' chest and, like a fisherman hooking a salmon, John yanked the rope taut and hauled the soldier and two comrades standing behind him backwards to crash down the steps on to the courtyard floor.

Our forward passage cleared, both Robin and I charged down the stone steps, smashing a couple of men-at-arms aside with our shields, and surging down to join up with Little John in the centre of the courtyard. Thomas was on my heels and behind him were a dozen mercenaries. Suddenly our men were all over the castle: the iron-studded door of the keep, at the northern end, was wide open, and I saw a wolfish mercenary jump down from the walkway on the north-eastern wall and cut down a half-dressed man who emerged bemused from its darkness; I saw a pair of knights in blue and white, cowards for sure, slipping over the western wall to make their escape. Another poltroon, a balding man-at-arms, hurled away his sword and began scrabbling in terror at the barred main gate, trying to claw it open so that he could flee to safety.

For a moment I stood still, panting with exhaustion, dripping sword in hand, my weight on my left leg, trying to master the waves of white agony flowing from my wounded calf.

Olivier, the skinny mercenary, had also battled his way down to the courtyard nearer the keep. I saw him, twenty yards away, take on two leather-jacketed enemy men-at-arms armed with pole axes, and drop one. But the second dodged Olivier's strike, slashed with his own weapon, and gashed Olivier's sword arm, rendering it useless, and finished him with an axe blow to the stomach that folded him in half. Two mercenaries nearby pounced on the axeman and took a swift revenge. But, as I watched, the skinny ruffian who would have happily burned out Roland's eyes died like a soldier on the castle's sanded floor, his bloody white and blue entrails bulging through his fingers.

I looked over towards a small chapel by the main gate and saw the Master for the first time that day. His expression was one of deep and terrifying fury. He had a naked sword in his hand – incongruous with his gaunt, ascetic features, his tonsure and the immaculate black robe that he wore. He glared at me briefly, his

347

mouth a white line, then fixed his eyes on Robin in the south of the courtyard.

And he stalked directly towards him.

A howling mercenary, tossed on the winds of madness, and wielding a bloody sword, hurled himself at the Master – but the former monk barely glanced at the battle-crazed man as he dispatched him with two swift, precise strikes of his own blade, leaving him bleeding and crying in the sand. The Master's eyes seemed to bore into Robin and he glided across towards him oblivious to the scramble of battle all about him, occasionally swatting men out of his path as if they were no more troublesome than late-summer flies. As he came on, surviving Knights of Our Lady seemed to coalesce around him, flocking to him as if he represented the only light in a world of darkness. Three, five, ten knights – and a gaggle of their men-at-arms gathered behind the Master's dark robe. Robin stepped in to meet his enemy, and at the same time both their swords licked out like bolts of lightning and cracked together with what seemed to my battle-heightened mind to be a shower of brilliant sparks.

The Master was fast, almost faster than any man I have ever seen – his sword was a flicker of light, a gleaming blur that probed and struck and sliced the air around Robin, and I remembered that he had been a Templar himself in his youth and had fought against the Moors of Spain and won much honour on those battlefields.

But my lord of Locksley was no stranger to the roar of battle either – as a youth he had been trained by the best sword-masters in England and had been fighting with a long blade ever since. So Robin blocked and parried, and counter-attacked with skill, smothering the Master's initial attack, and managing to keep his enemy's quick-silver blade from his flesh.

A bareheaded knight in blue and white charged at me and I could no longer observe the crash and wheel of the fight between the two lords of men. The knight's sword hacked down towards my head, but I got my shield up, just in time, taking the heavy blow on its already much battered frame and sweeping low with my own sword to thump the long blade into his mail-covered thigh just above the knee. He went down, but I found to my surprise that I was too weary to finish him – I watched Gavin leap forward and lance his sword-point into the man's white face. And, with that action – killing my opponent for me – the young bowman sealed his fate.

As Gavin bent to put his shoulder into the lunge, a Knight of Our Lady behind the fallen man jumped in and hacked his sword down into the back of the youngster's curly head, splitting his skull and burying the blade deep into his brains.

A great, deep animal-like cry of rage and despair came from behind us, and I was hurled off my feet as a force like a mighty whirlwind, an unstoppable, elemental impetus, barrelled past me, with a noise like the bellowing of a herd of fear-maddened bulls. I crashed painfully to the floor on my right shoulder, the helmet strap snapped and my steel cap fell forward to partially cover my eyes. And my impressions of the next few moments were of a huge shining axe blade swinging in a fine cloud of blood and a howling storm of terrifying noise as Little John, crazed with grief, barged straight into the crowd of enemy fighting men behind the Master – his last remaining knights – and began to hew and hack in a mindless, whirling, blood-spattering rage. At one point, I swear on my soul, I saw a severed arm fly through the air followed immediately by the upper half of a human head, still partially helmeted. And by the time I had painfully regained my feet, there was not a living enemy to be seen in the courtyard, save for a few gore-spattered men-at-arms, scrambling like cats over the walls to try and save their miserable skins.

And the Master.

The elemental fury of John's lone, whirlwind assault stopped the battle dead in its tracks. His rage seemed to have ended the carnage like a snuffed candle. The Master and Robin, both with their mouths agape in awe, were frozen a couple of yards apart with their swords raised, transfixed. They gawped as the big man laid down his axe and knelt among a ring of piled, mangled, knightly corpses, scooping up the limp body of his young friend in his arms, his blond, gore-speckled head pressed to Gavin's dark, broken poll, the giant's vast frame heaving with wild, lung-tearing sobs.

Robin recovered first. He reached out his sword and tapped the Master's blade, almost as if seeking to attract his opponent's attention, and purely by instinct, the Master delivered a lightning riposte, a low lunge that Robin had to scramble to avoid.

Robin took a long step backwards. 'Do you surrender?' he said to the Master. The monk was friendless in that courtyard, a circle of Robin's men was forming around him, yet he replied, 'And let you hang me? Or crop my fingers at your leisure? Oh, yes, that barbarous tale reached my ears. I think not!' And he lunged again, quick as thought, at Robin's chest, forcing my lord to parry and step away.

And again the Master attacked. A dancing step forward and huge vertical downward chop that seemed to contain all the fury and hatred in the world. The blade arced down – and was met by Robin's shield. But such was the power of the blow that the steel sliced halfway through the wood and leather of Robin's protector. My lord took a step backwards, his sword extended before him, warding the Master off, while he shook his left arm free of the flapping tatters of the shattered shield. The Master launched another manic offensive. Scything, double-handed diagonal cross-strikes from left and right, left and right. If any of these had landed, my lord, now shieldless, would be breathing his last. But Robin somehow, miraculously, each time got his sword between the Master's malice and his own skin. Their blades rang like bells, again and again, and Robin with every blow was being forced relentlessly backwards towards the wall.

The main battle was over. The only combatants in that yard were Robin and the Master. Every other man in the castle – unless dead, unconscious or grievously wounded – was watching the duel. Two men, two swords, in a circle of expectant blood-spattered faces. It was a fight to the death.

And Robin was losing.

The Master swung; Robin caught the powerful blow on his cross-guard, their blades locked, their bodies only inches apart . . .

I limped forward and hefted my sword. This was pointless – I would not allow my lord to die at the hands of this creature. I shoved a watching mercenary out of my way and stepped in . . .

'Stand back, Alan. Stand back, I tell you – that is an order!' My lord was nose to nose with the Master, his sword locked against his enemy's blade; they were panting spittal-breath into each other's faces, and yet he was speaking to me across ten yards of courtyard. 'This is my fight – I claim it. I will allow no man to come between us. Get back, Alan. That is a direct order!'

And Robin gave a mighty heave and hurled the Master away, forcing the monk to stagger back across the open space.

Then the Earl of Locksley showed his true quality.

He came on like a wild cat, a whirl of steel and speed, his sword lancing everywhere, probing at the Master's defences, and forcing his enemy to parry and block for his life. The Master seemed quite shocked by this sudden counterattack from Robin, but he rallied, he kept my lord at bay, and when Robin seemed to lose his footing and slip down on to his left knee, he rushed forward and pounded his blade savagely down at Robin's unguarded head.

It was a blow that my lord had clearly anticipated, for his sword swept up and across to his left, clanging against the Master's blade and forcing it out to thud harmlessly into the sand. Robin's body followed the direction of the parry that pushed the Master's sword aside. His weight transferred to his left knee; his right leg kicked out at the same time and swept across in front of him, parallel with the earth. His mailed right foot crashed into the Master's back foot an inch or so above the sand, followed through, and swept his enemy completely off his feet. The Master's legs flew up in the air, exposing bare, skinny shanks, and he crashed onto his back, just as Robin pulled in his leg and leaped to his feet. My lord stepped in and paced his sword tip, with exquisite delicacy, beneath the Master's chin, the point resting on his Adam's apple.

Both men were still for a dozen heartbeats – the only sound in the courtyard was their ragged breathing.

Then Robin spoke: 'If you surrender, you will not be harmed – but I will deliver you up to the Count of Foix for his judgment. Surrender now or you will die. I give you my word on that.'

The Master, sprawled on the sandy floor, glanced anxiously left and right. A dozen of Robin's armed men were within striking distance, blood-stained mercenaries, grim Companions, all with the hard glow of victory in their eyes. The Knights of Our Lady and their men-at-arms were nowhere to be seen – all dead, badly wounded or fled. The Master still held his sword in his hand, but wide of his body. It was clear that Robin could lunge forward and skewer his throat before he had time to strike. Yet still the Master hesitated.

'Surrender, right now, or die,' said Robin.

'Very well,' the Master mumbled. 'I shall take your word. I yield.' And he let the sword slip to the floor, and flopped down on his back, like a dead man.

The Castle of Montségur was ours but the fight for it had taken a heavy toll. Gavin had perished and Little John was inconsolable, his battered face streaming with tears as he wrapped his friend's corpse up tightly in a cloak and laid him with our other dead outside the main castle gate. Before he covered his dead friend's face with the cloak – I saw that iron-tough warrior bend down and swiftly, lightly, kiss the lips of the corpse. I shed a tear, too, at the sight.

Olivier was dead, as were another half dozen of his fellow mercenaries. Sir Nicholas had been wounded in the side, an axe blow had smashed several of his ribs early in the fight on the parapet, and although the knight's mail had kept the blade from his body, the iron links had been broken and twisted and had cut through the gambeson he wore under them and into his skin. The former Hospitaller was stoic under the pain, although the lines on his face seemed more deeply cut. 'It's a scratch, Alan, no more,' he said. 'I have taken worse and lived to laugh about it. We took the castle – that is what is important.'

My own wounded leg was on fire. As soon as the castle was secured, I asked Thomas to clean and rebandage it. It had stopped bleeding by then, but I feared that my exertions – I had scaled two stone walls and killed half a dozen men in the past half hour – had permanently damaged the muscle. Thomas washed it with water and wine, packed a cobwebby mess of Nur's into the wound and bound it very tightly with fresh linen. And I found that I could, with only a modicum of agony, walk about the courtyard. I took a moment to pray and give thanks St Michael, the warrior archangel, that I was not among the scores of dead and mortally wounded.

For me, though, the hardest blow I received that day was the discovery that Tuck's soul had left his body. Hobbling very slowly, I had led a party of mercenaries down to the cave to retrieve our belongings, and when I got there I found the empty shell of my friend on the altar at the back, his once-ruddy face white as milk against his dark robe. The young mercenary Anthony, who had been tending to him, told me that he had died a little before dawn. Tuck had just quietly stopped breathing and then the man had stripped and washed the body as well as he could and covered it with a blanket. I could not bear to move my old friend from the stone altar and so I left him there, with a final kiss on his broad, lined forehead, as we gathered up our belongings, spare weapons

353

and food – and the mercenaries bore it all on their backs up the hill to the castle. The tears rolled down my cheeks as I limped up that hellish slope once again.

By the time I made it back to the courtyard, something like good order had been restored after the chaos of battle. The dead had been placed outside by the main gate. They would be carried down to the saddle of land west of Montségur the next day, where we planned to bury them after a service conducted by Sir Nicholas. The wounded were being tended to by Thomas and Nur in the ground floor of the keep. The Master had been bound at the wrists and shut in an empty grain store room on the eastern side of the courtyard, with a stout oak bar across the door and a veteran mercenary on guard outside, a steady man, to make sure that the Master did not try to slip his bonds and use his tricks to escape.

I found Robin with Roland and a pale-faced Sir Nicholas by the door of the little chapel by the main entrance to the castle. Before I could tell him about Tuck, my lord said, 'Good, you're back, Alan – you should be here for this. Come inside', and he held open the door of the chapel and we all filed through into a small wooden room, not much bigger than a solar in a modest hall.

From the moment I had seen Robin holding open the door of the chapel, a voice inside my head had been calling insistently, urgently: 'He's found it, he's found the Grail. The blessed Holy Grail. I shall at last behold its wonder – and my beloved Goody, my poor, sick, dying Goody, shall be saved.'

At the end of the chapel was a wooden altar of smoothed beech planks covered with a white cloth, supporting a plain silver crucifix, a pair of iron candlesticks and a medium-sized box of some dark wood. Robin unbarred and pushed open a shutter set in the wall and allowed the grey light of day to seep into that dark space. Then he walked over to the box and threw back its lid.

I think, in my heart, I expected a fanfare of trumpets or a brilliant, blinding light or the sound of a Heavenly choir of angels all

354

singing Hosannas. Instead, there was a dull clunk as the box lid hit the silver crucifix behind it, and we all craned our necks forward to try and make out the object contained within.

Even Robin seemed a little nervous. He took a hank of his cloak, wrapped it around his hand and reached into the box, pulling out a smallish round object, which he placed on the pure white cloth of the altar. Roland, Sir Nicholas and I all took a step forward to examine it more closely in the dim light. It was a bowl about nine inches in diameter, and two inches in depth, perfectly round and made of a light honey-brown, almost golden wood, perhaps Mediterranean cedar. It was darkened with ancient dirt at the rim and on the outside by the touch of many hands, and I could see a few faint patches of what looked like white paint on the outside. The bowl was also slightly cracked in two places. It was clearly very old. Indeed, it looked extremely . . . ordinary. An old kitchen bowl. One that many a conscientious goodwife might have thrown away as a piece of rubbish.

I must confess, I was a little disappointed. Ever since I had first heard that the Grail might be a real object half a dozen years previously, I had been imagining what it might have looked like. In my mind, it had blossomed into a magnificent golden vessel, intricately carved, and set with precious stones, a vast bejewelled chalice radiating blinding light, an item more dazzlingly beautiful than any that had ever been crafted by the hand of Man.

And before me was merely an old cracked wooden bowl.

'It doesn't look like much, does it?' said Robin, voicing my thoughts exactly. 'Is this truly the Holy Grail?'

He sounded deeply disappointed.

'This is exactly the kind of bowl in which they would have mixed the wine at the feast – the last meal that Our Lord Jesus ate with his Apostles,' said Sir Nicholas, his voice filled with an almost greedy reverence. 'Christ and his disciples were not men of material wealth. Our Lord would not seek to flaunt the riches of this world.

He preached poverty and humility. This must be that blessed vessel, used at the Last Supper, and which also held the blood of Our Lord which he shed for us on the Cross. Can you not see it, my friends? Can you not feel its holy power? This is the Holy Grail! I'm as certain of it as I am of Salvation! This is the blessed Grail that we have so long searched for!'

Sir Nicholas fell to his knees and began to pray. I looked at Roland and we both knew that Sir Nicholas's words were no more than the pure truth. Christ would never have used an enormous, gaudily bejewelled golden cup at his Last Supper – he was the son of a poor carpenter. My cousin and I were of one mind, evidently. We, too, fell to our knees at the same moment and began to praise God with all our hearts. Only Robin remained standing. He had cocked his head on one side and was looking at the three of us on our knees before the altar. He was frowning.

But if my lord could not feel in his heart the holy power of this wondrous object before us, I felt only pity for him, as I pitied any human soul that is closed to the love of God. I shut my eyes and sent up a heartfelt paean to the Almighty for allowing me, by His boundless grace, to set my unworthy eyes on this divine artefact. Then I heard Sir Nicholas begin to say aloud those familiar words, that joyous litany that had been engraved on our hearts since childhood: 'Our Father, which art in Heaven . . .'

Roland and I joined him in saying the Lord's Prayer, and I felt our souls open like flowers in the spring and receive the blessings of God. When it was done we all fell into a deep and peaceful silence – I recalled my many sins, and humbly asked for God's forgiveness, and I prayed silently for Goody that she might live long enough to receive the blessing of health from this most Holy Grail. I opened my eyes and looked once more on the Grail – its simple purity, its venerable age, its sheer, unquestionable Godliness were all manifestly apparent. I felt hot tears, tears of joy, springing to my eyes and I saw that Nicholas was weeping, too.

I do not know how long we knelt there – praying, weeping and staring at that miraculous bowl, the ancient yellow-brown cedar wood glowing like the gold of my imagination in the drab daylight of the chapel – but it felt as if we had been there in that chapel all of our lives, and yet no more than a few moments as well. At some point I saw that Robin was gone – he had slipped out without a word or a noise, and without disturbing our meditations. Only we three Christian knights, we three Grail Knights, knelt before that holy vessel and worshiped the Lord of Hosts with all our hearts. Finally, Roland spoke. 'We must take it to the wounded,' he said, his voice thick and furred with emotion.

And he was right, for there were wounded men who must be allowed to drink from the Grail without delay.

I went in search of water, found it in the cistern behind the keep and returned with a brimming bucket. Sir Nicholas, careful not to touch the Grail with his naked fingers, filled the bowl with a few splashes from the bucket and, holding it with his cloak, blessed it with a long prayer and in turn, gave it to each wounded man to drink, while Roland supported the drinker's head, if he could not raise it himself. I maintained order in the line of men waiting to receive the Grail's blessing, and led away those, many of them on shaking legs, who had received the sacrament. And so, we three knights ministered to the wounded and hurt that afternoon, in imitation of our blessed Lord Jesus Christ. Amen.

Robin looked on as we distributed the Grail water to all of our wounded men, standing there by the castle wall with a faint smile on his face, his arms folded, but he said absolutely nothing. Sir Nicholas, who had been the first to drink, prayed loudly over every man who drank, and intoned that by God's power and the power of the Grail each man would now be made whole.

The atmosphere that day was extraordinary – Nur's thick mists of the morning had rolled away and once more bright sunshine filled the air with hope and joy. We had won our battle, and by an extraordinary feat of arms we had conquered an 'impossible' castle, and even our half dozen wounded seemed to be buoyed beyond their pain by our possession of the wondrous Grail – for word had spread fast among those who had not known our true mission. And after drinking just a sip or two, each wounded mercenary confessed to being filled with light and grace, all of them claiming to feel happier, stronger and more spiritually whole.

I must set this down for all to know, for this is the true miracle of that miraculous day – not one of the seven men who had been wounded, some severely with blades deeply puncturing their bodies, subsequently perished of his wounds. Not one. I truly believe that the power of the Grail saved their lives that day. I swear this to you on my honour as a knight: not one of those men died of their wounds.

When it came to my turn, when all the other men in our company, including Robin, had drunk, I found I was shaking with happiness. The draft of water that I sipped from that plain old wooden bowl tasted like cool, liquid silver as it slid down my throat. I could feel the blessed liquor spreading its holy balm throughout my body. The bandaged wound in my right calf seemed to throb suddenly as that draft of holy water pooled in my belly. It was as if the hurt had been touched with a cauterizing iron – but cold, rather than hot. The deep cut seemed to flare under its bloody cloth swaddling as if touched by an icy blade and I could feel the healing power of the Holy Grail begin its work. Of course, I was not instantly healed but the pain became noticeably less. My whole body seemed lighter and filled with a strange and holy joy.

To the delight of Vim and his men and, I suspect, to Robin's great relief, Thomas discovered a strongbox filled with silver coins in the keep. There were also various other items of value: a pair of jewelled broaches, a fine ivory statue of the Virgin and Child, some bolts of expensive silk cloth from far beyond the Saracen lands and a bag of gold and silver finger rings. When I asked Robin where these treasures might have come from, he gave me a sly, contented smile.

'Long as I've known him, the Master has always loved material wealth. For all his vaunted piety, he really only seeks money and power – just like everybody else,' Robin said. 'I doubt he was here for a month before he had his men pillaging these lands for taxes or contributions to support the dignity of the Knights of Our Lady or whatever he might have called it. Count Raymond of Foix admitted as much to me, so I knew he must have more than a little silver and a bauble or two tucked away.'

Robin took possession of the strongbox but immediately distributed a generous reward in silver to each of the surviving mercenaries, and ordered that a cask of wine – we had found several in the castle store rooms along with a cache of javelins, shields, swords and other spare armaments – be opened and served out to all of us. We ate and drank and admired our silver and our treasures, feeling the warmth of pride in a task well accomplished.

Sir Nicholas insisted that a holy service of thanksgiving be said in the courtyard, the chapel being too small, and, with himself officiating – and the Grail prominently displayed – we all gave our thanks to God for the victory and lifted our voices in song.

Towards eventide, Robin and I paid a visit to Tuck's corpse in the now empty cave below the castle. I brought with me a beaker of Grail water, carried carefully on our descent so as not to spill its holy contents, which Sir Nicholas had blessed. The Grail itself had been replaced in the chapel, set there between two lighted candelabra, so that those who wished to pray before it might be afforded the opportunity.

When Robin and I reached the bottom of the mountain, and had made our way into the cave, dusk was falling. Tuck's body was in exactly the same position as when I had last seen it – lying on the stone altar, and by the guttering light of pine torches, Robin and I tipped a little of the Grail water into our friend's slack mouth, and used the rest to wash his torn head.

Alone with Robin, I took this opportunity to ask him when we might depart the castle. We had the Grail and I was afire to fetch it home to Goody. But my lord seemed distracted, perhaps by his grief for Tuck, and the best I could extract from him was a promise that we would begin our homeward journey soon.

Alas, Robin and I did not see a further miracle that night – Tuck was not raised from the dead by the magic of the Grail. Although, in honest truth, I had not expected it. I did not doubt that the Grail had enormous power but I reasoned that after God had called a soul into Heaven, that happy being would not willingly return to Earth at the command of mortal men. And no one had claimed that the Grail could bring men back to life as Jesus did with Lazarus.

I knelt by the altar on which Tuck slept, and said a prayer for his soul, with Robin looking on from the shadows of the cave.

'We should leave him here when we return to England,' said my lord after a little time had passed. 'We cannot take him with us and this would make a more than fitting tomb for our friend, bigger than the death vault of a duke. There's something about this place, something special, that I think would befit Tuck. What do you say, Alan? Shall we let him rest here until the end of time?'

'Until Judgment Day,' I said, correcting Robin's unchristian phrase without thinking. But I knew my lord was right. I had sensed it from the first and it had unsettled me even then – this cavern was no mountain womb, as Nur had called it, it was a natural tomb.

Chapter Twenty-three

I was eager to leave Montségur as soon as we were able to do so. The next morning was, by my rough calculations, the seventh or eighth day of May, and I felt the pressing need to bring the Grail back to Goody as soon as possible. In my head, I figured that I had to begin the return journey by the ides of May, the middle of that month, to have a reasonable chance of getting home before the curse was fulfilled. Yet a sea voyage back to England was a chancy thing – who knew how long it might take in adverse weather. Or when a ship might be available to take us back home. And the alternative – to ride up through the territory of France could take just as long or longer and would mean travelling through the war-torn areas where Prince Arthur and King John were contesting for mastery.

So I wanted to depart immediately, and tried my best to persuade Robin of this course. But my lord went through the calculations of the journey with me and persuaded me that we could spare a few more days at Montségur, perhaps three or four more, to allow the wounded to rest a little longer before they were forced to endure the pain and disruption of a horseback journey.

While the Grail, I was quite certain, had saved many of their lives, holding back Death as we had been promised it would, the deep sword cuts suffered by our men did not magically close, and neither did broken limbs suddenly mend. And the wound on my calf was still bloody, although it did indeed feel much better. But I was still bone tired – we had been riding and fighting hard for weeks now with little rest or sleep – and I allowed Robin to persuade me that we could afford to spare a little time in recuperation before we began the arduous return. It was, he said, more than the fighting men's due. I could not but agree with him.

I took a blissful day of rest, and Thomas and I spent the time chatting and sitting in a patch of sunshine, cleaning and oiling our war equipment. My squire was in high spirits – he had fought well, killed several men and emerged more or less unscathed. It occurred to me, not for the first time, that he was a young man who was becoming extremely accomplished in the arts of war. Like everyone else in the castle, he had drunk from the Grail and he was now filled with a youthful energy and zest that made me feel – a man not yet twenty-six – like a broken-down old cripple.

The next morning, I spent some hours in the chapel, kneeling before the Grail, and praying earnestly that God would shield Goody from the malevolence of the curse for long enough for me to return home and minister to her with the Grail water. I prayed long and hard, and when I emerged from the chapel, blinking in the sunlight, I felt confident that merciful God would keep Goody safe for another day or so.

As I gazed around the courtyard of the castle in a mood of placid contentment, I saw that the veteran mercenary, a man called Philip, who had been given the task of guarding the Master in his store-room prison, was waving to attract my attention and calling my name. I walked over to him and was surprised to hear him say that the Master had been asking to speak to me for some hours.

'I'm sorry, sir, I would have come to find you earlier but I didn't dare. The Earl's man, that big fellow they call Little John, told me that if I left this spot for an instant, even to relieve myself, he'd castrate me with a bowstring and feed me my own collops.'

I reassured Philip that it was fine and that there was no urgency – but I will admit that my curiosity was piqued. Why would the Master wish to speak to me? We had nothing of great import to say to each other, or nothing that I was aware of.

I pushed open the door of the store room, and waited while the mercenary barred it behind me. On the other side of the space, a yard or two away, a pathetic figure sat on the bare ground with his back to the wall of the store house. The place was badly, or more probably, hastily constructed of planks of wood nailed to a box frame and enough light leaked through the gaps between them to allow me to observe the prisoner with moderate ease. The Master had been stripped of his robe and wore only a tattered grey-white chemise, that made him look even thinner than usual. His hands were still tied, and he held them low against his flat belly. His pock-marked face was gaunt and I saw that the shaved patch of his tonsure was covered in a light grey fuzz in striking contrast to the brown ring of hair that surrounded it. How different he seemed, I reflected, to the tall commanding figure on the battlements who had parleyed with Robin three days ago. He looked old and weak, small and deflated, like a punctured bladder.

'I was told that you wished to speak to me,' I said brusquely. 'What do you want?' I rested my hand on my hilt. I remembered that this punctured bladder had destroyed my father; his henchman had killed my good friend Hanno while he was bound to a chair and helpless; he had sent his men to burn my home and threaten my family. A small flame of anger ignited in my belly, a rage that began to grow and burn more fiercely the longer I looked at him.

'I was born not far from here, Sir Alan – did you know that?' The Master spoke in a low voice, trembling with strong emotion.

I shrugged. Every word he uttered seemed to add fuel to the rage-fire in my guts.

'A little town called Mirepoix – a beautiful place with a fine stone church. That is where I first learned to love God. That is when I first became aware of His glory. My mother took me twice a day to pray there and it was so quiet and beautiful and holy, so . . . pure that I knew that I wanted to devote my life to the Church.'

'Fascinating,' I murmured and glanced at the locked door behind me. For a moment, I seriously thought about killing him. Taking his head, there and then. The sentry would not protest. But I knew that Robin would be angry if I summarily put him to death. He had given his word of honour . . .

'It was at Mirepoix, sitting on the knee of my grandfather, who was a man of the southern mountains, that I first heard the tales about . . .' the Master was staring intently at me, he had paused significantly before saying, '. . . the Grail.'

'I'm sorry,' I said, 'but I do not care to hear your family reminiscences. Shall I tell you about *my* father? The innocent man whose life you ruined, whose ignominious death you arranged?'

The Master ignored my question. 'It was at Mirepoix, as a child, that I first heard the tales of the Grail – wonderful tales,' he said, his voice had become louder, more insistent. 'It was there too that I first heard about the Holy Lance . . .'

'Have you anything of the slightest importance to say? Because, if not, I will take my leave before I lose my temper.'

'But it was only when I took possession of both of these objects – the Lance and the Grail – that I realized that, of the two, the Lance has the greater power.'

'What?'

'Ah, so now I have your attention.' The Master smiled at me unpleasantly. 'I said that the Holy Lance has more power than the Grail. Can a simpleton such as you grasp that? I spent many years possessing these items, as you know, and many years studying them, chasing down obscure documents in dusty libraries, sending out men to the four corners of the world to find the least scrap of information about the Lance and the Grail. Would you like to know what I found?'

I admit he did have my attention, but I could not bring myself to ask what he had discovered. I shrugged, but my eyes were fixed on his face now, my belly anger dampened by curiosity. For the Master this, evidently, was answer enough, and he continued. 'For hundreds of years these two holy objects had been on this Earth,' he said. 'I believe they were gifts from Heaven, talismans for those who would use them in the service of God. They represent the male and female elements of the universe, the dual nature of all life – day and night, good and evil, Heaven and Earth. The Grail is feminine, of course, it represents the life-giving womb, and its power is creative and restorative – as I think you have already discovered. Yes?'

I said nothing. I just stood there fingering my sword hilt.

'The Lance is masculine – a symbol of the male member, and its power is destructive. It kills men, rather than healing them, but' – here the Master paused for emphasis; he held up his bound hands, both the index fingers steepled, his eyes were bright, shining in the gloom. I could clearly see the twin thumbs on his left hand – 'it has the power to translate a human soul directly to Heaven. To kill a man with the Lance is to send him to Heaven – no matter what sins he committed on Earth. It is the weapon that pierced Our Lord Jesus Christ's side and his Father decreed that while that blade retains its power to kill, He would always show mercy to its victims.'

'I have heard these tales before,' I said. I could still feel my anger like hot weight inside my gut. I wanted him to stop talking, to be silent so that I could leave. 'Is that all you have to tell me?'

'Oh, there is much more than that, you fool. So much more.' The Master's features seemed to have come alive as he spoke about the Grail and the Lance. The years seemed to fall from him and it was as if he were filled with an energy or force.

'What do you think would happen, fool, if the male and the female principles were to be brought together?' The Master almost shouted his question. 'What would happen? The Grail and the Lance united in a simulacrum of the act of love – there is a ceremony, known only to a very few men, a simple series of acts, the right place, somewhere high and remote, the right time, a prayer or two, and what do you think could happen? Can you even conceive of it, you bumbling English simpleton?'

The Master was raving at me by this point. He did not move from his seated position, but he seemed to be humming with a strange force and, oddly, by some trick of the dim light, he appeared to be floating an inch above the floor.

'Power,' the Master bawled at me. 'More power, simpleton, than you can possibly imagine. Bring together the Lance and the Grail in the right circumstances and the result would be un-believable: an avalanche of holy fire, cataracts of flame, a storm of molten starlight – the awesome power of God Almighty Himself! The man who united the Grail and the Lance would have the strength of thousands, he could uproot forests, crush mountains in his fists . . .

The door of the store room crashed open and the guard stood there, somewhat embarrassed. 'Is everything all right, sir? Only I heard a lot of shouting and I wondered . . .'

'Everything is fine, Philip,' I said. 'Do not concern yourself – the prisoner was merely telling me about some foolish fancies of his. Close the door behind you, if you please.'

The guard retreated pulling the door shut and I rubbed my eyes and looked again at the Master, and saw that he was just a skinny bound man in a threadbare chemise sitting on the floor of his prison. The only indications of his former passion were two pink spots on each cheek and a dying gleam in his eye.

'You wanted us to come here,' I said with a sudden blaze of inspiration. 'You lured us all here from Toulouse.'

The Master nodded. 'I lured *you*, the bearer of the Lance, from *England!*'

'And Gilles de Mauchamps was seeking the Lance when he came to Westbury and burned my home to the ground?'

'It has always been about the Lance, you fool. De Mauchamps destroyed your inconsequential little farm on my orders. I knew that with your manor destroyed, you would give up the soft, dull, uxorious life you had chosen and come south to find me. And I knew that you would bring the Lance with you. To me.'

'But how did you . . .'

'I spread the word of my presence in Casteljaloux across Bordeaux. I knew that would bring you there. And when Amanieu d'Albret failed to take you, I had a man in Toulouse get word to you that I was in Foix . . .'

'Is Tronc one of your creatures?'

'Who? Viscount de Trencavel? He's just a foolish brat who flirts with heresy, he's of no importance.'

The rage was boiling again in my belly. This ridiculous stick-thin figure, puffed up with his own importance, drunk on ridiculous dreams of God-like power, who had not only killed my father and burned my home, but who had also manipulated me across half of Europe – once again it crossed my mind simply to kill him there and then, and apologize to Robin afterwards. But, with an effort, I controlled myself.

I let out a long, cleansing breath. 'What did you want to speak to me about? Tell me quickly for I do not wish to be in your foul presence any longer than necessary.'

The Master eyed me slyly.

'Do you have it near at hand?' he asked.

'What?'

'Do you have the Lance nearby?'

367

I ducked my head forward and down and tapped the T-shaped handle that was just visible between my shoulder blades.

'Ah!' The Master released a sigh of deep satisfaction. 'I knew that I could feel its presence. I knew it. Tell me, Sir Alan, what is your heart's desire? What do you wish for more than anything?'

His question took me aback and, in my surprise, I answered him absolutely truthfully: 'I want to go home to my wife.'

'No, no, no – how can you be so small-minded? You could have the world at your feet. You could have riches and titles – a dukedom, a kingdom no less, a harem of willing women, money and power beyond imagining. You and I – with the Lance and the Grail united – we could rule the whole of Christendom together.'

I thought about great wealth, and harems of women and ruling over the whole of Christendom . . . for no longer than about two fast heartbeats. Then I said, 'No, I tell you truly, I would rather go home to my wife.'

It was the truth. As God is my witness, I did not want the world at my feet. I wanted Westbury and Goody and some sons and daughters to follow me. I wanted a well-stocked wood pile that would last the whole winter through, a few pigs running in my woods, a cow or two in the pasture. I wanted good fresh bread to eat, and yellow butter and Goody's bramble preserves and a cup of decent wine from time to time. I truly did not want to be the emperor of the world. I wanted to go home.

So I turned for the door.

'Wait!' the Master called, too loudly. His bravado had melted like frost on a sunny spring morning. 'Wait, Sir Alan, I beg you.'

I turned back. 'What is it?'

'May I see it? May I see it one last time?'

I shrugged, and reached over my shoulder to pull my lance-dagger out from its sheath. Its iron blade looked dull and ordinary in the dim light. But the Master fixed his eyes upon it hungrily.

'Let me hold it! Let me hold it one last time.'

'You call me simpleton. Do you truly think I am that much of a fool?' I said, irritated now rather than enraged. 'Do you think I would just hand you a deadly weapon to use against me?'

'I swear to you, Alan, I swear on my soul, I swear on Our Lady and the Grail and by all that I hold dear, that I will not try to harm you – but I would hold the Lance in my hand one last time. The Count of Foix will execute me, for certain, perhaps in a slow and horrible way. Grant a condemned man one last harmless request. Let me hold the Holy Lance one more time before I die.'

And you may call me a fool, or a simpleton, but I did. He sounded pathetic, desperate, weak – and despite everything he had done, I felt a stir of pity for him. Perhaps the Master was using the last dregs of his odd power to command my mind – and perhaps I *am* feeble-willed. But then, perhaps, in my heart of hearts, I wanted what was to happen next to happen. In any case, I gave the lance-dagger over to the pleading wretch on the store-room floor.

I drew Fidelity, and with my sword cocked in the air above his head, as cautiously as I was able, I passed the Master the blade with my left hand. He took it in his two bound hands, lifted the old pitted iron to his lips and kissed it once. He stared deeply at the blade as if communing with its ancient legend. Then, before I could stop him, he tossed the knife over in the air, flipping it until the blade pointed towards him, and with one powerful surge of his bound hands he drove the point deep into his own chest, into his beating heart.

The Master laughed weakly as his soul slipped away, blood spilling down his chest and over his hands which were still clasped tightly on the handle of the lance-dagger, a ribbon of blood flowing between the tiny thumbs on his left hand. He managed a few whispered words to me before he died: 'You are a kindly fool, but a fool nonetheless. May God grant that I meet you in Heaven . . .'

What I did next was deeply unpleasant, and might seem a trifle odd, but I have never regretted it. The task took me less than a quarter of an hour, and by the time I pushed past the startled sentry outside the store room, and strode across the courtyard towards the keep, I was feeling decidedly light-headed. I found Nur stirring a bread poultice at the big table in the centre of the room on the second floor of the keep.

She looked up when I came barging in and she eyed the big bundle that I was holding in my right hand. The grey cloth of it was stained with gore and, as I set it on the table before her, a little red fluid oozed from the bottom.

'This is a gift for you, Nur,' I said, and then relapsed into silence as the witch began to untie the knotted linen at the top of the bundle and peel back the sticky cloth to reveal her prize. It was the Master's severed head, freshly hacked off moments after that evil creature had breathed his last.

Nur cooed over it as if it were a newborn.

'Oh Alan, you always were a kind boy,' she said happily. 'The things I can do with this! You have no idea of the power of this fresh head – its eyes, and brains, the skull itself, of course . . .'

'Don't speak to me about power,' I said. Then realizing that I had sounded harsh, I smiled tightly at her. 'And I have something else to say to you . . .' But I stopped, for I had no idea how to express what needed to be said.

'I'm sorry,' I said, and stopped again. Then, all in a rush, I said, 'I am deeply sorry about the way that I treated you after you were so cruelly hurt by my enemies in Outremer. I behaved dishonour-ably, perhaps even in a cowardly manner, and I am truly sorry. I did love you for a time, but after, but after . . .'

Then I ran dry of words.

370

Nur was looking at me intently, her brown eyes glowing almost golden above her habitual black covering. 'You found that you could not love me after this had happened,' she said it for me. Then she reached to the side of her face and untied a string, pulling the veil away from her face to reveal its awful destruction.

I stared at the ruin of her features, the nose gone, and the ears, the lips cropped to display her teeth, now mostly rotten or missing, but I found that I could look at her without flinching, or feeling horror or disgust, or even pity – this was only Nur, a young woman whom I had once loved. Our eyes met and I looked deeply into the infinite sadness of her soul – and saw my own reflection.

'How could you love me, Alan?' she said softly. 'How could you love me when I looked like this. No man could. But we shared a little happiness, for a time, you and I, and now I have a new life. The spirits guard me, and I have found myself an honoured place as their servant. Perhaps our love was never meant to be, perhaps it was the spirits who chose me and took me away from you.'

I felt a wave of relief wash through my whole body, from the top of my head to my toes, and I felt clean, renewed, whole. I smiled with deep, joyous gratitude at the young woman I had so sorely wronged.

'And Goody?' I ventured.

'I cannot lift the curse, Alan – with great regret, I cannot lift it. The curse is a law unto itself. But we have the Grail now, so, go, take it to her, let her drink from it and she will surely recover.'

'You are certain that she still lives?'

Nur reached into the neckline of her robe and pulled out the leather bag that always hung there on a thong. She cleared a space on the wooden table and emptied the contents on the surface. A cascade of tiny grey-white bones clattered on to the wood. The witch peered intently at the pattern that had been created. For a long while she said nothing. Then . . .

'She lives, Alan. Goody yet lives – but her doom is near!'

I felt my heart give a skip – a feeling of intense relief mingled with fear.

'You are certain?' I said.

Nur looked at me. 'Do you know what these bones are?' she said. 'Do you know what power of divination they possess?'

I shook my head.

'Do you remember our love aboard that ship? With the King? On the sea journey to Outremer?'

I nodded – and I knew with a horrible creeping dread exactly what she was about to say.

'We made a baby, Alan – the spirits granted us a child, which began to grow in my womb the day we made love below decks.'

I could not speak, my throat had closed itself like a fist.

'It died – when you took your love away, it died. It was born dead a few months after you left me and that accursed land. A boy. A tiny perfect boy. My grief was like a madness and before I buried the child, our son, I took his little right hand, I cut it off and held it in mine. All the while when I journeyed, over mountain and desert, suffering, starving – following you, Alan. Walking in your footsteps. For all of that terrible trek, I had the hand of our child in mine. When I did not know which way to go, I asked our child and his spirit guided me to the right path. When I was in doubt or in fear, I asked our son and he showed me the way. He still shows me the way, he still speaks to me, even now . . . and he tells me that your Goody yet lives.'

The skin on my neck was crawling at her words. My heart was an autumn gale of emotions: horror, pity, remorse, disgust . . .

'He has forgiven you, Alan,' said Nur looking intently into my face. 'Our son forgives you. All is well, and all will be well.'

I could look at her no longer, nor could I look at the pathetic scatter of childish finger bones on the table. I turned to go, but as I reached the door, I heard Nur say behind me, 'Thank you,

Alan . . .' She coughed, seeming to have something caught in her throat. 'I thank you for your gift.'

I went in search of fresh air – and Robin – and found both at the foot of the mountain, where my lord was overseeing the burial of our dead. As half a dozen mercenaries thudded into the turf with pick and shovel, I told him what had happened with the Master, how he had taken the lance-dagger and ended himself, and humbly begged my lord's pardon. He was, in fact, not particularly angry with me.

'At least you did not kill him yourself,' he said. 'My word has not been broken. But whatever possessed you to give him that old weapon, I will never understand. Are you soft in the head? Still, it saves us having to hand him over to the Count of Foix for torture and execution – and who knows, he might have been able to weasel out of that fate, somehow. No, I'm content that he's no more; good riddance to him.'

Nur's words were preying on my mind – about Goody's doom being near – and my own words to the Master were also echoing in my head – and I asked Robin when we might begin our journey home.

'All right, all right, Alan, I know you're very keen to set off – shall we say the day after tomorrow? We'll give the wounded one more day of rest, and ourselves time to pack our traps, and still have plenty of time to get back to Goody before the first day of July. Would that satisfy you?'

It would. I returned to the castle lighter of heart in the sure knowledge that we would very soon be heading home.

Chapter Twenty-four

I awoke from a deep slumber a little after midnight. Something was very wrong. I had been sleeping on the ground floor of the keep, near the door, and I disturbed nobody as I grabbed my sword belt and slung it with its heavy scabbard over my shoulder and went out into the courtyard in my chemise, my legs feeling the chill of the May night air. All was quiet as the grave. By the faint starlight and a sliver of moon, I could see a huddle of sleeping men under an awning by the kitchens, and a few over by the store rooms. I ran my eye over the crenellated line of the battlements, east, south, west, noticed nothing, stopped and looked again. In the dim light, I could just make out what looked like a small round lump on the southern part of the western wall between two perfectly square tooth-like shapes of the fortifications. For an instant, the gap between the 'teeth' was completely filled, and then it disappeared – was that a body, a person? The smaller lump seemed to still be there. Had it been merely a trick played by my midnight eyes? It crossed my mind to sound the alarm but I hesitated; fear that I had made a mistake silenced me, I think, and the certain knowledge that we had no foes around for miles – and the sight, if my eyes had not deceived me, of someone going out of the castle, and not trying to come in. All these factors meant that I did not rouse the garrison. Instead, I trotted over to the stone steps and bounded up them to the walkway below the parapet, determined to look again at this strange gap between the fortifications' teeth, that had filled and then mysteriously emptied.

I found myself looking down at a man, hanging from a knotted rope attached to one of Little John's war hooks. He was climbing slowly down the outside of the castle walls. I must have been still fuddled by sleep for it took three heartbeats before I realized that the man now looking up at me from the bottom of the rope was my old friend and comrade Sir Nicholas de Scras.

The former Hospitaller was just reaching the ground. He looked up, released the rope and put a finger to his lips and made a shushing noise. I was intrigued. Where could he be going at this time of night? He beckoned me wordlessly to come down to him and, stepping through the crenellations and with Fidelity in its scabbard slung across my shoulders, I clambered down. Sir Nicholas had moved away from the wall, down the steep slope a score or so paces on to a flattish patch of the mountainside about the size of a moderate riding cloak. As I scrambled down the rocky ground to join him, I saw with a feeling in my gut like water draining out of a gutter that he had baggage beside him, a bedroll, a bundle of weapons, a sack of food, and a cloth bag of thin material which showed the edges of a square box inside.

I stared at the cloth-wrapped box and then looked up at Sir Nicholas's face. The thin moon was high behind his right shoulder and his familiar features were hidden in deep shadow.

'You are stealing it,' I said incredulously. 'In God's name, are you seriously attempting to make away with the Holy Grail?'

Sir Nicholas spoke: 'Come with me, Alan – leave this place, leave your evil lord and come with me. You are better than this.'

I still could not quite compass what Sir Nicholas was doing.

'You are trying to take the Grail from Robin – from Robin?' I said stupidly. 'The Grail is his; we all agreed, right from the very beginning, that he should have it in his sole possession.'

'He is not worthy of it.' The words came out as a hiss. 'He is a thief and a murderer, Alan – a Godless man of corruption. We both know this, and how you can serve him, I do not understand. Come with me, Alan, I beg you – leave this villainous so-called Earl, come with me and serve the blessed Grail for the glory of God.'

I said, as calmly as I could, 'You cannot do this, Sir Nicholas. You cannot. Let us go back inside the castle, we will return the Grail to its place in the chapel and we will forget this happened.'

'He is not worthy of the Grail,' Sir Nicholas said. 'He is a dirty thief – he stole the Templars' silver. I know it. You know it.'

'You call him a thief and claim some kind of moral superiority,' I said, 'and then use this moral superiority as a reason to steal from him. Which makes you equally a thief.'

But while I was saying this, a part of me was thinking that Sir Nicholas did not sound quite himself. He sounded to me like another man altogether, and his hidden face added to this illusion.

'The Earl of Locksley does not understand the power of the Grail. He cannot even see its true holiness. Why should a man like that have it in his possession? He does not love God. He does not worship Him. He respects none of God's laws; he takes what he wishes and does whatever he likes, regardless of the teachings of the Church. He is evil and it is the duty of all good Christians to stand in his way, to impede him in all his Devilish designs. The thought of allowing him – him! – to be the keeper of the Grail, the cup of Christ itself, is an abomination. But you, Alan, you are a good Christian, you know how he is – you can be saved from his evil. Come with me; follow me and leave that wicked man. The Grail will save us both!'

A chill ran down my spine at Sir Nicholas's words. I knew that tone now: he sounded, more than anything else, like the pock-marked man whose tonsured head I had hacked off that very morning, a man who had also asked me to join him in his dreams of power. Could the Master's evil soul have somehow entered this good and true knight's living body and infected him with his own peculiar madness? Or did the Grail itself drive people to madness?

'I cannot let you take the Grail,' I said flatly.

'Stand aside, Alan, for I will have it,' Sir Nicholas said.

And suddenly we both had our swords in our hands.

Yet both had a reluctance to strike the first blow.

'Let us go back,' I pleaded. 'See – the rope still hangs there. We will return the Grail to the chapel, go to our beds and never speak of this meeting again. Nicholas, my old friend, please, I beg you, let us unmake this evil night before it is too late.'

'Stand aside, Sir Alan.' The knight spoke through gritted teeth.

'I will not.'

'Then to Hell with you!' he said. And struck.

He was dressed in mail, I in a flimsy chemise; he was angry and disgusted with Robin, and I think more than a little mad – but I was determined that he should not make away with the object of our quest, the prize that had cost the lives of Tuck and Gavin, the prize that I must have in order to save Goody's life. So I struck back.

There was not much to tell between us as swordsmen. My youth and speed were balanced against his battle experience, but I think the wound in his left side, an axe blow into his ribs from one of the Knights of Our Lady as he came over the wall, turned the tables in my favour.

His first strike, a double-handed overhand vertical blow at my head came unbelievably fast, and I was slow, but just speedy enough to sweep it away as it came down towards my skull, stumbling two steps to my right down the rocky slope and almost losing my footing altogether. My right calf muscle protested at the sudden jar, but that stumble saved me, too, for it made me duck my head to find my balance and in his next blow the steel came whistling no more than an inch above my blond locks. But then I forgot that Sir Nicholas was my friend and saw him, through a film of sweaty battle-fear, as the man who might very well end my life in the next two or three heartbeats.

I blocked his next slice with my cross-guard, and thrust Fidelity's point at his eyes, making him take a fast step back up the slope. I saw that he was feeling his wound, favouring his left side. And I used that weakness without the slightest scruple – attacking that side relentlessly, hard blow after blow aimed at his ribs, all of which he parried, but which made him wince in pain with every blocked strike. I could see that the wound had opened and blood, black in the moonlight, was blooming on his surcoat. I could also see that our battle cries and the sharp ringing of steel had roused the castle and dark heads were appearing, and red torches too, at the battlements. He saw them as well and knew that he was lost – for now there could be no silent, secret escape for him with the Grail box slung over his back. But even though he knew that he must lose – Robin's men would be out of the gates in a few moments – he still did his best to cut me down. He still tried to kill me.

But, in the finish, with his wounded side, he was no match for me, and I killed him before Robin's men came within ten paces. He stumbled on the uneven slope, went down on one knee, tired, bleeding, and was a fraction of an instant slow to block my swinging strike at his unprotected head. Fidelity smashed into his blade and such was the power of my blow that it carried on, burying itself two inches into his skull, just above the ear.

And he was dead.

God have mercy on my soul, and his – for I killed one good friend in the service of another that night. Sir Nicholas de Scras was a fine warrior and a true knight, a good man, and I will remember him as such, not as the skulking thief who, driven mad by the lure of the Grail, tried to cheat Robin and do me to death. I can feel the tears rising as I write, and remember him as the man he truly was.

I have killed men, so many men, in war and out of it – for spite, for duty, by accident, and very occasionally for the pleasure of seeing the light go out in their eyes. Their shades know me and sometimes they form up in squadrons, dress their ranks, lower their lances and charge me in my dreams. I did not wish to kill Sir Nicholas de Scras – but I did so. I killed him for Robin, for a principle, but mainly, I swear, just to prevent him from killing me.

I must lay down my quill for a little while now.

The dawn, when it came, was warm and bright and Robin decreed that we would be leaving the very next day. I was glad – the death of Sir Nicholas lay heavily on my soul, and I still grieved sorely for Tuck as well. This quest, this strange adventure, may have been successful in that we now possessed the Grail and the Master was dead and his knights killed or scattered – but the toll had been a crushingly heavy one. I wanted to be home with Goody with no more delay. Thomas and I spent the morning packing our weapons and belongings into waterproof leather sacks in preparation for the long journey – and I spent a good deal of time praying in the chapel before the Grail, which had been restored to its place there and now was flanked by two armed guards on either side of the altar.

I was on my knees, trying to ignore the bored, much-scarred and slightly odiferous mercenaries, and focus on an image in my head of my beloved wife, when I heard the sentry calling for Robin from the roof of the keep. There was an urgency in his voice, almost a note of panic, that made me straighten up, abandon my prayers and run out into the sunny courtyard.

Robin and Little John and half a dozen mercenaries were already standing on the flat roof of the keep when I reached the top of the wooden ladder that was its only method of access. And looking west, I felt the water in my bladder chill. For coming along the track around the small hill to the north-west of our refuge was an army – more than a hundred, perhaps two hundred men, mostly in black surcoats over mail, but a score or so in white cloaks, well equipped for war, riding well-trained horses.

The Templars had come to Montségur.

I looked over at Robin, who was wearing the particularly serene expression I knew so well, and which meant he was deeply troubled, and said, 'We're not leaving tomorrow, are we?'

He looked over to me and smiled warmly. 'Let's just see what they want with us before we start despairing, shall we?'

Nevertheless, I saw him a few moments later in the courtyard ordering Vim to call in all the mercenaries engaged in tasks on the mountainside, and conferring with Little John about the place-ment of men on the walls. I stayed on the roof of the keep and watched the horsemen spill on to the bald saddle of land to the west below the castle. Despite what I had said to Robin, I don't remember feeling fear or despair or any particular emotion when I saw these fresh enemies in their hundreds, dismount and begin to set up their encampment.

I was tired and melancholic after the fight with Sir Nicholas and I looked on with a dull, almost uninterested eye as the drama unfolded far beneath us. It seemed to me to be as clear as sunshine that our pathetic handful of surviving men – perhaps some twenty effectives – could be overrun by the Templars whenever they chose to do so, and I and everybody else would die on these accursed walls. And when that had happened, Goody would die alone in

England because I had failed to bring the Grail to her in time. But all I felt was a remote sadness, an empty feeling rather than a raging grief – the way you do when you discover that a far distant relative has been gathered unto God.

All the rest of that day I watched from the keep as the Templars busied themselves below. They sent men around the mountain to the north and south, set up a ring of sentries around the whole eminence and established a small detachment at the base of the eastern ridge. We were trapped – surrounded, and outnumbered at least ten to one – yet the Templars made no move to attack, nor did they send an embassy to toil up the slope under a white flag to negotiate our surrender. I was puzzled until Thomas supplied the answer for me.

'They do not wish to talk,' said my squire. 'They do not seek information from us, nor do they seek our surrender. They have come here to slay us, and I believe they will attack in the morning with all their strength. Can we hold them off the walls, do you think, Sir Alan?'

I was about to tell him the truth, that we were doomed, then changed my mind. What would Robin say in these circumstances?

'Of course we can hold them,' I said, lifting my chin, squaring my shoulders and smiling confidently into his earnest brown face. 'This castle is damn near impregnable – you'd need a train of mighty castle-breakers and thousands of men to take it, not that handful of Templar cavalry down there.'

'We took it,' said Thomas mildly.

'Yes, but we had the help of a witch. I can't see the Templars having much truck with witchcraft. Ha-ha! No, we can certainly keep them out. We just have to hold our nerve and do our duty as men-at-arms.'

With such foolish words are men consigned to their deaths. Not that we had much choice in the matter. They had made no move to parley with us and our only choice was to go down there and

381

abjectly surrender to them – which would mean an ignoble death for Robin and perhaps for all of us – or to fight.

We would fight.

We did not fight the next day. Nor the day after that. For three days, the Templars thoroughly scouted the lower slopes of the mountain, and presumably came to the same conclusions we had – that there were only two ways to assault the castle, from the west surging up to the front door, so to speak, and from the east along the spur of land that we had chosen. Those three days were torture. I tried to resign myself to death from the first moment I saw the long column of Templars riding up on to the saddle of land to the west, and to Goody's death. But I could not. For me, it was not the despair that was so agonising: it was the hope. As each new day dawned, and the Templars declined to attack, I hoped against hope that they would miraculously withdraw and leave us in peace. Or that Robin would find us a way out of the trap. I dared to hope that I would be able, somehow, to get back to England in time to give Goody a life-saving drink from the Grail.

On the second day after the Templars had besieged us, I was standing on the battlements looking out over their camp, easing my back after a bout of brutal labour and indulging in a mood of particular melancholy, when I turned to find Nur standing next to me. She was offering a cup of watered wine and a piece of honey cake. I wiped the sweat from my brow – I had been carrying dozens of huge rocks from the courtyard up to the parapet, missiles that we were planning to rain down on the enemy when he came at us – and smiled sadly at the witch.

'Fear not, Alan, you will not perish here,' she said. 'I have consulted the bones. It is not your time. You will die a very old man. I have seen it.'

I shuddered at her mention of the finger bones of our dead child.

382

I had spent some time, during several sleepless nights, wondering what manner of boy – and man – he would have been, had he lived. A mingling of Nur and myself: would he be dark or blond, tall or short? Would he be able to ride and fight like a knight? Would he have turned to sorcery and evil spirits? That little bundle, which had never truly lived, haunted me with his death. Most of all, I hated to think of his little innocent hand, severed from his body and rotting down to bare bones as it was carried across the expanses of Europe by the witch who stood before me.

'I am not concerned for my own life, Nur,' I told her. 'It is Goody that I fear for. I worry that I shall not be able to bring the Grail back to her in time to save her.'

Nur cocked her head on one side for a few moments considering, then she said, 'You do not need to take the Grail to her – all that is necessary is that she drink a liquor that has been cradled in the Grail's embrace. Why do you not fill a flask with water from the Grail – I will give you the three drops of my blood which are required – and simply go to her, leave at this very hour, with the flask? Or, if you will not leave, send someone else.'

I must admit that I was astounded. This elegant solution had never occurred to me. I hurried off the wall and down into the courtyard, shouting for Thomas and for my lord of Locksley almost in the same breath. I gathered these two men together by the kitchens and began to babble out my plan to them.

After a few moments, Robin stopped the almost unintelligible flow of my words with a hand on my arm. 'Let me see if I have this right, Alan,' he said, 'You want Thomas to slip out of the castle tonight with a quantity of Grail water, and journey all the way back to Bordeaux and then England alone and administer the water to Goody, so saving her life – is that it?'

I nodded, having spent all my words.

'Why do you not go yourself? I would give you leave, if you asked me.'

I shook my head. 'My leg is not fully healed, and a certain youthful nimbleness and speed will be required to slip past the Templar sentries on the mountainside. And I will not shirk this fight. I must stand with you, my lord, and face our enemies – and Thomas shall go in my stead.'

'Would you do this?' Robin was looking at Thomas.

'With the greatest respect, my lord, my true place is here by Sir Alan's side,' my squire replied.

'Well, yes, it would be rather dangerous,' Robin said. 'I can see why you might be frightened. You'd have to slip through the net here at Montségur and go hundreds of miles through war-torn country, then there would be a perilous sea voyage . . .'

'It is not the danger!' Thomas was looking hard at Robin. I do not think I have ever heard him interrupt anyone before, let alone our lord. 'My place is here beside Sir Alan – the test of battle is looming; I cannot desert him in his hour of need.'

'Goody is my life,' I said. 'If you wish to help me – go to her. If you can save her life, you would be rendering a far, far greater service to me than you would by dying beside me on these damned walls.'

'Why do we not all go?' said Thomas.

'We have wounded men,' said Robin, 'and even if we were all able to slip away quietly, the Templars would see we were gone, or hear us blundering around in the darkness on the slopes, and we would be hunted and hounded through the countryside of Foix and cut down in the open. Our best chance of defence is here behind these walls. But one man, one quick, silent man would have a very good chance . . .'

'If you will go, you will earn my undying gratitude,' I said.

'And mine,' said Robin. 'Go!'

Thomas slipped away that night, climbing down the almost sheer northern face of the mountain with the aid of one of Little John's war hooks and a long rope. He took with him – slung over his shoulder on a stout cord – the sturdy leather bottle that I had purchased in Toulouse, containing a pint of water from the cistern that had been stirred together with a few drops of Nur's blood in the Holy Grail. I said a prayer over the red-streaked water in the Grail and embraced Thomas, instructing him to kiss Goody from me. Then my squire departed, and I watched him climb hand over hand down the knotted rope and disappear into the scrubby brush of the mountain slope. I strained my ears for an hour or so afterwards – trying to make out the sounds of alarm or combat that would have indicated Thomas had been intercepted. But, to my enormous relief, I heard nothing.

The attack finally came on the morning after Thomas's departure. The Templars chose the front door, up the path, and it appeared to be almost leisurely, as if our enemies believed that they had already broken into our defences and it was only a matter of polishing off the survivors. But we had not been idle. Robin had ordered us to collect stones from the mountainside and to pile them in cairns every five yards around the walkway of the battlements; he had also distributed the castle's stock of javelins – we had found about four score of them in the keep – in small heaps up behind the walls. Finally, he had arranged for a great fire to be set up, but not lit, in the middle of the courtyard, on which cauldrons of water could be boiled up and then dumped on our enemies' heads.

But we were so few. Vim now commanded only a dozen unhurt mercenaries and five men who we classed as walking wounded and who, thanks to the power of the Grail, were ready to fight; another three men, too badly injured to stand upright on the walls, were bedded down in the keep. Of the nine Companions of the Grail who had set out from Bordeaux just over a month before, only five remained in the castle: Robin, Little John, Roland and myself – and Nur, of course. We had twenty-one effective men-at-arms – and one skinny Arabian witch – with which to combat some two hundred Templar knights and their sergeants.

When they came up the hill, it was on foot and at a gentle pace. It was a cool cloudy day and the snow-capped Pyrenees that had been visible for nearly a week by now were shrouded in grey. I was dreading another fog of the type that had allowed us to approach the summit of Montségur without being seen – and, indeed, perhaps that is what the Templars had also been waiting for. But it did not materialize and so they came slowly up the slope in great numbers. Robin placed one man on the eastern wall to watch over the spur, but the rest of us lined the parapet on either side of the main gate and we waited for them.

I said a prayer to St Michael, the warrior archangel, my favourite of all the saints, as I watched our enemies approach, for the fear of death was upon me once again. I asked him to come to our aid with his fiery sword and sweep our enemies from the mountainside. I consoled myself with the thought that Thomas must have got away safely. But at the back of my mind was the suspicion that this was all a cruel joke: a feeling that God had arranged for Goody to live and for me to die. So be it. When I had last seen my beloved, I had asked God to spare her and take me in her stead – it was time, clearly, to pay that price.

There were, I suppose, about a hundred men who came against us that morning: mostly tough, well-armed Templar sergeants with black surcoats over their mail, but with about a dozen or so knights among them, too. As they swarmed up that lung-crushing slope, I saw at the back of the first wave of men, perhaps two hundred yards away, a knight with a full helmet obscuring his face, urging on the sergeants to climb more swiftly. I noticed him because he had only one hand, his sword hand. On the other side his mail sleeve flapped emptily and he carried no shield. I had no doubt that it was Gilles de Mauchamps – the man who had burned Westbury and slaughtered my friends and servants. The first flush of anger warmed my blood.

At fifty yards, our two mercenary crossbowmen loosed their quarrels at the scrambling men, and Robin, who had a position on the parapet directly above the main gate, took the first of their lives with his war bow. He had admitted to me that he had only a handful of arrows left and so he would be husbanding his shafts carefully, but we were well stocked with quarrels. Unfortunately, so were they – at least forty of the sergeants coming on towards us seemed to be armed with big, wicked-looking T-shaped bows and, once within range, we on the battlements found ourselves ducking behind the crenellations as their bolts whistled over our heads and cracked and sparked against the battlements.

They had ladder-men too, a dozen of them, and I heard them roaring as they surged towards the gate and hurled themselves at the base of our walls. I stood straight then, ignoring the crossbow peril, with a javelin in each hand and a killing rage in my heart, and hurled the light spears down into the boiling mass of red-faced infantry below, skewering one man through the neck and missing completely with my second missile. I roared defiance at them, then I bent again and seized a jagged rock the size of a firkin of ale, hefted it over the battlements and hurled it on to the seething crowd of enemies below. On either side of me mercenaries and Companions were doing the same, bending, lifting and hurling, over and over again. The devastation we wreaked was appalling – men were crushed like weeds under a ploughman's boot, limbs snapped, heads pulped. I saw Robin out of the corner of my eye, carefully choose a victim, draw and loose his bow, and smile with quiet satisfaction. But there were too many of them – a raging sea of humanity surged below our walls, a huge jostling, screaming herd of blood-crazed mankind – and while we crushed them with rock after rock, and pierced them with bolt and arrow and javelin, the ladders were swinging upwards. Five, six, seven ladders, swinging up and banging against the stonework, and I heard the thunking sound of sharp steel on wood and, as I leaned out to thrust a javelin down into a yelling face twenty feet below, I saw that they had two men with long woodsmen's axes chopping methodically into the main gate, while a quartet of knights warded our missiles off with big shields held defensively over their heads.

It could only be a matter of moments before we were overwhelmed.

There were scores of men on the ladders now, brave men, bounding up the frail, bouncing wood. I grasped a rock the size of my head, ran to the nearest ladder and hurled the stone down into the body mass of a rapidly climbing knight. It crashed into his chest with an awful muted thud and swept him and the two fellows behind him down to the rocky floor below. I shoved the ladder away and it fell atop their broken bodies. But there were too many ladders, too many men surging up the walls, and the splintering crunches below of the axes on the door was relentless. Philip, the veteran mercenary who stood to my left, died then with a quarrel in his eye, and I saw that beyond him an enemy, a Templar knight, was in the very act of climbing over the parapet. I sprinted towards him, leaping over Philip's body. I reached the Templar just in time, Fidelity's naked blade in my right hand, and took his head off with one pounding chop, then booted his slack torso back over the wall, but another man-at-arms popped up in his place and he managed to deflect my next sword thrust with his own blade, and thrust me back with his shield, then he was over the wall and we were chest to chest, snarling in each other's faces, butting and biting. I hurled him backwards and just managed to find the room to swing my sword and lop his right arm at the elbow; and he reeled away screaming, spurting, dying. But the walls had been breached in several places by now. I pulled out my mace from its place tucked into my belt at the small of my back and ran back north to batter and slice into a man with two feet on the walkway in the place I had been defending a dozen heartbeats before. He died with Fidelity in his guts but, when I had ripped out my blade and chanced to look behind me, south again, another two Templar sergeants had appeared from nowhere and were tumbling over the battlements in a panicked tangled of swords, scabbards and shields. I felt all the blood in my body change in some subtle way, becoming lighter and seemingly as corrosive as acid, and I charged them, screaming, 'Westbury!' fit to burst my lungs, with my long sword swinging, my immortal soul soaring up to Heaven, my eyes misting red.

Chapter Twenty-five

We held that wall by the skin of our balls for what seemed like several hours but which, in reality, must have been less than a quarter of an hour. We struggled and killed, chopped and sliced, bit and swore, bled and died. We hurled back men and ladders; and crushed bone and skull by plummeting lethal rocks down upon the heads of those yet trying to scale the walls; we poured pots of boiling water on the men below and jeered at their scalded screams – at one point Little John, frothing white at the mouth like a moon-crazed idiot, cleared half a dozen enemies who had made it to the parapet in one unstoppable, howling charge, his great axe swinging around his head like a solid, circular sheet of steel. I was battling a Templar knight, a raging lion of a fighter, and had finally managed to drop him with a smashed jaw – feint from Fidelity and a sideways flick of my mace – when I heard Robin's battle-voice shouting my name above the clamour of a dozen death cries, the awful shrieks of wounded men and the clatter of iron on stone, steel on wood.

'Alan, Roland – the courtyard. Get down there both of you. The gate is falling. They're breaking through. Get down now.'

The pressure from the ladder-men on the wall seemed to have eased, and the parapet was a mass of stirring bodies, wounded and dead, ours and theirs, and I sprinted over the bloody backs of friend and foe for the stone steps that led down, with Roland at my shoulder.

When I hit the flat, sanded courtyard, I could see daylight through the wood of the door and with every further blow, its giant frame shuddered and sagged a little more. As I skidded to a halt just before it, the door split open and two big men wielding axes burst through, shedding long splinters of wood, followed by a Templar sergeant and a shieldless knight in a white surcoat with a sword in his only hand.

It was Gilles de Mauchamps.

He saw me, recognized me and ran at me snarling. Our blades arced out and clashed together once, and I counter-swung the mace at his head – and he pulled back just in time. There were more Templars bursting through, men-at-arms and knights, and my enemy was jostled away by the men coming in behind him. I killed a man-at-arms, and another. Roland was fighting like a Trojan beside me. I heard a roar from above and Little John jumped from the battlements to land with a thud in the sand. Then he was up, his great axe swinging. I ducked under a massive sword cut from a Templar knight, bobbed up and crushed his shoulder joint with a wind-milling mace blow. Roland had boldly engaged two men at once but was now struggling to fend them both off – I saw him take a blow to the head and stumble – and yet more Templars were crowding through, menacing shapes filling the bright light of the entrance.

In that moment, with the main gate breached and a dozen Templars inside our walls, we were beaten; the castle was theirs, we were all as good as dead.

Yet as I hacked Fidelity deep into the waist of a ferret-faced man-at-arms and ripped out his innards, I was dimly aware of a hideous noise coming from my right – a foul sound somewhere between a shriek and a drone – and into the mêlée in the courtyard charged a small, slight figure that looked as if it had been conjured from a wine-parched feverish nightmare. A pale emaciated body, naked but for a tattered black loincloth, rushed furiously out from the keep. Her body had been whitened with chalk and then painted with coal-black and blood in weird fantastical shapes and patterns. A pair of dry, empty, bone-white breasts, stippled with tiny black circles flapped on her skinny chest. The shortish grey hair had been stiffened with blood until it stood out straight from the scalp in a dark, spiky ball like an enormous gory hedgehog. But the terrible face under that macabre, prickled helmet was worse: a noseless, lipless, earless monstrosity, painted a ghoulish white and black to resemble a leering skull, the eyes burning with manic rage like those of a foul fiend from the uttermost depths of Hell.

In her left hand, this creature carried a foreshortened spear with a grisly burden mounted on the sharp tip: a severed human head, similarly adorned with white chalk and bloody designs etched with a knife into the dead skin, the tonsured hair similarly spiked with dried blood, the mouth wedged open with a pair of short sticks and the tongue, painted deathly white, lolling freely as the head jiggled in the running witch's hand. In her right hand was a small but wicked-looking hatchet.

Nur howled and keened appallingly as she hurtled towards the knot of struggling men in the centre of the courtyard – and I swear, she caused every man in the battle, even those who knew her well, to pause for just an instant and stare at her shockingly hideous appearance. And in that tiny pause, Robin struck. I saw him standing on the parapet directly above the main gate, draw back his bow and aim almost vertically down into the courtyard. He loosed three shafts in as many heartbeats, one, two, three, plucking the arrows from the bag at his waist, nocking them, and shooting almost faster than the eye could see. Three times he loosed his shafts, and three enemies were transfixed. The first to fall was Gilles de Mauchamps – the one-armed knight crunched down to his knees, half a bow shaft protruding up from the hollow beside his collar bone. The next was a sergeant, who took an arrow straight down through his mail coif and into his brain, and the last was the axeman, a few paces into the courtyard, standing over the body of my cousin Roland, his weapon raised. Robin pierced his broad back with his final arrow, but it was Nur, screaming her weird war chant, who sent his soul to Hell.

The witch leaped at him with hatchet in one hand and the Master's head on a stick in the other and savaged him with both, butting his face with the bizarre severed-head-mace and hacking at his knees with the hatchet. When he was down, she finished him with a couple of scything hatchet blows to the back of the skull – then she drove on, into the astonished group of enemy men-at-arms standing flat-footed by the splintered gate, screaming at them and lunging madly with her awful weapons. Little John and I renewed our onslaught against the remaining Templars with a fresh wave of fury. We drove them towards the gate, killing, screaming, shoving them backwards with our steel. I found myself beside Nur by this point; we were shoulder to shoulder, cutting, slicing, lunging and – praise God – somehow corralling the pack of them, forcing them back, back to the shattered main gate.

Then Little John was beside me, too, with a plank of wood from our dinner table in his hands, slamming the end mercilessly into the faces crowding in the entrance and, by main force, pushing the crowded enemy out with a foot-wide, six-foot length of roughly cut timber.

Faced by the three of us – a blood-covered maniac swinging sword and mace, a giant wielding a long lump of wood and a naked battle-crazed fiend from Hell – our enemies wilted. They paused, they hesitated, they froze in their terror when they should have surged forward. One man-at-arms, blinded on the threshold, his face a mask of gore, was shrieking, 'The Devil, the Devil, the Devil is against us!' I killed him with a thrust to the throat from Fidelity – but I heard the cry taken up by more of the men outside. 'The Devil is with them! The fiend is loose! God preserve us!'

Miraculously, as we three shoved and struggled and hacked at them, the pressure began to slacken. And they finally began to pull back from the doorway and out of sight.

When John had secured the door with another plank wedged into the frame and a stout locking bar dropped into its brackets, I limped up the stone stairs and looked out over the departing enemy, running down the hill in the manner of a flock of sheep panicked by a wolf. I could still hear faint cries of 'Beware the Devil! The Devil is loose!' from the running men.

The Templars were in full retreat – I could hardly believe it. More than a hundred trained men had come against us that morning – and now more than a third of them lay crushed and broken outside and inside our walls. They had been frightened away from our broken gates by a skinny, naked, body-painted witch-woman who was not quite right in the head.

Gilles de Mauchamps was still on his knees, a yard or two inside the courtyard. Five or six of his dead comrades lay about him but he still breathed, and he was tugging ineffectually at the arrow that jutted beside his neck, as the blood bubbled and spilled on to the white surcoat that sagged over his chest and belly. Beyond him, I saw Roland still lying on the floor, blood running down his temple, and Nur on her haunches beside my cousin, covered in battle-filth and dust, and seemingly trying to wake him. She leaned back and silently reached her skeletal white arms up to the sky as if imploring God or the spirits to come to her aid, and I saw that a black stick seemed to have sprouted from her emaciated, paint-spotted left breast – and then I realized with a cold, drenching shock that it was the latter half of a crossbow quarrel, I could even make out the leather fletchings. I was amazed that someone with such a frail-looking body had lasted as long as she had, for she must have taken her wound when we were pushing the enemy out of the gate. But even Nur's powerful life force could not endure a pierced heart and she slumped down then and there, as I came down the stone steps towards her, falling gently sideways on to the courtyard floor, stretching out her bony white arm to touch Roland's unconscious blond head.

By the time I reached him, Gilles de Mauchamps had managed to undo the straps on his helmet one-handed and wrestle it from his head. He was clearly unable to rise and he remained on his knees like a penitent, swaying left and right. Blood covered the whole of his front, and was running freely from the corners of his slack mouth. He looked at me as I approached, his dark eyes questioning, seeming to ask the eternal query of the dying man – why me? – and he mumbled something that was too muffled by his own clotted gore to be comprehensible.

I looked at him there, on his knees, dying. I paused for a heartbeat and stared into his face. Fidelity twitched in my hand, the blade seeming to have a soul of its own. I wanted to tell him that this death was the price of his cruel deeds at Westbury. That this was God's judgment. I thought about cutting his head from his shoulders, or spitting in his face, or taunting him with some clever remark. But, to be honest, I was just too tired. Instead, I looked into his eyes for a few moments, while he struggled to speak and the blood bubbled from his lips, then I shrugged and moved on.

Nur was dead when I reached her but my cousin yet lived. Her white hand had found its way to his cheek, and in death the slight grubby fingers of the witch seemed to caress the shiny burn scar that marked the side of his face. Roland had a fresh wound to his sword arm, a gash that had ripped through his mail, probably a spear thrust, and a deep sword cut over his left ear, which I assumed came from the blow that had felled him. But he was breathing steadily and, God willing, I was fairly sure that he would live.

The enemy did not come again that day. We stacked our dead by the walls, folded their arms and closed their eyes, and we hurled the enemy corpses – including that of Gilles de Mauchamps – over the steep cliff on the north-eastern side of the castle. We tended to our wounded, which was almost all of us – I had acquired a shallow sword cut across the back of my neck below the line of my helmet, which was irritatingly painful whenever I moved my head, and a deep cut in my right thigh, just above the knee – and all managed to have a drink from the Grail, which Robin said would not only heal our wounds but also put heart into us for the final battle.

Roland remained unconscious – breathing shallowly but regularly, his wounds bathed in Grail water and bound up. He looked peaceful and, in my exhausted state, I had to struggle hard not to envy his seemingly delightful sleep.

We ate a little, prayed, mourned the dead, set the sentries on the walls and all managed to take some measure of rest that night – I fell into a deep but disturbed slumber an hour or two after dusk in which I dreamed that I was trapped at the bottom of a deep well, while Nur and Goody looked down on me from above and mocked my impotent efforts to climb the slimy stone sides and escape my doom. I was awoken by Vim not long after midnight who told me gruffly that it was my turn to stand sentry duty and that all was quiet on the mountain – but when I tried to rise from my blankets, my whole body felt as if it had been beaten with cudgels for days or weeks on end.

It was chilly on the ramparts, and what was worse was the knowledge that we could never manage to repulse another assault as ferocious as the one the day before. Only five mercenaries yet lived, including Vim – and with myself, Robin and Little John – who was a mass of minor cuts, bruises and punctures – we had only eight fighting men with which to repel any attack. I prayed that my death would be swift, when it came. And I wondered how Thomas was faring – had he managed to elude the Templars and make his way north? In a weak moment, just before the dawn, I even briefly considered taking my own life with the lance-dagger, as the Master had done, to ensure my everlasting reward in paradise. But I soon began to scold myself for such weakness – thank the Lord – and at the first pinky-grey light of dawn I felt entirely different about the matter of my life and death, and went over to the keep to wake Robin and report on an uneventful night.

The Templar embassy came a little before noon. A lone knight walking up the path that lead to the main gate, unarmed except for a sword at his waist and carrying a beautiful, snowy white flag on a long ash pole over his shoulder. As he drew nearer, I saw that it was the handsome, red-haired knight I had seen that day with Gilles de Mauchamps at the Maison des Consuls in Toulouse.

'God save you all,' he sang out, as he came close to the walls, stopping about ten yards away and smiling cheerfully up at the ramparts – which had every defender who could drag himself upright lined up on them on Robin's hurried orders.

'What can we do for you, sir?' The Earl of Locksley's tone was perfectly polite, and I marvelled at his composure. He had taken a blow to the ankle the day before and while the joint was not broken it was swollen to twice its normal size and I knew that Robin, just by standing upright, was being battered by waves of pain.

'Well, without wishing to disparage your magnificent defence yesterday – it was most impressive, my congratulations – I have come to discuss your surrender.'

'What makes you think, sir, that we are ready to surrender?' Robin's words once again were mild as buttermilk, polite, utterly courteous.

'My dear fellow – how many men have you left under arms? Twenty? Thirty, perhaps? I have more than a hundred men-at-arms down there and thirty knights. And I have just sent off a rider to Toulouse to fetch another hundred. With the greatest respect for your valour, you cannot keep us out for ever. I thought we might come to some accommodation to save unnecessary bloodshed.'

'I have no problem with shedding your blood, none at all,' said Robin, but he was smiling down at this charming Templar.

'Quite, quite – but, you see, I'm afraid I rather do. I am Guy d'Épernay, by the way. The Seigneur de Mauchamps, our gallant captain, has tragically fallen, and that means that as Preceptor of the Templars of Toulouse, I am now the leader of our forces. I think you will find me far more open to reasonable discussion than poor old Gilles, may he rest with God. And I think I might be able to persuade my Order to overlook certain, erm, financial transgressions on your part in exchange for a certain rather special something, a unique holy relic, shall we say, that you currently have in your possession. Do you understand me?'

'I think, sir, that you'd better come inside,' Robin said.

The gate had been barricaded with fresh wood and nailed shut at this point and so the Templar knight had to be hoisted up on a rope to the ramparts above the main gate. He passed along the line of wounded men with many a nod and a smile – and although he may have been surprised at how few we were and how knocked about our shrunken company was, he gave no sign of it and followed Robin amiably into the keep, where, once I had brought them a flagon of wine and two goblets, they remained alone for more than an hour.

When they emerged, there was not a single man in Montségur who did not scan their faces for hopeful news. And the news was plain to see. Robin wore his usual serene expression, but with a little smile tugging at the corner of his lips; Guy d'Épernay looked openly delighted. Suddenly every bloody, bandaged, exhausted face in the castle was beaming. The Templar was courteously lowered back down the outside of the wall, after many a friendly slap on the back as he passed along the parapet, and the hard-bitten mercenaries actually waved to him and called out good wishes as he clambered down the mountain to the Templar camp.

'Saved at the last minute, Alan – plucked out of the slavering jaws of Death!' Robin was allowing himself to be openly jubilant.

'Do you think we can trust him?' I asked, for the sake of saying something. I knew we had no choice in this matter.

'I believe so, God, I really hope so – it turns out that I know some of his people in Épernay; and his father was a great tournament rival with my father back in King Henry's day. He's a friend of the Viscount de Trencavel, as well. He seems to be a decent fellow; a man of his word, I'd say. He was also in a rare sweat to acquire the Grail for the Templars. He kept on asking me about it, all the way through our negotiations – he's never seen it himself, of course, but he had heard all the extravagant tales. I think he would agree to almost anything to get his hands on it.'

'So we must give it up?' I asked.

'It's the Grail or all our lives,' Robin said. 'We can march out of here, heads held high, with all our weapons and our wounded – we can even take the Master's silver hoard with us. We will have enough to rebuild Westbury, if that is what is troubling you. But the truth is that we have no choice. Do you want to stay here and die for the Grail, when we can go free? Do you want all of them to die for it?' He waved a hand across the courtyard at the mercenaries who were already happily engaged in tearing down the planks from the patched main gate.

There was no need to reply to my lord's question.

Robin personally handed over the Grail to Guy d'Épernay in a brief ceremony the next day that followed the burial of our dead at the foot of the mountain. One of our erstwhile enemy priests obliged by saying the prayers over the mass grave and then we all gathered in the Templar camp in the saddle below Montségur, with our wounded and our horses and our baggage, and my lord presented the square wooden box to a visibly ecstatic Guy d'Épernay.

Guy opened the box slowly, reverently, and I caught a bright flash of gold, before he looked away, as if the very sight of the Grail were searing his eyes, and gently closed the lid. Laying the box down on a portable altar, he fell to his knees, followed in this example by all of his men, who were gathered eagerly around him. He lifted his face to the Heavens and began to utter a loud and lengthy prayer to God Almighty, thanking Him for delivering this blessed vessel into his unworthy care. When he had finished, he led his fellow Templars in a psalm, the singing pure, high and deeply wonderful in that lonely place, the music seeming to bounce off the peaks of the far Pyrenees. But while the Poor Fellow Knights of Christ and the Temple of Solomon raised their solemn voices to God and praised his holy name – Robin and the handful of survivors of the bloody struggle for Montségur climbed stiffly, painfully into their saddles and slipped away, pointing their horses' heads north towards Toulouse.

When we had travelled a couple of miles down the road and were well out of sight of the saddle of land, the singing having died away behind us, I dug my heels into my horse's ribs and rode up to the head of the column until I was trotting along knee to knee with my lord.

'I saw it,' I said.

'I beg your pardon, Sir Alan,' said Robin. 'You saw what?'

'I saw the Grail.'

'Well, congratulations, my lad. What a blessed day for you!'

'Where is the real one?'

'The real one? Whatever can you mean? The one and only Holy Grail – the cup of Christ, a transcendently beautiful, finely wrought vessel of solid gold, intricately carved and encrusted with priceless jewels – now rests with the noble Order of the Knights Templar. I have just given it to them in fair exchange for our lives. And don't you *ever* say, or even dare to think, otherwise.'

'So you still have the real one?'

Robin did not answer for a few moments, then he said, 'Have you ever thought about how many people that we know have died for that damned bowl? Your father, Hanno, Sir Nicholas, the Master, Tuck, Gavin – even poor Nur. And many, many more have perished in its name – think of all the Master's victims, for a start. All those men and women are dead because of a piece of ancient wood that some people are convinced, for some reason, once held a few drops of Christ's blood. Oh, and it was also used as a wine container at a rather dull farewell party that your precious Lord and Saviour once threw in Jerusalem.'

It was my turn to be silent – I hated this irreverent, blatantly blasphemous side of Robin, but I could not deny that a vast lake of blood had been spilled in the name of the Holy Grail.

Robin continued: 'I went to see the Master in that little store room, when he was our prisoner, did you know that?'

I shook my head.

'I had something that I wanted to ask him urgently before I handed him over to the Count of Foix. Can you guess what I wanted to know?'

'Did you want to know if the Grail was genuine?'

'No – nobody can say that for sure after all these years. You either believe it is genuine or you don't. You either have faith in the Grail and its power or you don't. I went to see the Master because I could not understand why I had been unable to find the Grail after we took Château Chalus-Chabrol and I wanted him to explain it to me. Do you remember?'

I did. It was around the time that King Richard had died. We had captured the Master and searched the tiny Castle of Chalus-Chabrol high and low and found not a trace of the Grail. Then the Master had escaped, and somehow he had regained possession of the sacred vessel a few months later.

'Did he tell you what he did with the Grail?'

'He did,' said Robin. 'He told me that, when it became clear that the castle would fall, he threw it over the walls and into the midden.'

I was shocked. The idea of the Master, who so venerated the Grail, tossing it into the stinking mound of garbage, vegetable peelings, animal bones, broken crockery and human waste that polluted one area outside every large habitation, filled me with a deep disgust. And I had drunk from this Grail – twice!

Robin could see my face and, as he often did, he seemed to be reading my mind – he laughed.

'Don't worry, Alan, I am sure that after he retrieved it, he gave it a thorough wash. But my point is this: we did not find it because the Holy Grail was hidden in a mound of refuse. I even had some of our men poke about in the midden, if I remember correctly, but they didn't find the Grail because they didn't know that they were actually looking for a cracked old wooden bowl, the kind of item that might well be thrown away by a house-proud goodwife and find its way into the midden.'

'A clever hiding place,' I muttered. Somehow I could faintly taste something stinking and rotten on my tongue.

'No – you don't understand, Alan. The Grail was not out of place in the filth and rubbish of the midden because, from one perspective, it is just that – rubbish – a dirty, cracked old bowl. The thing that makes it a wondrous relic, an object that can cure wounds and hold back Death, is belief. If you have faith in the Grail, a cracked old bowl becomes a priceless treasure.'

'So do you still have it? I know that the thing you gave the Templars was the golden cup we stole from Welbeck.'

Robin said nothing for a while, and I did not press him. We had many miles to travel that day.

Finally he said, 'You must keep all of this under your hat, agreed? Seriously, Alan, no loose tongues on this matter? The Templars have Malloch's golden cup, yes, but they will believe it is the real Grail unless somebody tells them otherwise. It looks exactly as people imagine the Grail to be. And when I saw an opportunity to deceive them, I could not resist . . .

'But I do not have the real Grail – if it is indeed that – either. After I had spoken to the Master, I began to think about that old bowl and the many pointless deaths it has caused. It may be nothing more than a piece of rubbish, but I think it is an unlucky piece of rubbish. I think that, through their honestly held beliefs a good many people would be prepared to kill for that ancient piece of rubbish – and they might certainly seek to kill the person who possessed it, in order to take it from them. I decided that I did not want to burden myself, or my family, with that perpetual risk. So, to answer your question, no, I do not have the real Grail.'

I held my breath, and counted to five in my head.

'What did you do with it?' I asked.

'I gave it to someone who now has no fear of death. I kept my word to my old friend Tuck, the promise that I made on his deathbed. Right now, the Grail is clutched in his cold dead hands in that hidden cave under the mountain. I hope it will remain there, out of the world, in his safekeeping, until the end of time.'

Chapter Twenty-six

We travelled slowly because of our wounded and were delayed in Bordeaux for a week before we could find a ship willing to take us to England, but I was not unduly dismayed that we did not set sail until the first of June because I had heard from friends of Robin at the docks that a young Welsh man-at-arms by the name of Thomas had boarded a ship to England on the eighteenth day of May.

My squire had apparently made it thus far unscathed and, God willing, he should be with Goody almost two weeks before I arrived there myself, perhaps by the middle of June. We parted company with Vim and his surviving mercenaries at Bordeaux. Some of the more seriously wounded were lodged in the Abbey of St Andrew under the care of the monks, but the rest of the men – five hard-bitten fighters – found themselves to be pleasantly wealthy by their standards and no longer required by Robin.

Although they had lost so many of their number in battle, the proportion of the silver hoard of Montségur that each man received was correspondingly greater, and so they parted with the Earl of Locksley amicably, with jingling pouches and many a jest. A couple of the men were planning to return to their homes in Brabant province and buy small holdings and take up the placid life on the land; others – disappointed by the news that King John of England and King Philip of France had recently signed a treaty at Le Goulet in Normandy and were now formally at peace – seemed determined to spend every penny on drink and women in the less salubrious parts of Bordeaux. Vim, who had naturally appropriated a larger share than his men, was planning to put a goodly amount of his silver into the wine trade with England – he had dreams of hanging up his sword and becoming a rich merchant.

I know that Robin had hoped to see his countess Marie-Anne and his two sons in Bordeaux, but as part of Eleanor's *ménage* they were obliged to follow the old Queen and were now in Chinon, in the county of Anjou. So he sent messages to them by courier, told them of his plans to return to Westbury with me, and we embarked for England on a small ship called *The Holy Trinity*.

The sea voyage was a melancholy one, long and dull, and the four of us – Robin, Little John, Roland and I – were constantly reminded of our comrades who had died in this fruitless quest: Tuck's happy red face haunted me, as did Sir Nicholas's stern mien. Little John still grieved deeply for Gavin. I even found myself thinking not unkindly of Nur when the *Trinity* found itself becalmed and enveloped in a thick fog off the Norman coast. The notion of our dead son and his tiny severed hand was often in my thoughts as well. And I prayed every morning and night that Thomas had met with no mishap on the journey home and that Goody had been cured by the power of the Grail.

I had plenty of time at sea to think about Robin's disposal of the Grail. Although I did yearn to see it once more, and to drink its cool healing waters again, I could see the reasoning behind his actions, and while they seemed to make the quest into a bloody and painful waste of time, I found to my surprise that I agreed with what he had done. If he possessed the Grail, word would get out

405

sooner or later, and he and his family would be in constant mortal danger. If the Templars discovered his trick, their wrath would know no bounds, and possession of the true Grail is not something that could be kept a secret indefinitely.

There was also something else that I had discovered about the Grail that I did not esteem. It seemed to make men act against their true nature; indeed, it seemed to have the power to turn them into madmen. I thought about Sir Nicholas still trying to kill me even when he had no further hope of escape. I thought about the Master – a good man, once, but turned towards evil. No, I decided, it was better that Tuck's spirit should guard it through the ages. I had drunk from it – twice. The vessel that had contained Christ's sacred blood had nourished me and touched my soul. And that is a share of holiness that is given to few mortals.

It did my heart good to see Westbury – not only for the familiar joy of a homecoming as we galloped up the Great Northern Road on hired nags in the last days of June – but because it was un-familiar. The place was the same yet different. I had last seen it as a blackened ruin, but in the months I had been away my steward Baldwin had rebuilt the manor from the ground up – and added a few improvements. The wooden palisade that marked the perim-eter of the courtyard had been extended by perhaps a third. The hall was bigger and shaped like the letter L, the guest hall had been enlarged, there were half a dozen more outbuildings than I remembered and the whole compound smelled cheerfully of cut wood.

But my greatest joy was not the construction of a finer residence, but the sight when we came trotting through the wide-open gates of Westbury of a slim figure with bright blonde hair clad in a dark-blue dress sitting on a stool by the door of the new hall. And in her arms was a little bundle of white cloth with a tiny pink face poking out from the folds.

Is there any greater joy for a man than the sight of his first-born son? I can honestly tell you that there is – it is the sight of his beloved wife, well and strong and fully returned to health, and holding that baby son in her arms outside the door of his newly made hall, waiting to greet him with a loving kiss.

I was too overcome to speak as I took my family in my embrace, squeezing Goody and my month-old son Robert in my arms as if I would hold them for ever and praising God with all my heart for preserving them for me.

I heard the full story of Goody's recovery from Thomas who was waiting to greet me with a basin of hot water and a towel with which to wash away the dust of the road. I was scrubbing my damp face with the towel and babbling my thanks to him for reaching my beloved in time with the Grail water when he stopped me with a gentle outstretched hand.

'It was not my doing, Sir Alan,' said this honest fellow. 'She was in blooming health when I returned two weeks ago, and had been safely delivered of Robert, too. I did nothing – indeed I still have the Grail water in its leather bottle, untouched.'

I was astounded. It took Goody a long while to explain to me what had occurred. In short it was not the Grail that had cured her, but the wise-woman Brigid's care. After Robin and I had left England, Goody had remained in her pitiful state of sickness for some weeks, but Brigid had used her wisdom and all of her powers of healing to bring my beloved back to the land of the living – and she had even managed to keep the baby alive in her womb as well, and that, it seemed, had been Goody's chief preoccupation while she was suffering from her illness.

'I am not sure that it really was a curse,' Goody told me the next day. 'Brigid believed that the malaise was magical but she claims that every misfortune is caused by unearthly powers – rain at harvest time, an old grandfather who dies suddenly in his sleep, a chicken that won't lay, everything. It could just as well have been a sickness of some kind. I'm not sure that I wholly believe in curses, it often seems like a lot of silly nonsense to me.'

I had forgotten how refreshingly forthright my lovely wife could be.

Just then little Robert began to cry and Goody – although like most gentlewomen in her position, she had hired a wet nurse – rushed over to his cot to see that he was being cared for. I wandered over to the guest house to speak to Robin and Little John, who had taken up residence there with Roland.

Robin spoke vaguely about moving back to the caves in Sherwood, but I could see that he was quite comfortable in the guest hall at Westbury and I did not really mind if he made the place his permanent home. Likewise Roland had made some noises about returning to Paris and his father's house, but he did not seem in any hurry to leave Westbury either. I think the truth was that none of us wanted the quest to end – it had been an extraordinary journey, and we had seen wonders and miracles and performed feats of valour and, despite the pain of so many lost comrades, deep down not one of us wished the camaraderie of the adventure to end. Besides, we had a solemn ceremony to perform the next day and I wanted as many of the Companions of the Grail to be there as possible.

The next day, I took Thomas to the Westbury bath house before dawn for a thorough cleansing in hot and cold water, and then, with my squire dressed in a simple white shift with a good quality dark-green cloak over the top, he and I and Robin and Roland – along with Goody and Baldwin and the entire household – trooped down to the little stone church in the village of Westbury and participated in a Mass for the souls of our dead friends conducted by Father Arnold, the village priest. When the service was over, in the presence of the whole community of village and manor, Thomas shrugged off the cloak and knelt humbly before the Earl of Locksley.

Robin drew his sword and lightly tapped Thomas on the

shoulders with it and, with a straight face, he invoked God Almighty and St George, and bade him take on the onerous duties of a knight.

'I dub thee Sir Thomas Blood,' my lord of Locksley said, before lifting my erstwhile squire to his feet, embracing him and presenting him with a pair of fine silver spurs. While Robin was taking Sir Thomas's homage – for from that moment onward he would be Robin's man and no longer mine – I leaned over to Roland and asked him quietly about the change of name.

'Oh, Sir Thomas feels that Blood is a less confusing surname for a knight serving an English lord than "ap Lloyd". You know that he has no family in Wales left and he has not set foot there since he was a lad, so he let it be known to Robin that he would be Sir Thomas Blood henceforth – and it is a good warlike name for a knight, I would say.'

We feasted Sir Thomas in the courtyard at Westbury on a fine July afternoon, and many of us made him gifts suitable for his new rank. Robin gave him a fine sword, and Roland a new hauberk of iron links, and Little John presented him with a beautifully painted shield. While we were enjoying nuts and sweetmeats with the last of the wine, seated at a three-sided square of trestle tables, one of the grooms, a nervous fellow who had been hired while I was in the southern lands, led out my special gift to Sir Thomas.

It was Shaitan, my destrier, glossy, mettlesome and black as pitch, but well mended from the cut on his back and as big and strong as a plough ox. I was a little sad to part with the warhorse for we had been together for some years now and I had fought many times from his broad back, but I wanted to make the lad a magnificent gift on the occasion of his knighting that matched the gratitude I felt towards him for his many years of loyal service.

The groom held Shaitan's head while I began a long speech about Thomas's virtues – I had spent the previous day preparing it and I felt I owed the young man a proper recitation of his courage and steadfastness as my squire. While I spoke, Goody, her maid Ada and the servants cleared the tables and brought out more dainties to be enjoyed. The day was uncomfortably hot and we had all consumed a good deal of wine, as well as having partaken of a hearty meal, and while I talked on I noticed some of my guests nodding in the strong sunshine, their eyes closing momentarily. I had got no further than listing Thomas's valorous service with me in Normandy against King Philip's men, when I noticed this somnolence and I remember clearly thinking to myself that I really must bring my speech to a speedy close as I had even sent poor Shaitan off to sleep, for I saw that his dark, liquid eyes were closed and his long black head was drooping.

At that moment Goody came out of the hall carrying a large tray filled with a dozen flagons of watered ale and a tower of stacked earthenware cups, for some of the guests had been complaining of thirst, asking for something with less body than our good red wine. She was walking towards the feasting tables, and was halfway across the courtyard when she tripped on her long skirts and sent the tray and the flagons and the cups crashing to earth with a deafening clatter. It was a simple accident, something that might happen any day, to any one – but I have relived that moment in my mind a thousand times since then.

Shaitan woke with a start at the loud noise behind him and reacted in a way that any highly strung destrier might. Being jerked so suddenly from his slumbers, he conceived himself under attack from the rear by some predator and lashed out behind him with his massively powerful hooves. His two black limbs surged out and his off hind hoof cracked directly into the top of Goody's skull.

My sweet wife had not even been looking at the horse, she was bending down to gather up the broken fragments of cheap earthenware when Shaitan's hoof thudded into her skull. Goody was immediately flung several paces across the courtyard and she landed in a heap of skirts and limbs and, to my horror, I saw a bright trickle of scarlet running out from beneath them.

I thrust the table out of my path scattering plates and cups and one unlucky guest and charged over to her fallen body. I was beside her in two heartbeats, cradling her blonde, broken head in my hands, feeling the blood trickle through my splayed fingers. She looked up at me, opening her beautiful violet-blue eyes and gazing up into mine one last time. I could feel the bones of her head moving ever so slightly in my palms, and through the matted golden hair I could see a dent the size of my fist above her right eyebrow filled with jelly and blood. She smiled once and tried to speak, but then her gaze shifted, just fractionally, to beyond my shoulder and fixed on something that no living eye could see. Quite slowly, with a little tired sigh, the soul went out of her body.

I remember little of the next few days and weeks. I was drowning in a grief so deep as to block out almost all memory. But for some strange reason I could not shed a single tear. Robin and Thomas, Roland and Little John took turns to sit with me but I scarcely moved or spoke and only ate and drank tiny amounts and sat dry-eyed with an empty expression and a cold, echoing numbness in my heart.

The weeks passed, and the business of Westbury continued around me. Baldwin was a competent steward of the manor, and the harvest was brought in without the slightest participation from me. I swam silently in my grief, alone inside my head, quietly torturing myself with thoughts of how I might have saved her. Should I not have brought Shaitan out of the stables? Should I have had him hobbled? Why on earth had I thought that he would make a suitable gift for Sir Thomas Blood? But the truth was, and I was finally forced to accept this, that there was nothing I could have done to save her or to prevent her death. Yet I still had not shed a single tear.

One thing stuck in my mind, and kept going around and around in my head like a spinning cartwheel: Goody died on the second day of July in the year of Our Lord twelve hundred. It was exactly one year and one day after Goody and I had been wed. Nur's curse had come to pass.

Grief fades with time, of course, although to the griever himself, this can seem an impossibility. But one morning in September, I found myself sitting in the sunshine outside the hall, staring dry-eyed into space, as had been my habit for many long weeks, when I heard a sound. It was a baby crying inconsolably. And I thought swiftly, angrily, *Where is that wet nurse? Where is the servant who is supposed to be caring for my son? How dare they allow him to disturb my grief?* I looked around for Robin or Thomas to send them to fetch somebody for the infant, but there was nobody within sight and the crying continued, on and on, grating on my soul.

At last, I struggled to my feet and went to comfort the child myself, and, as I plucked that bawling, neglected baby from its basket and took him into my arms, I looked into his violet-blue, tear-stained eyes and saw Goody looking back at me, a small, perfect, madly sobbing, pink-faced version of my one true love.

I squeezed my only living son to my breast, feeling his warm, wriggling body against mine. Feeling his frailty, his strength, his wildly beating little heart. And, as I rocked him back and forth, with my big, clumsy arms wrapped tight around his tiny, fragile frame, his tears at last subsided and finally ceased.

And mine began to flow.

Epilogue

At my daughter-in-law's urging, I paid a visit last night to the village of Westbury and to the humble cott of two of my tenants. The woman of the household, Martha, had recently been delivered of a baby. She and her aged husband, you will remember, were the beneficiaries of the first miracle of the Flask of St Luke – and there have been two more since then; that is, two more that I know about. I admired their baby for a little while, a sturdy sleeping boy, and gave his father Geoffrey a silver penny with which to celebrate the birth at the alehouse.

The weight of my own baby son in my arms had rescued me from despair in the weeks after Goody died, a deep melancholy in which I might well have ended my own existence. My son Robert truly saved my life, I believe, but for some reason other men's sons do not have the same joyous effect on me. I am happy to admire a child, briefly, and it pleases me to see them grow, but these days I find I am feigning interest much of the time in visits of this sort.

But, as Marie and I walked back to the manor that long August evening after our little call in the village, I pondered the riddle of the false flask and the 'miracles' it has apparently engendered.

A rock-like belief, it seemed to me, was the key to many of the wonders that the world contains. In a word, faith. Martha and Geoffrey believe absolutely that their child was a miraculous gift from God – they asked for His mercy and received it. In one way of seeing it, it was their faith in God that granted them a child. Another way of looking at it is that the flask, having once contained water from the Grail – and a few drops of Nur's blood – may have had some supernatural power that allowed Martha to conceive. I do not believe that. I prefer to believe that the couple's deep, unshakeable faith allowed them to create new life.

Was Nur's curse truly responsible for the death of Goody? I do not know – it may have been no more than a sad accident. But I do not choose to put my faith in curses and foul magic – and so I say no, it was not the witch's malediction that killed my beloved. I am deciding to believe, I do believe, that it was a cruel coincidence.

Was the Holy Grail truly able to heal all hurts and hold back death? Certainly Vim's men fought better at Montségur knowing that the Grail was with them – they had faith in it, I did too – and none of the wounded died after drinking from the Grail. That blessed bowl certainly had a potency of some kind. I know it.

Faith and belief might sometimes be misplaced, I concluded silently, but they have a vast power to affect our lives. And, as in the case of Martha and Geoffrey, affect our lives for the better.

'Marie,' I said, as we approached the manor, 'can you arrange for Father Anselm to come to see me tomorrow.'

'Of course, Alan,' said my daughter-in-law. 'But I thought you didn't care for him. What shall I say you want him for?'

I took a step or two before I answered her, then I said, 'You may tell him that, after careful deliberation, I have decided to purchase a fine golden relic-casket for our little church.'

Historical Note

Barcelona instantly became my favourite city in the world after a weekend there with my wife last summer. The authorities screen movies in the public squares, bar-hopping's a genuine art form, there's cool architecture everywhere and nobody eats dinner till ten at night. And, as if that wasn't enough, I was also privileged enough during my visit to see some of the earliest images ever made of the Holy Grail.

In the heart of the Museu Nacional d'Art de Catalunya (MNAC), the interior of a small twelfth-century church has been partially reconstructed. The original church of St Clement still stands in the remote village of Taüll in the Valley of Boí high in the Pyrenees, but when the stunning Romanesque frescos the church contained were discovered at the beginning of the twentieth century, and foreign 'entrepreneurs' began chipping off bits of the masonry and carrying them away, the Spanish authorities acted swiftly. Using a near-miraculous chemical process, in which strips of treated cloth are pressed on to the church walls and then peeled off, these ancient paintings were painstakingly removed from the walls of the church of St Clement and taken to Barcelona, where they have been lovingly restored and housed in MNAC.

When I saw them there in June 2012, I was astonished by their remarkable beauty and power. The main apse of the reconstructed church is the setting for the superb painting of *Christ in Majesty*, which shows the Saviour enthroned in Heaven and looking down on mortal sinners with a stern yet compassionate expression. The curve of the apse gives the fresco a strangely three-dimensional effect, and the colours – royal blue, warm ochre, creamy white and blood red – appear to be as vibrant as the day they were painted, probably in 1123. Christ is surrounded by various saints and apostles and below his bare right foot and slightly to the left is a panel containing an image of the Virgin Mary.

Her expression is serene, she holds up her right hand, palm out in a gesture of blessing, or perhaps of warning, and in her left hand, covered by her rich blue mantle, she is holding a shallow bowl, painted white, which seems to be filled with fire and has rays of reddish-orange light shooting out of it.

This is one of the very earliest representations of the Holy Grail, an object that shortly afterwards began to appear regularly in religious art all over the Pyrenees. Of course, the object in her hand was not regarded then as the Holy Grail, as we think of it today – it was a *graal*, the word in the medieval language of the region for a common, broad, shallow dish of the kind that might be used to hold a cooked fish when it was served at the table. And it was 'holy' because Mary the Mother of God was holding it, not in her bare palm, but in a hand covered by her blue mantle.

Opinion is divided on what the graal is supposed to symbolize – other Christian dignitaries have their symbols, useful icons for identifying them in medieval art today, as then: St Luke, for example, is often pictured with an ox; St Peter holds a set of keys; on the picture of *Christ in Majesty*, in the panel to the right of Mary's, St John is seen supporting a book in his right hand, the

416

hand also covered in a mantle, like the Virgin's, to indicate the book's holiness. Some scholars suggest the graal pictured in this magnificent painting might be a container of Christ's blood, reminiscent of the Saviour's words repeated in the Eucharist – 'This is my blood of the new covenant, which is shed for many . . .' – others suggest the graal might hold sacred oil – chrism – a holy unguent used in consecration and other important Christian rituals. Personally, I think Mary's graal is a symbol of her womb, in which she conceived Christ by the Holy Spirit and carried him for nine months. What more powerful symbol could a holy mother display than the space inside her body in which she nurtured her child and from which issued the future Saviour of Mankind?

But whatever the graal was originally intended to mean – and nobody can be absolutely certain – the symbol was to have a profound effect on Christendom. By the middle of the twelfth century, graillike objects were appearing regularly in the hands of the Virgin in religious art, particularly in the southern lands of western Europe – in the Languedoc in France, northern Spain and northern Italy. Sometimes they were bowls, sometimes cups or chalices, sometimes they appear to be oil lamps.

However, it was not until the end of the twelfth century that the Holy Grail made its literary debut. *Perceval, Le Conte du Graal* (*Percival, The Story of the Grail*) was written by the French poet Chretien de Troyes sometime between 1180 and 1190 – perhaps sixty years or more after the graal was pictured in the Virgin's hands in the Pyrenees – and the work was an almost instant hit in European aristocratic circles. The Grail appears as a golden bowl encrusted with precious jewels, paraded about by mysterious denizens of a mysterious castle in the company of a shining lance, a pair of candlesticks and a silver carving platter. (See my previous novel *Warlord*.)

In Chretien's story the graal is a receptacle for the host of the Eucharist, and such is its power that one wafer of holy bread a day is enough to sustain the lord of the mysterious castle. Beyond that, Chretien does not say much about the Grail, and indeed his poem *Le Conte du Graal* was never finished. But the Grail was now loose in the literary domain and it had begun to exert its strange fascination over writers, which has continued ever since. Around 1200, a Bavarian poet called Wolfram von Eschenbach produced an operatic retelling of Chretien de Troyes's story called *Parzival*, embellishing it considerably, and conceiving of the grail as a precious stone that had fallen from the sky. But the version of the Grail story that I have chosen to adopt comes from Robert de Boron, a Burgundian knight, who wrote *Joseph d'Arimathie or Le grant estoire dou graal* (*Joseph of Arimathea or the Great History of the Grail*), sometime in the 1190s. His take on the legend is the one that would be most recognizable to readers today, in that his Grail is both the cup used at the Last Supper and the vessel used to catch the blood of Christ as he died on the Cross.

I would recommend that anyone interested in the story of the Grail read Professor Joseph Goering's excellent book *The Virgin and the Grail: Origins of a Legend* (Yale University Press, 2005) for more details on the medieval Grail poets. Indeed, I must acknowledge him as the inspiration behind my own take on the Holy Grail in this novel and my source on its origins and, perhaps, its physical reality. Because I think that there might really have been a physical object which people in the twelfth and thirteenth centuries considered to be the Holy Grail.

And it might even still exist.

Let's return to the beginning of the twentieth century and the Valley of Boí in the high Pyrenees. At the same time that the marvellous painting of *Christ in Majesty* was discovered in St Clement of Taüll, a set of wooden sculptures was found in another church dedicated to St Mary a few hundred yards away. These figures were part of a tableau, dated to about the same time as the fresco in St Clement's church, which is most likely to depict the

Descent from the Cross – statues of Mary and Joseph of Arimathea, and perhaps Nicodemus, helping to bring down Christ's dead body after the Crucifixion. In other contemporary examples of this sort of tableau, Christ's hand is seen as dangling over a wooden bowl held by his mother, in a manner such that a few drops of his blood might fall into the bowl. The wooden statue of Mary bears a striking resemblance to the image of the Virgin in the painting in St Clement's. Both have the same clothing, the same posture, the same expression – indeed the resemblance is so striking that scholars believe that one must have been a copy of the other, although it is impossible to say whether the painting inspired the wooden statue or vice versa.

But, for me, the most interesting thing about the statue of the Virgin, which is now housed in the Fogg Art Museum at Harvard University is that the left hand, the hand that would have been holding the bowl that caught the Saviour's precious blood, is missing. It has been cut off at some point and neither the hand nor the wooden bowl it once undoubtedly held have ever been found.

I like to think that this missing twelfth-century wooden bowl, from a group of statues in a remote church in the Pyrenees, might have been the origin of the physical, the actual Holy Grail. Perhaps this was the sacred objective of real quests, by real medieval knights. And, perhaps, somewhere in a Swiss vault in a wealthy man's private collection, or in some secret dusty annex of the Vatican, it sits to this day.

Cathars and castles in the air

Montségur, of course, is a real castle twenty miles south-east of Foix in the shadow of the Pyrenees, and was the site, in 1244, of the heroic last stand of the Cathars during the Albigensian Crusade. But forty-four years earlier, when my fictional heroes and villains occupied the place, it was in reality a ruined fortress that had been abandoned by the Counts of Foix as too remote to bother with. Ruined or not, it still would have been a formidable bastion and, I think, very nearly impregnable after only minor repairs to the walls. A man standing on the battlements can see for miles in all directions, and the sides of the mountain are incredibly steep, and fairly exhausting to climb in a T-shirt and shorts on a sunny May day – let alone in heavy armour and under fire from all manner of lethal medieval missiles. It took ten thousand crusaders nine months to subdue the castle in 1243–1244, and this presented me, as a twenty-first-century novelist, with a bit of a problem.

When I had puffed and panted my way up the tourist path to the main entrance on the western side in hot sunshine, and clambered all over the existing walls of the castle, I was left with a magnificent view and absolutely no idea how a handful of men – even superb warrior-heroes such as the Companions of the Grail – could possibly capture it in the year 1200. I knew that the crusaders forty years later had attacked up the narrow spur of land to the east of the castle (as my heroes eventually do) but, like Alan Dale, I could still not see how the Companions could successfully attack on such a narrow front under sustained fire from the castle. A couple of well-aimed mangonel or trebuchet strikes and a volley or two of crossbow bolts would have destroyed such a small number of assailants.

I went back down the mountain in a state of mild despair, had supper and went to bed early. The next morning I was awoken at dawn by a terrible noise that sounded like something between machine-gun fire and a seventies drum solo. A powerful hail storm was battering the terracotta roof of my auberge and hailstones the size of golf balls were bouncing waist-high off the stone floor of the courtyard below. After the bright sunshine of the day before this came as something of a shock, and when the hail ceased a thick fog descended on the village of Montségur, weather so dense that you could barely see ten yards. I stayed in the hotel most of that day – except for a very pleasant visit to the excellent

Montségur museum – but I was quite happy to be inactive, indeed, I was elated. I had found a plausible plot device that would allow me to get my heroes close to the castle walls without being seen: Nur's sudden magical mist. The weather there, so close to the Pyrenees, is very changeable, and if I hadn't witnessed it myself, I would never have dared to include something quite so preposterous in the story.

As well as outlandish weather, Montségur is also well supplied with a satisfying quantity of strange myths. There are many legends of the Cathars hiding their lost treasure in secret caves, and of travellers well into the twentieth century having visions of a lady dressed all in white appearing to them on the steep slopes. My kind hosts at the auberge told me that there was a large hidden cave burrowed into the rock directly under the castle itself, but the official French gatekeeper of the castle grumpily denied it and despite a long, hot exhausting search I could not find it. Nevertheless, there may well be large caves in the rock of Montségur, as yet undiscovered or just forgotten, and in my imagination, in one of them, at a stone altar far at the back lies an ancient skeleton with an even older plain wooden bowl in his bony grasp.

Angus Donald
Tonbridge, Kent, December 2012

Acknowledgements

A book is always a collaborative process – I get to have my name in big letters on the front, of course, but it wouldn't exist without a great deal of help from a great many people. I would firstly like to thank my agent Ian Drury, of Sheil Land Associates, for his unfailing support and encouragement of the Outlaw Chronicles over the years and also his colleague in the foreign rights department Gaia Banks. My talented editors at Sphere, Ed Wood and Iain Hunt, deserve high praise for wrestling this book into its current shape, and Anne O'Brien did her usual excellent proofreading job.

I owe a debt of gratitude to Professor Joseph Goering of the University of Toronto for his marvellous book *The Virgin and The Grail*, which inspired me to put my Robin Hood and his Holy Grail in the same novel. On my trip to Barcelona last summer to look at some extraordinary twelfth-century images of the Grail, I was looked after very well by Anna Portabella, and lavishly wined and dined by Daniel Fernandez, my Spanish publishers. And I must also thank the kind staff at the Museu Nacional D'Art de Catalunya, who showed me around the reconstructed Pyrenean church of St Clement of Taüll in the basement of their fine museum and other jewels of their collection and patiently answered all my questions. Finally, I would like to thank Philip and Camilla Drinkall, who lent me their iPad charging lead at the auberge in Montségur and allowed me to join them for a wonderful evening, and without whom my research trip would have been far less enjoyable.